D0447936

Also by Bryan Doerries

The Theater of War
All That You've Seen Here Is God

THE ODYSSEY OF SERGEANT JACK BRENNAN

THE ODYSSEY OF SERGEANT JACK BRENNAN

This is a work of fiction. Names, characters, places, and incidents either are the product of the author's imagination or are used fictitiously. Any resemblance to actual persons, living or dead, events, or locales is entirely coincidental.

Copyright © 2016 by Theater of War Productions Limited Liability Company

All rights reserved. Published in the United States by Pantheon Books, a division of Penguin Random House LLC, New York, and distributed in Canada by Random House of Canada, a division of Penguin Random House Canada Ltd., Toronto.

Pantheon Books and colophon are registered trademarks of Penguin Random House LLC.

Library of Congress Cataloging-in-Publication Data
The Odyssey of Sergeant Jack Brennan / Bryan Doerries.
Doerries, Bryan.
pages cm
ISBN 978-0-375-71516-7 (trade pbk. : alk. paper).
ISBN 978-1-101-87099-0 (eBook).
1. Soldiers—Comic books, strips, etc. 2. Veterans—Comic books, strips, etc.
3. Homer. Odyssey—Adaptations. 4. Graphic novels. I. Title.
PN6727.D655O39 2016   741.5'973—dc23   2015023578

www.pantheonbooks.com

Jacket art by Joëlle Jones (illustration) and Mike Luckas (colorist)
Courtesy of Theater of War Productions LLC
Jacket design by Janet Hansen

Printed in China
First Edition
2 4 6 8 9 7 5 3 1

Doerries, Bryan,
The Odyssey of Sergeant
Jack Brennan /

11/29/16

ODYSSEY OF SERGEANT JACK BRENNAN

BRYAN DOERRIES

PANTHEON BOOKS, NEW YORK

FOR JOEY MANLEY

INTRODUCTION

While waiting to fly home after a challenging seven-month deployment to Afghanistan, Sergeant Jack Brennan gathers his war-weary infantry Marines at a U.S. air base in Kyrgyzstan to tell them—in his own words—"the oldest war story of all time."

In forty-eight hours, they'll be stepping off a plane in San Diego, returning to the world they left behind. Most of them are too tired or too numb to "decompress," as they've been ordered to do, let alone to talk about their feelings or what might await them back home. None of them is very much interested in sitting through a lecture. But they all respect Brennan, and—out of respect—they agree to hear him out.

For as long as he can remember, Brennan has been obsessed with military history. Over the past ten years, he has devoured everything from Thucydides's *History of the Peloponnesian War* to the most recent edition of the *Counterinsurgency Field Manual*. In all his reading, no war story has ever captivated or touched him more than Homer's *Odyssey*, especially after returning from his first tour to Iraq.

The ancient Greek epic about the warrior Odysseus's ten-year journey home from the Trojan War, and the many losses and setbacks he faced along the way, spoke directly to Brennan, as if it had been written specifically for him. And so throughout his last two deployments—to Ramadi, Iraq, and Helmand Province, Afghanistan—Brennan has carried a dog-eared copy of the *Odyssey* in his rucksack and read it religiously, like a guide for navigating the rough and stormy seas veterans sometimes encounter on the way home from war.

As a squad leader, Brennan now feels a deep responsibility for his Marines, especially the younger ones, who will be returning home for the first time. He wants to see all of them safely back to the States. More crucially, he wants to make sure that once home they do not lose their way or stray off course. As Brennan has experienced in the past, the abrupt return to barracks and civilian life following deployment can be jarring for Marines. He understands that the challenges of combat can sometimes pale in comparison to those of homecoming, but he also knows that many of his men are unaware of the trials that may await them stateside.

This night is the last time the squad will be together "in-country" before heading back to San Diego. And so, assembling his Marines at dusk, Brennan resolves to tell them his version of Homer's *Odyssey* in order to give them the strength, awareness, and resolve they'll need to sail through the potentially turbulent waters ahead.

PROLOGUE

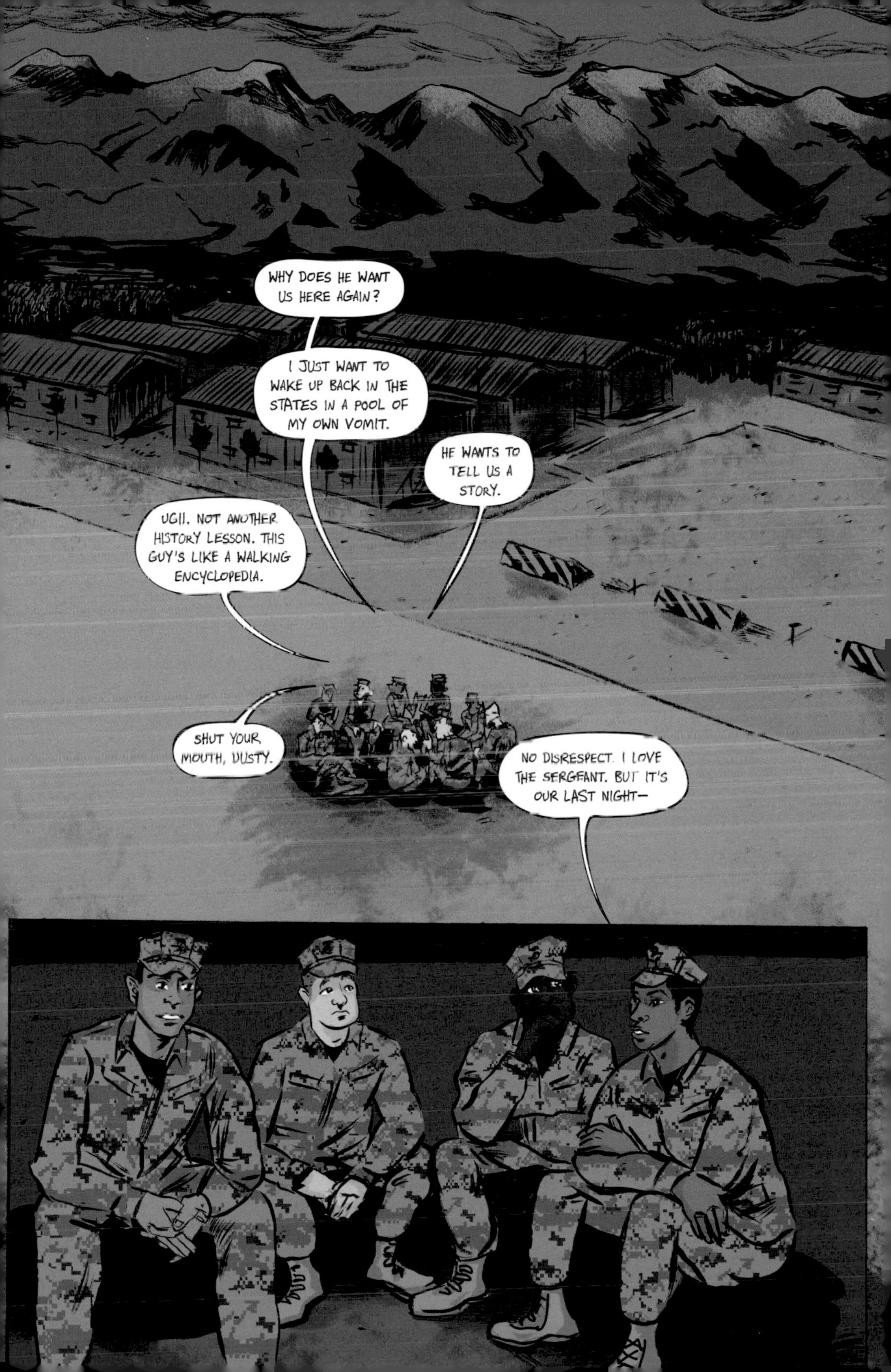
WHY DOES HE WANT US HERE AGAIN?
I JUST WANT TO WAKE UP BACK IN THE STATES IN A POOL OF MY OWN VOMIT.
HE WANTS TO TELL US A STORY.
UGH. NOT ANOTHER HISTORY LESSON. THIS GUY'S LIKE A WALKING ENCYCLOPEDIA.
SHUT YOUR MOUTH, DUSTY.
NO DISRESPECT. I LOVE THE SERGEANT. BUT IT'S OUR LAST NIGHT—

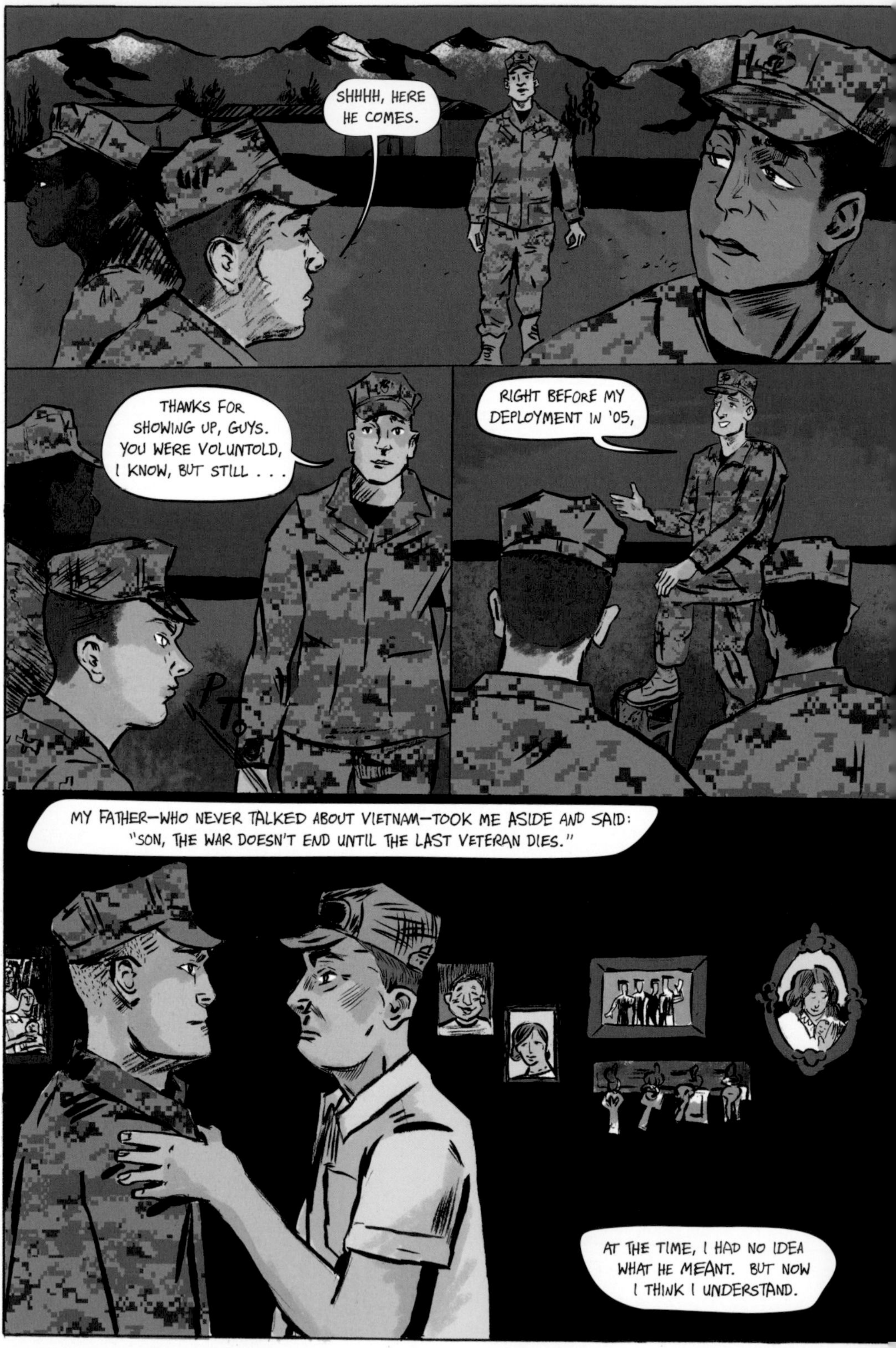
SHHHH, HERE HE COMES.
THANKS FOR SHOWING UP, GUYS. YOU WERE VOLUNTOLD, I KNOW, BUT STILL . . .
RIGHT BEFORE MY DEPLOYMENT IN '05,
MY FATHER—WHO NEVER TALKED ABOUT VIETNAM—TOOK ME ASIDE AND SAID: "SON, THE WAR DOESN'T END UNTIL THE LAST VETERAN DIES."
AT THE TIME, I HAD NO IDEA WHAT HE MEANT. BUT NOW I THINK I UNDERSTAND.

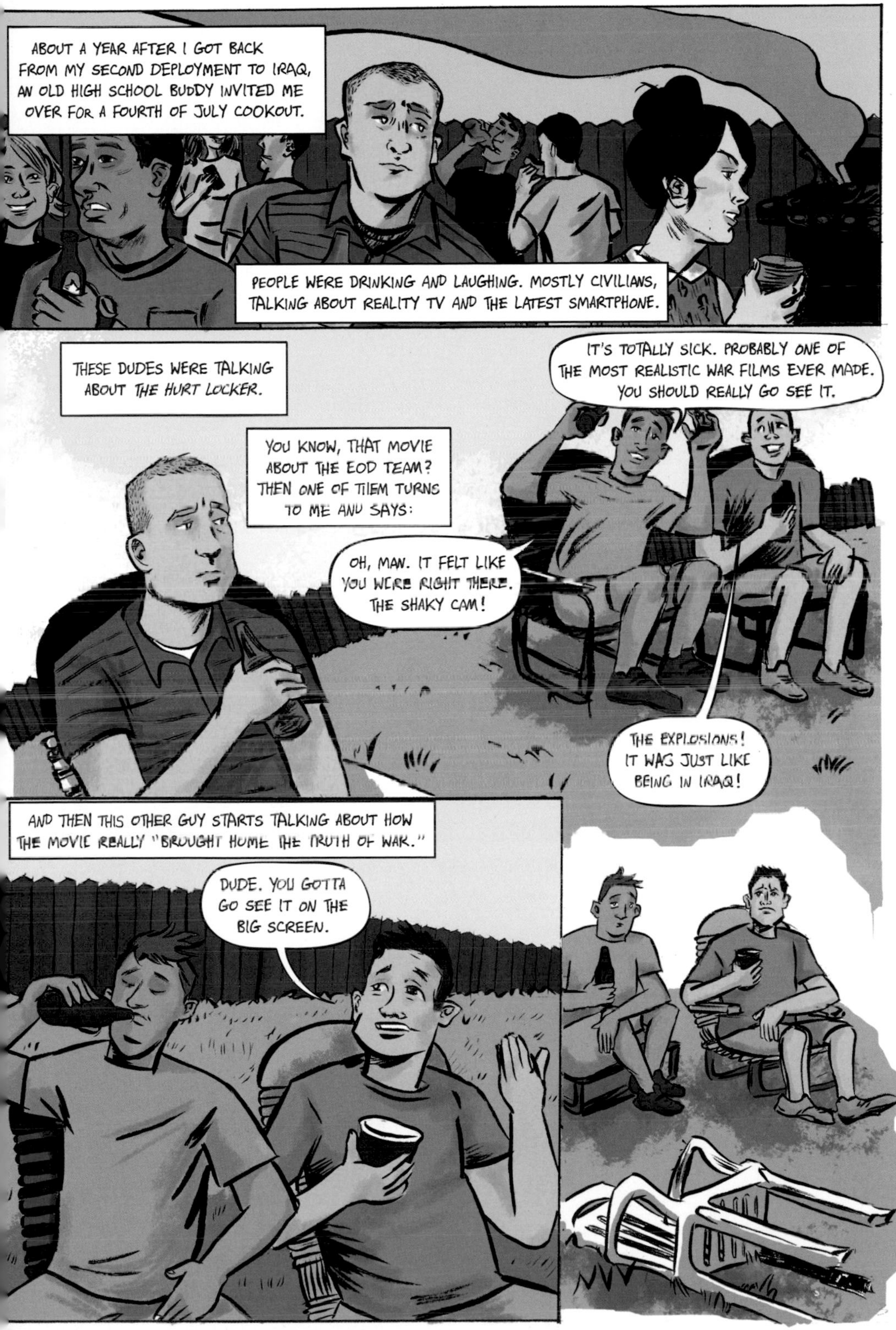
ABOUT A YEAR AFTER I GOT BACK FROM MY SECOND DEPLOYMENT TO IRAQ, AN OLD HIGH SCHOOL BUDDY INVITED ME OVER FOR A FOURTH OF JULY COOKOUT.
PEOPLE WERE DRINKING AND LAUGHING. MOSTLY CIVILIANS, TALKING ABOUT REALITY TV AND THE LATEST SMARTPHONE.
THESE DUDES WERE TALKING ABOUT *THE HURT LOCKER*.
IT'S TOTALLY SICK. PROBABLY ONE OF THE MOST REALISTIC WAR FILMS EVER MADE. YOU SHOULD REALLY GO SEE IT.
YOU KNOW, THAT MOVIE ABOUT THE EOD TEAM? THEN ONE OF THEM TURNS TO ME AND SAYS:
OH, MAN. IT FELT LIKE YOU WERE RIGHT THERE. THE SHAKY CAM!
THE EXPLOSIONS! IT WAS JUST LIKE BEING IN IRAQ!
AND THEN THIS OTHER GUY STARTS TALKING ABOUT HOW THE MOVIE REALLY "BROUGHT HOME THE TRUTH OF WAR."
DUDE. YOU GOTTA GO SEE IT ON THE BIG SCREEN.

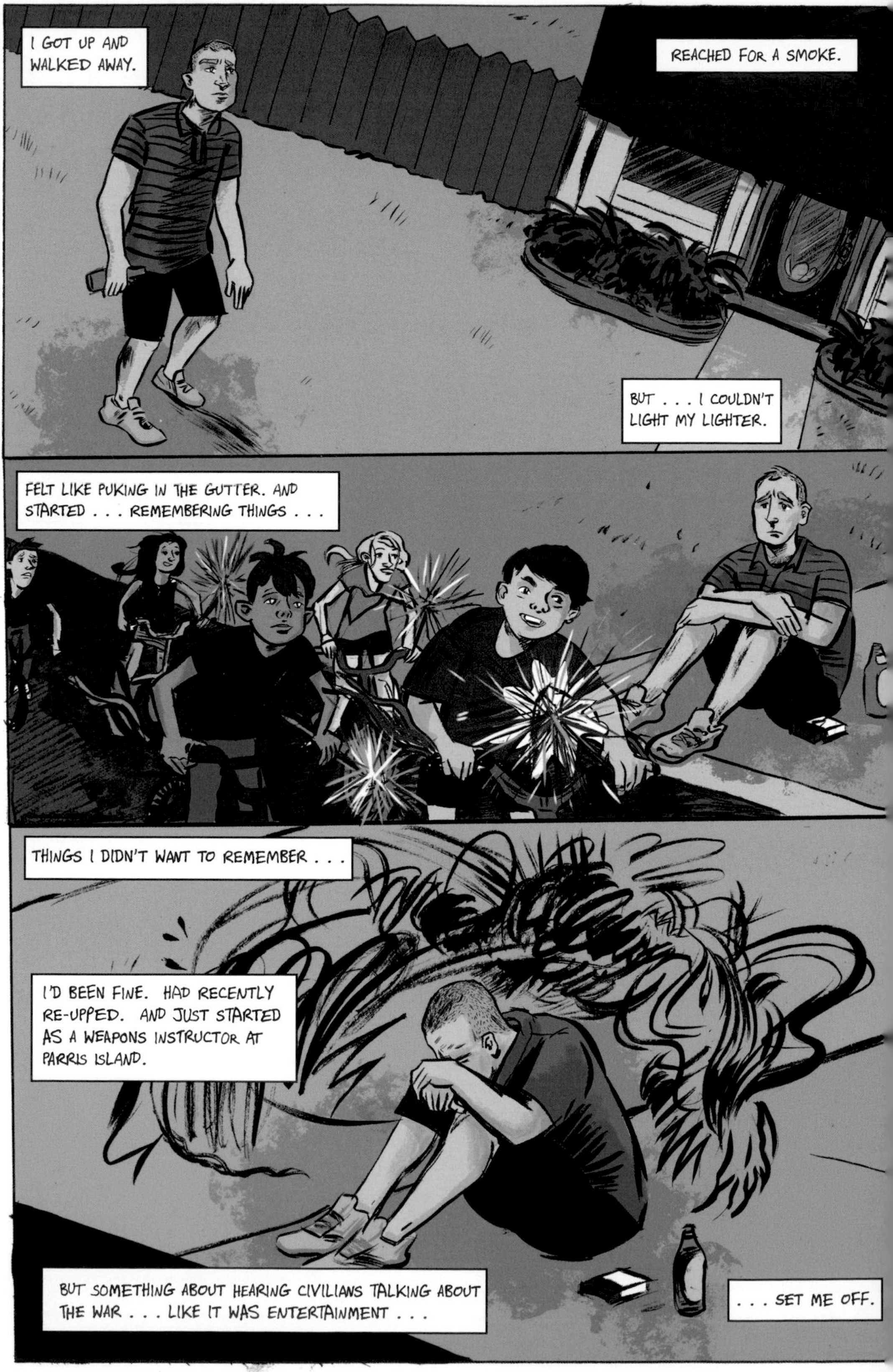
I GOT UP AND WALKED AWAY.
REACHED FOR A SMOKE.
BUT . . . I COULDN'T LIGHT MY LIGHTER.
FELT LIKE PUKING IN THE GUTTER. AND STARTED . . . REMEMBERING THINGS . . .
THINGS I DIDN'T WANT TO REMEMBER . . .
I'D BEEN FINE. HAD RECENTLY RE-UPPED. AND JUST STARTED AS A WEAPONS INSTRUCTOR AT PARRIS ISLAND.
BUT SOMETHING ABOUT HEARING CIVILIANS TALKING ABOUT THE WAR . . . LIKE IT WAS ENTERTAINMENT . . .
. . . SET ME OFF.

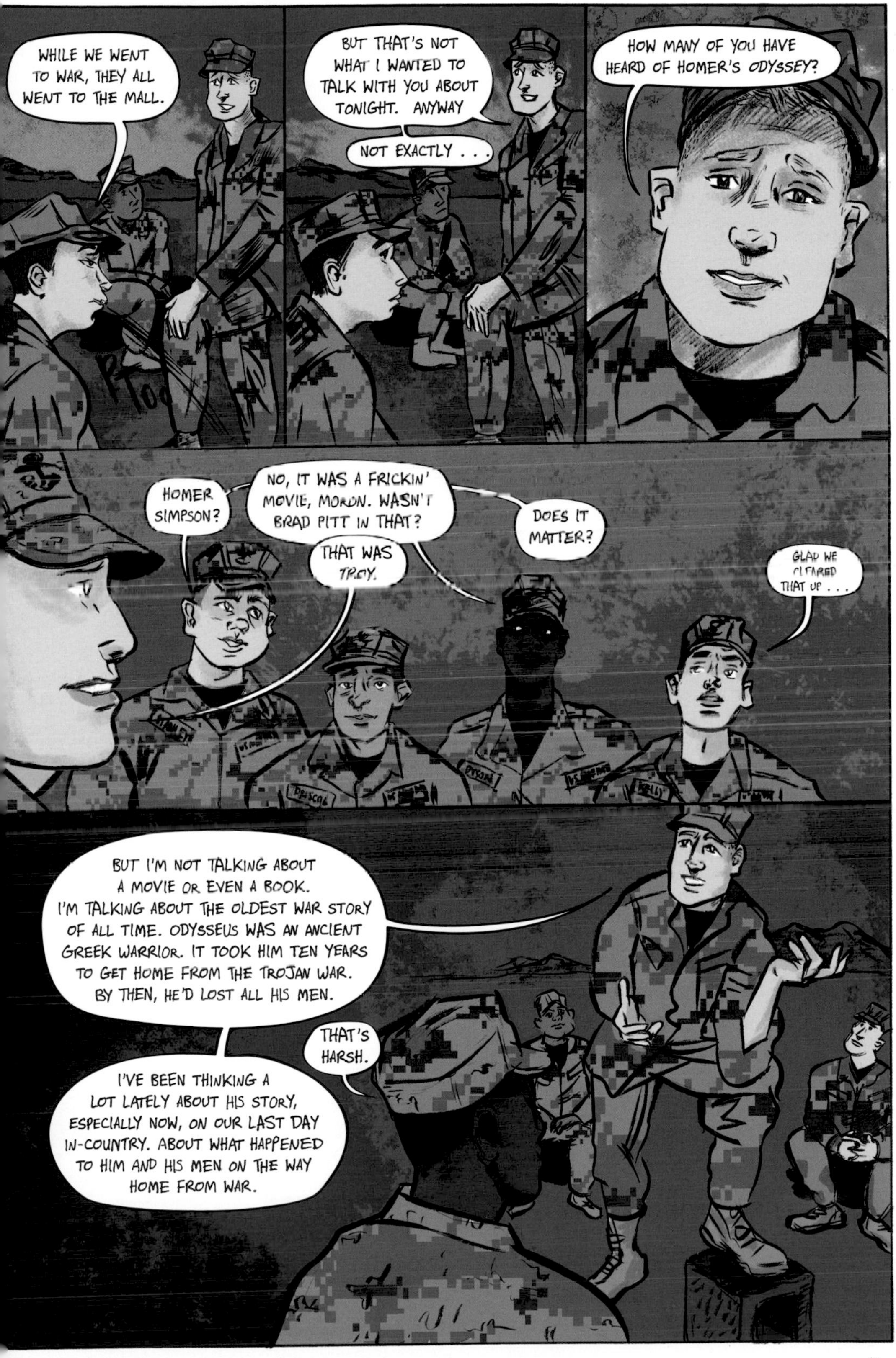
WHILE WE WENT TO WAR, THEY ALL WENT TO THE MALL.
BUT THAT'S NOT WHAT I WANTED TO TALK WITH YOU ABOUT TONIGHT. ANYWAY
NOT EXACTLY . . .
HOW MANY OF YOU HAVE HEARD OF HOMER'S ODYSSEY?
HOMER SIMPSON?
NO, IT WAS A FRICKIN' MOVIE, MORON. WASN'T BRAD PITT IN THAT?
THAT WAS TROY.
DOES IT MATTER?
GLAD WE CLEARED THAT UP . . .
BUT I'M NOT TALKING ABOUT A MOVIE OR EVEN A BOOK. I'M TALKING ABOUT THE OLDEST WAR STORY OF ALL TIME. ODYSSEUS WAS AN ANCIENT GREEK WARRIOR. IT TOOK HIM TEN YEARS TO GET HOME FROM THE TROJAN WAR. BY THEN, HE'D LOST ALL HIS MEN.
THAT'S HARSH.
I'VE BEEN THINKING A LOT LATELY ABOUT HIS STORY, ESPECIALLY NOW, ON OUR LAST DAY IN-COUNTRY. ABOUT WHAT HAPPENED TO HIM AND HIS MEN ON THE WAY HOME FROM WAR.

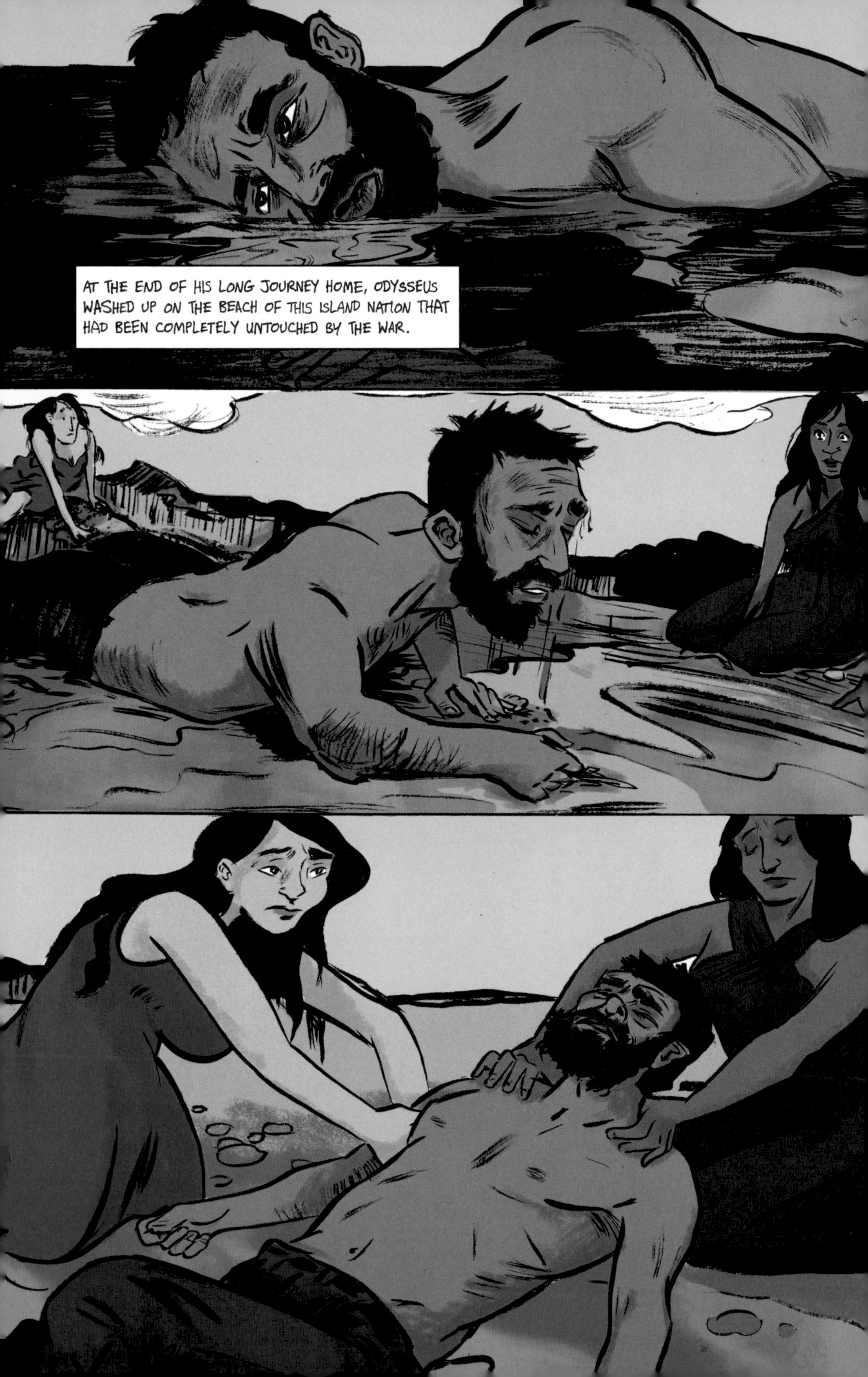
AT THE END OF HIS LONG JOURNEY HOME, ODYSSEUS WASHED UP ON THE BEACH OF THIS ISLAND NATION THAT HAD BEEN COMPLETELY UNTOUCHED BY THE WAR.

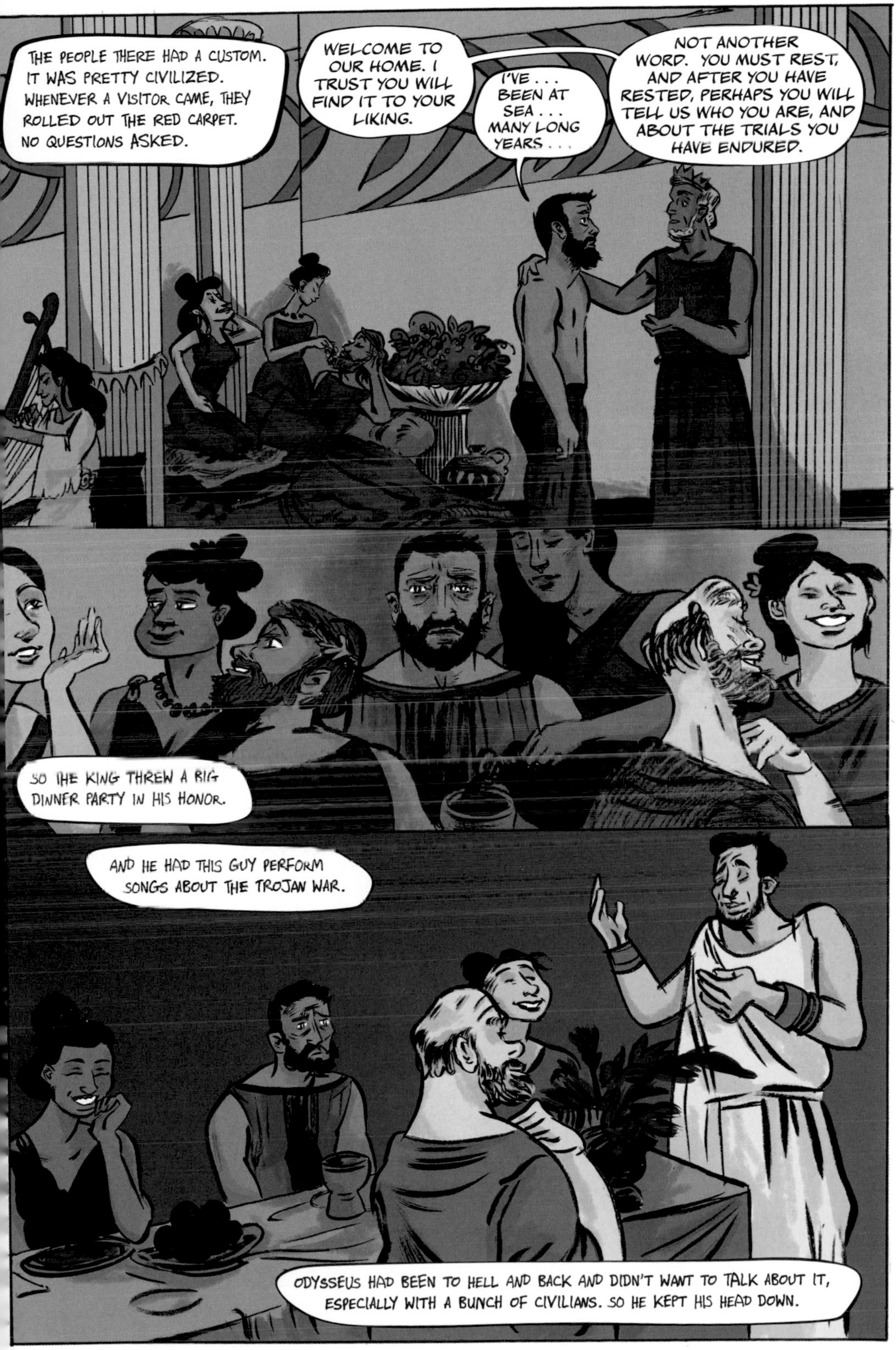
THE PEOPLE THERE HAD A CUSTOM. IT WAS PRETTY CIVILIZED. WHENEVER A VISITOR CAME, THEY ROLLED OUT THE RED CARPET. NO QUESTIONS ASKED.
WELCOME TO OUR HOME. I TRUST YOU WILL FIND IT TO YOUR LIKING.
I'VE . . . BEEN AT SEA . . . MANY LONG YEARS . . .
NOT ANOTHER WORD. YOU MUST REST, AND AFTER YOU HAVE RESTED, PERHAPS YOU WILL TELL US WHO YOU ARE, AND ABOUT THE TRIALS YOU HAVE ENDURED.
SO THE KING THREW A BIG DINNER PARTY IN HIS HONOR.
AND HE HAD THIS GUY PERFORM SONGS ABOUT THE TROJAN WAR.
ODYSSEUS HAD BEEN TO HELL AND BACK AND DIDN'T WANT TO TALK ABOUT IT, ESPECIALLY WITH A BUNCH OF CIVILIANS. SO HE KEPT HIS HEAD DOWN.

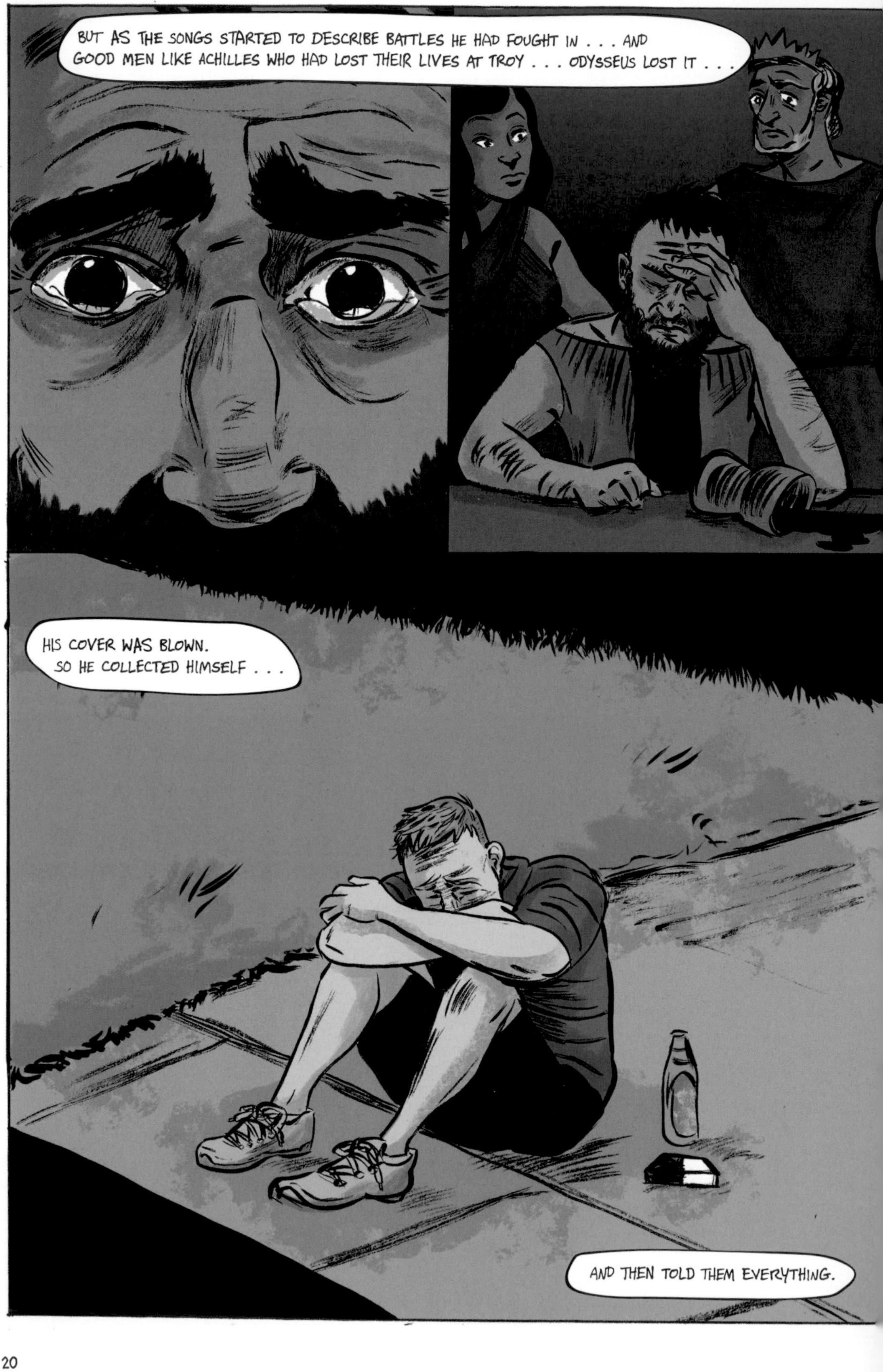
BUT AS THE SONGS STARTED TO DESCRIBE BATTLES HE HAD FOUGHT IN . . . AND GOOD MEN LIKE ACHILLES WHO HAD LOST THEIR LIVES AT TROY . . . ODYSSEUS LOST IT . . .
HIS COVER WAS BLOWN. SO HE COLLECTED HIMSELF . . .
AND THEN TOLD THEM EVERYTHING.

CHAPTER I

THE WAR NEVER ENDS

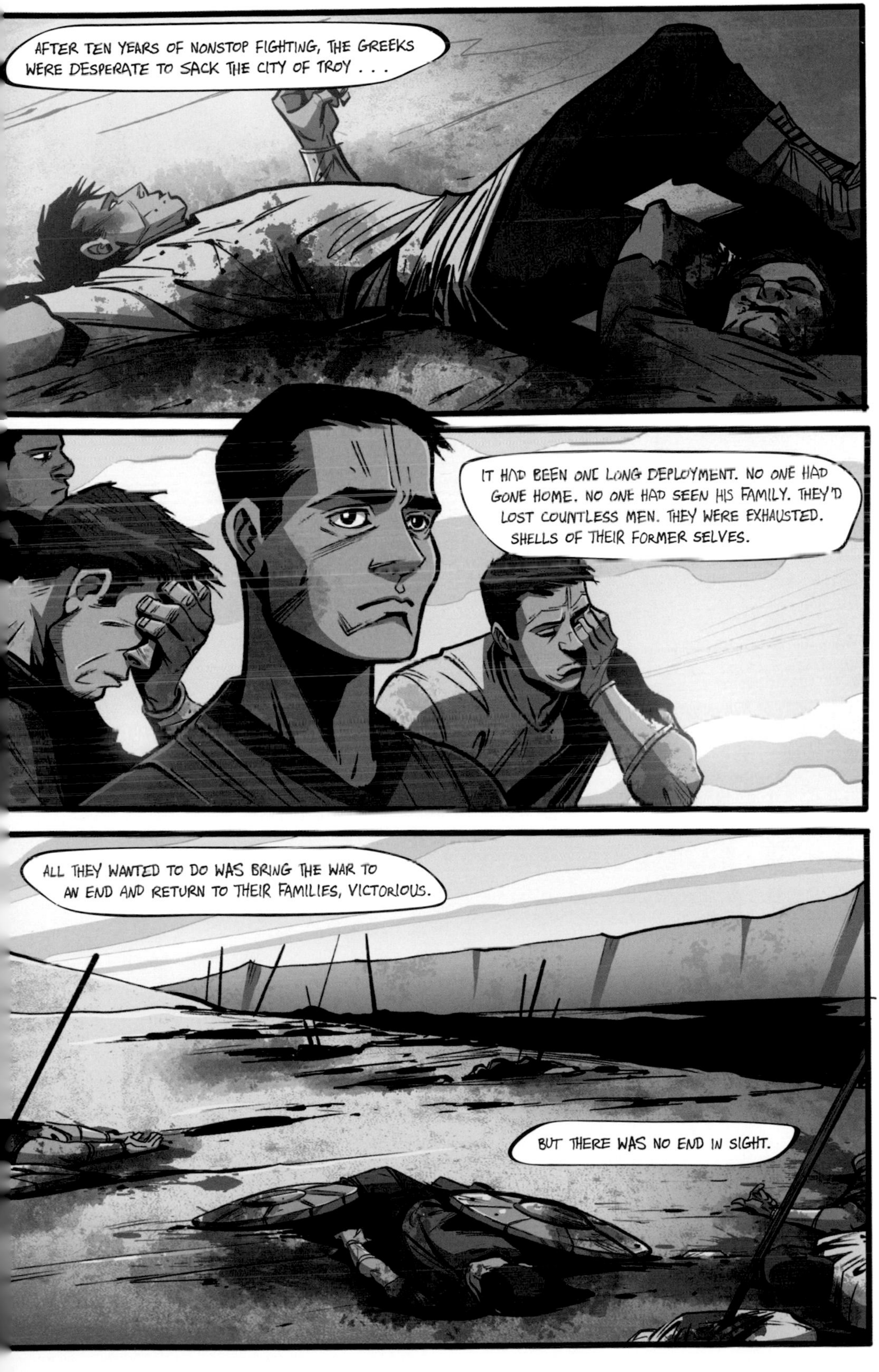
AFTER TEN YEARS OF NONSTOP FIGHTING, THE GREEKS WERE DESPERATE TO SACK THE CITY OF TROY . . .
IT HAD BEEN ONE LONG DEPLOYMENT. NO ONE HAD GONE HOME. NO ONE HAD SEEN HIS FAMILY. THEY'D LOST COUNTLESS MEN. THEY WERE EXHAUSTED. SHELLS OF THEIR FORMER SELVES.
ALL THEY WANTED TO DO WAS BRING THE WAR TO AN END AND RETURN TO THEIR FAMILIES, VICTORIOUS.
BUT THERE WAS NO END IN SIGHT.

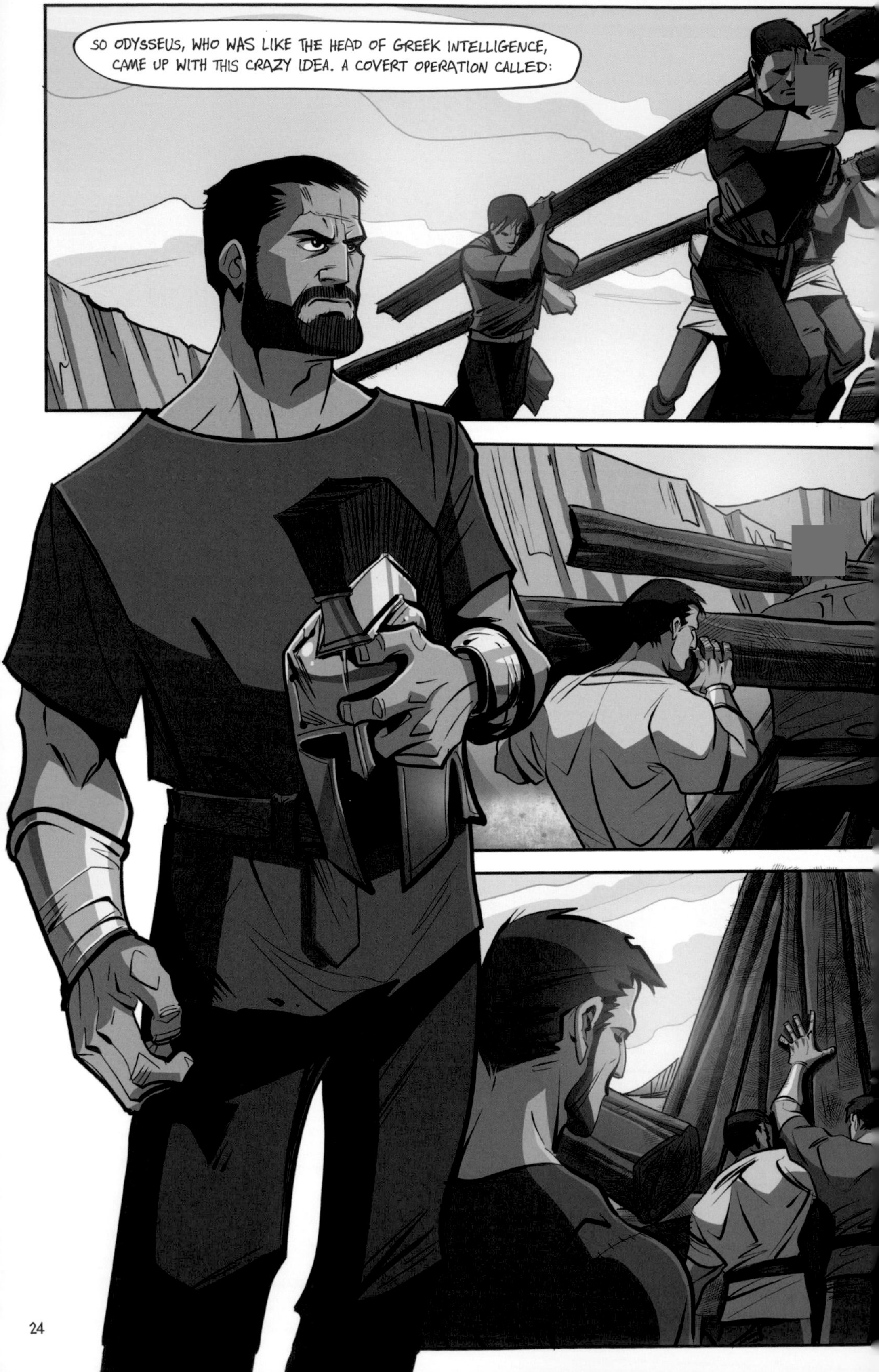
SO ODYSSEUS, WHO WAS LIKE THE HEAD OF GREEK INTELLIGENCE, CAME UP WITH THIS CRAZY IDEA. A COVERT OPERATION CALLED:

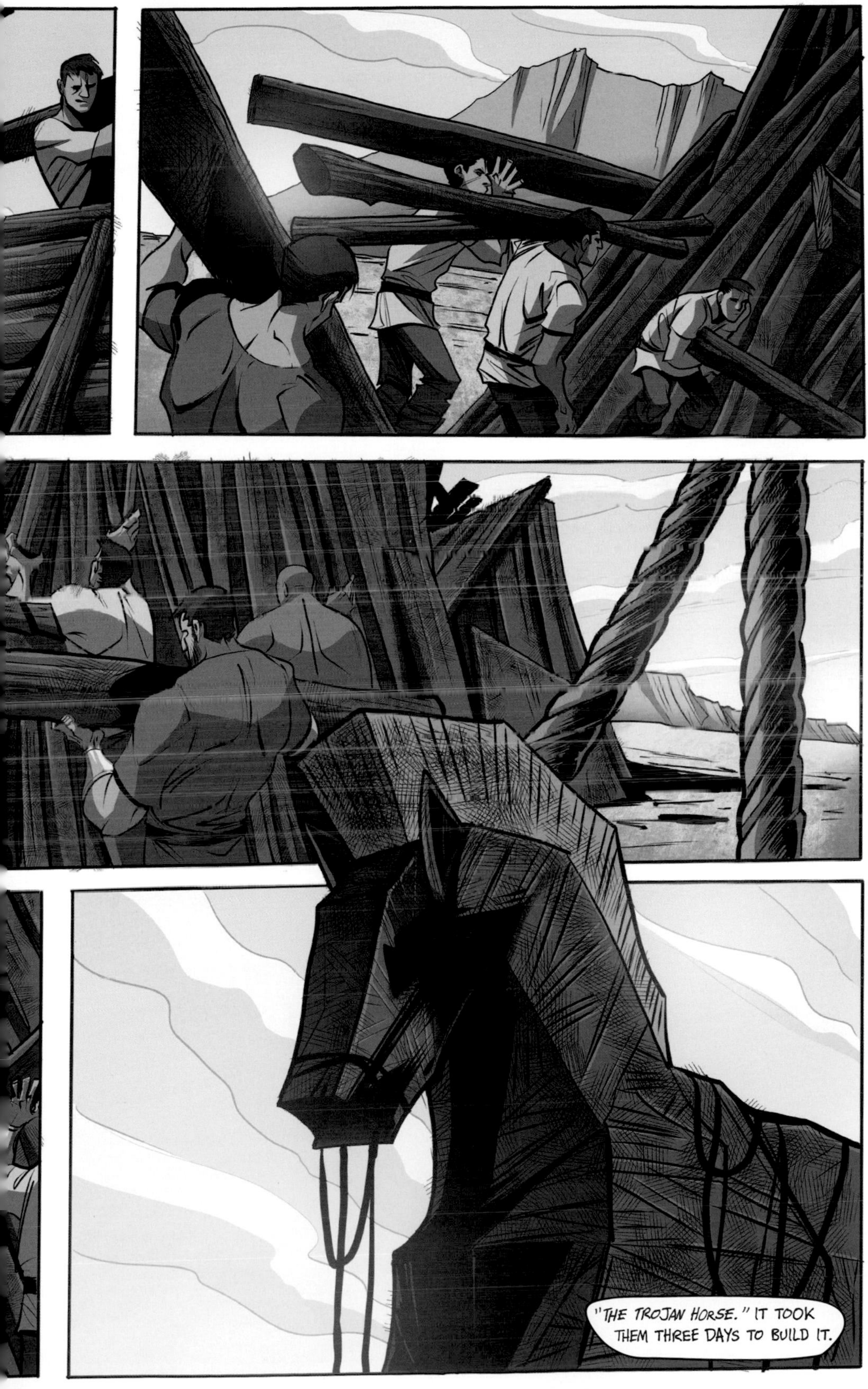
"THE TROJAN HORSE." IT TOOK THEM THREE DAYS TO BUILD IT.

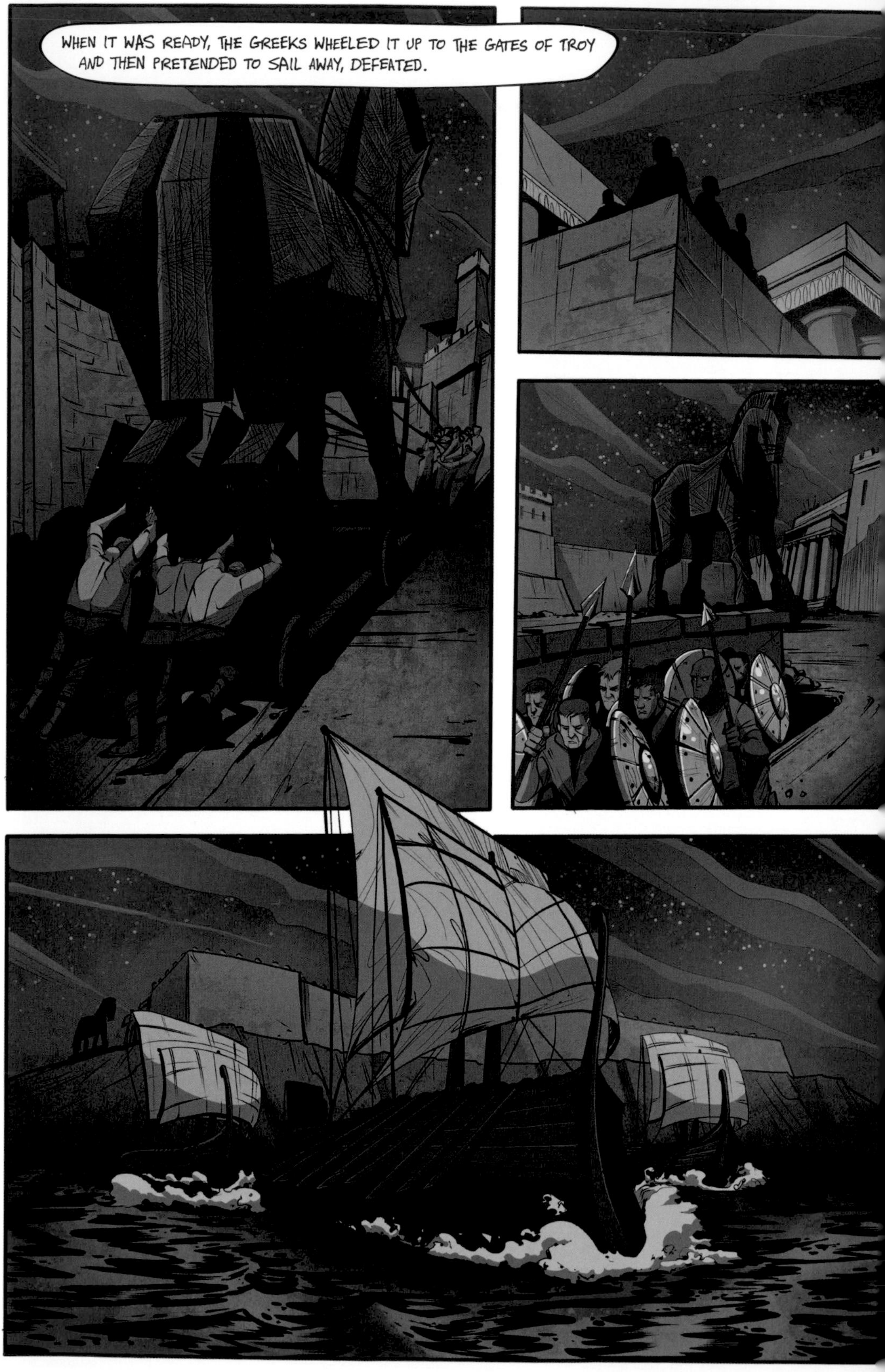
WHEN IT WAS READY, THE GREEKS WHEELED IT UP TO THE GATES OF TROY AND THEN PRETENDED TO SAIL AWAY, DEFEATED.

AND THE TROJANS—WHO KNOWS WHAT THEY WERE THINKING?

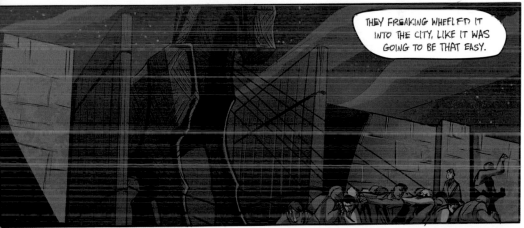

THEY FREAKING WHEELED IT INTO THE CITY, LIKE IT WAS GOING TO BE THAT EASY.

AT LONG LAST, VICTORY IS OURS!

AIAIAIAIAI AIAIAIAIAI!

THE GREEK SPECIAL OPS WAITED ALL DAY AND MOST OF THE NIGHT INSIDE THE HORSE.

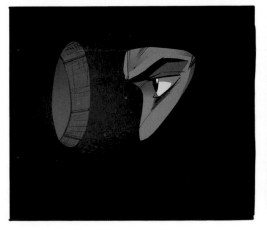

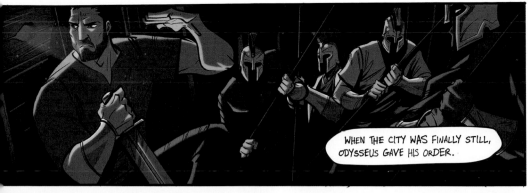

WHEN THE CITY WAS FINALLY STILL, ODYSSEUS GAVE HIS ORDER.

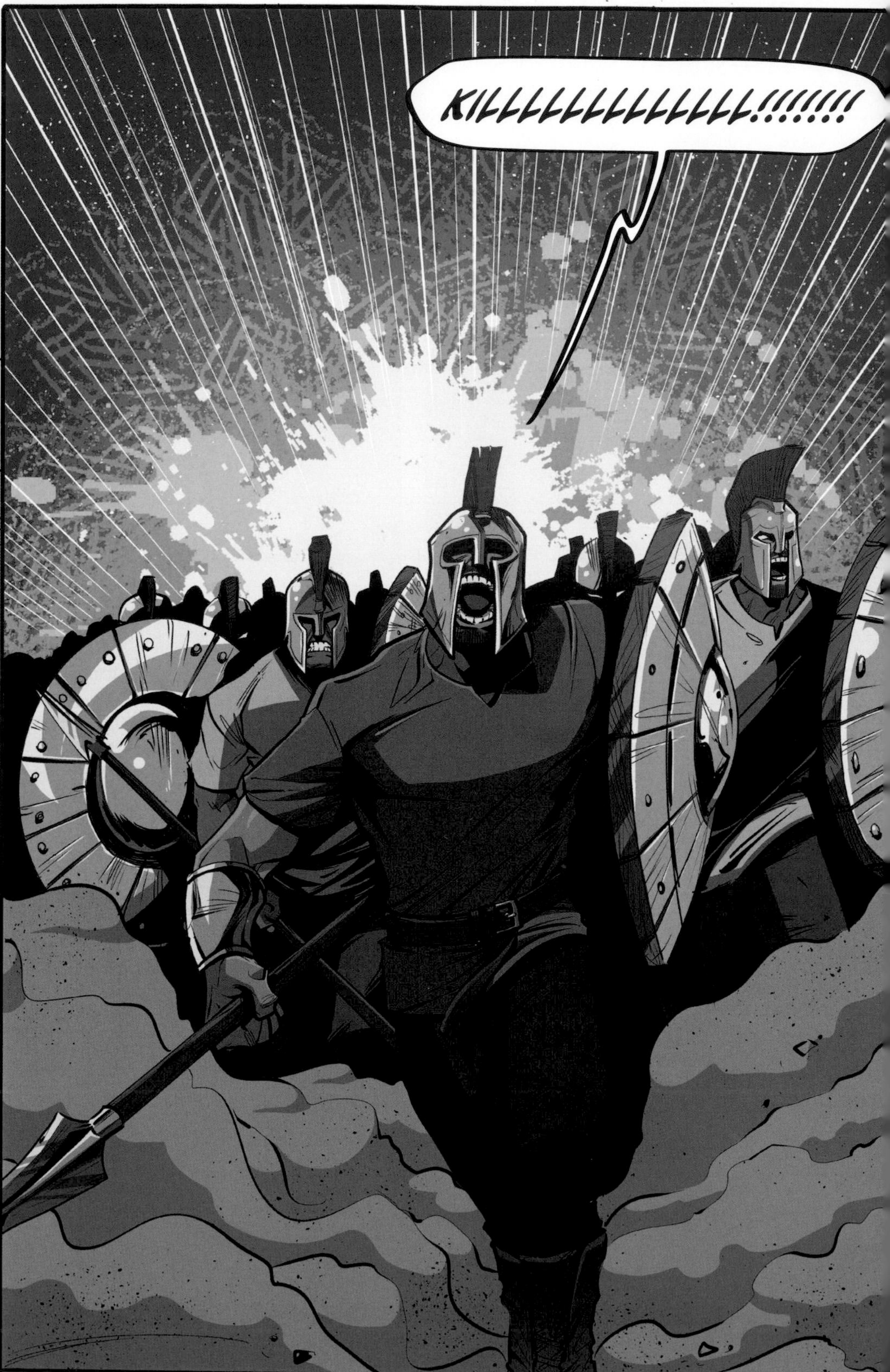
KILLLLLLLLLLLLLLL!!!!!!!!

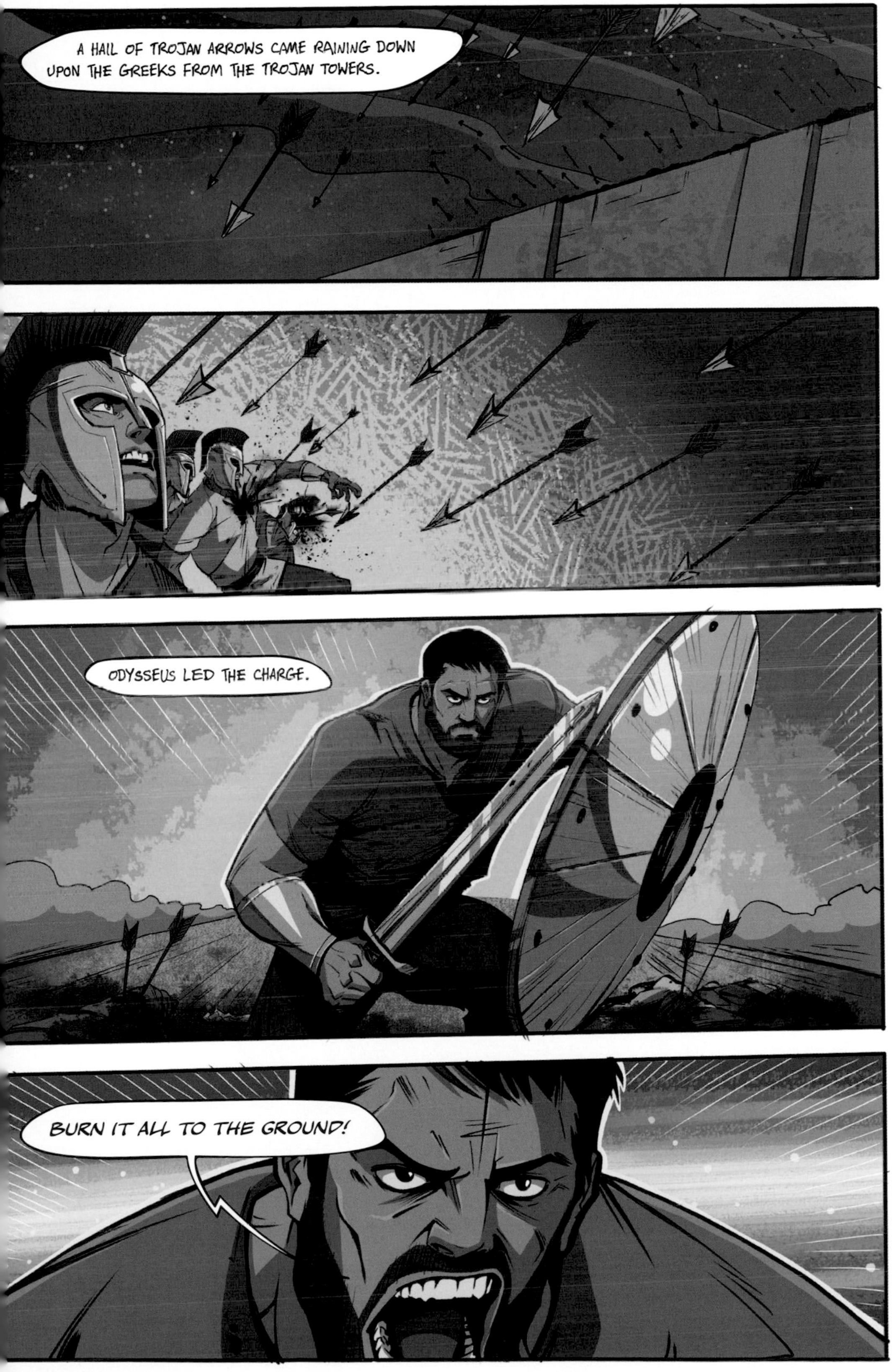
A HAIL OF TROJAN ARROWS CAME RAINING DOWN UPON THE GREEKS FROM THE TROJAN TOWERS.
ODYSSEUS LED THE CHARGE.
BURN IT ALL TO THE GROUND!

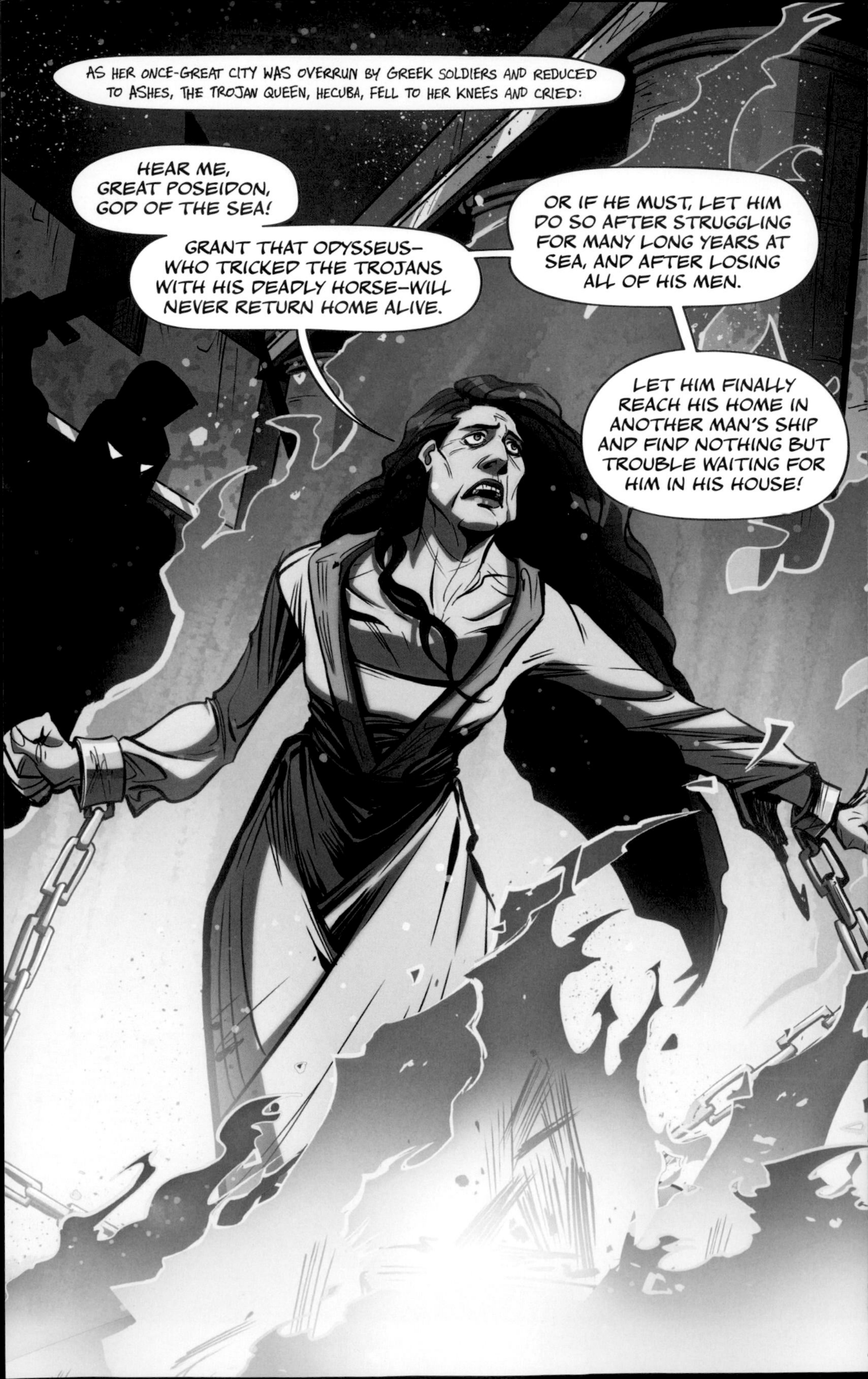
AS HER ONCE-GREAT CITY WAS OVERRUN BY GREEK SOLDIERS AND REDUCED TO ASHES, THE TROJAN QUEEN, HECUBA, FELL TO HER KNEES AND CRIED:
HEAR ME, GREAT POSEIDON, GOD OF THE SEA!
GRANT THAT ODYSSEUS—WHO TRICKED THE TROJANS WITH HIS DEADLY HORSE—WILL NEVER RETURN HOME ALIVE.
OR IF HE MUST, LET HIM DO SO AFTER STRUGGLING FOR MANY LONG YEARS AT SEA, AND AFTER LOSING ALL OF HIS MEN.
LET HIM FINALLY REACH HIS HOME IN ANOTHER MAN'S SHIP AND FIND NOTHING BUT TROUBLE WAITING FOR HIM IN HIS HOUSE!

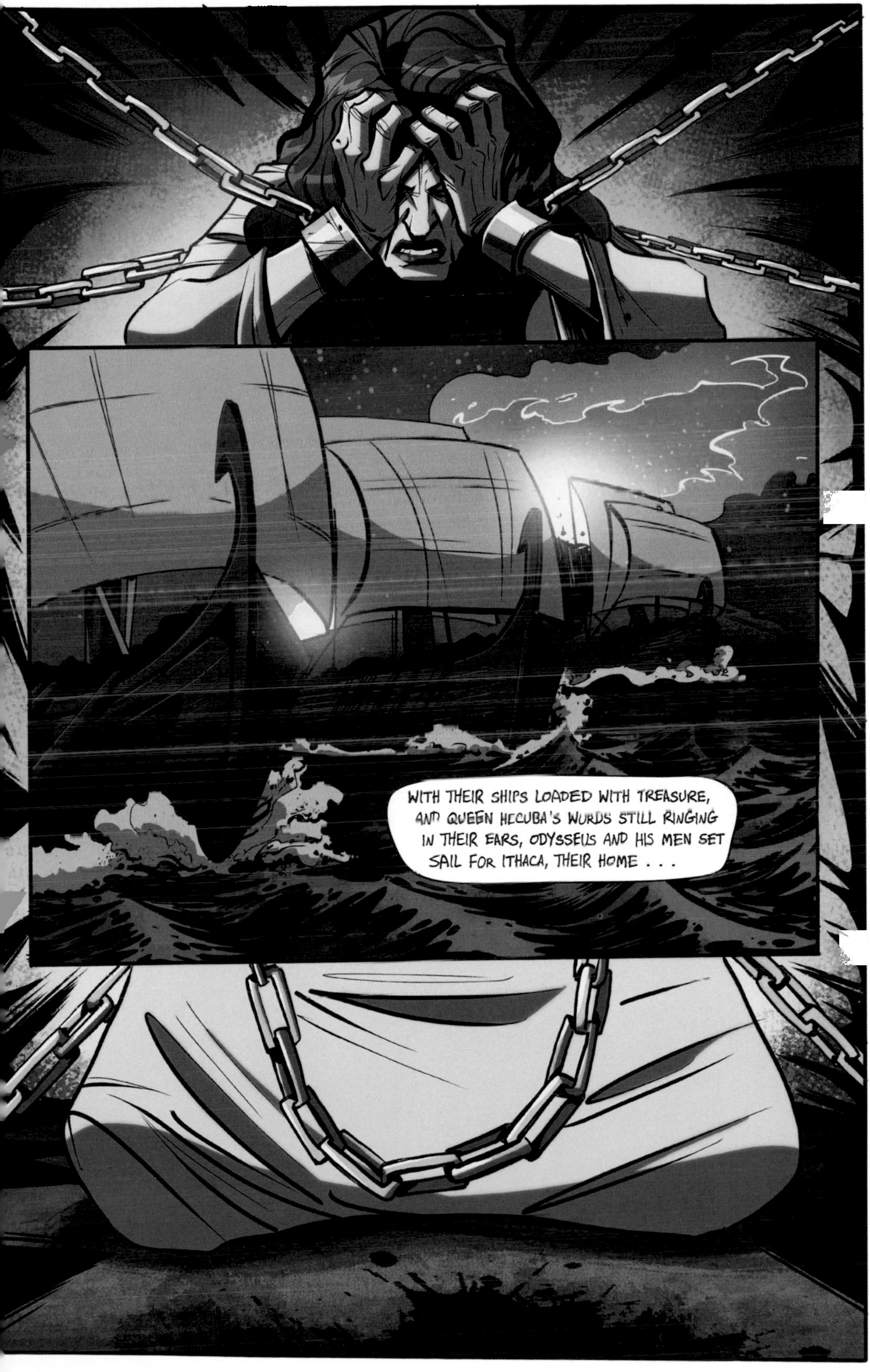
WITH THEIR SHIPS LOADED WITH TREASURE, AND QUEEN HECUBA'S WORDS STILL RINGING IN THEIR EARS, ODYSSEUS AND HIS MEN SET SAIL FOR ITHACA, THEIR HOME . . .

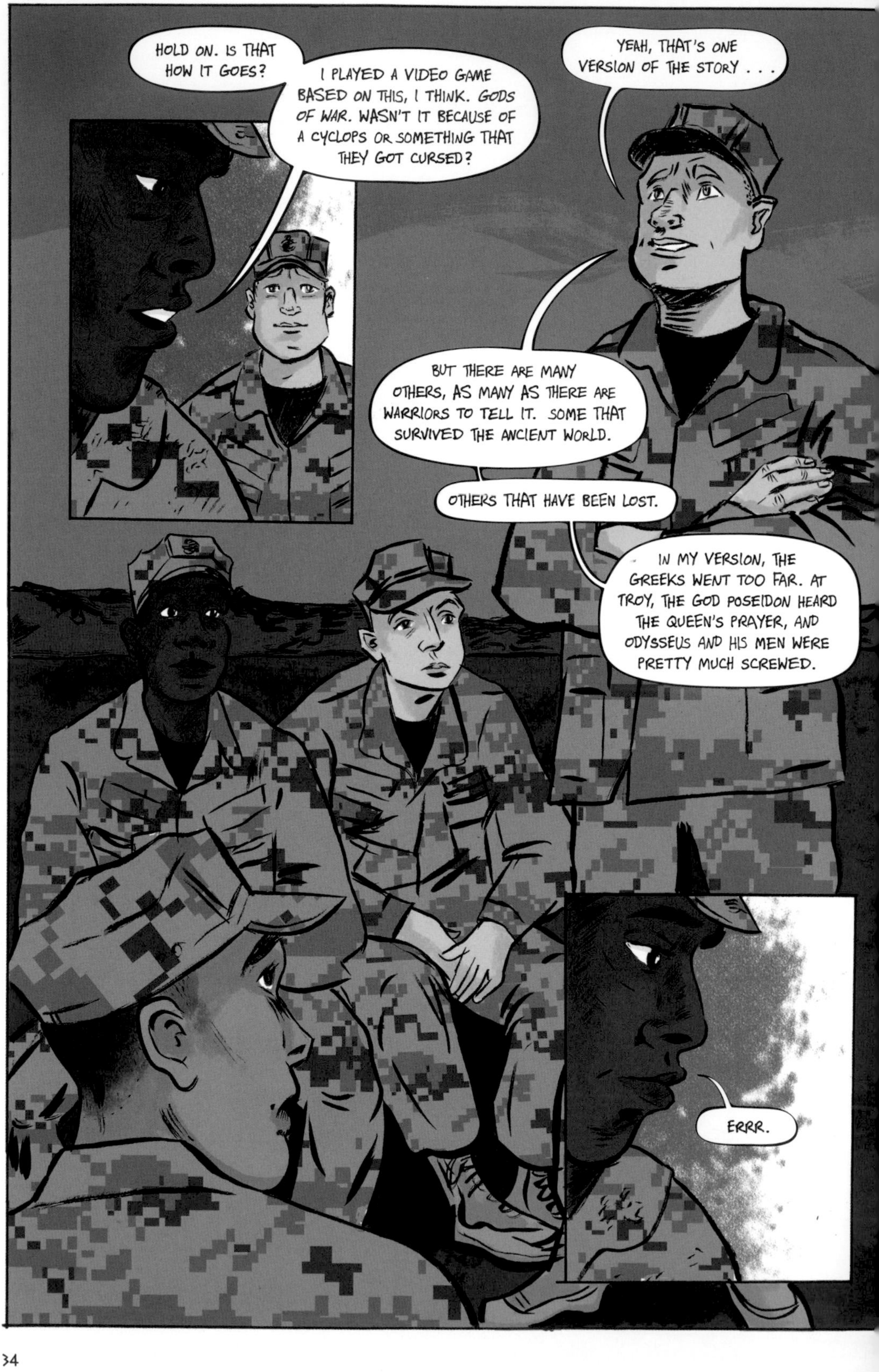
HOLD ON. IS THAT HOW IT GOES?
I PLAYED A VIDEO GAME BASED ON THIS, I THINK. GODS OF WAR. WASN'T IT BECAUSE OF A CYCLOPS OR SOMETHING THAT THEY GOT CURSED?
YEAH, THAT'S ONE VERSION OF THE STORY . . .
BUT THERE ARE MANY OTHERS, AS MANY AS THERE ARE WARRIORS TO TELL IT. SOME THAT SURVIVED THE ANCIENT WORLD.
OTHERS THAT HAVE BEEN LOST.
IN MY VERSION, THE GREEKS WENT TOO FAR. AT TROY, THE GOD POSEIDON HEARD THE QUEEN'S PRAYER, AND ODYSSEUS AND HIS MEN WERE PRETTY MUCH SCREWED.
ERRR.

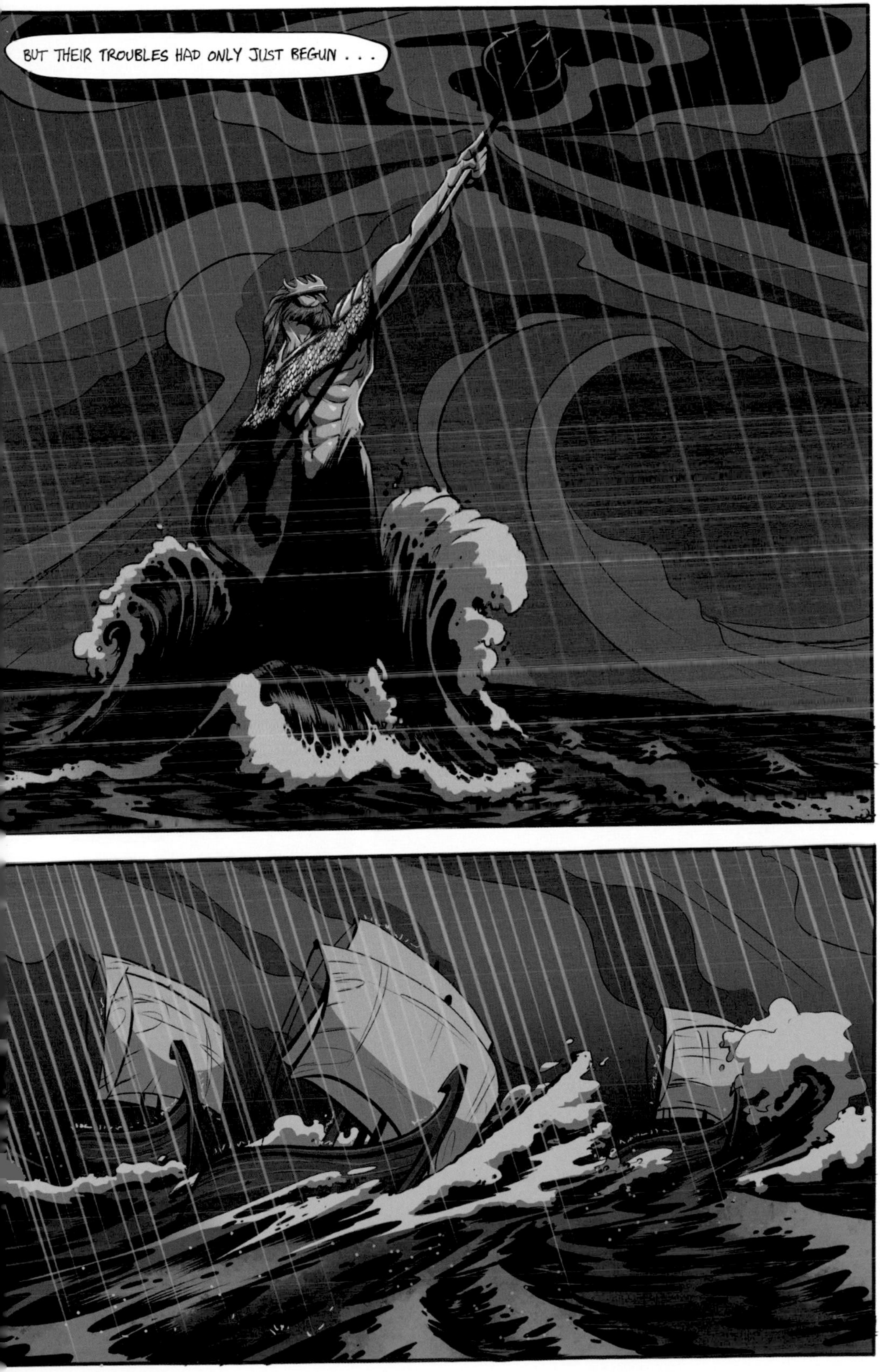
BUT THEIR TROUBLES HAD ONLY JUST BEGUN . . .

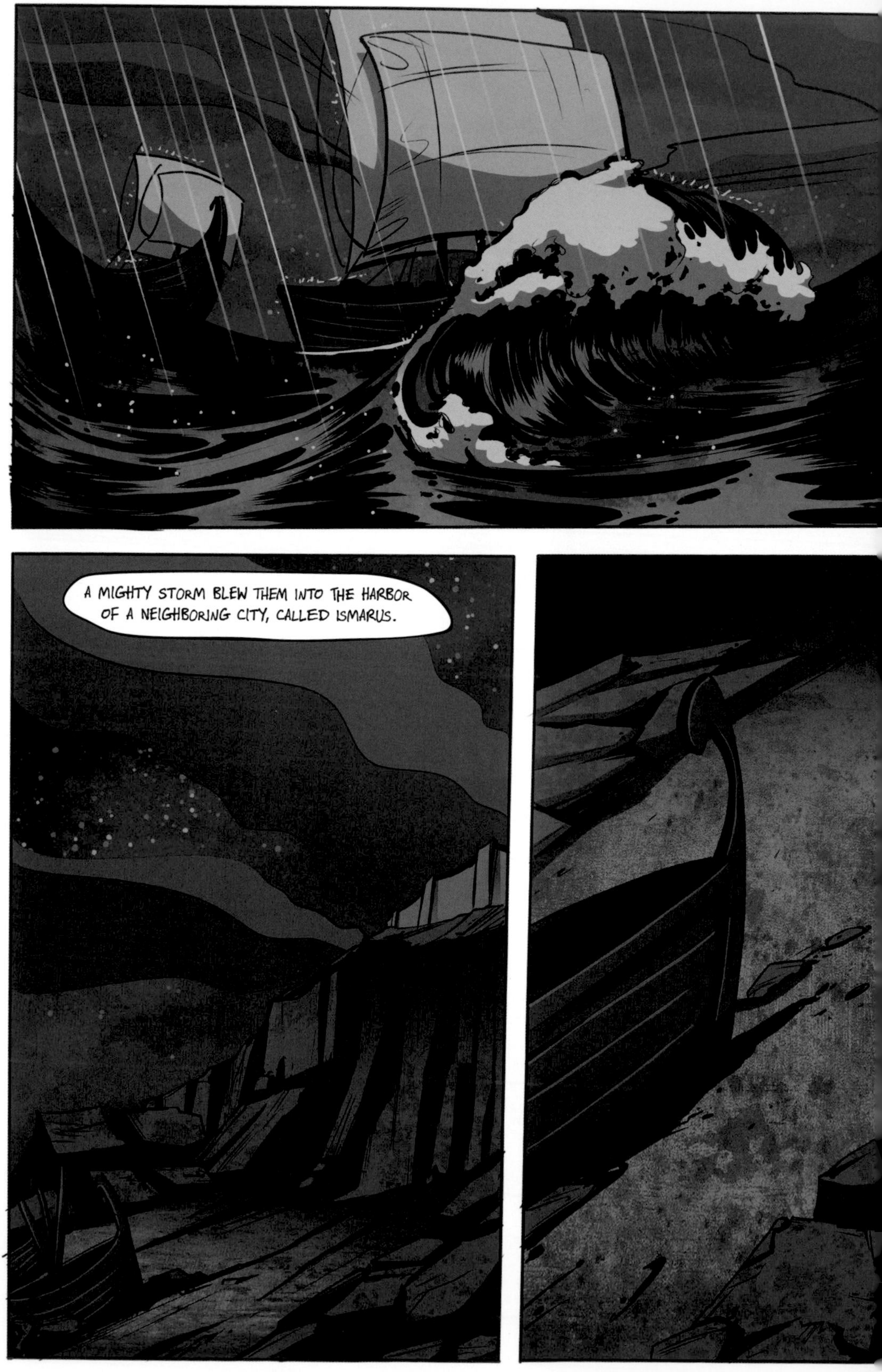
A MIGHTY STORM BLEW THEM INTO THE HARBOR OF A NEIGHBORING CITY, CALLED ISMARUS.

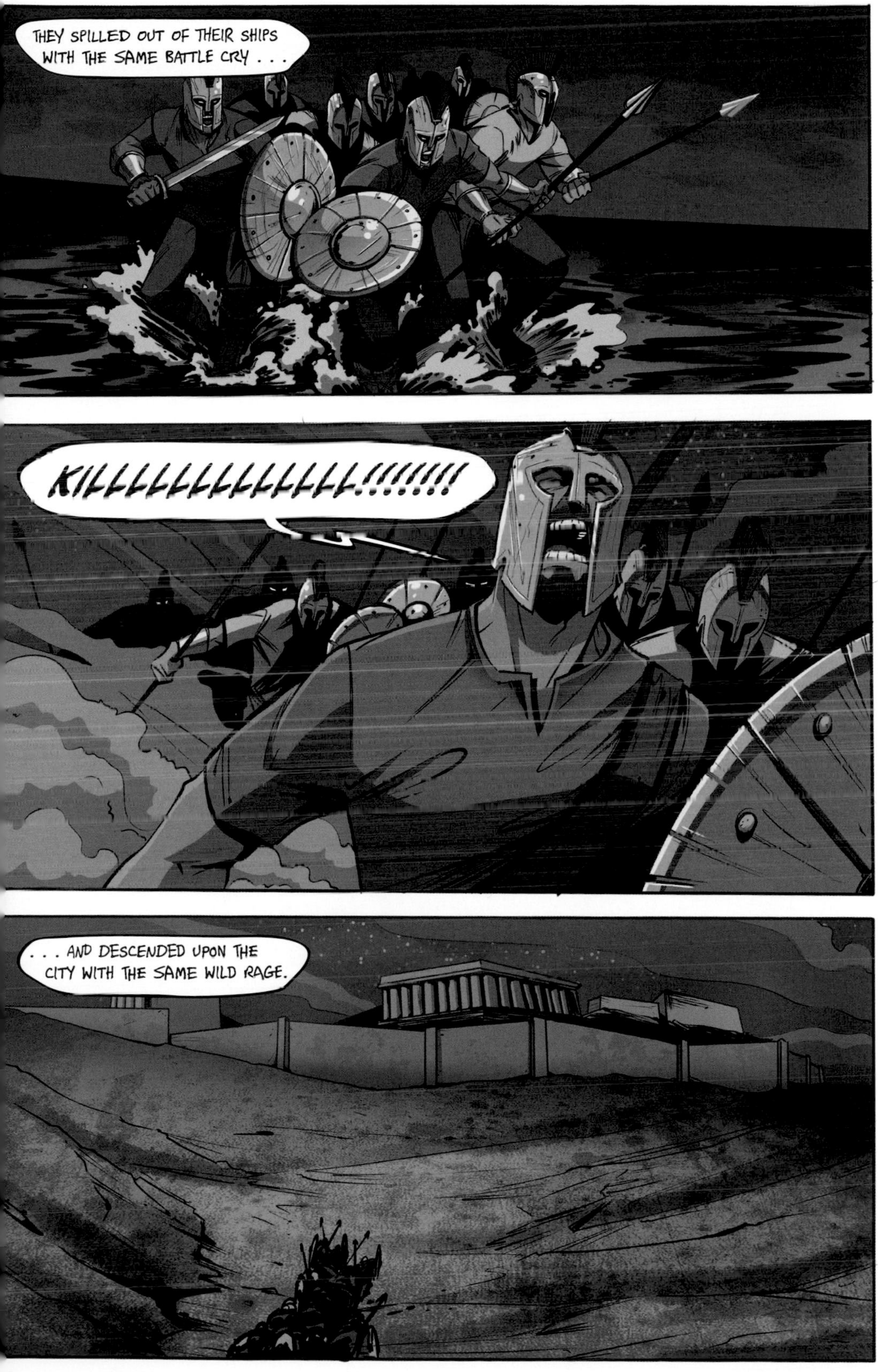
THEY SPILLED OUT OF THEIR SHIPS WITH THE SAME BATTLE CRY . . .
KILLLLLLLLLLLLLL!!!!!!!!
. . . AND DESCENDED UPON THE CITY WITH THE SAME WILD RAGE.

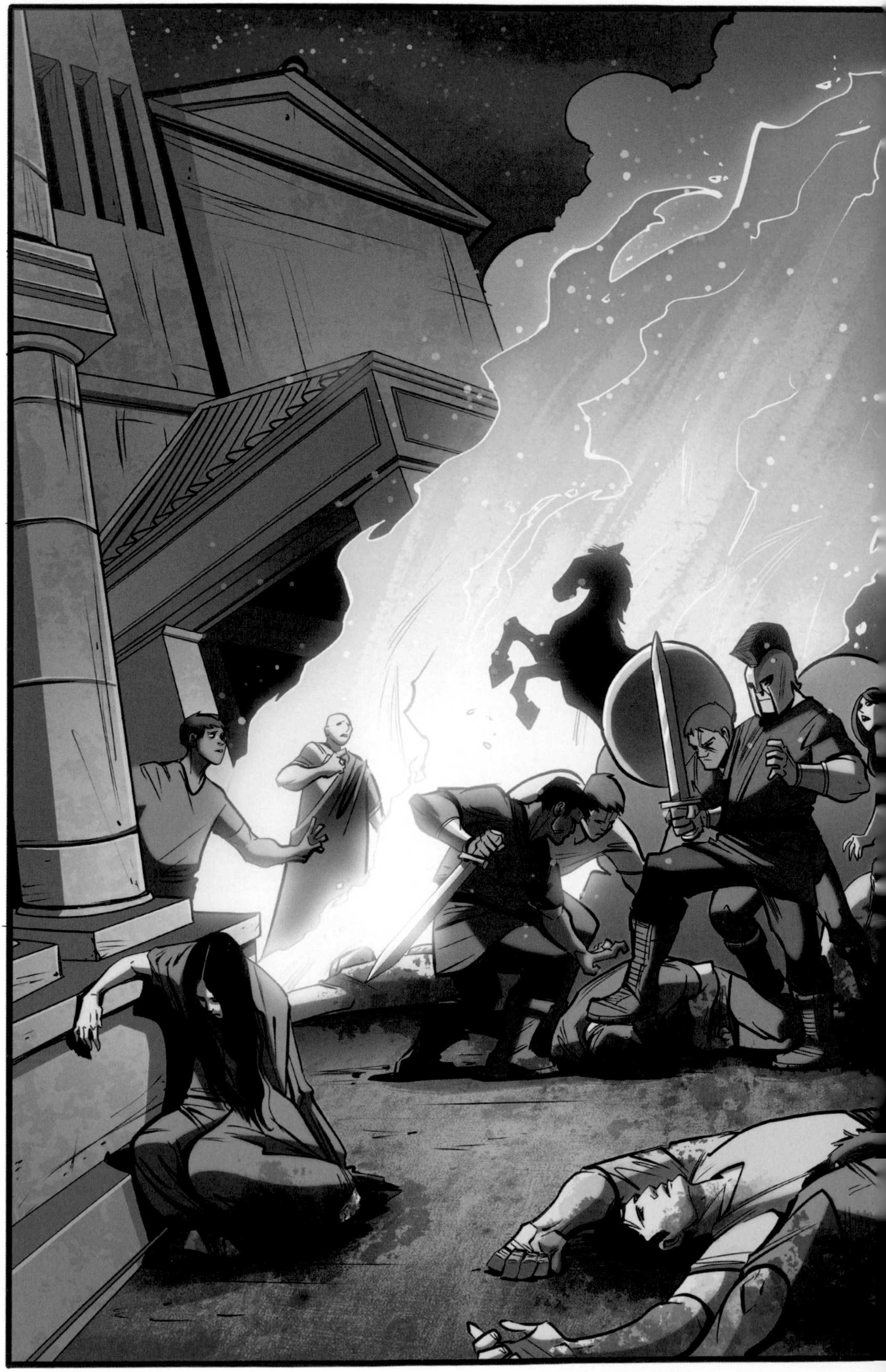

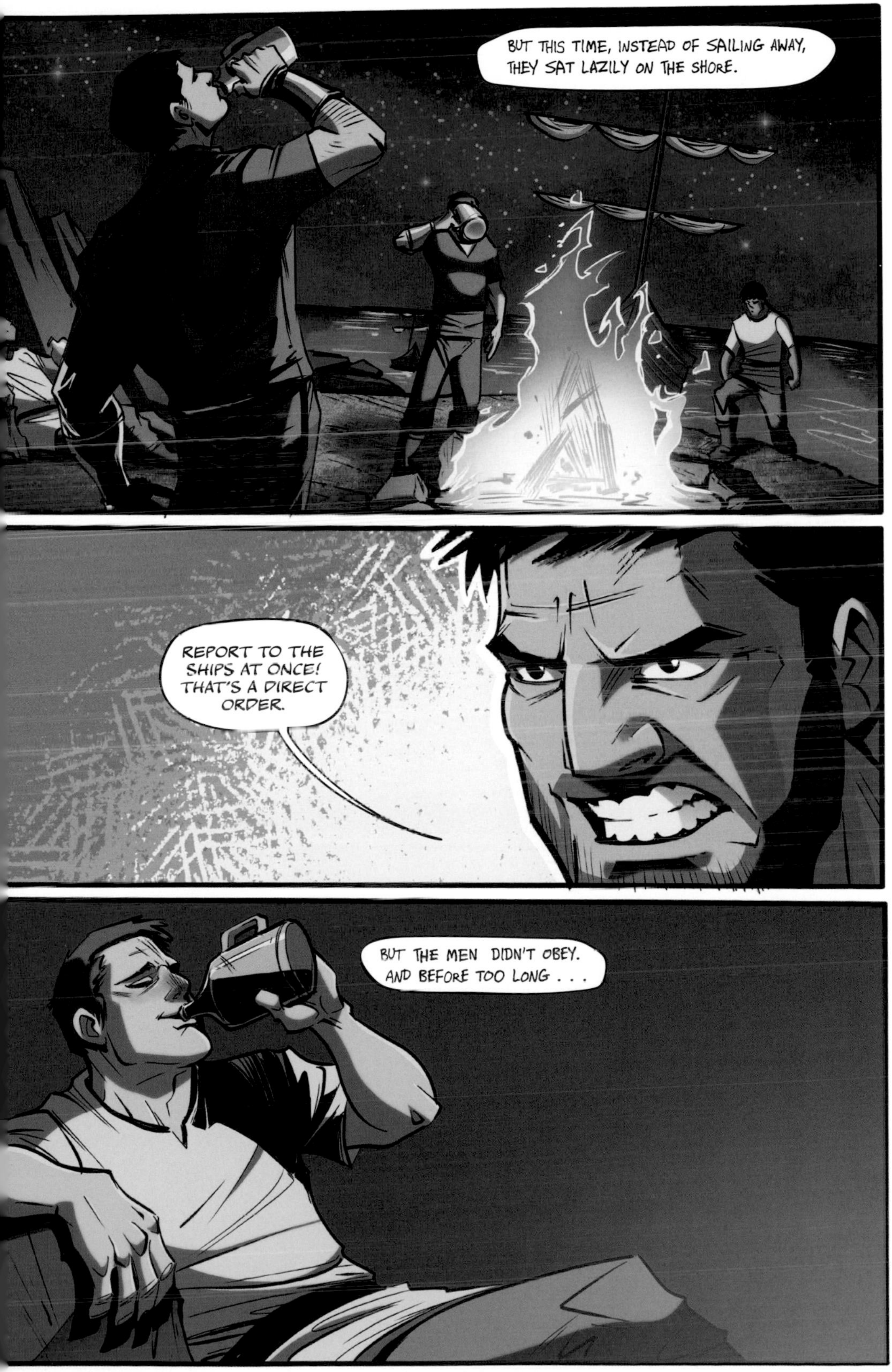
BUT THIS TIME, INSTEAD OF SAILING AWAY, THEY SAT LAZILY ON THE SHORE.
REPORT TO THE SHIPS AT ONCE! THAT'S A DIRECT ORDER.
BUT THE MEN DIDN'T OBEY. AND BEFORE TOO LONG . . .

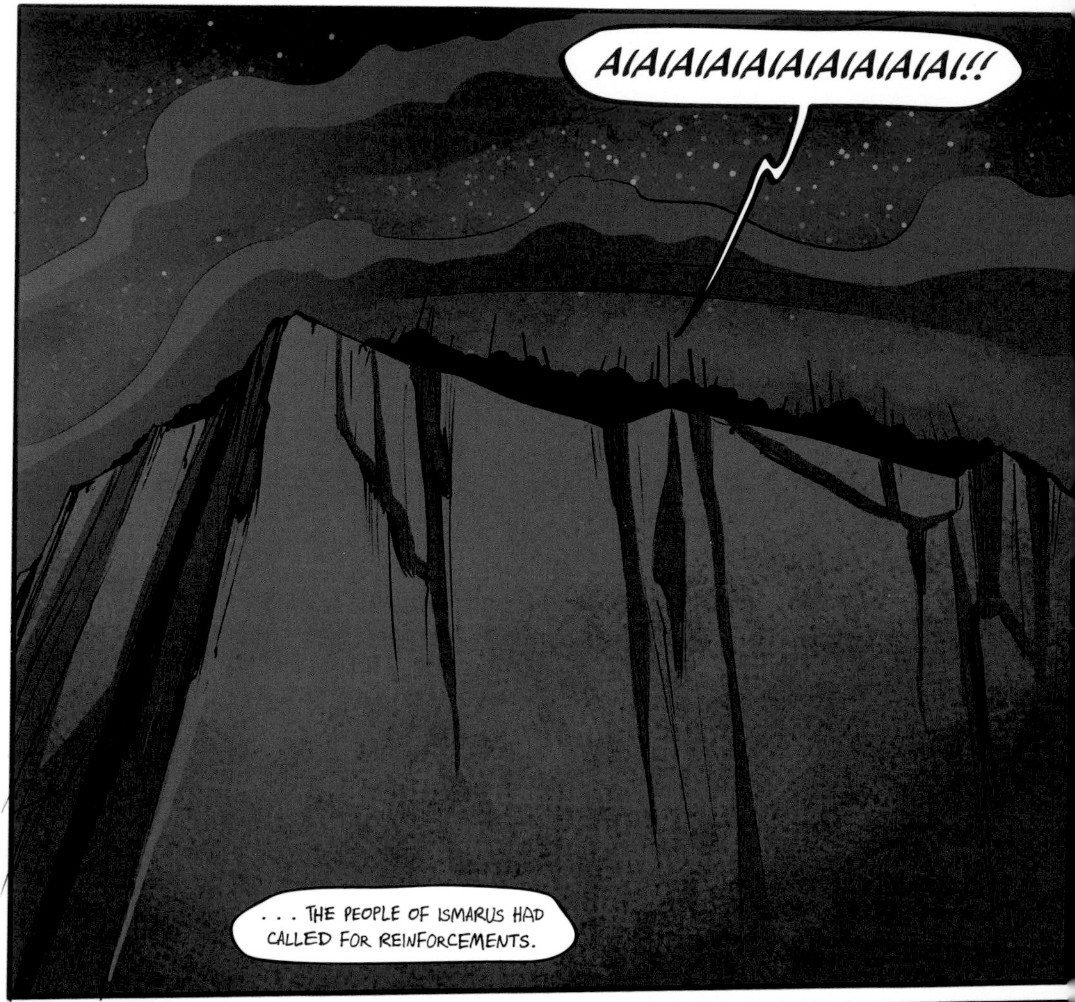
AIAIAIAIAIAIAIAIAIAI!!
. . . THE PEOPLE OF ISMARUS HAD CALLED FOR REINFORCEMENTS.

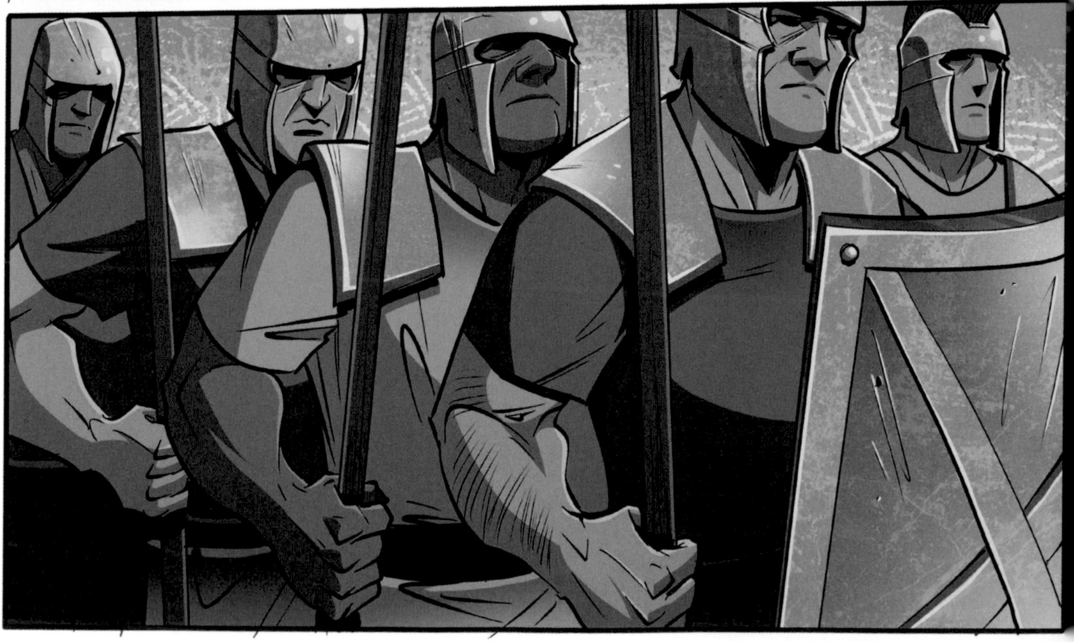

ON MY ORDER, MEN!

KILLLLLLLLLLLLLL!!!!!!!!!!!!!!!

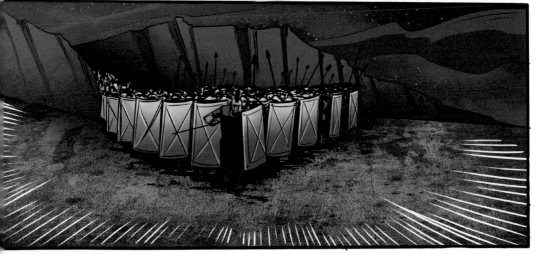

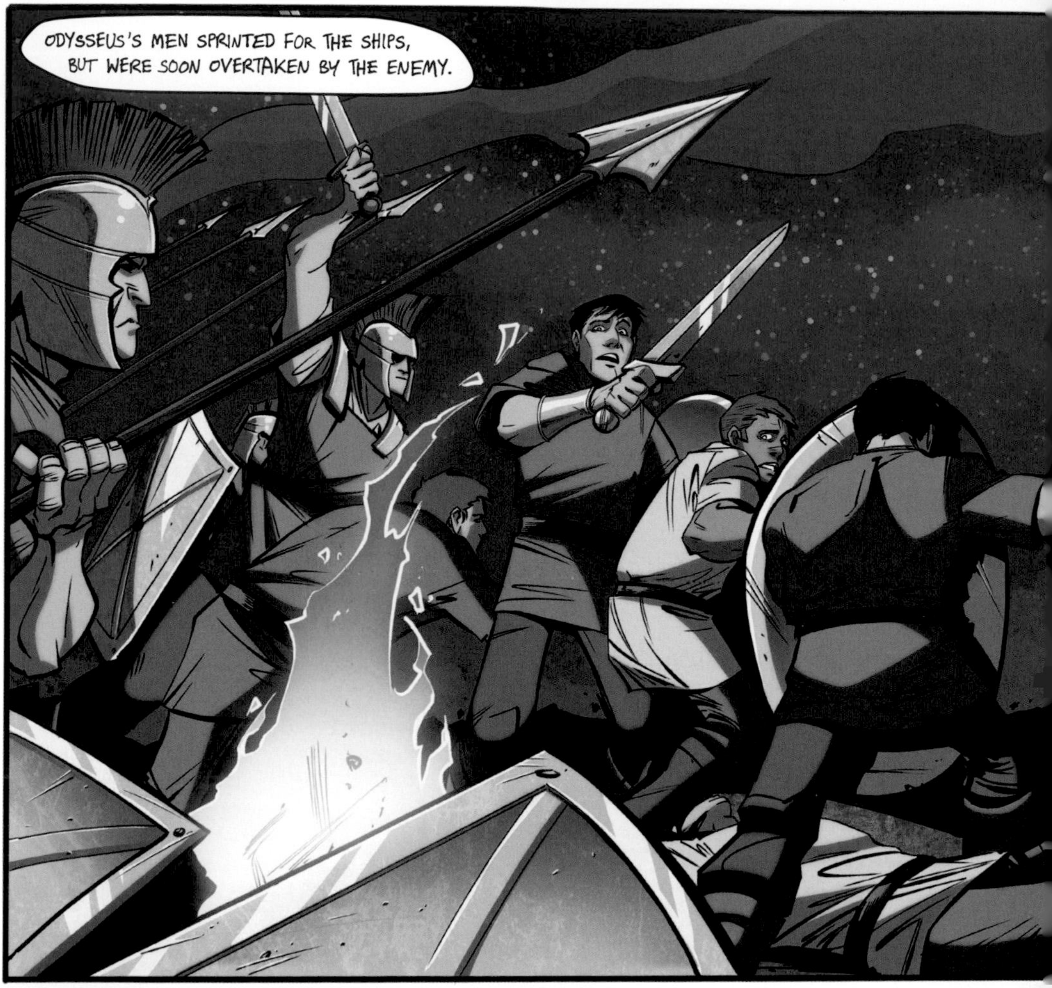
ODYSSEUS'S MEN SPRINTED FOR THE SHIPS, BUT WERE SOON OVERTAKEN BY THE ENEMY.

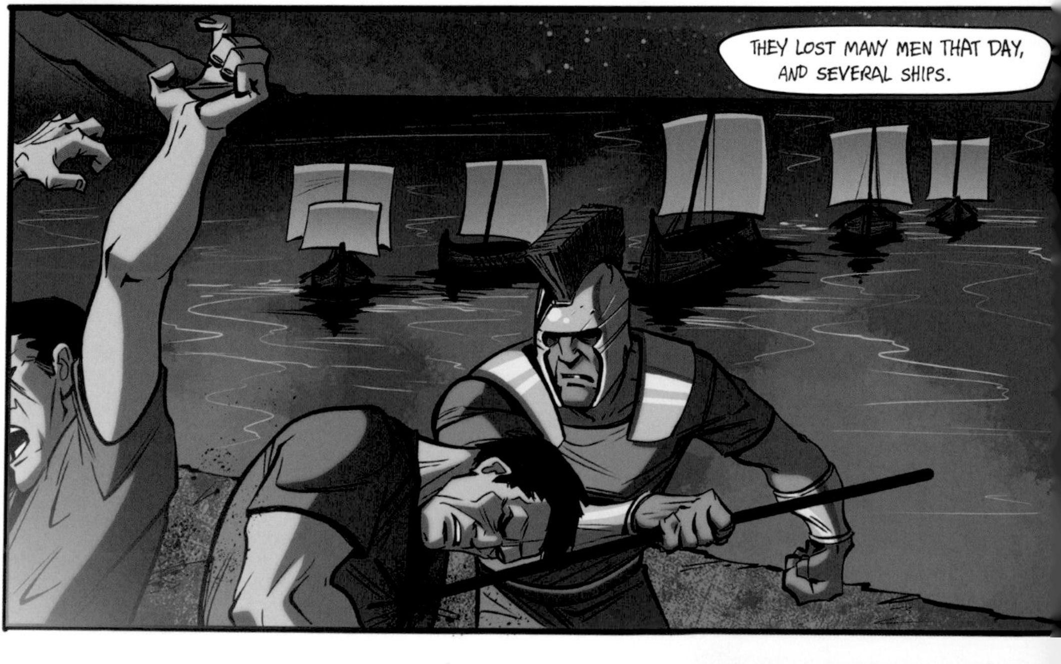
THEY LOST MANY MEN THAT DAY, AND SEVERAL SHIPS.

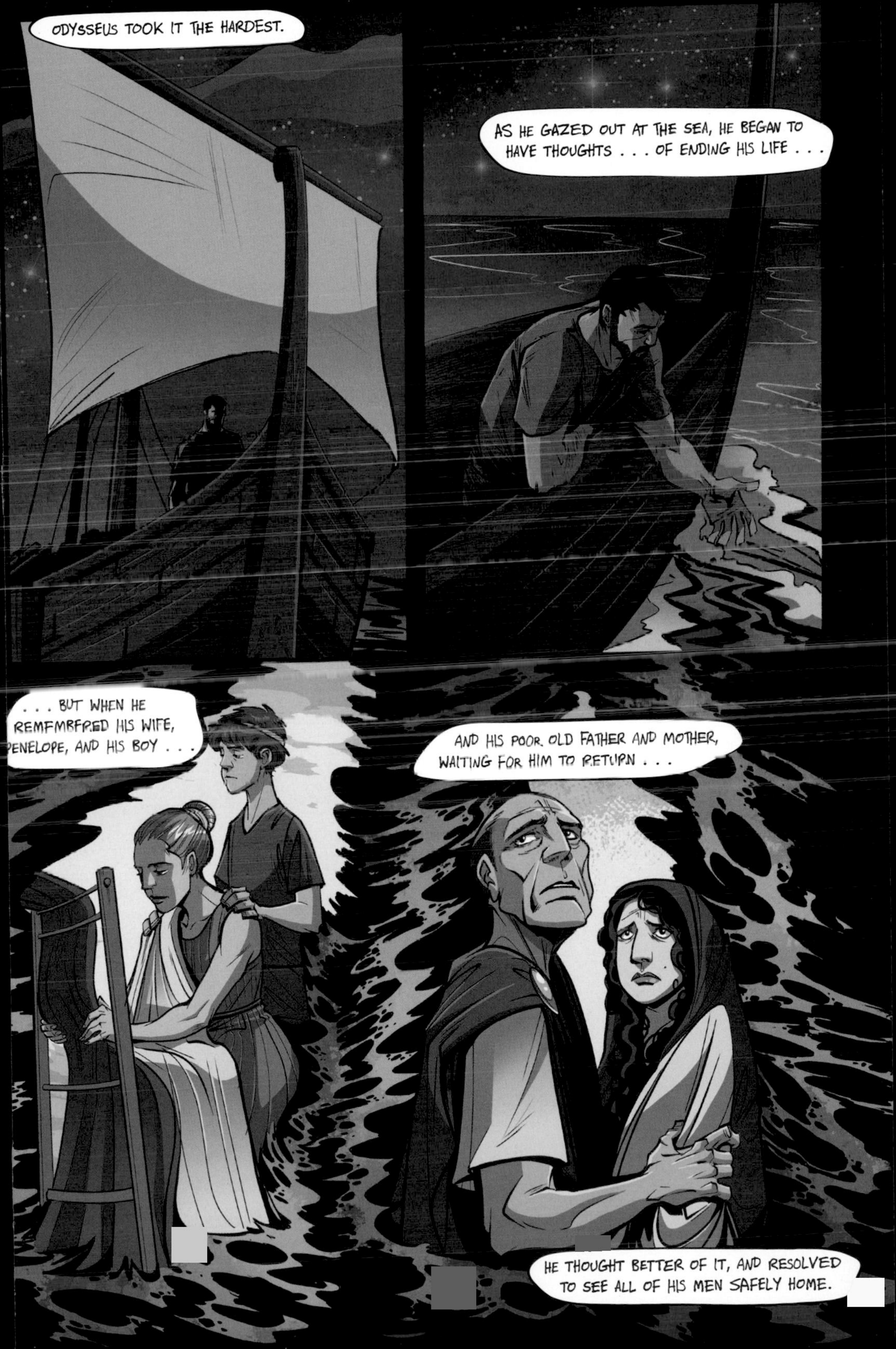

ODYSSEUS TOOK IT THE HARDEST.
AS HE GAZED OUT AT THE SEA, HE BEGAN TO HAVE THOUGHTS . . . OF ENDING HIS LIFE . . .
. . . BUT WHEN HE REMEMBERED HIS WIFE, PENELOPE, AND HIS BOY . . .
AND HIS POOR OLD FATHER AND MOTHER, WAITING FOR HIM TO RETURN . . .
HE THOUGHT BETTER OF IT, AND RESOLVED TO SEE ALL OF HIS MEN SAFELY HOME.

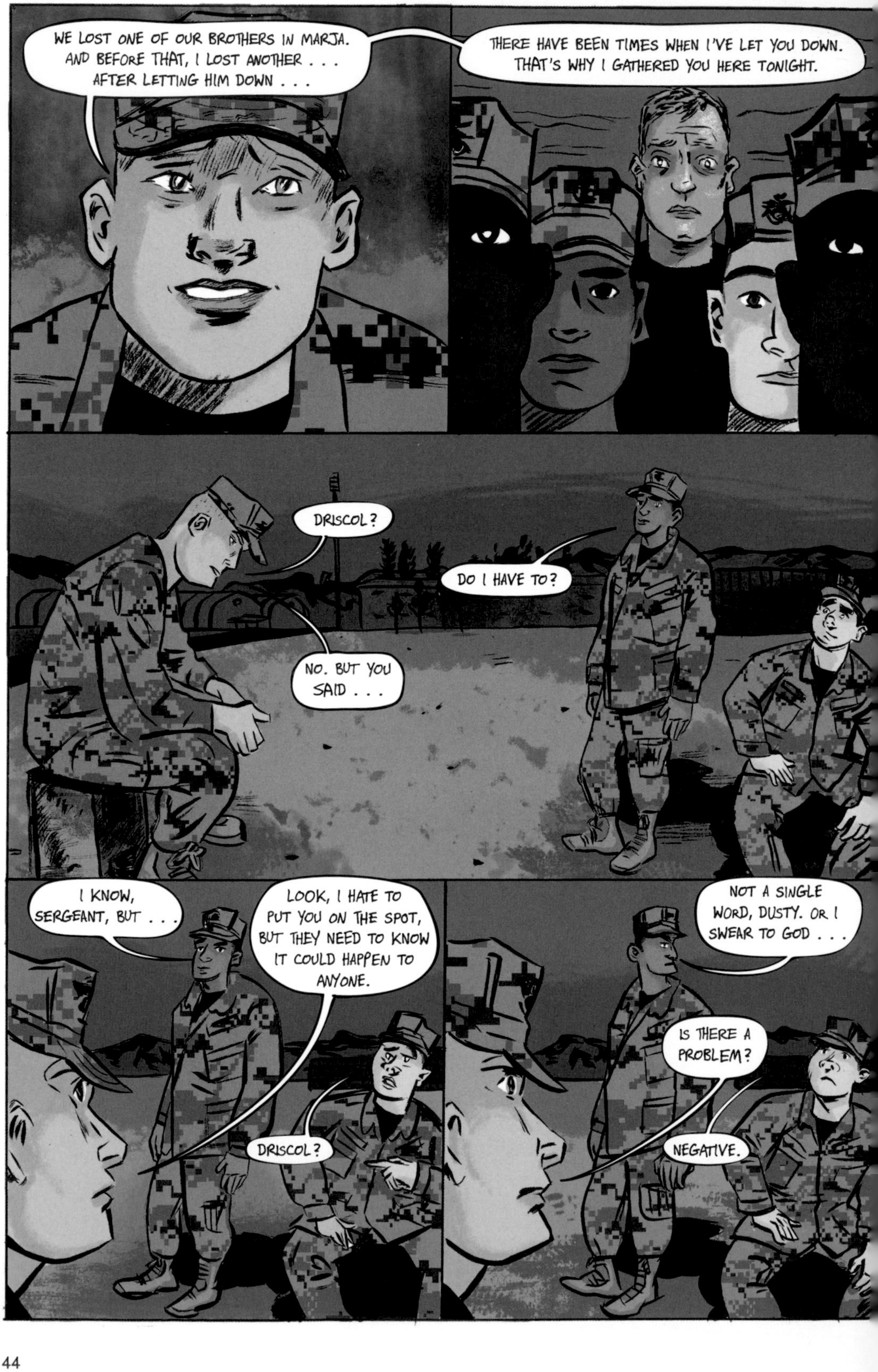
WE LOST ONE OF OUR BROTHERS IN MARJA. AND BEFORE THAT, I LOST ANOTHER . . . AFTER LETTING HIM DOWN . . .
THERE HAVE BEEN TIMES WHEN I'VE LET YOU DOWN. THAT'S WHY I GATHERED YOU HERE TONIGHT.
DRISCOL?
DO I HAVE TO?
NO. BUT YOU SAID . . .
I KNOW, SERGEANT, BUT . . .
LOOK, I HATE TO PUT YOU ON THE SPOT, BUT THEY NEED TO KNOW IT COULD HAPPEN TO ANYONE.
DRISCOL?
NOT A SINGLE WORD, DUSTY. OR I SWEAR TO GOD . . .
IS THERE A PROBLEM?
NEGATIVE.

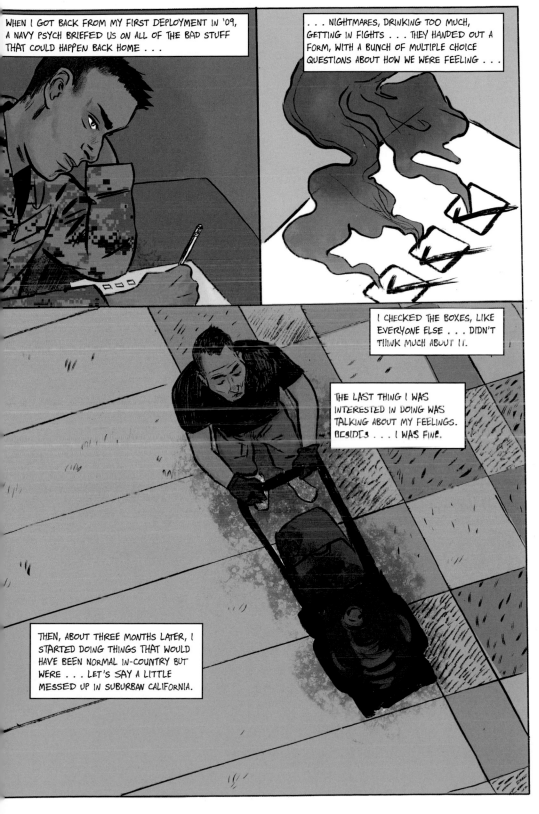

WHEN I GOT BACK FROM MY FIRST DEPLOYMENT IN '09, A NAVY PSYCH BRIEFED US ON ALL OF THE BAD STUFF THAT COULD HAPPEN BACK HOME . . .

. . . NIGHTMARES, DRINKING TOO MUCH, GETTING IN FIGHTS . . . THEY HANDED OUT A FORM, WITH A BUNCH OF MULTIPLE CHOICE QUESTIONS ABOUT HOW WE WERE FEELING . . .

I CHECKED THE BOXES, LIKE EVERYONE ELSE . . . DIDN'T THINK MUCH ABOUT IT.

THE LAST THING I WAS INTERESTED IN DOING WAS TALKING ABOUT MY FEELINGS. BESIDES . . . I WAS FINE.

THEN, ABOUT THREE MONTHS LATER, I STARTED DOING THINGS THAT WOULD HAVE BEEN NORMAL IN-COUNTRY BUT WERE . . . LET'S SAY A LITTLE MESSED UP IN SUBURBAN CALIFORNIA.

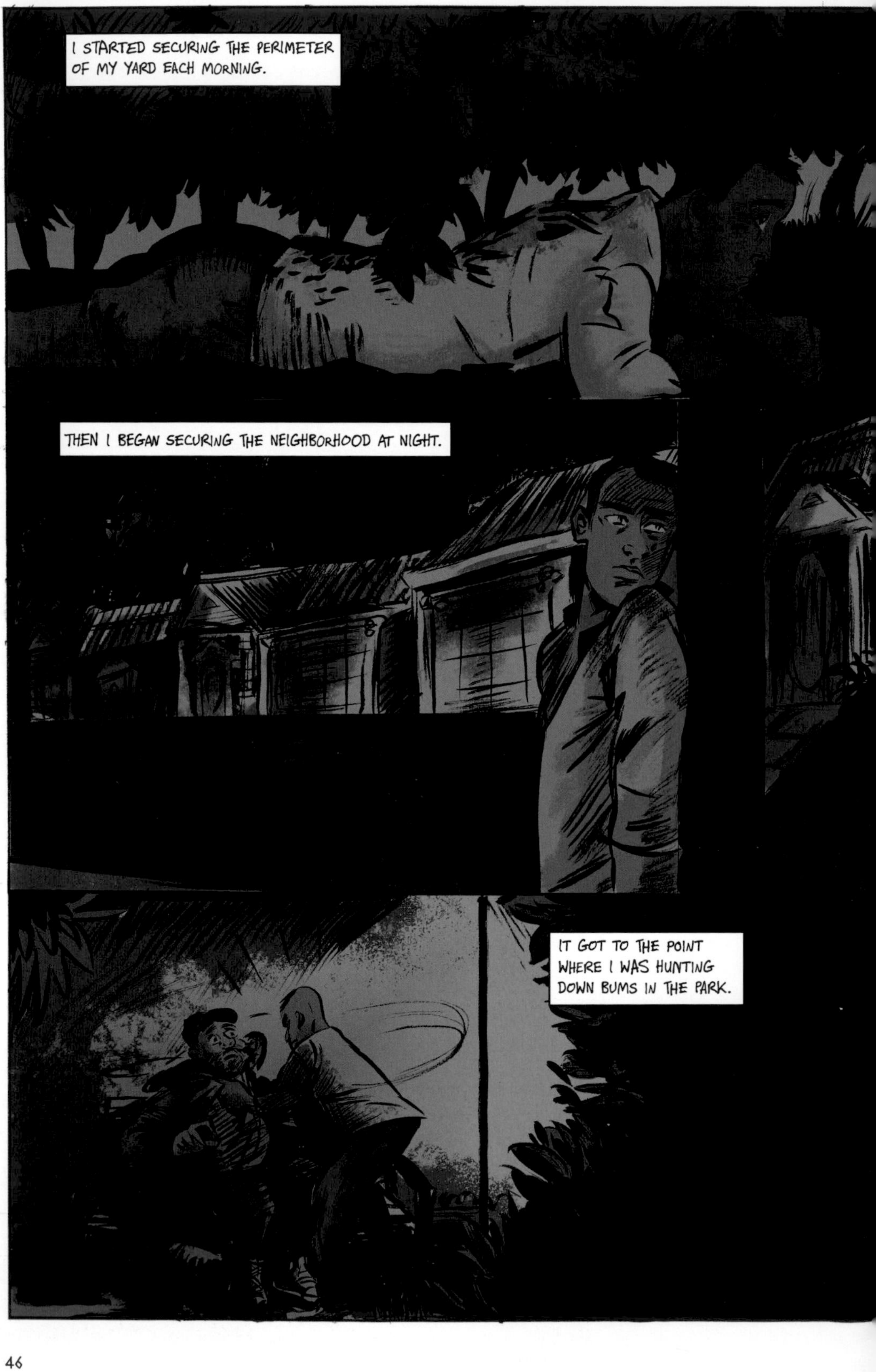
I STARTED SECURING THE PERIMETER OF MY YARD EACH MORNING.
THEN I BEGAN SECURING THE NEIGHBORHOOD AT NIGHT.
IT GOT TO THE POINT WHERE I WAS HUNTING DOWN BUMS IN THE PARK.

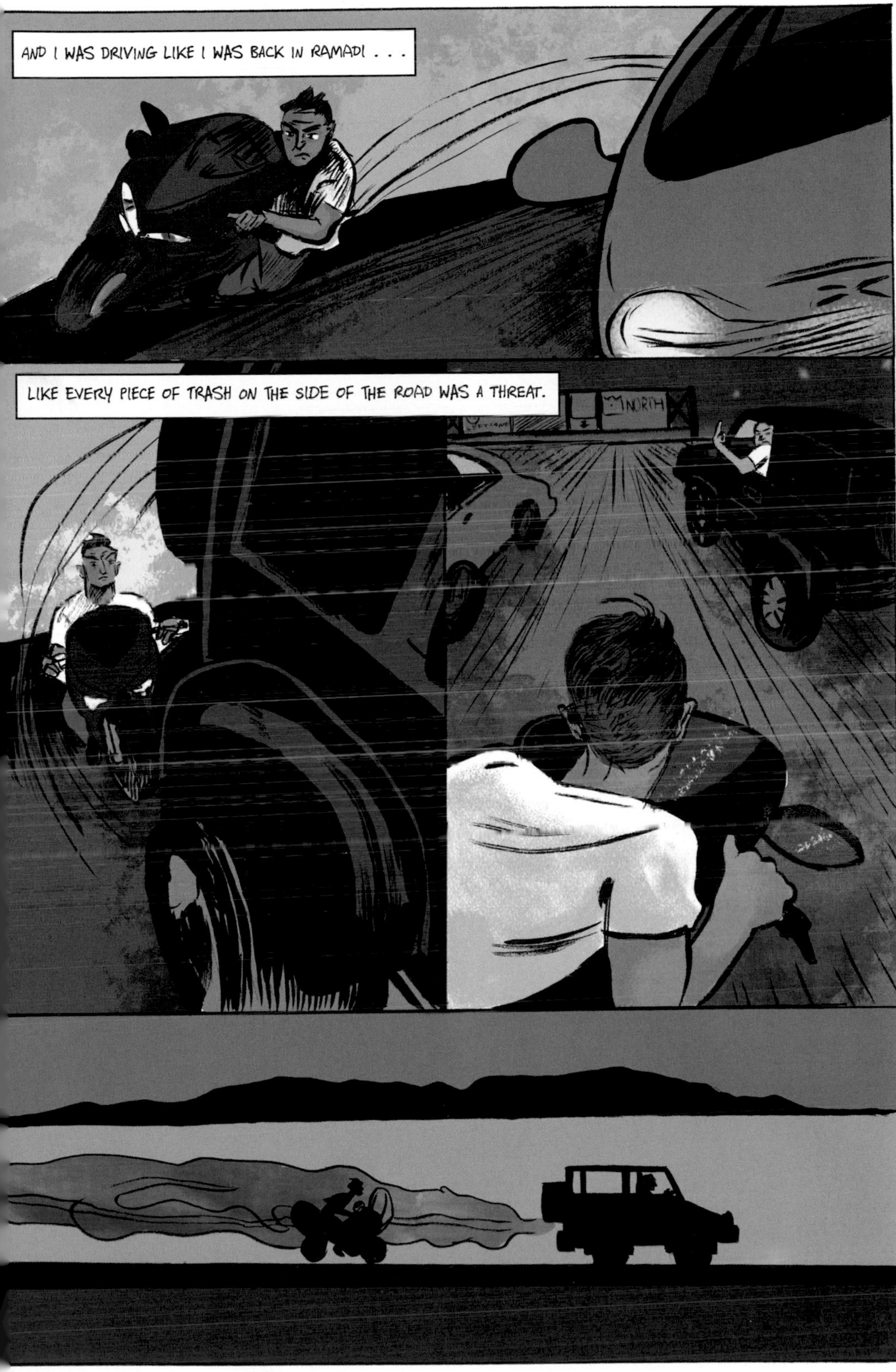
AND I WAS DRIVING LIKE I WAS BACK IN RAMADI . . .
LIKE EVERY PIECE OF TRASH ON THE SIDE OF THE ROAD WAS A THREAT.
NORTH

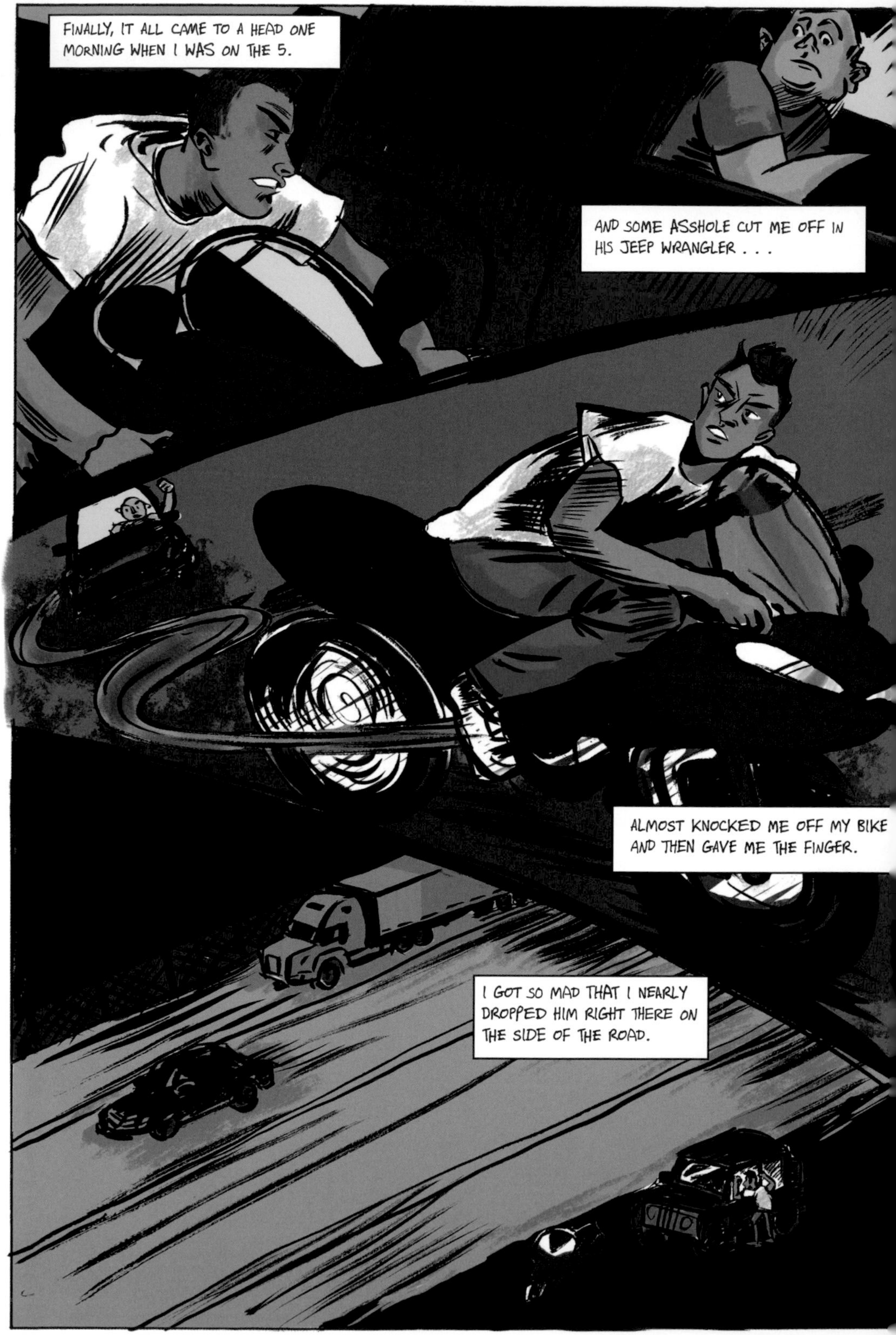
FINALLY, IT ALL CAME TO A HEAD ONE MORNING WHEN I WAS ON THE 5.
AND SOME ASSHOLE CUT ME OFF IN HIS JEEP WRANGLER . . .
ALMOST KNOCKED ME OFF MY BIKE AND THEN GAVE ME THE FINGER.
I GOT SO MAD THAT I NEARLY DROPPED HIM RIGHT THERE ON THE SIDE OF THE ROAD.

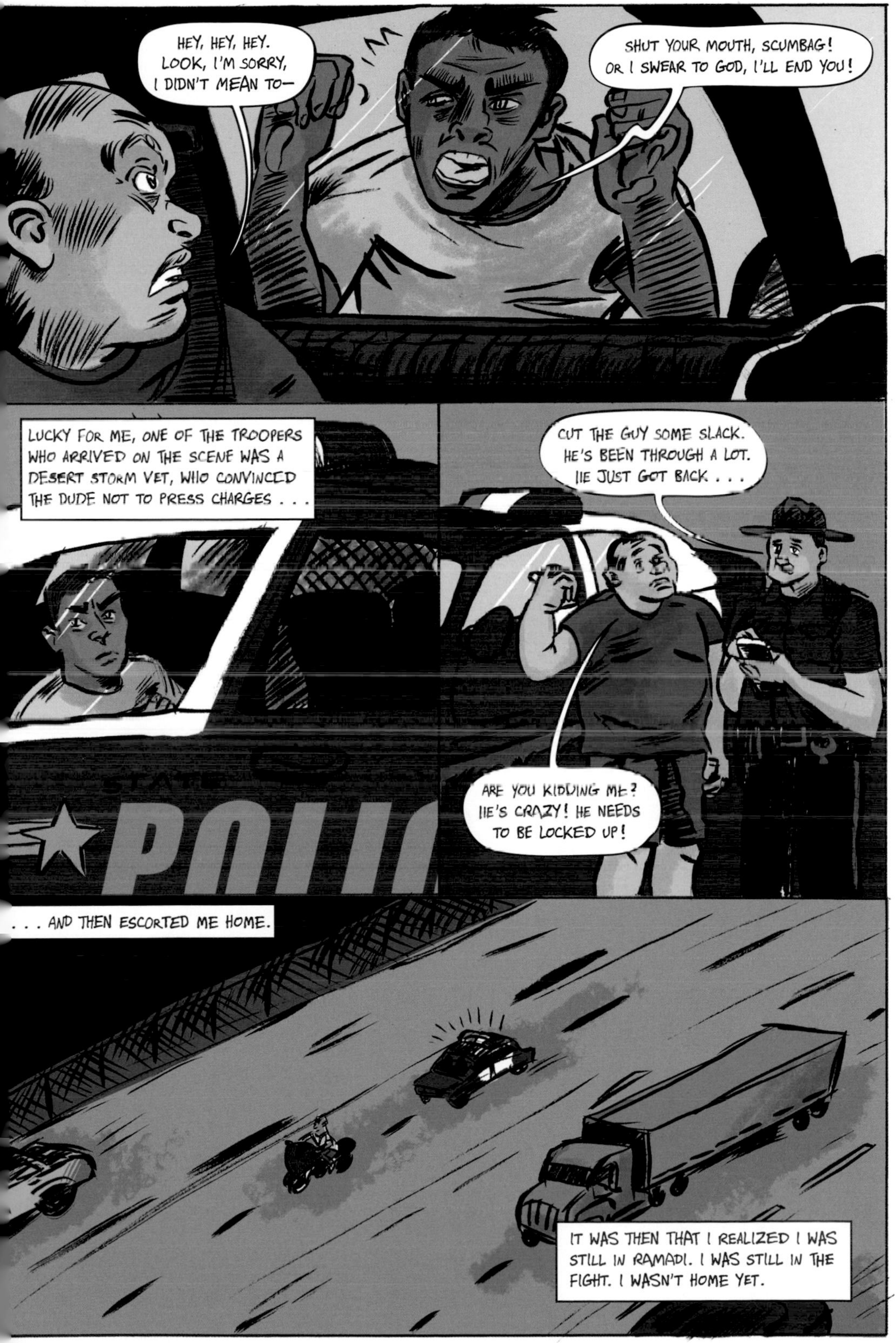
HEY, HEY, HEY. LOOK, I'M SORRY, I DIDN'T MEAN TO—
SHUT YOUR MOUTH, SCUMBAG! OR I SWEAR TO GOD, I'LL END YOU!
LUCKY FOR ME, ONE OF THE TROOPERS WHO ARRIVED ON THE SCENE WAS A DESERT STORM VET, WHO CONVINCED THE DUDE NOT TO PRESS CHARGES . . .
STATE
POLI
CUT THE GUY SOME SLACK. HE'S BEEN THROUGH A LOT. HE JUST GOT BACK . . .
ARE YOU KIDDING ME? HE'S CRAZY! HE NEEDS TO BE LOCKED UP!
. . . AND THEN ESCORTED ME HOME.
IT WAS THEN THAT I REALIZED I WAS STILL IN RAMADI. I WAS STILL IN THE FIGHT. I WASN'T HOME YET.

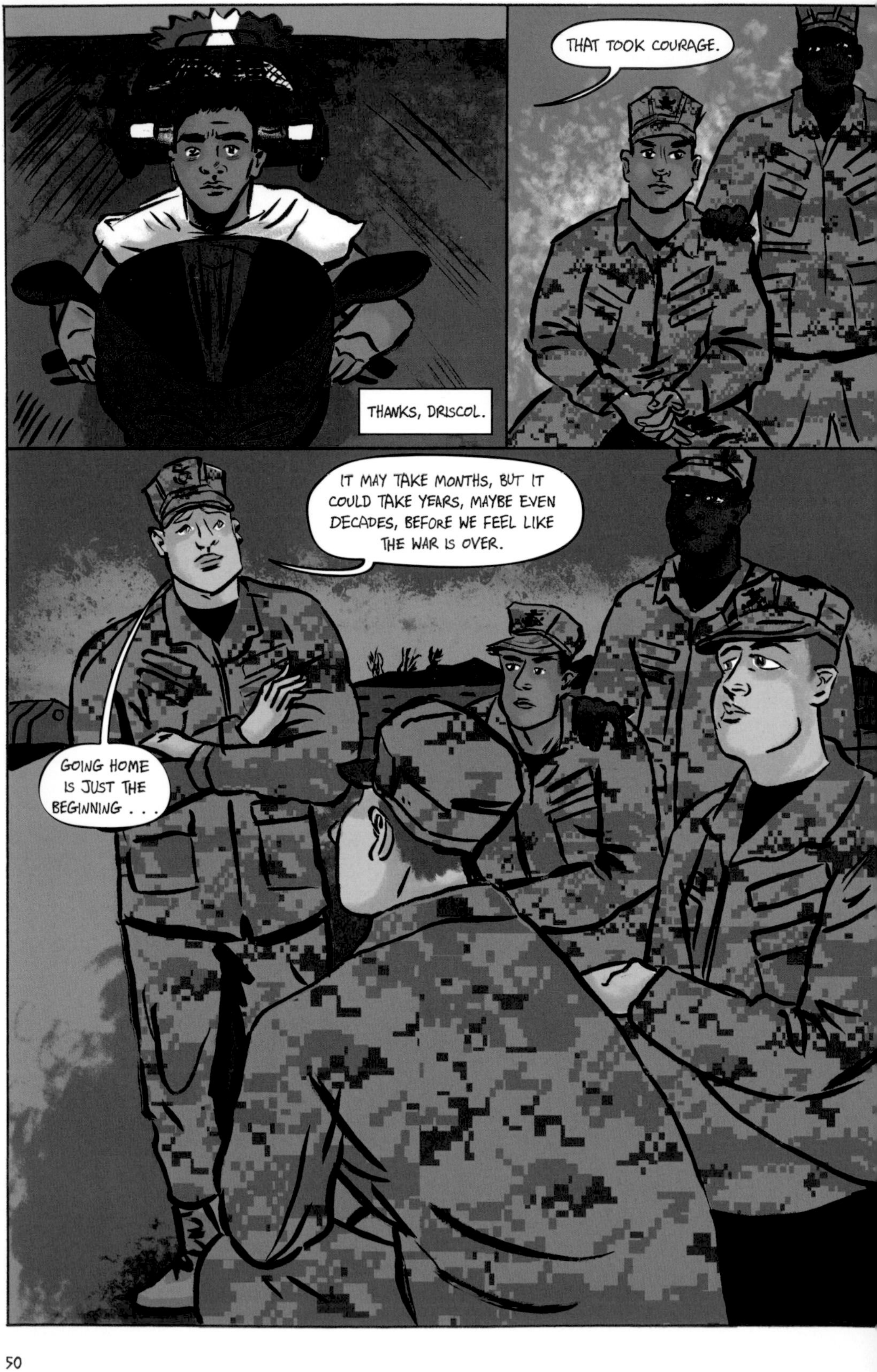
THANKS, DRISCOL.
THAT TOOK COURAGE.
IT MAY TAKE MONTHS, BUT IT COULD TAKE YEARS, MAYBE EVEN DECADES, BEFORE WE FEEL LIKE THE WAR IS OVER.
GOING HOME IS JUST THE BEGINNING . . .

CHAPTER 2

STRAYING OFF COURSE

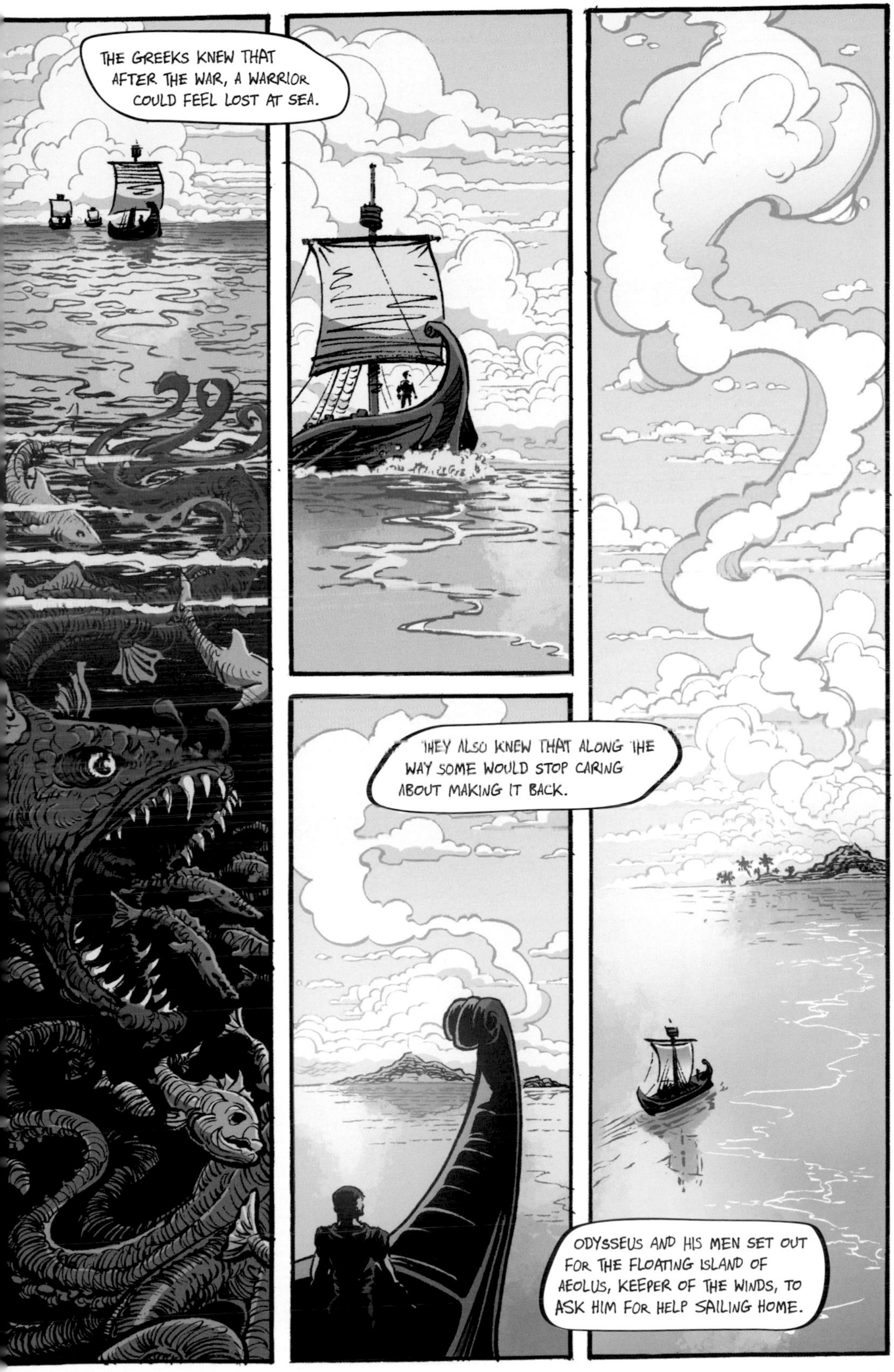
THE GREEKS KNEW THAT AFTER THE WAR, A WARRIOR COULD FEEL LOST AT SEA.
THEY ALSO KNEW THAT ALONG THE WAY SOME WOULD STOP CARING ABOUT MAKING IT BACK.
ODYSSEUS AND HIS MEN SET OUT FOR THE FLOATING ISLAND OF AEOLUS, KEEPER OF THE WINDS, TO ASK HIM FOR HELP SAILING HOME.

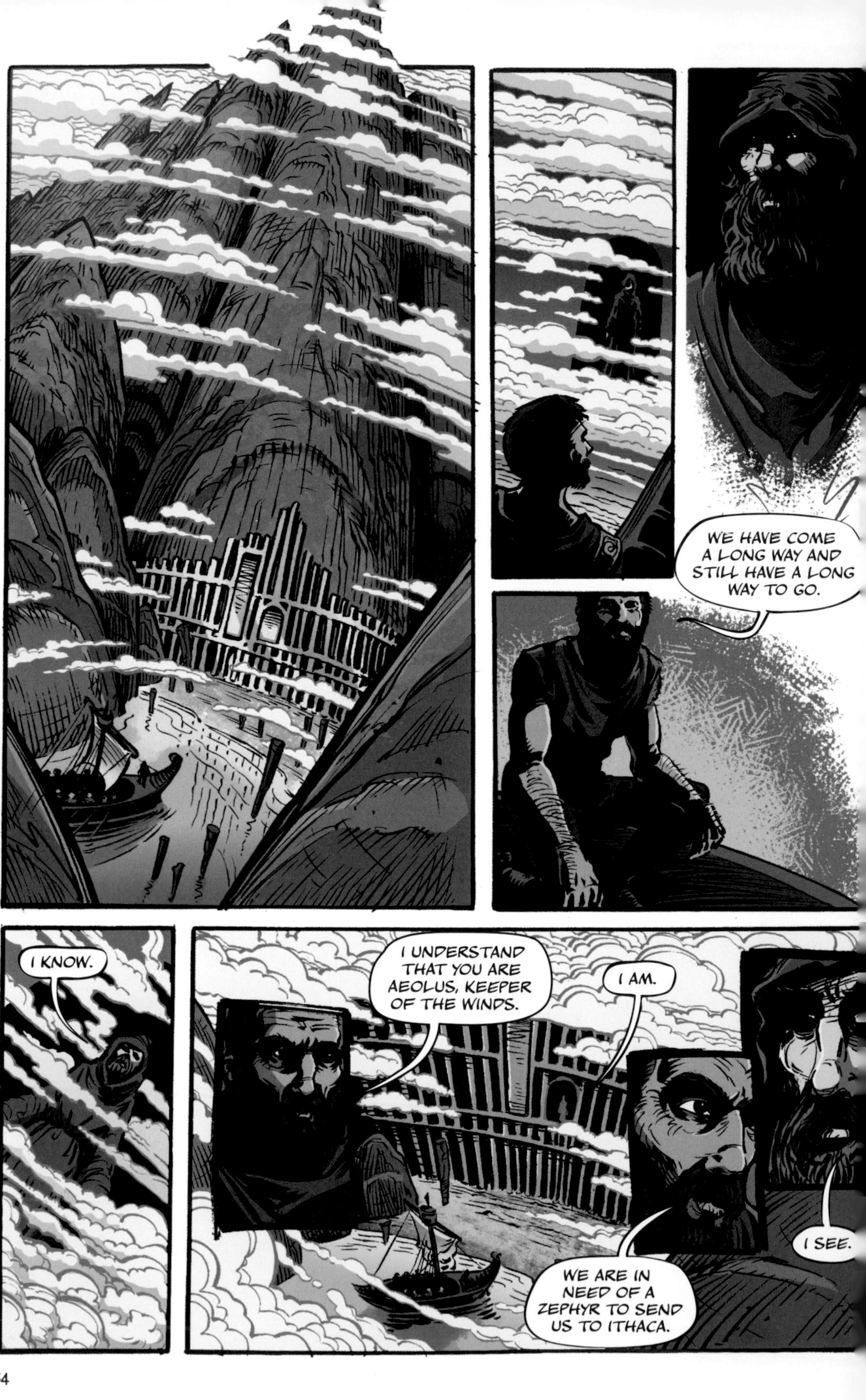
WE HAVE COME A LONG WAY AND STILL HAVE A LONG WAY TO GO.
I KNOW.
I UNDERSTAND THAT YOU ARE AEOLUS, KEEPER OF THE WINDS.
I AM.
WE ARE IN NEED OF A ZEPHYR TO SEND US TO ITHACA.
I SEE.

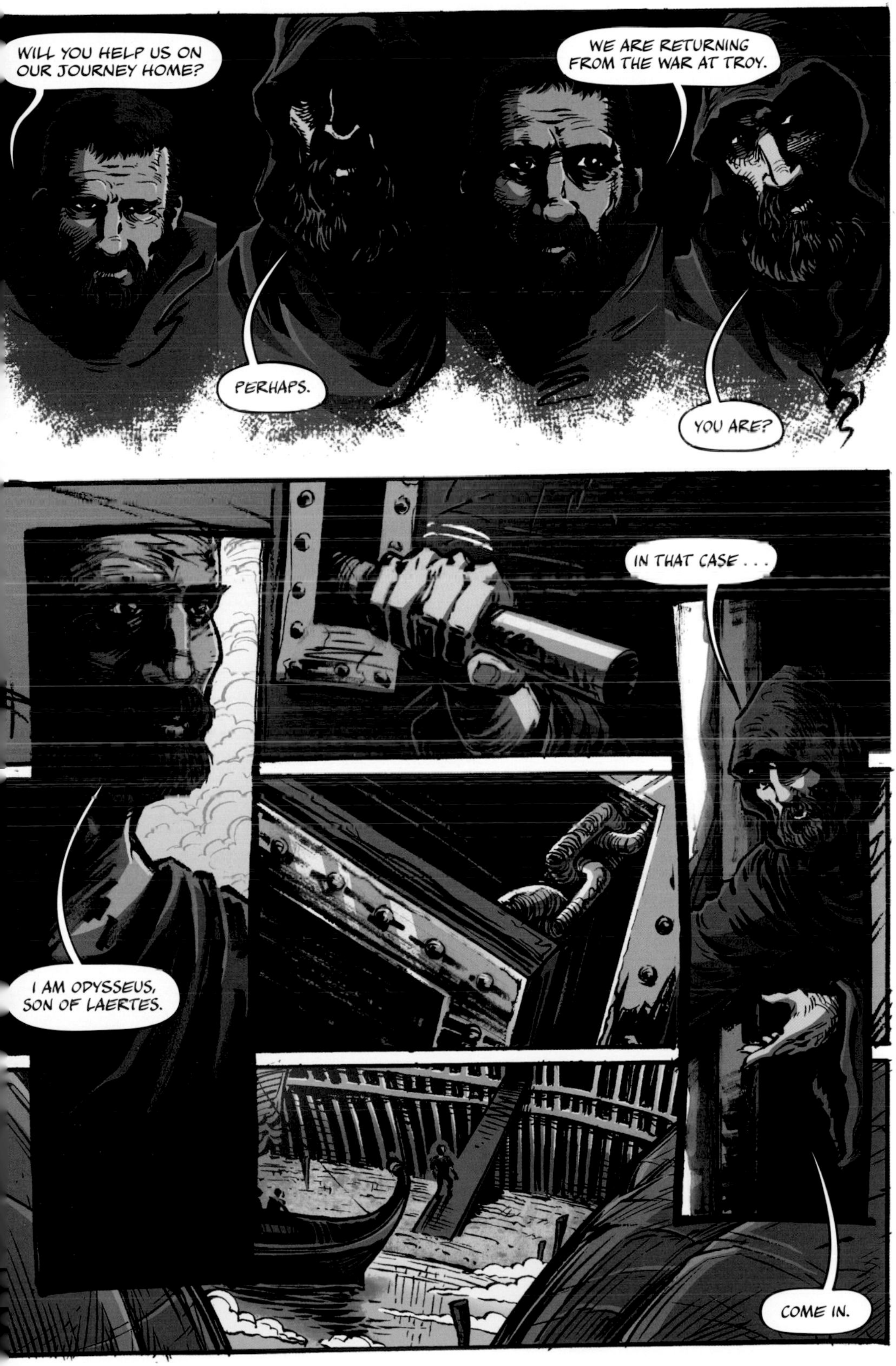
WILL YOU HELP US ON OUR JOURNEY HOME?
PERHAPS.
WE ARE RETURNING FROM THE WAR AT TROY.
YOU ARE?
I AM ODYSSEUS, SON OF LAERTES.
IN THAT CASE . . .
COME IN.

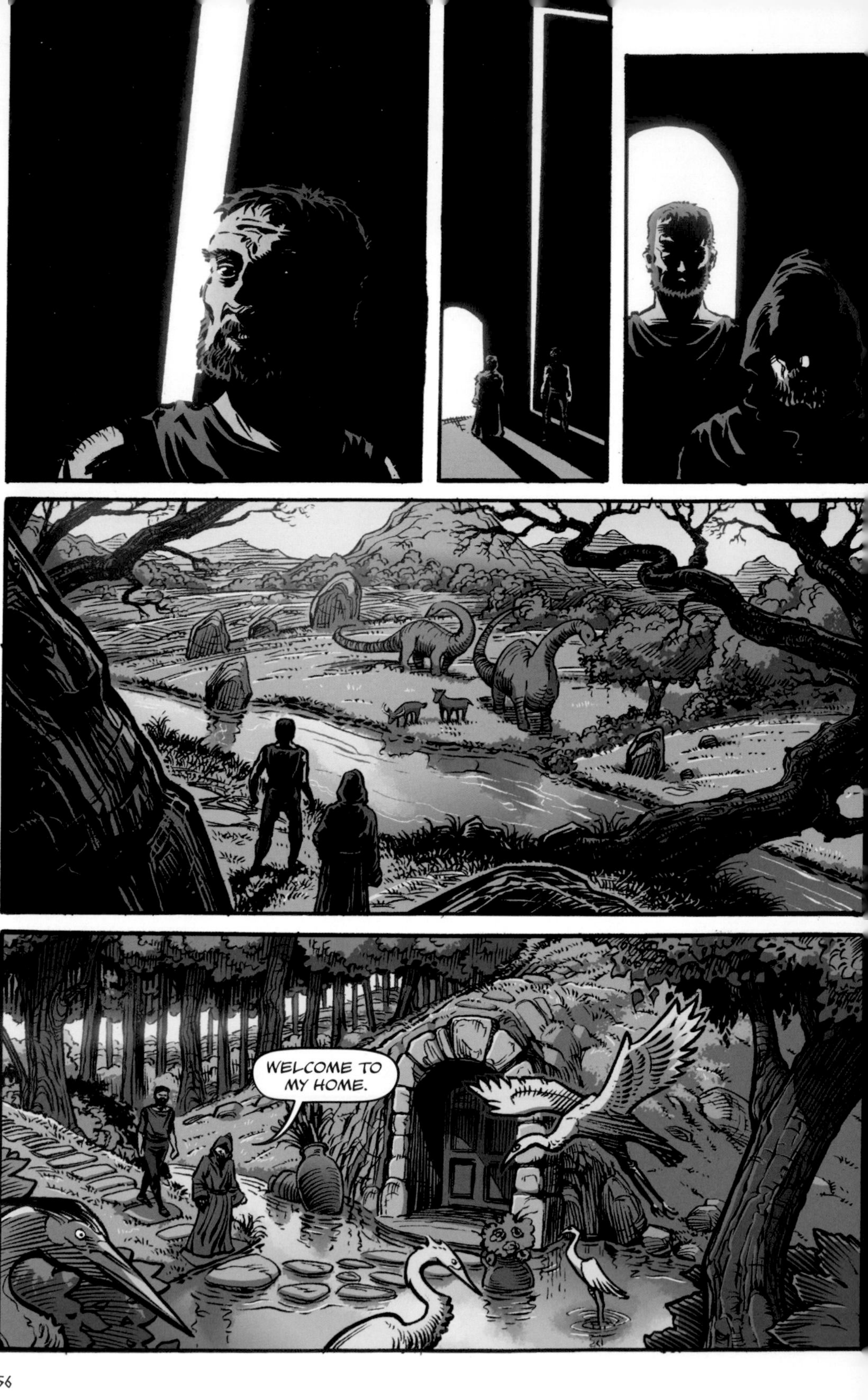
WELCOME TO MY HOME.

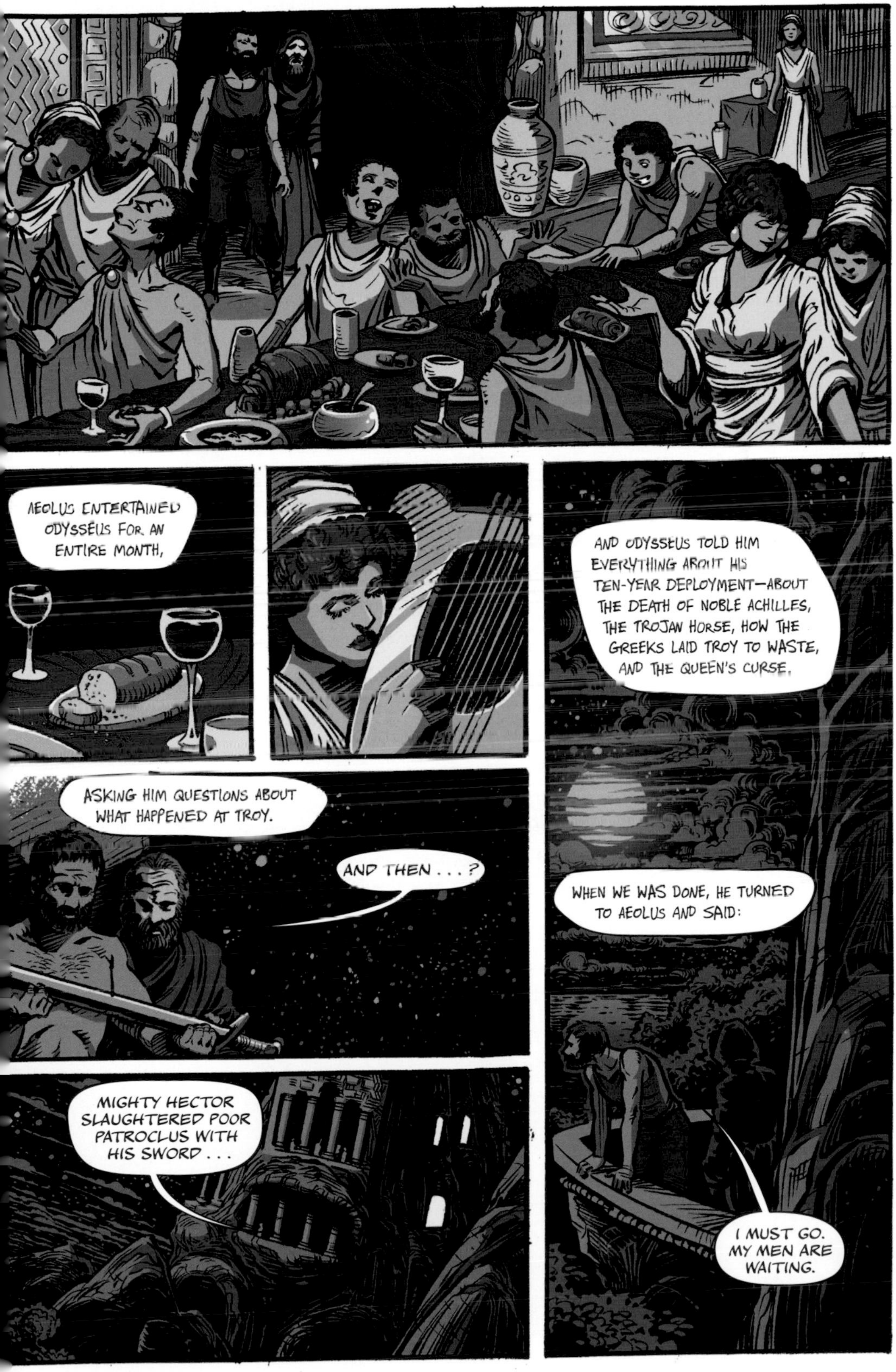
AEOLUS ENTERTAINED ODYSSEUS FOR AN ENTIRE MONTH,
ASKING HIM QUESTIONS ABOUT WHAT HAPPENED AT TROY.
AND THEN . . . ?
MIGHTY HECTOR SLAUGHTERED POOR PATROCLUS WITH HIS SWORD . . .
AND ODYSSEUS TOLD HIM EVERYTHING ABOUT HIS TEN-YEAR DEPLOYMENT—ABOUT THE DEATH OF NOBLE ACHILLES, THE TROJAN HORSE, HOW THE GREEKS LAID TROY TO WASTE, AND THE QUEEN'S CURSE.
WHEN WE WAS DONE, HE TURNED TO AEOLUS AND SAID:
I MUST GO. MY MEN ARE WAITING.

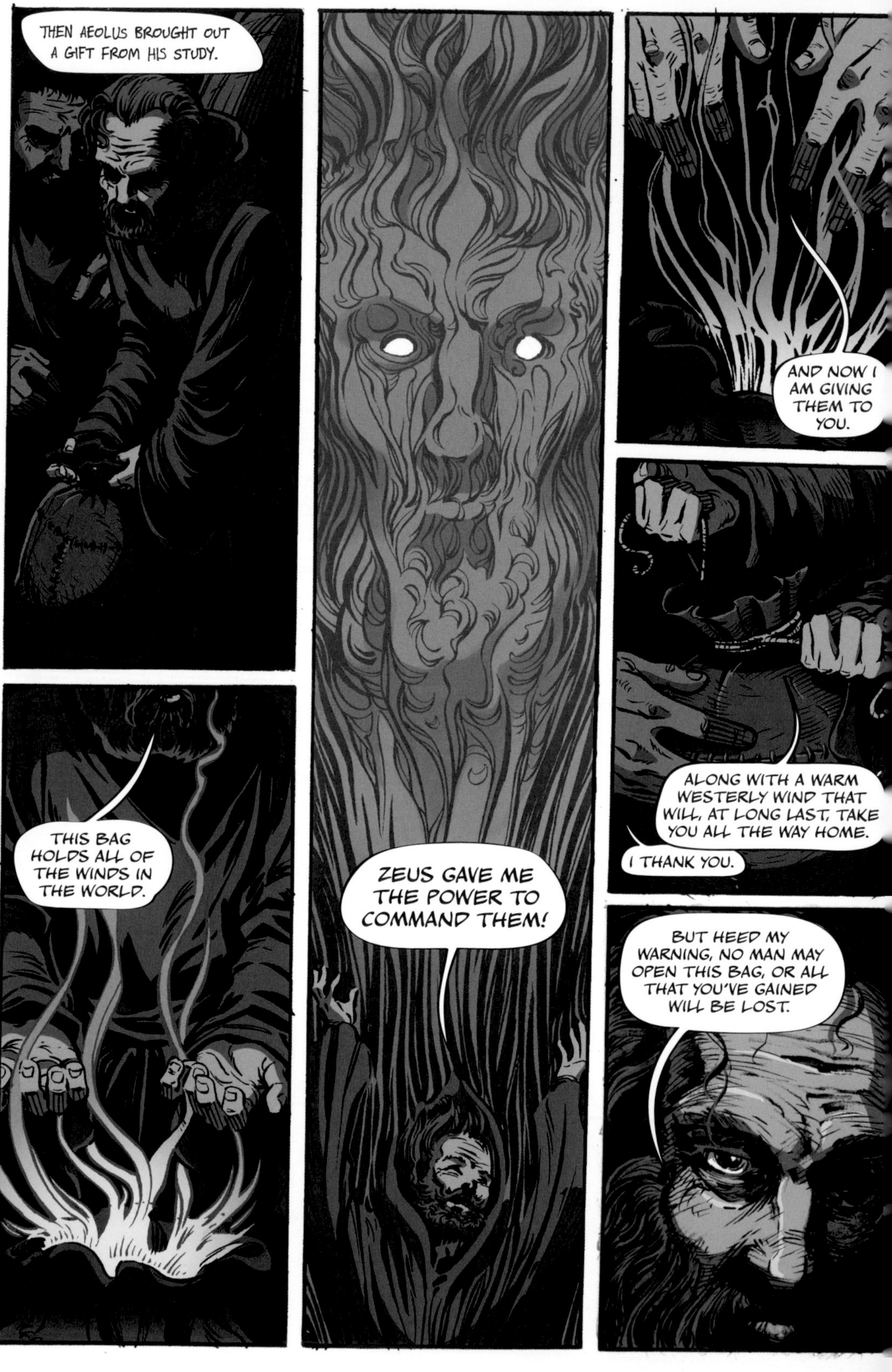
THEN AEOLUS BROUGHT OUT A GIFT FROM HIS STUDY.
THIS BAG HOLDS ALL OF THE WINDS IN THE WORLD.
ZEUS GAVE ME THE POWER TO COMMAND THEM!
AND NOW I AM GIVING THEM TO YOU.
ALONG WITH A WARM WESTERLY WIND THAT WILL, AT LONG LAST, TAKE YOU ALL THE WAY HOME.
I THANK YOU.
BUT HEED MY WARNING, NO MAN MAY OPEN THIS BAG, OR ALL THAT YOU'VE GAINED WILL BE LOST.

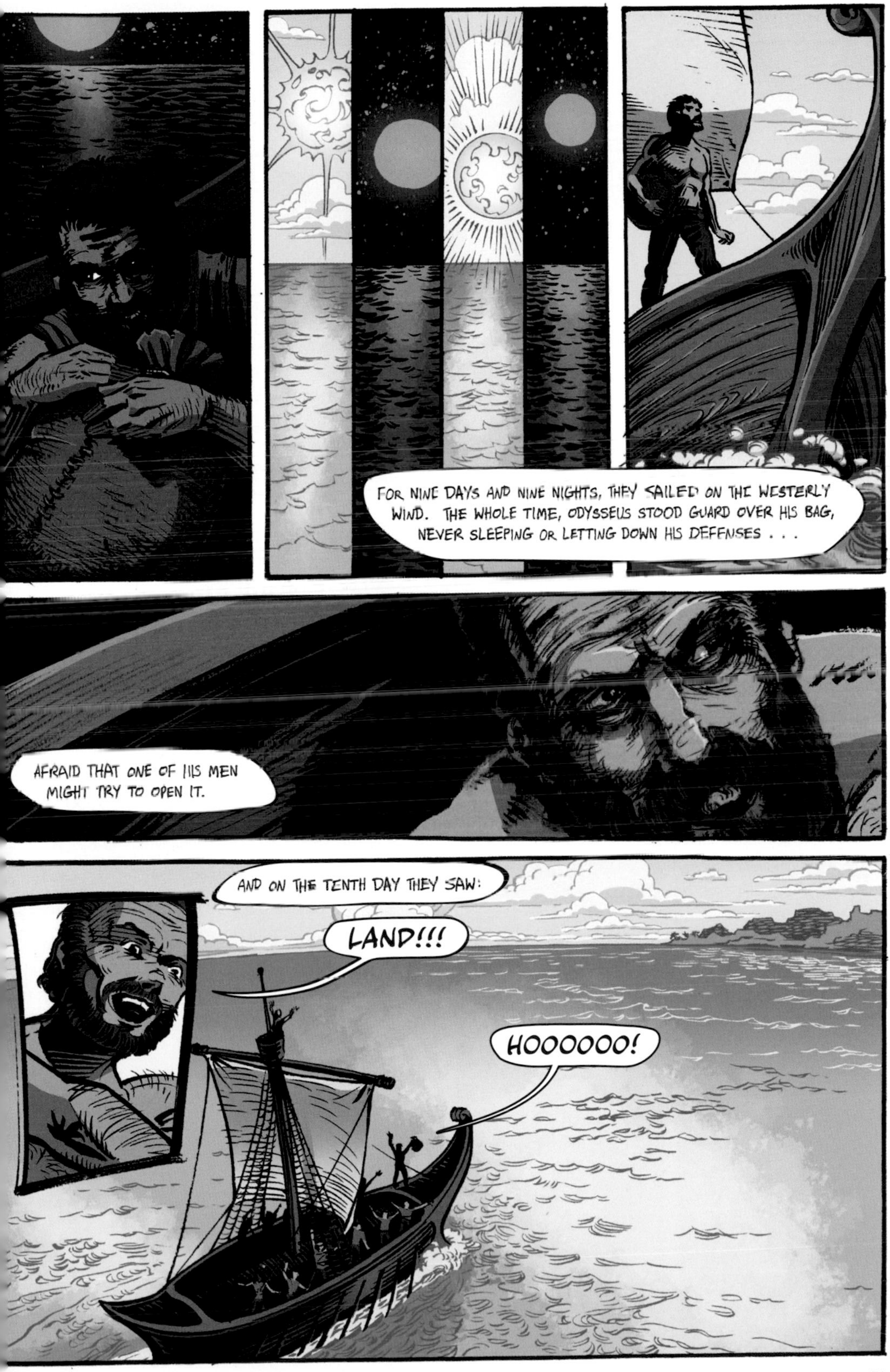
FOR NINE DAYS AND NINE NIGHTS, THEY SAILED ON THE WESTERLY WIND. THE WHOLE TIME, ODYSSEUS STOOD GUARD OVER HIS BAG, NEVER SLEEPING OR LETTING DOWN HIS DEFENSES . . .
AFRAID THAT ONE OF HIS MEN MIGHT TRY TO OPEN IT.
AND ON THE TENTH DAY THEY SAW:
LAND!!!
HOOOOOO!

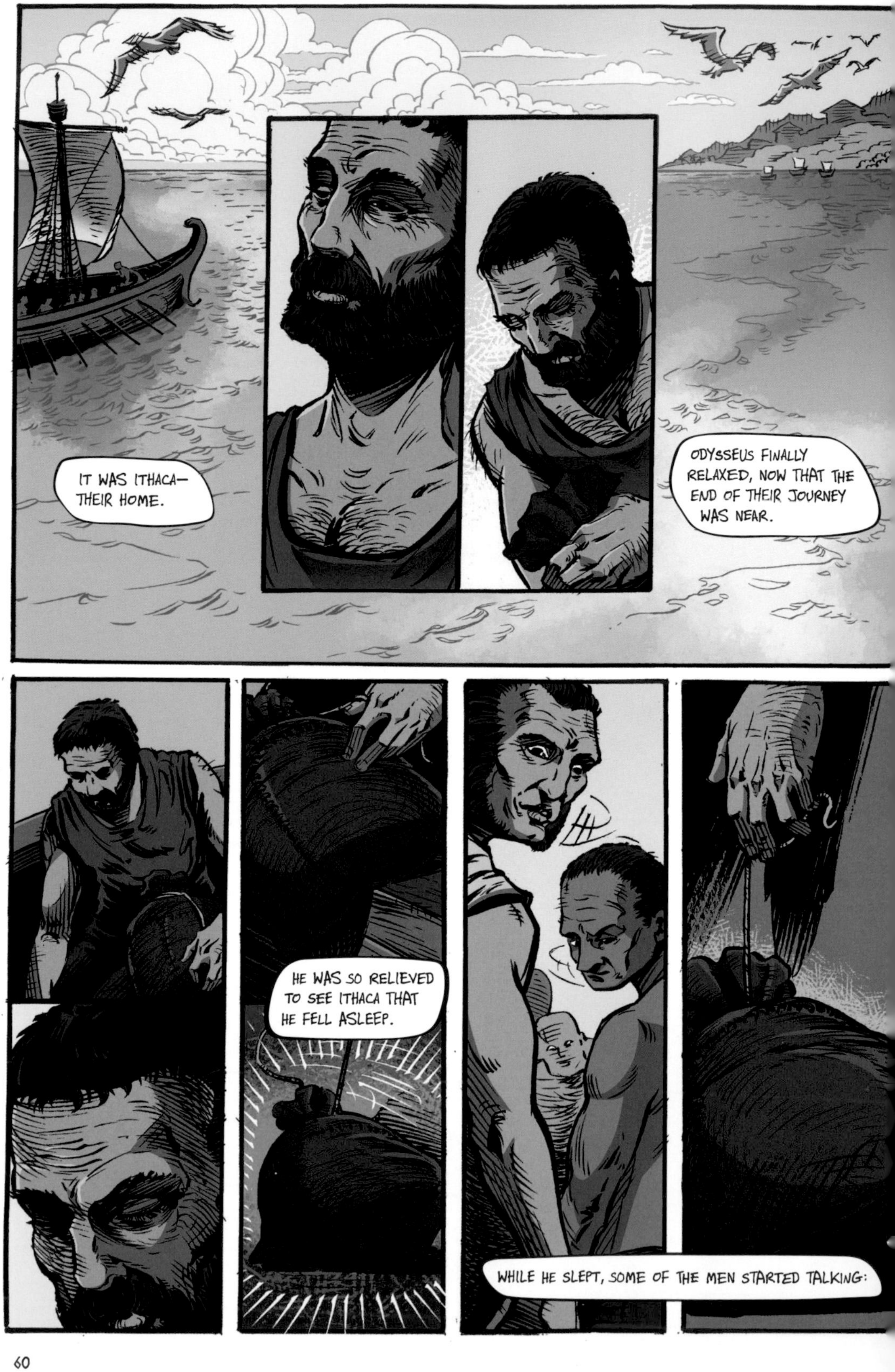
IT WAS ITHACA—
THEIR HOME.
ODYSSEUS FINALLY RELAXED, NOW THAT THE END OF THEIR JOURNEY WAS NEAR.
HE WAS SO RELIEVED TO SEE ITHACA THAT HE FELL ASLEEP.
WHILE HE SLEPT, SOME OF THE MEN STARTED TALKING:

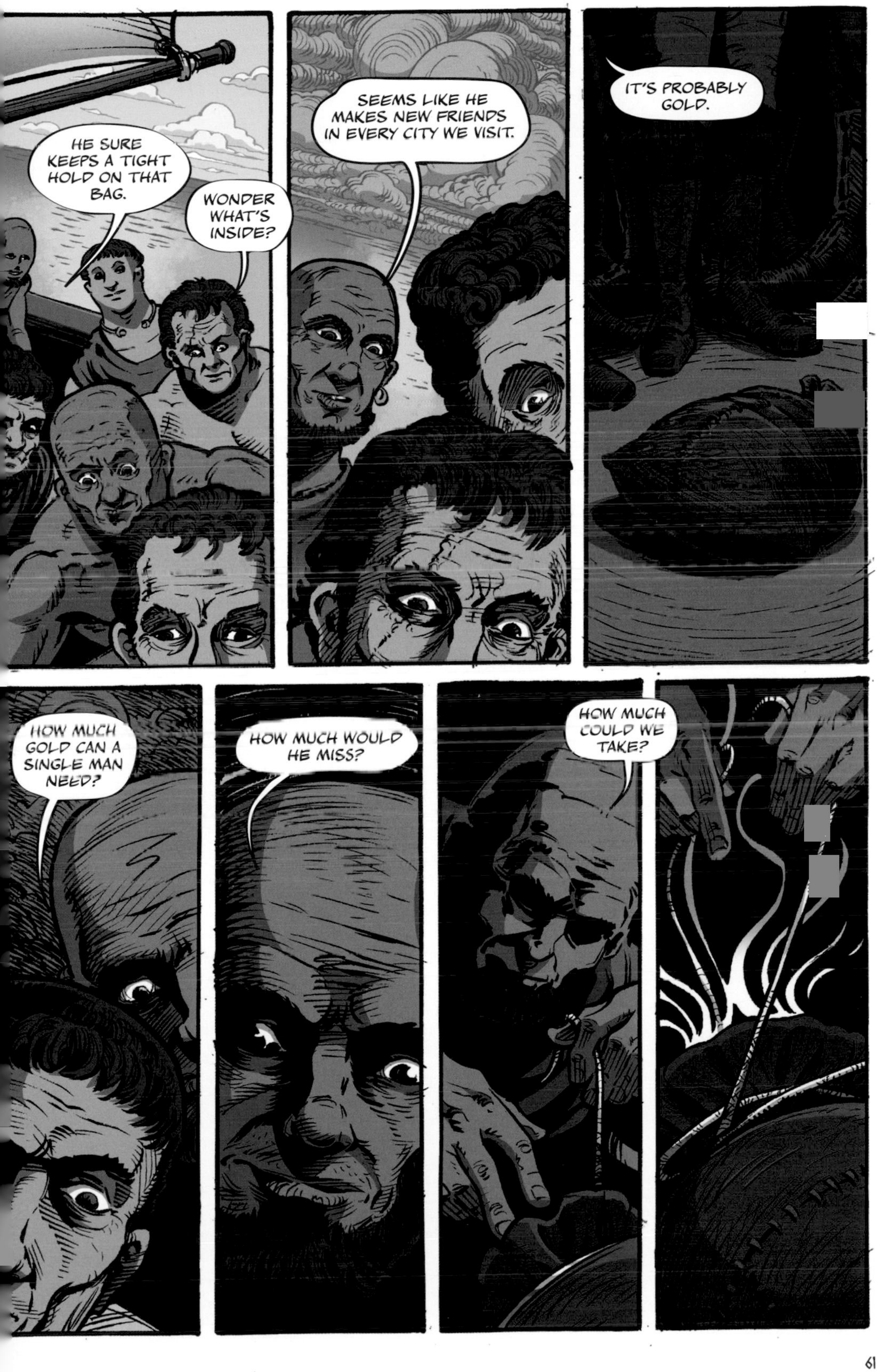
HE SURE KEEPS A TIGHT HOLD ON THAT BAG.
WONDER WHAT'S INSIDE?
SEEMS LIKE HE MAKES NEW FRIENDS IN EVERY CITY WE VISIT.
IT'S PROBABLY GOLD.
HOW MUCH GOLD CAN A SINGLE MAN NEED?
HOW MUCH WOULD HE MISS?
HOW MUCH COULD WE TAKE?

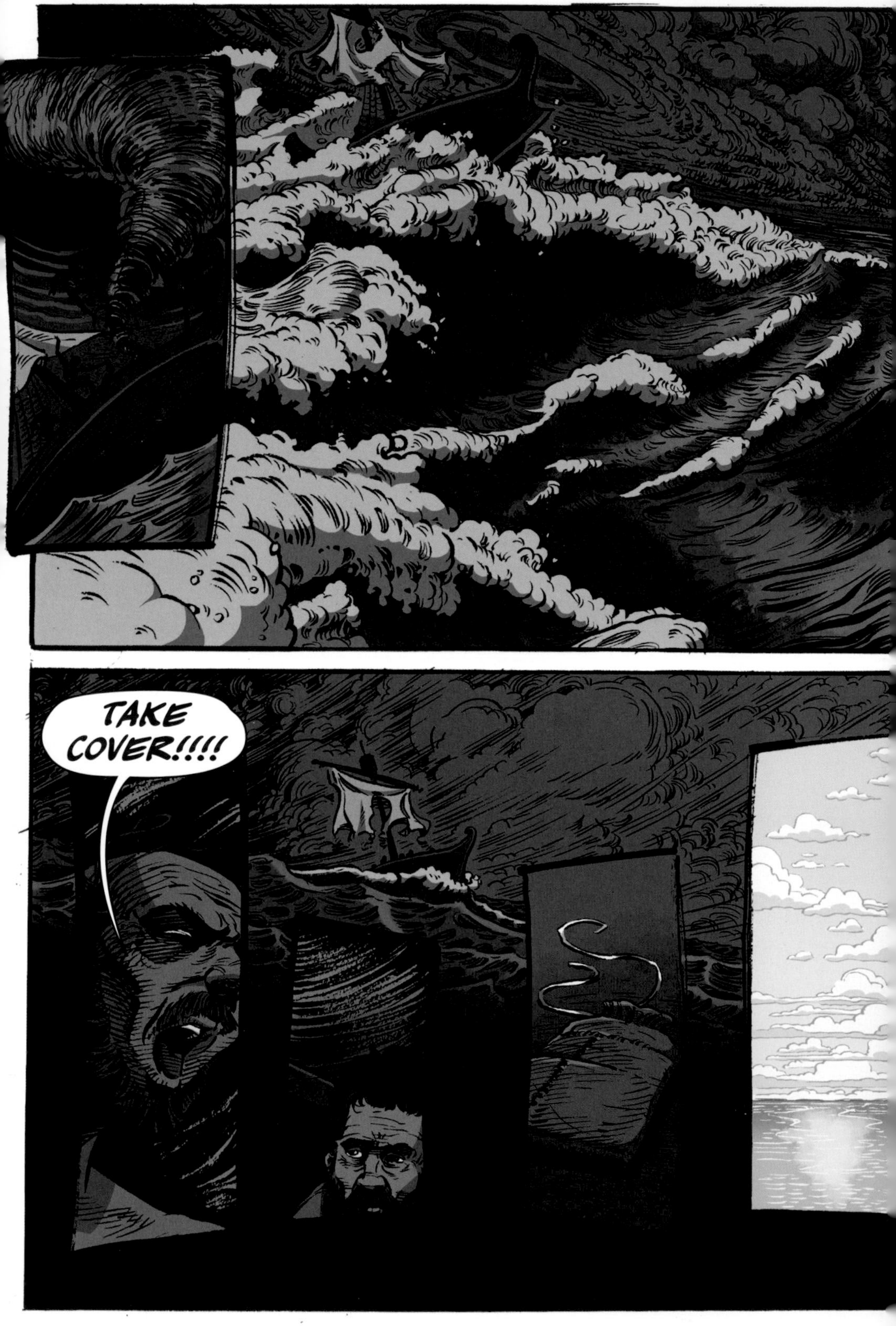
TAKE COVER!!!!

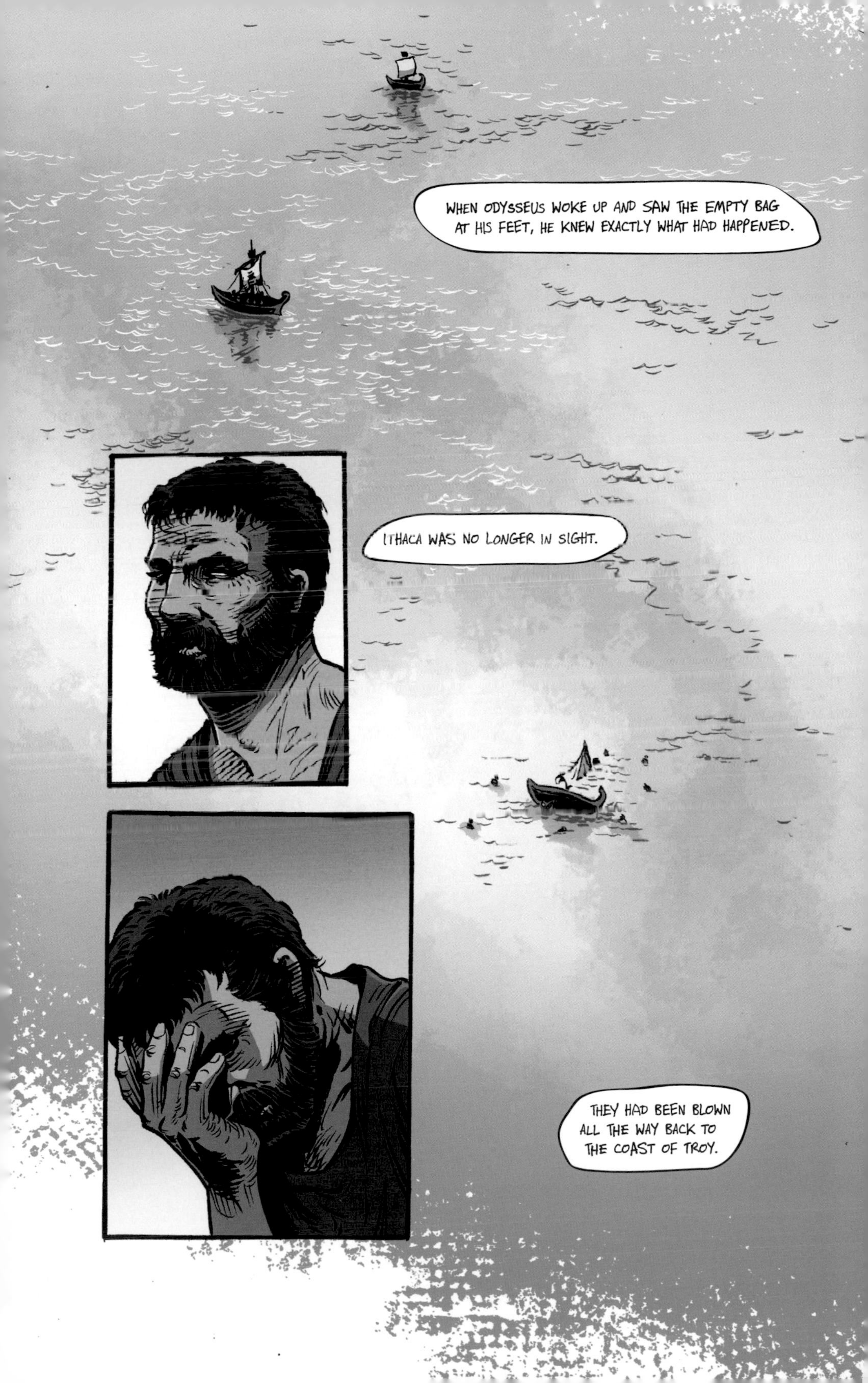
WHEN ODYSSEUS WOKE UP AND SAW THE EMPTY BAG AT HIS FEET, HE KNEW EXACTLY WHAT HAD HAPPENED.
ITHACA WAS NO LONGER IN SIGHT.
THEY HAD BEEN BLOWN ALL THE WAY BACK TO THE COAST OF TROY.

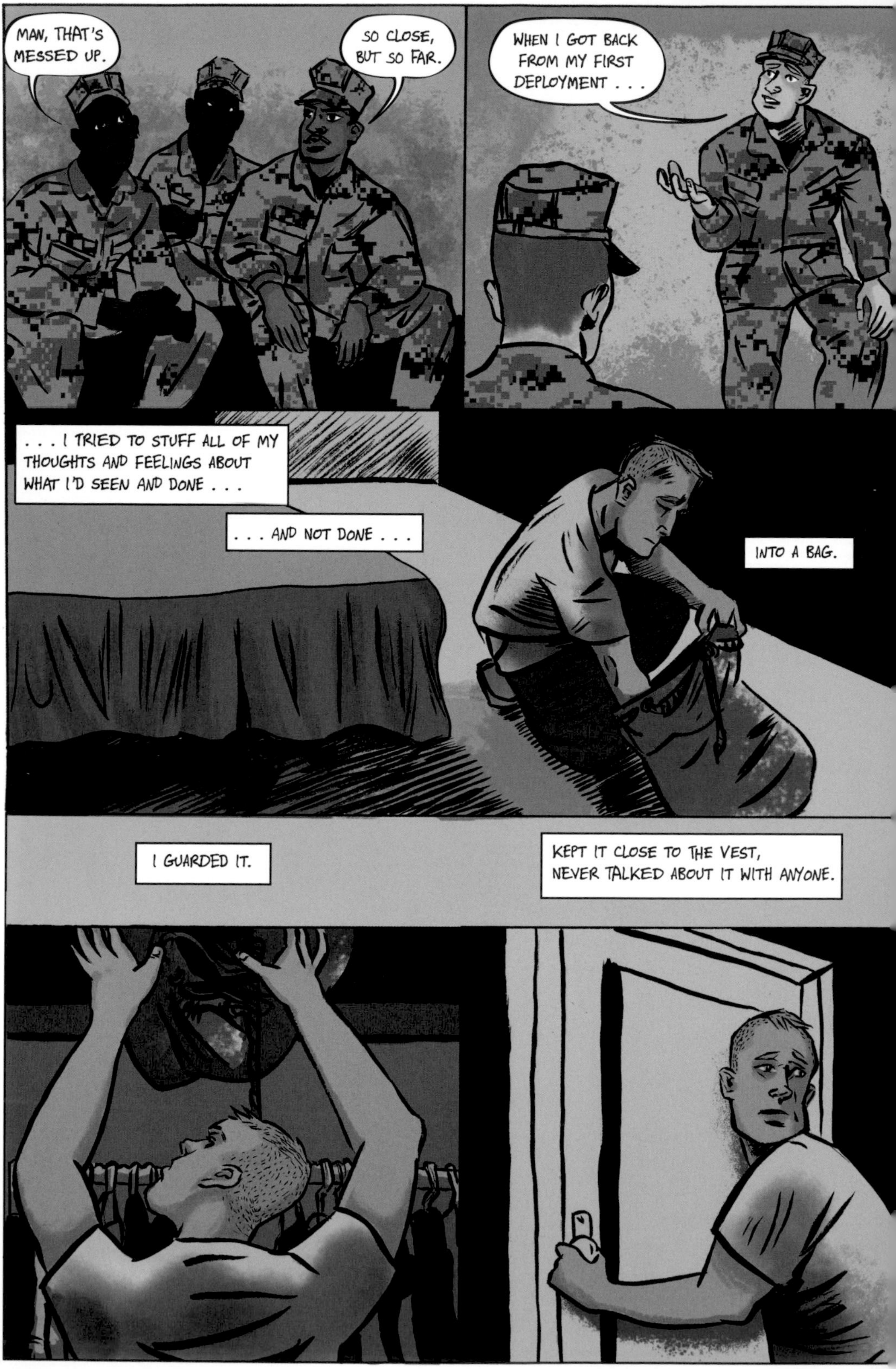
MAN, THAT'S MESSED UP.
SO CLOSE, BUT SO FAR.
WHEN I GOT BACK FROM MY FIRST DEPLOYMENT . . .
. . . I TRIED TO STUFF ALL OF MY THOUGHTS AND FEELINGS ABOUT WHAT I'D SEEN AND DONE . . .
. . . AND NOT DONE . . .
INTO A BAG.
I GUARDED IT.
KEPT IT CLOSE TO THE VEST, NEVER TALKED ABOUT IT WITH ANYONE.

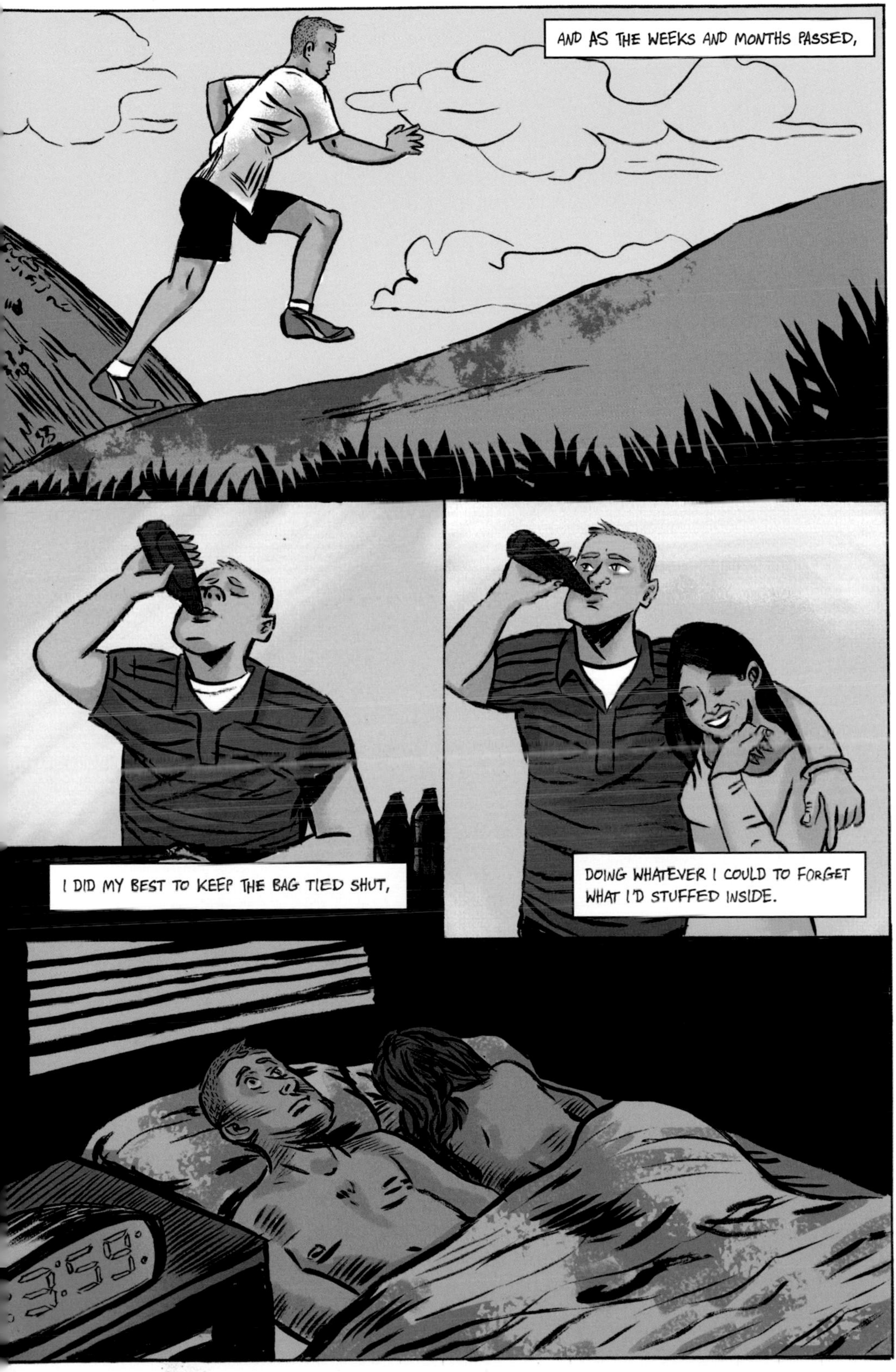
AND AS THE WEEKS AND MONTHS PASSED,
I DID MY BEST TO KEEP THE BAG TIED SHUT,
DOING WHATEVER I COULD TO FORGET WHAT I'D STUFFED INSIDE.
3:59

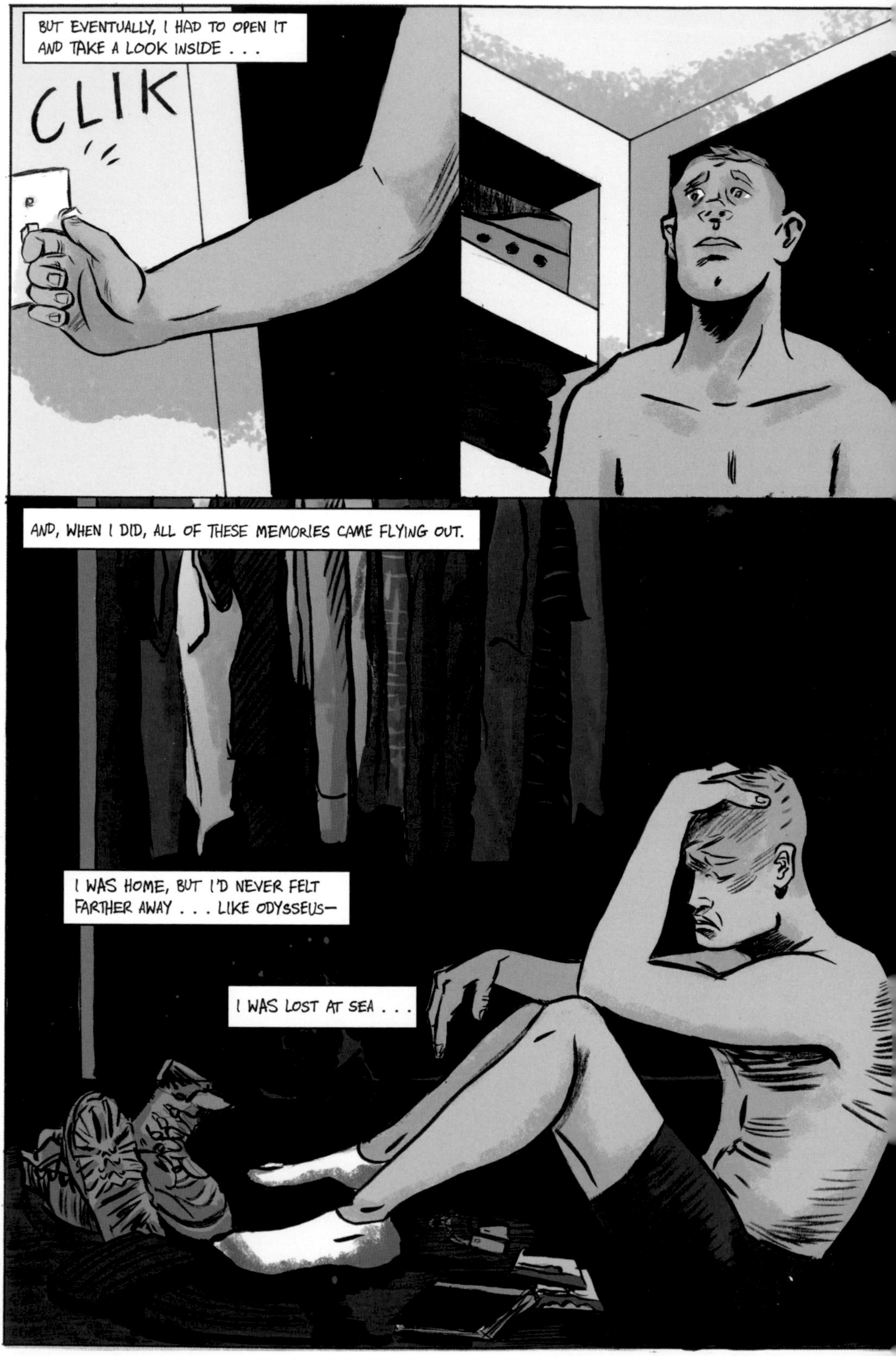
BUT EVENTUALLY, I HAD TO OPEN IT AND TAKE A LOOK INSIDE . . .
CLIK
AND, WHEN I DID, ALL OF THESE MEMORIES CAME FLYING OUT.
I WAS HOME, BUT I'D NEVER FELT FARTHER AWAY . . . LIKE ODYSSEUS—
I WAS LOST AT SEA . . .

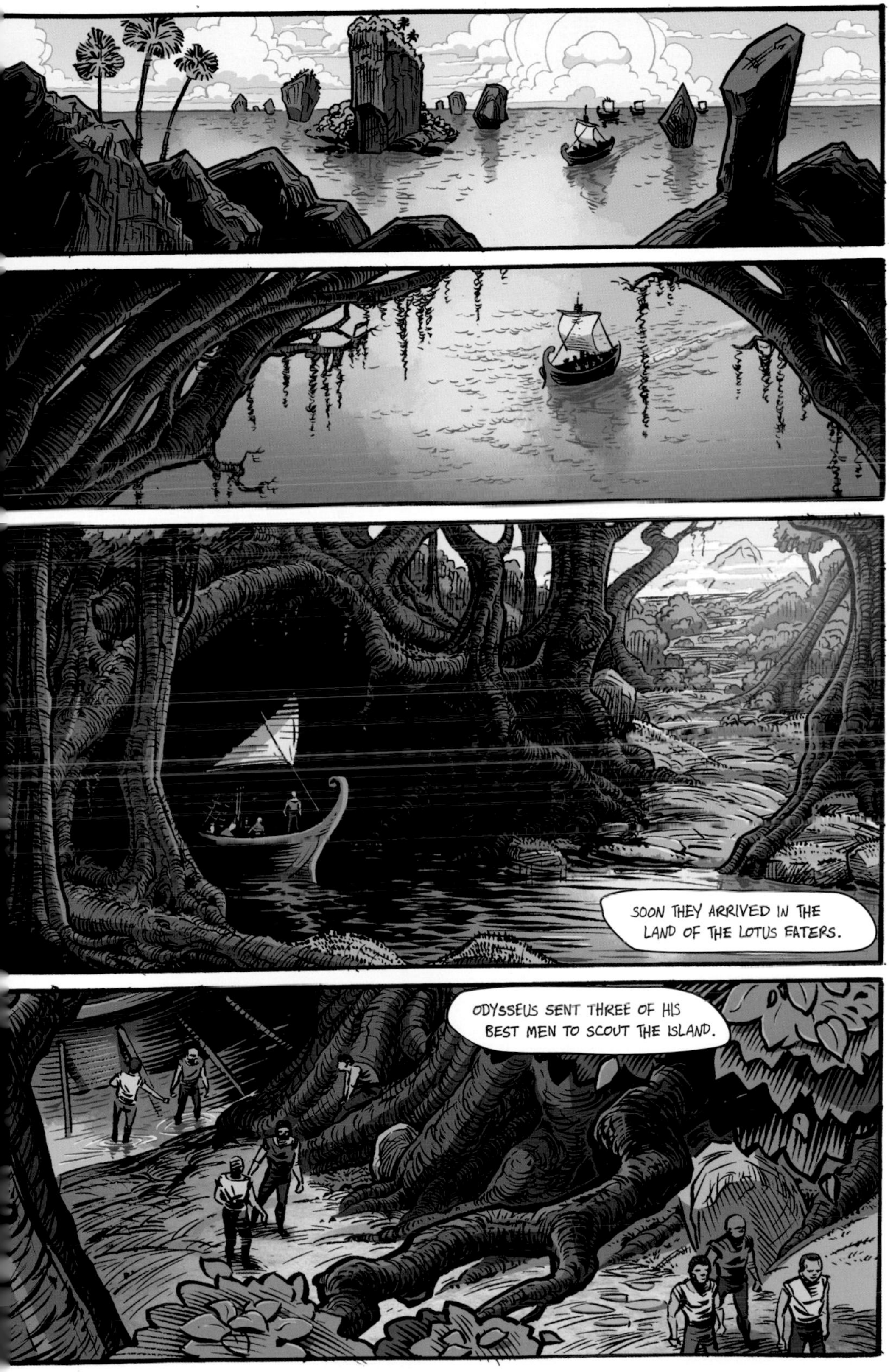
SOON THEY ARRIVED IN THE LAND OF THE LOTUS EATERS.
ODYSSEUS SENT THREE OF HIS BEST MEN TO SCOUT THE ISLAND.

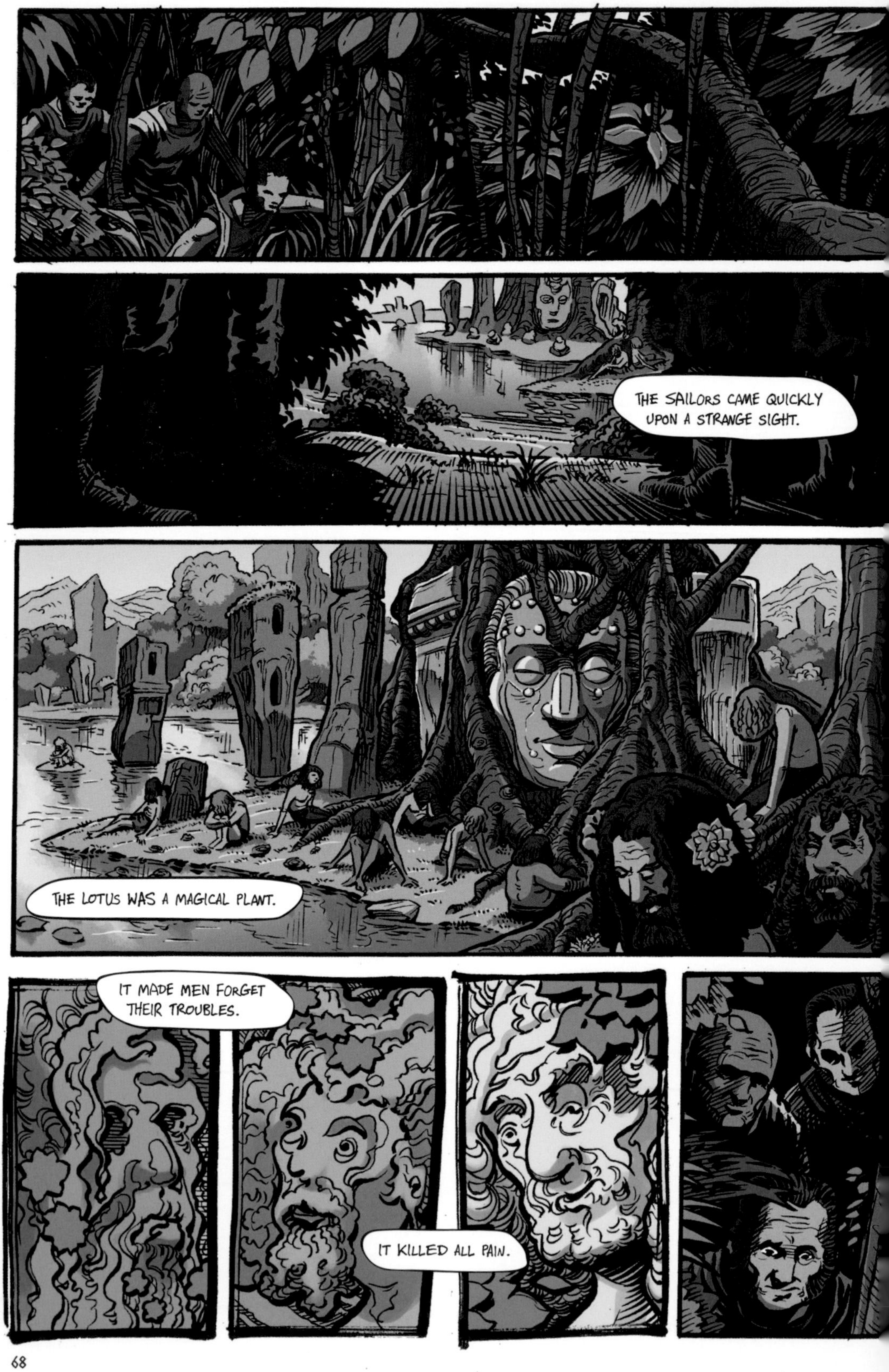
THE SAILORS CAME QUICKLY UPON A STRANGE SIGHT.
THE LOTUS WAS A MAGICAL PLANT.
IT MADE MEN FORGET THEIR TROUBLES.
IT KILLED ALL PAIN.

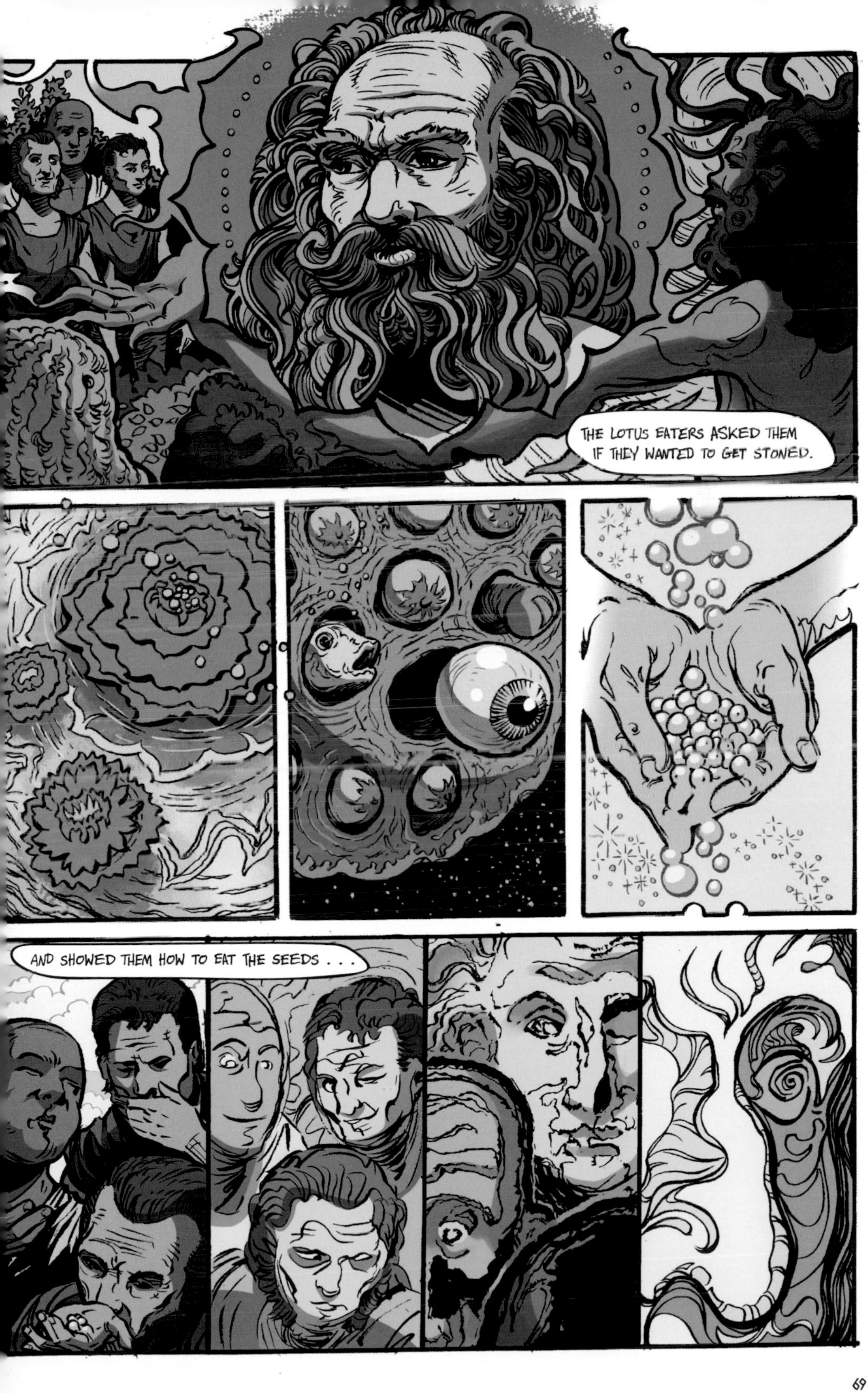
THE LOTUS EATERS ASKED THEM IF THEY WANTED TO GET STONED.
AND SHOWED THEM HOW TO EAT THE SEEDS . . .

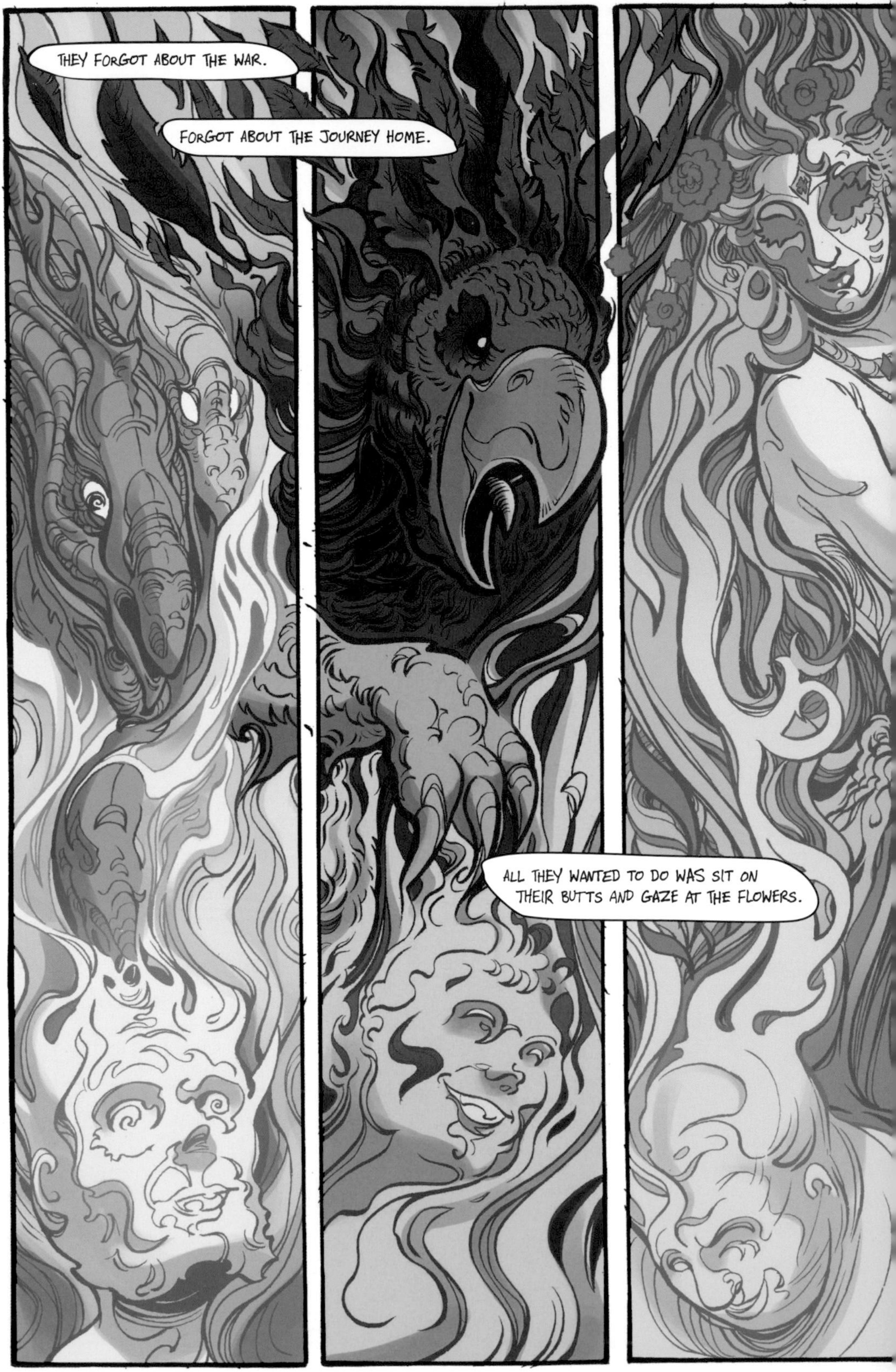
THEY FORGOT ABOUT THE WAR.
FORGOT ABOUT THE JOURNEY HOME.
ALL THEY WANTED TO DO WAS SIT ON THEIR BUTTS AND GAZE AT THE FLOWERS.

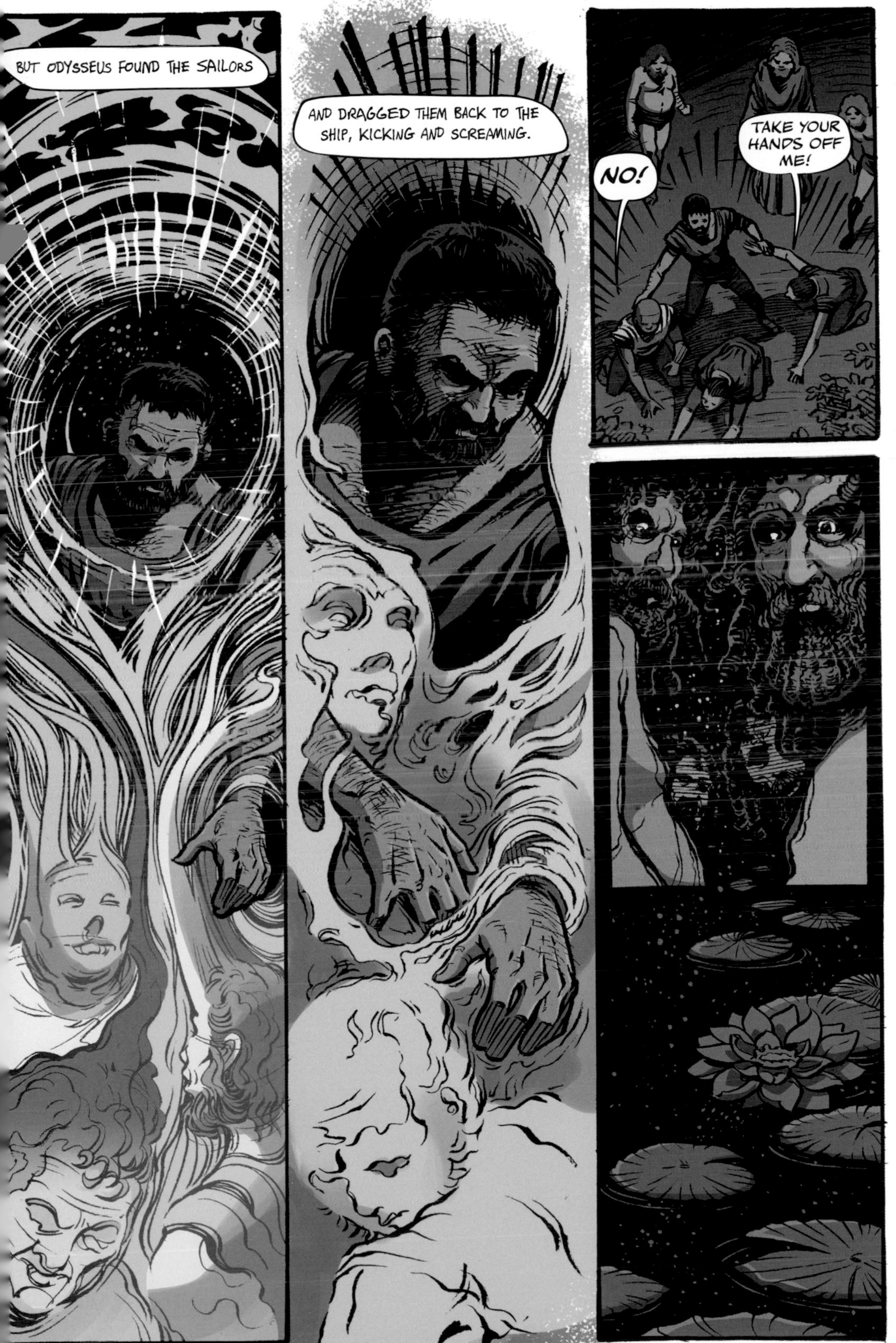
BUT ODYSSEUS FOUND THE SAILORS
AND DRAGGED THEM BACK TO THE SHIP, KICKING AND SCREAMING.
NO!
TAKE YOUR HANDS OFF ME!

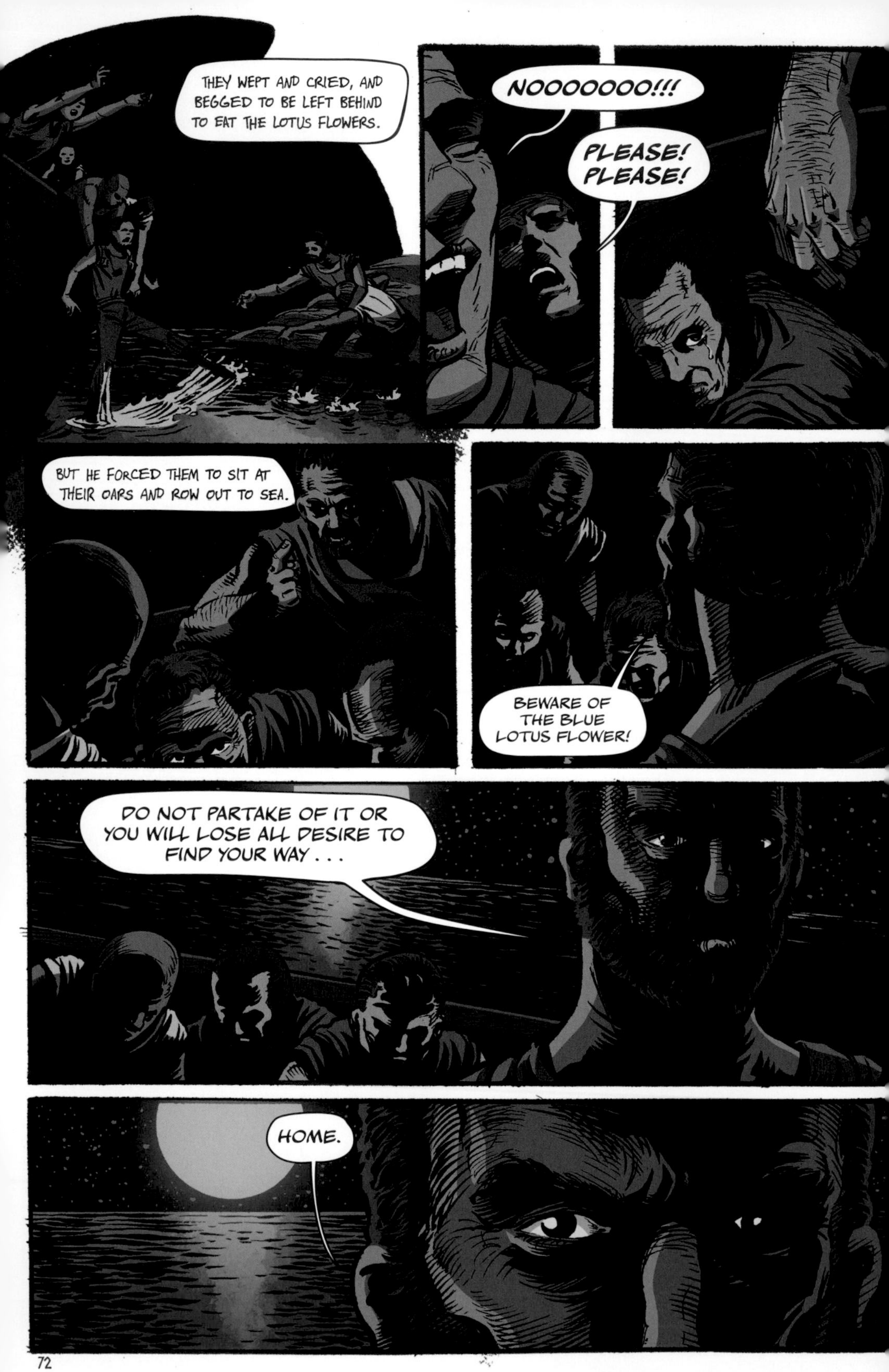
THEY WEPT AND CRIED, AND BEGGED TO BE LEFT BEHIND TO EAT THE LOTUS FLOWERS.
NOOOOOOO!!!
PLEASE! PLEASE!
BUT HE FORCED THEM TO SIT AT THEIR OARS AND ROW OUT TO SEA.
BEWARE OF THE BLUE LOTUS FLOWER!
DO NOT PARTAKE OF IT OR YOU WILL LOSE ALL DESIRE TO FIND YOUR WAY . . .
HOME.

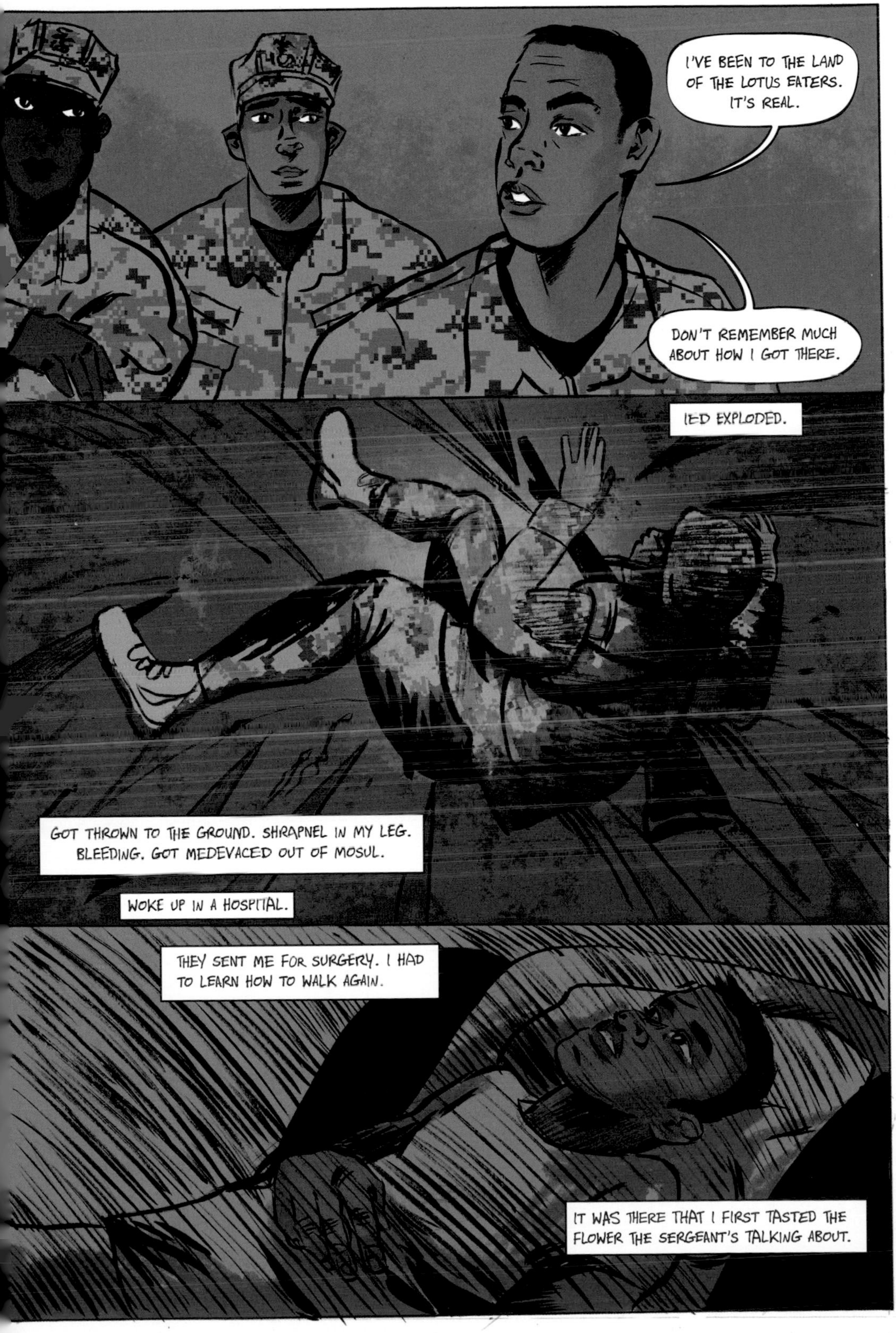
I'VE BEEN TO THE LAND OF THE LOTUS EATERS. IT'S REAL.
DON'T REMEMBER MUCH ABOUT HOW I GOT THERE.
IED EXPLODED.
GOT THROWN TO THE GROUND. SHRAPNEL IN MY LEG. BLEEDING. GOT MEDEVACED OUT OF MOSUL.
WOKE UP IN A HOSPITAL.
THEY SENT ME FOR SURGERY. I HAD TO LEARN HOW TO WALK AGAIN.
IT WAS THERE THAT I FIRST TASTED THE FLOWER THE SERGEANT'S TALKING ABOUT.

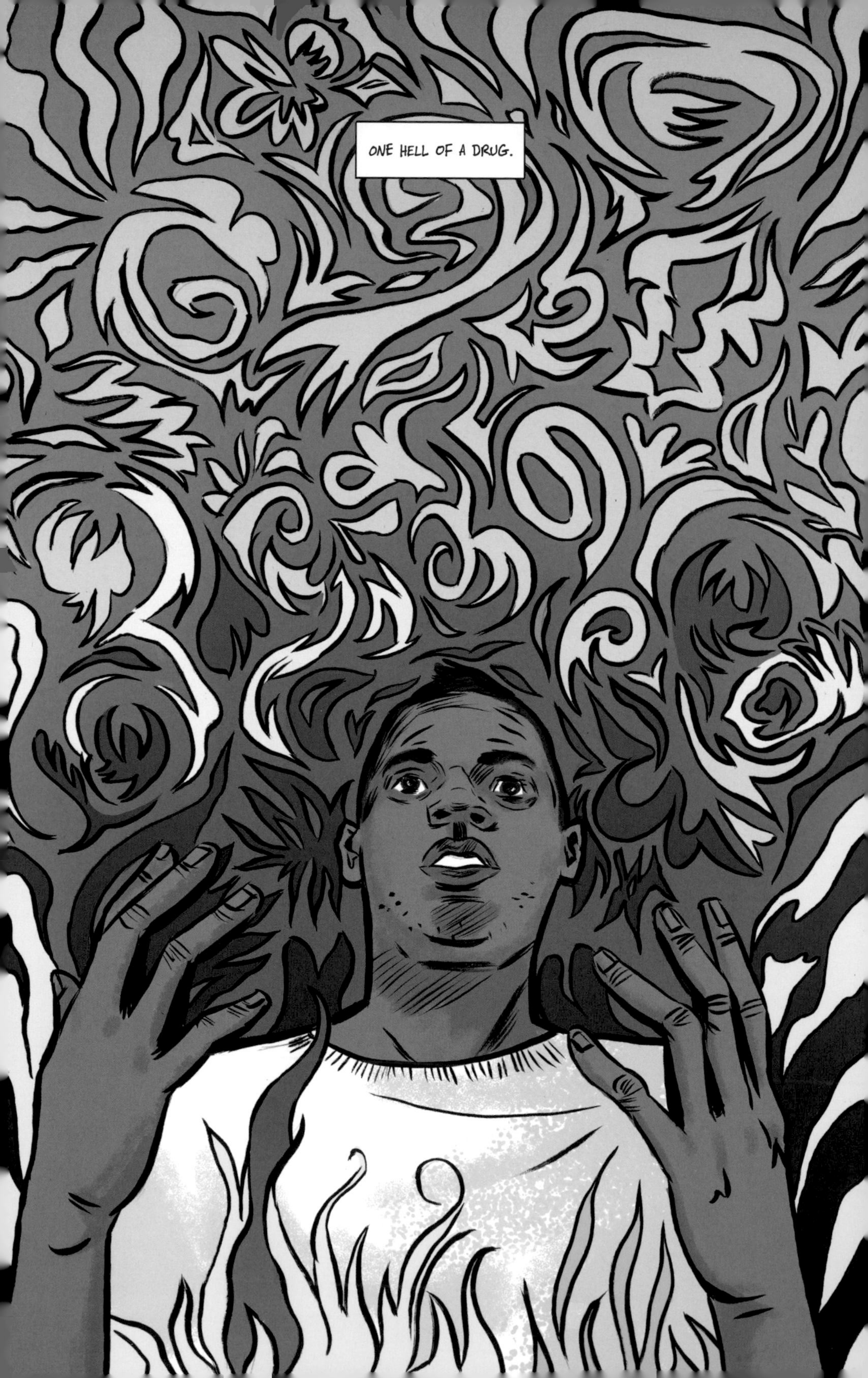
ONE HELL OF A DRUG.

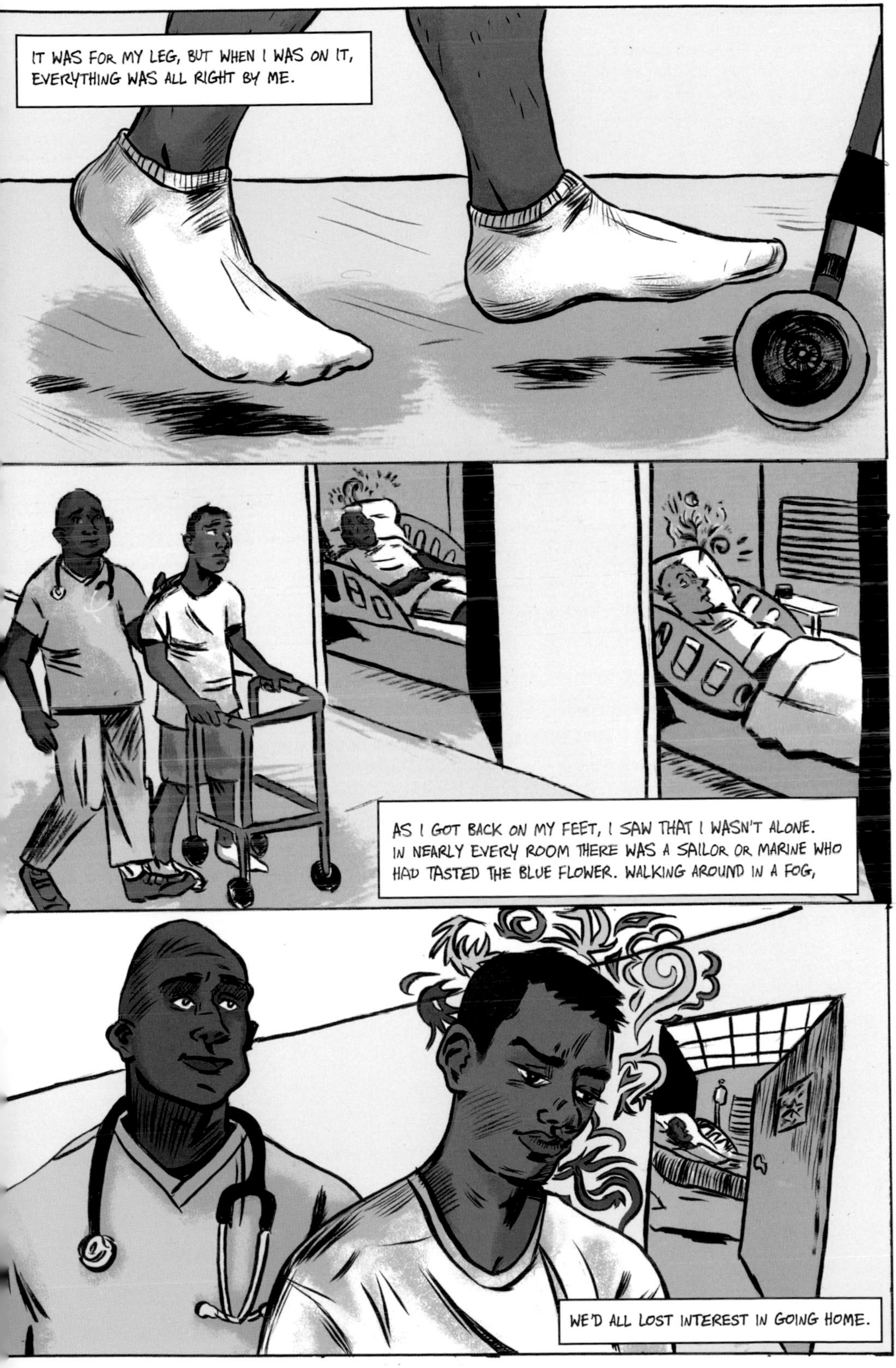
IT WAS FOR MY LEG, BUT WHEN I WAS ON IT, EVERYTHING WAS ALL RIGHT BY ME.
AS I GOT BACK ON MY FEET, I SAW THAT I WASN'T ALONE. IN NEARLY EVERY ROOM THERE WAS A SAILOR OR MARINE WHO HAD TASTED THE BLUE FLOWER. WALKING AROUND IN A FOG,
WE'D ALL LOST INTEREST IN GOING HOME.

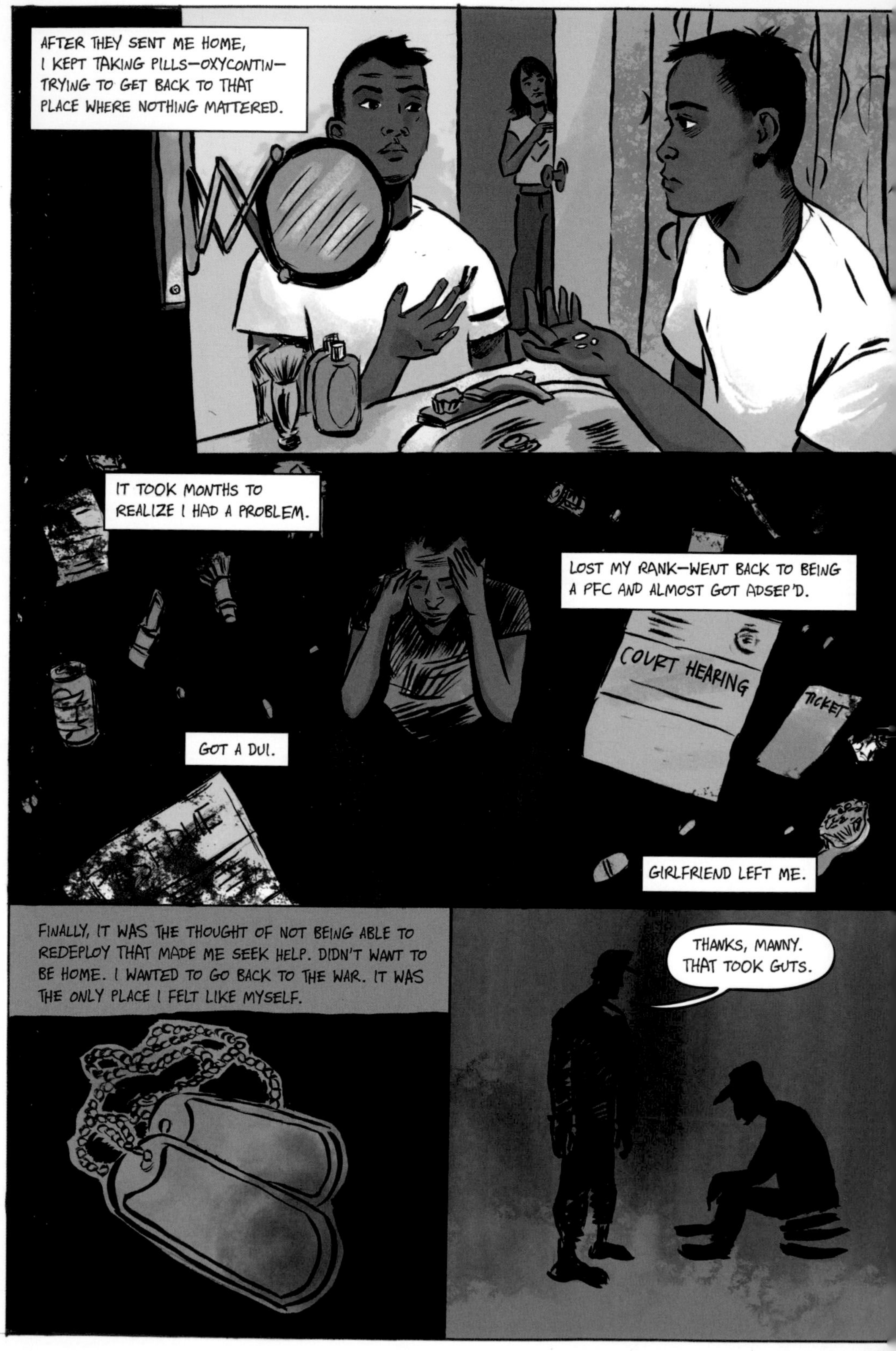
AFTER THEY SENT ME HOME, I KEPT TAKING PILLS—OXYCONTIN—TRYING TO GET BACK TO THAT PLACE WHERE NOTHING MATTERED.
IT TOOK MONTHS TO REALIZE I HAD A PROBLEM.
LOST MY RANK—WENT BACK TO BEING A PFC AND ALMOST GOT ADSEP'D.
COURT HEARING
TICKET
GOT A DUI.
GIRLFRIEND LEFT ME.
FINALLY, IT WAS THE THOUGHT OF NOT BEING ABLE TO REDEPLOY THAT MADE ME SEEK HELP. DIDN'T WANT TO BE HOME. I WANTED TO GO BACK TO THE WAR. IT WAS THE ONLY PLACE I FELT LIKE MYSELF.
THANKS, MANNY. THAT TOOK GUTS.

CHAPTER 3

BREAKING THE SPELL

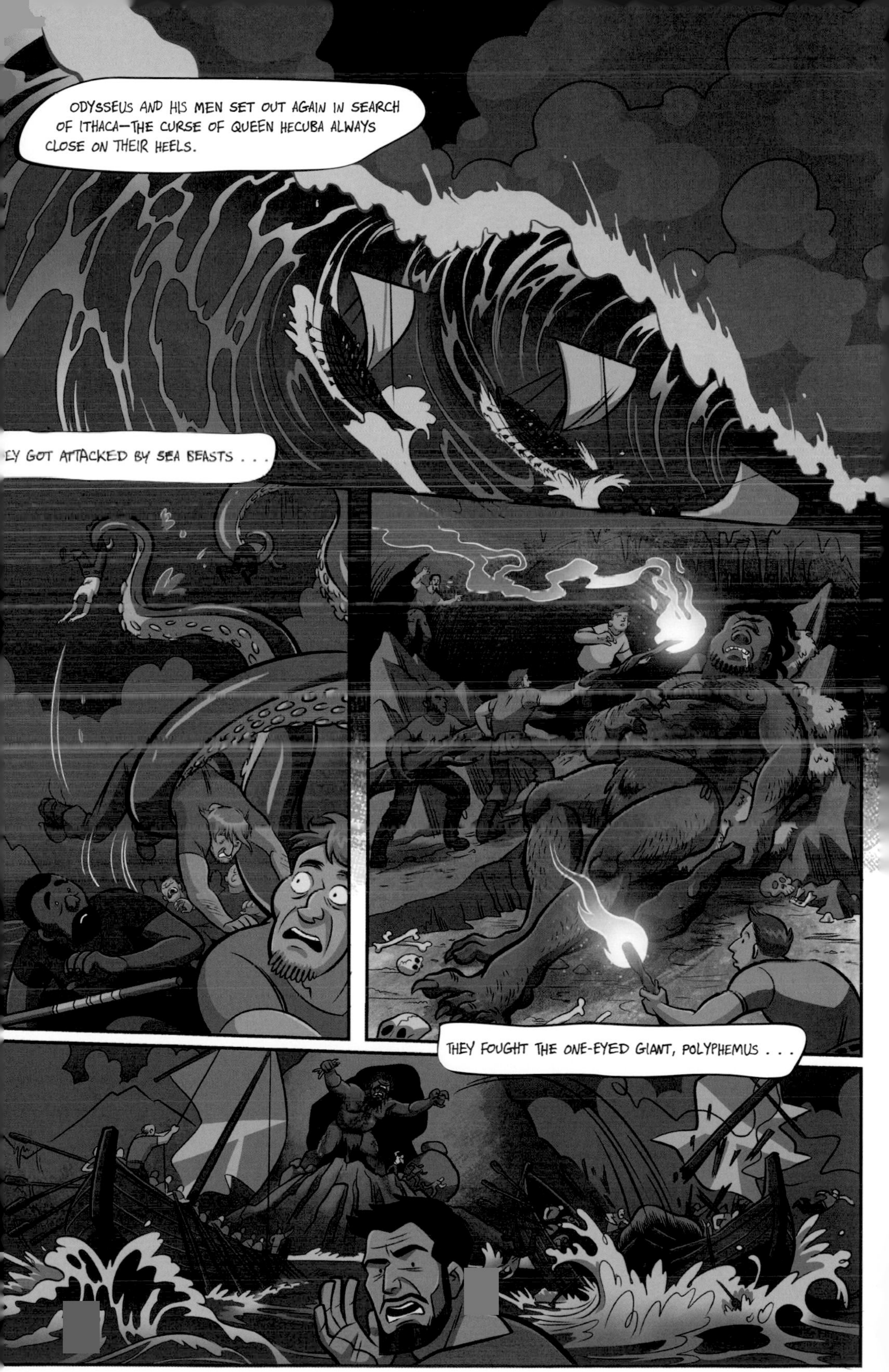
ODYSSEUS AND HIS MEN SET OUT AGAIN IN SEARCH OF ITHACA—THE CURSE OF QUEEN HECUBA ALWAYS CLOSE ON THEIR HEELS.
EY GOT ATTACKED BY SEA BEASTS . . .
THEY FOUGHT THE ONE-EYED GIANT, POLYPHEMUS . . .

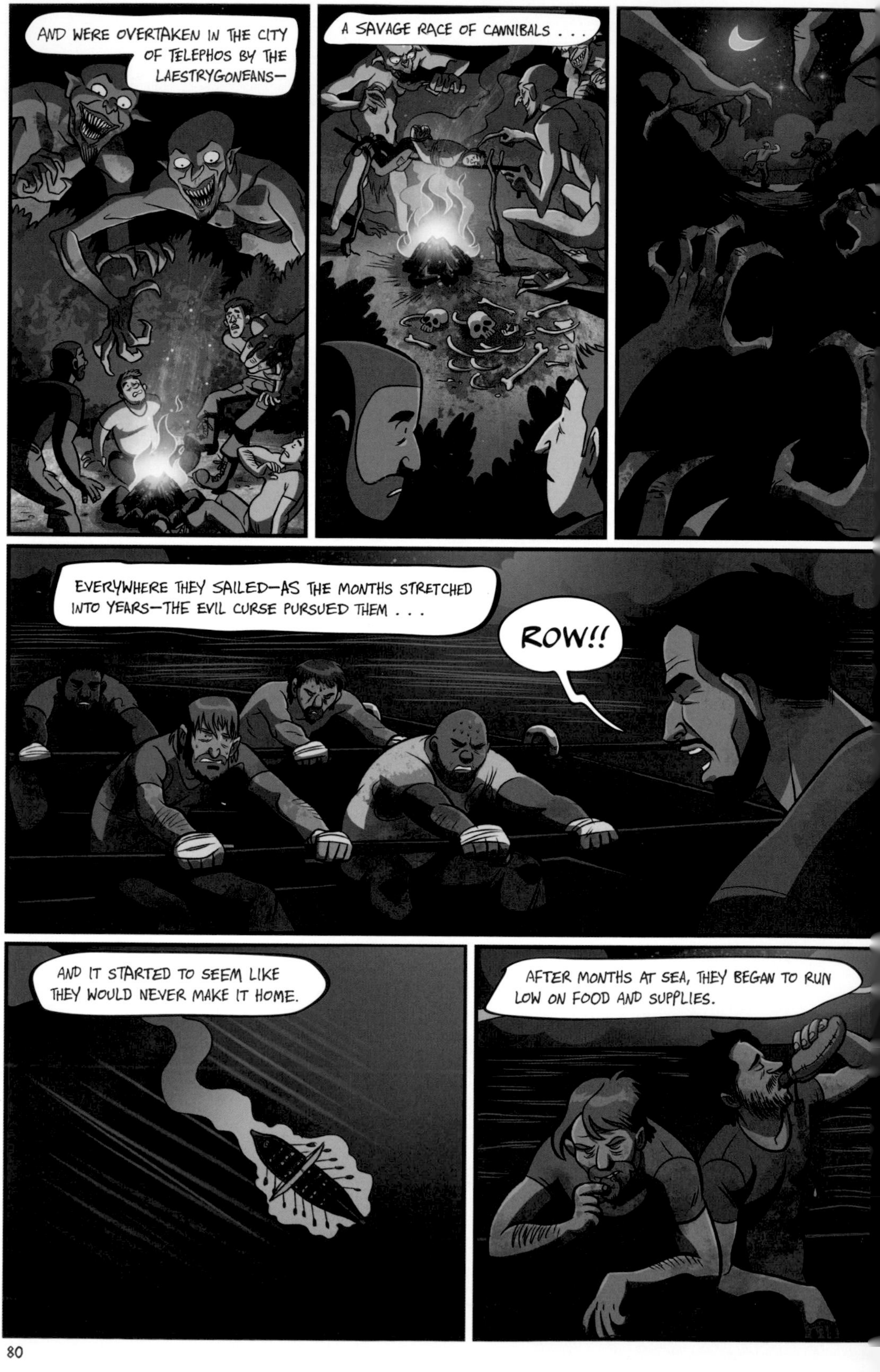
AND WERE OVERTAKEN IN THE CITY OF TELEPHOS BY THE LAESTRYGONEANS—
A SAVAGE RACE OF CANNIBALS . . .
EVERYWHERE THEY SAILED—AS THE MONTHS STRETCHED INTO YEARS—THE EVIL CURSE PURSUED THEM . . .
ROW!!
AND IT STARTED TO SEEM LIKE THEY WOULD NEVER MAKE IT HOME.
AFTER MONTHS AT SEA, THEY BEGAN TO RUN LOW ON FOOD AND SUPPLIES.

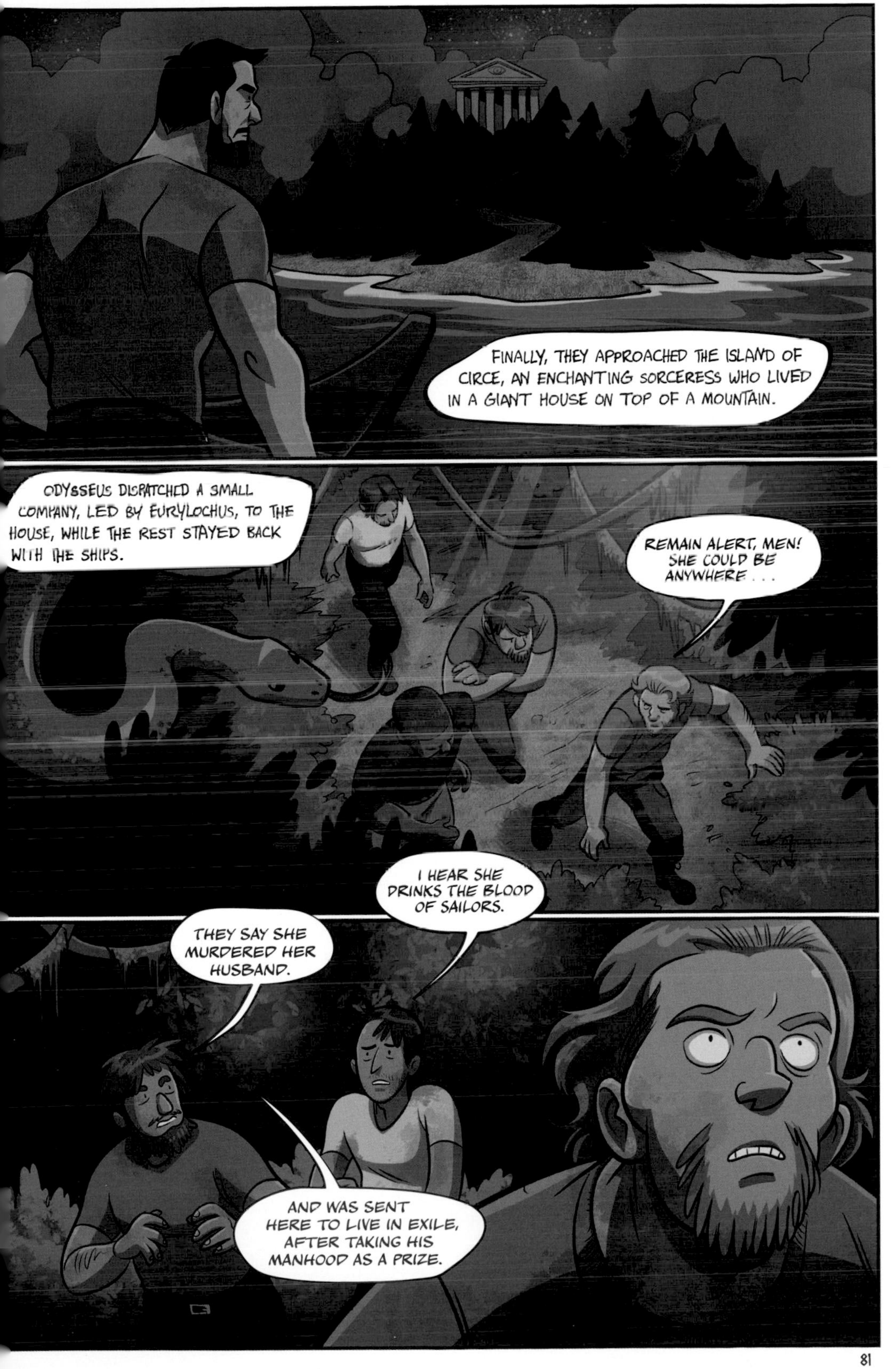
FINALLY, THEY APPROACHED THE ISLAND OF CIRCE, AN ENCHANTING SORCERESS WHO LIVED IN A GIANT HOUSE ON TOP OF A MOUNTAIN.
ODYSSEUS DISPATCHED A SMALL COMPANY, LED BY EURYLOCHUS, TO THE HOUSE, WHILE THE REST STAYED BACK WITH THE SHIPS.
REMAIN ALERT, MEN! SHE COULD BE ANYWHERE . . .
THEY SAY SHE MURDERED HER HUSBAND.
I HEAR SHE DRINKS THE BLOOD OF SAILORS.
AND WAS SENT HERE TO LIVE IN EXILE, AFTER TAKING HIS MANHOOD AS A PRIZE.

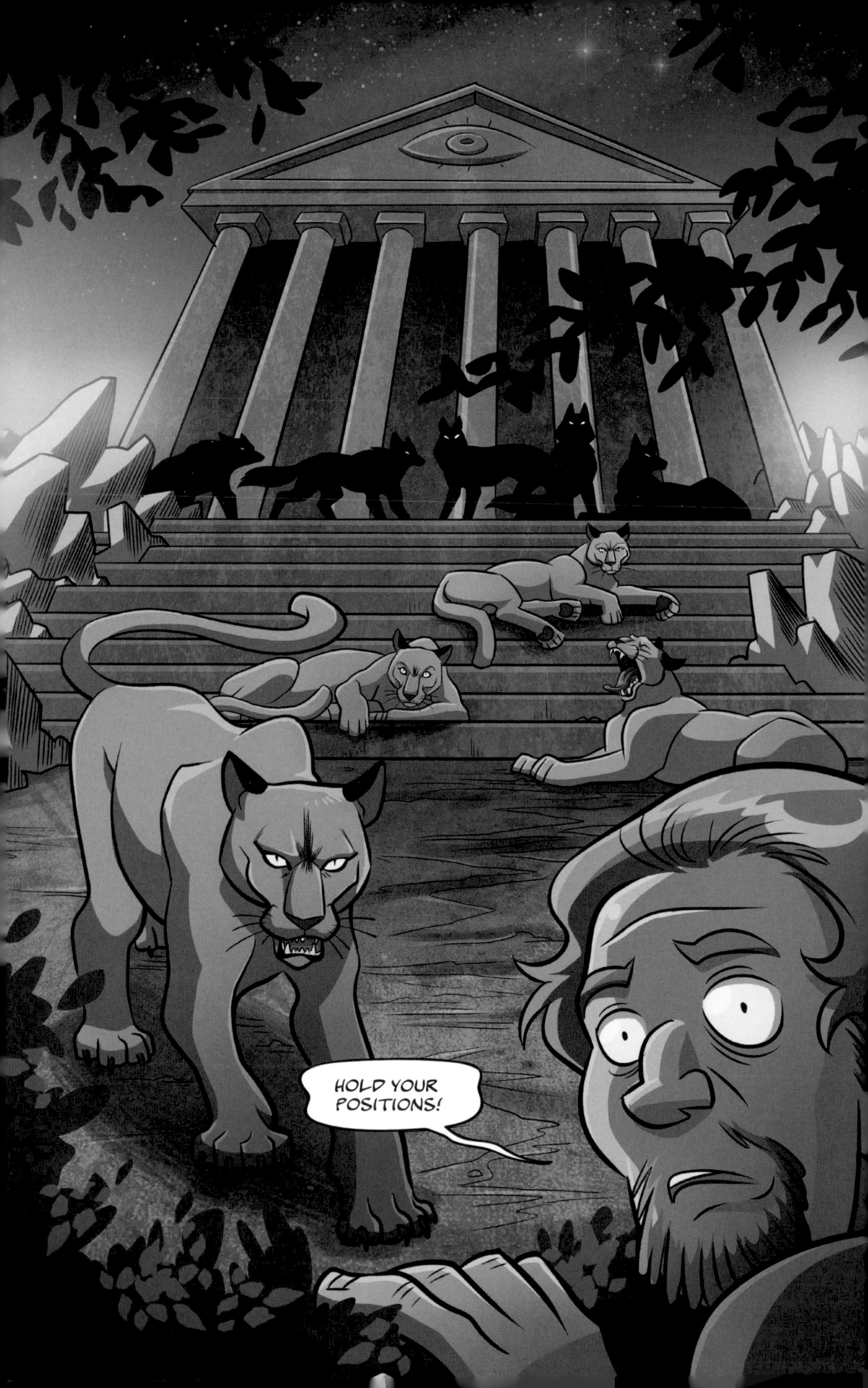
HOLD YOUR POSITIONS!

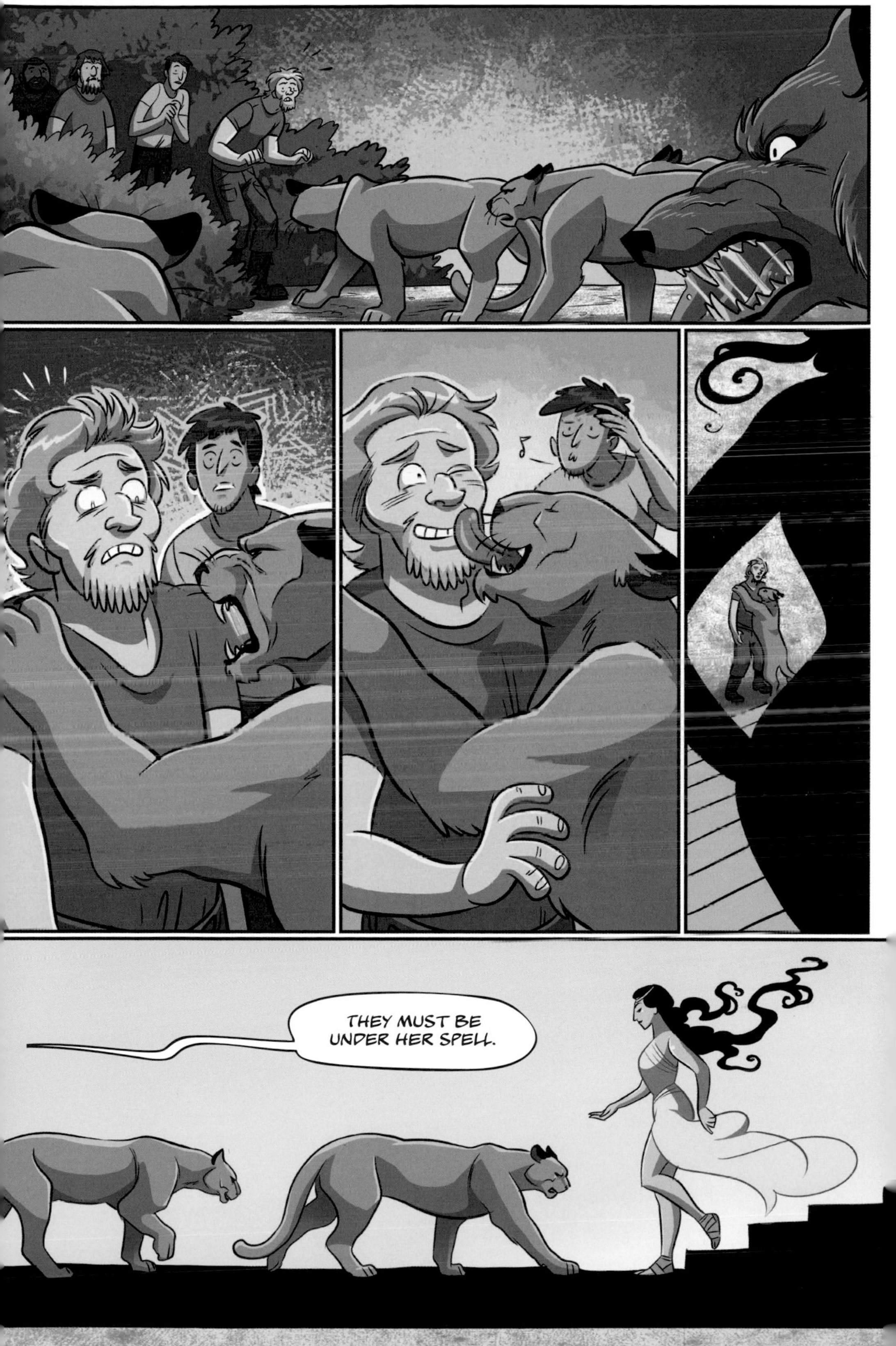
THEY MUST BE UNDER HER SPELL.

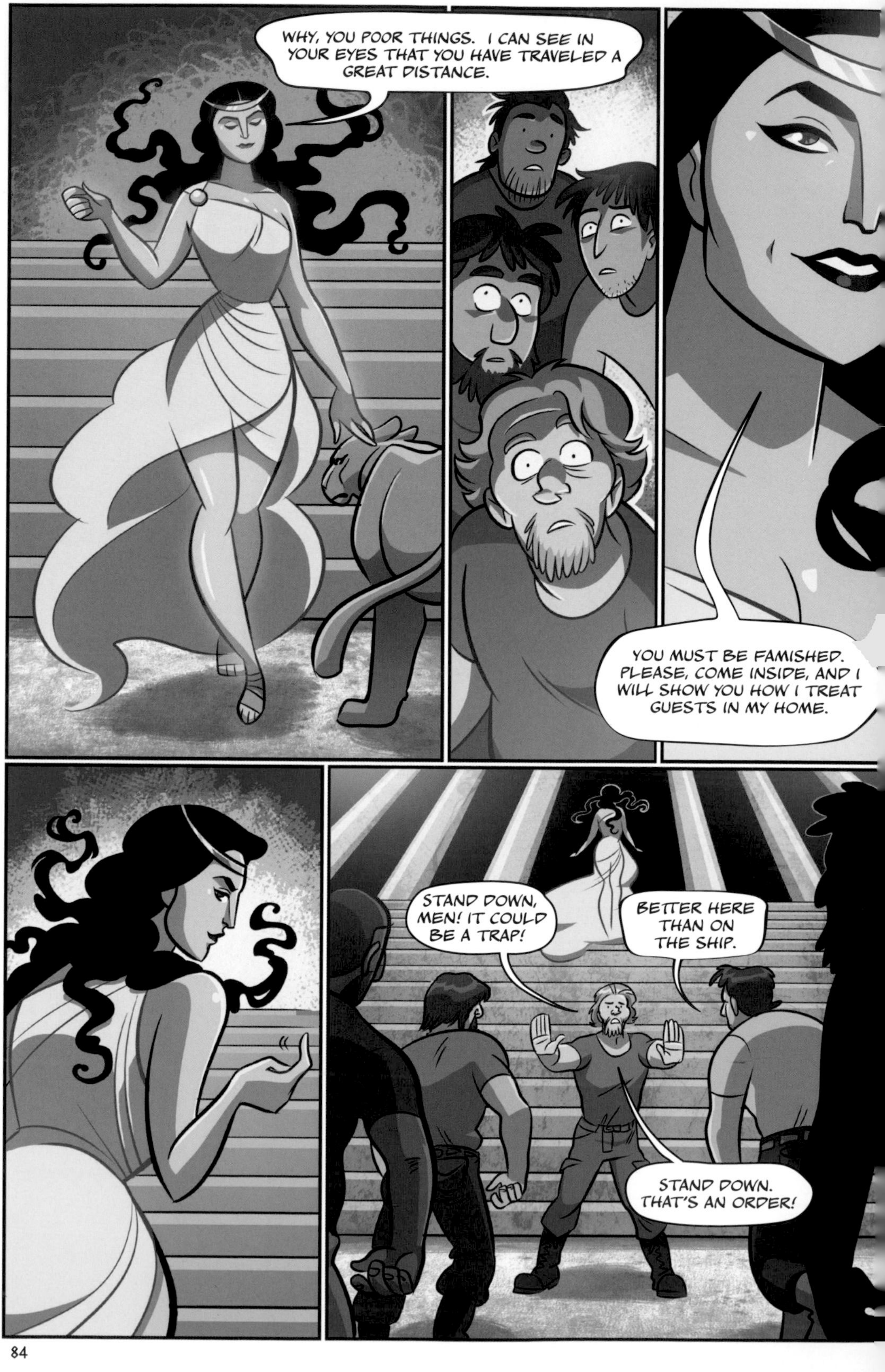
WHY, YOU POOR THINGS. I CAN SEE IN YOUR EYES THAT YOU HAVE TRAVELED A GREAT DISTANCE.
YOU MUST BE FAMISHED. PLEASE, COME INSIDE, AND I WILL SHOW YOU HOW I TREAT GUESTS IN MY HOME.
STAND DOWN, MEN! IT COULD BE A TRAP!
BETTER HERE THAN ON THE SHIP.
STAND DOWN. THAT'S AN ORDER!

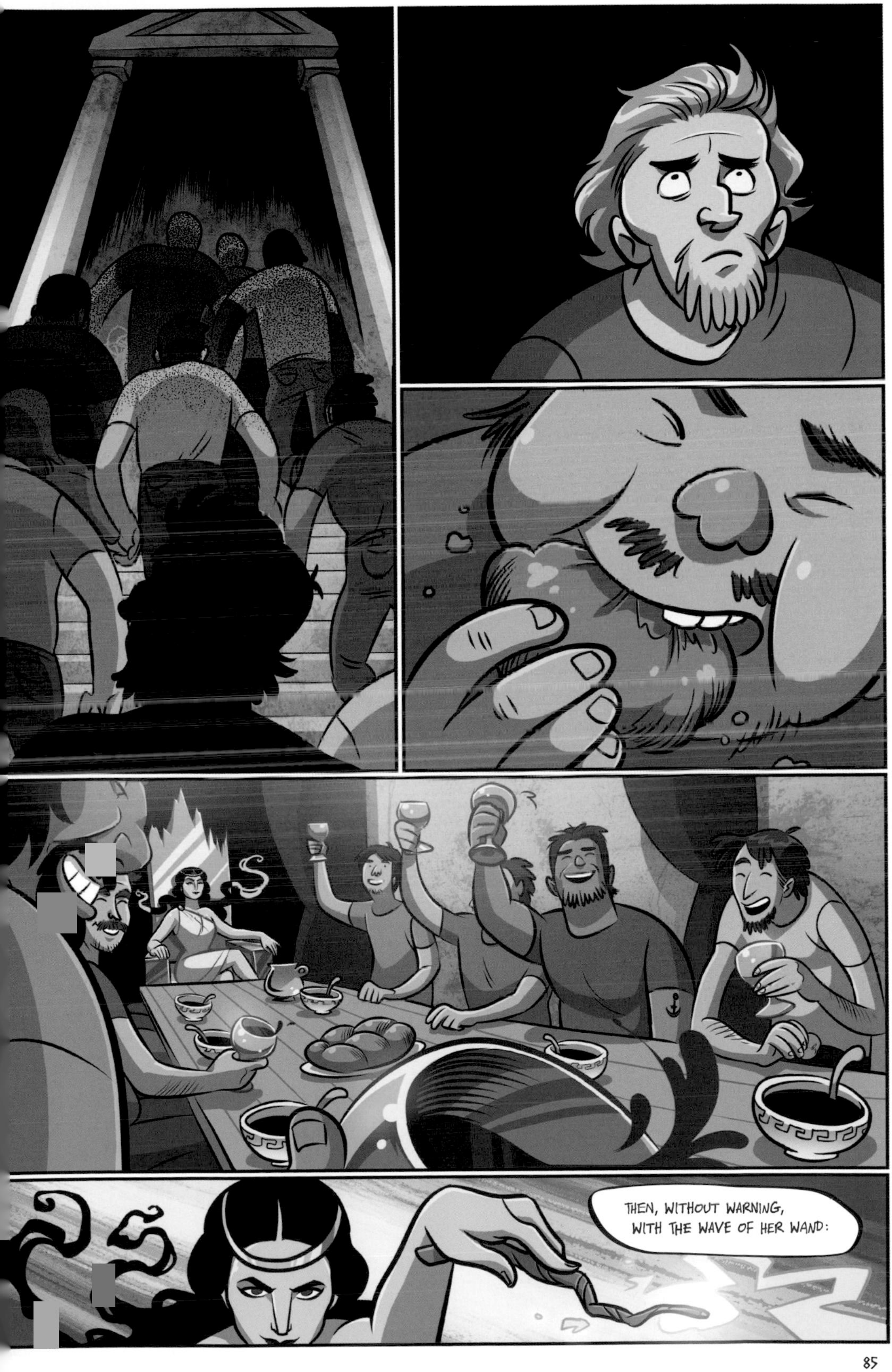
THEN, WITHOUT WARNING, WITH THE WAVE OF HER WAND:

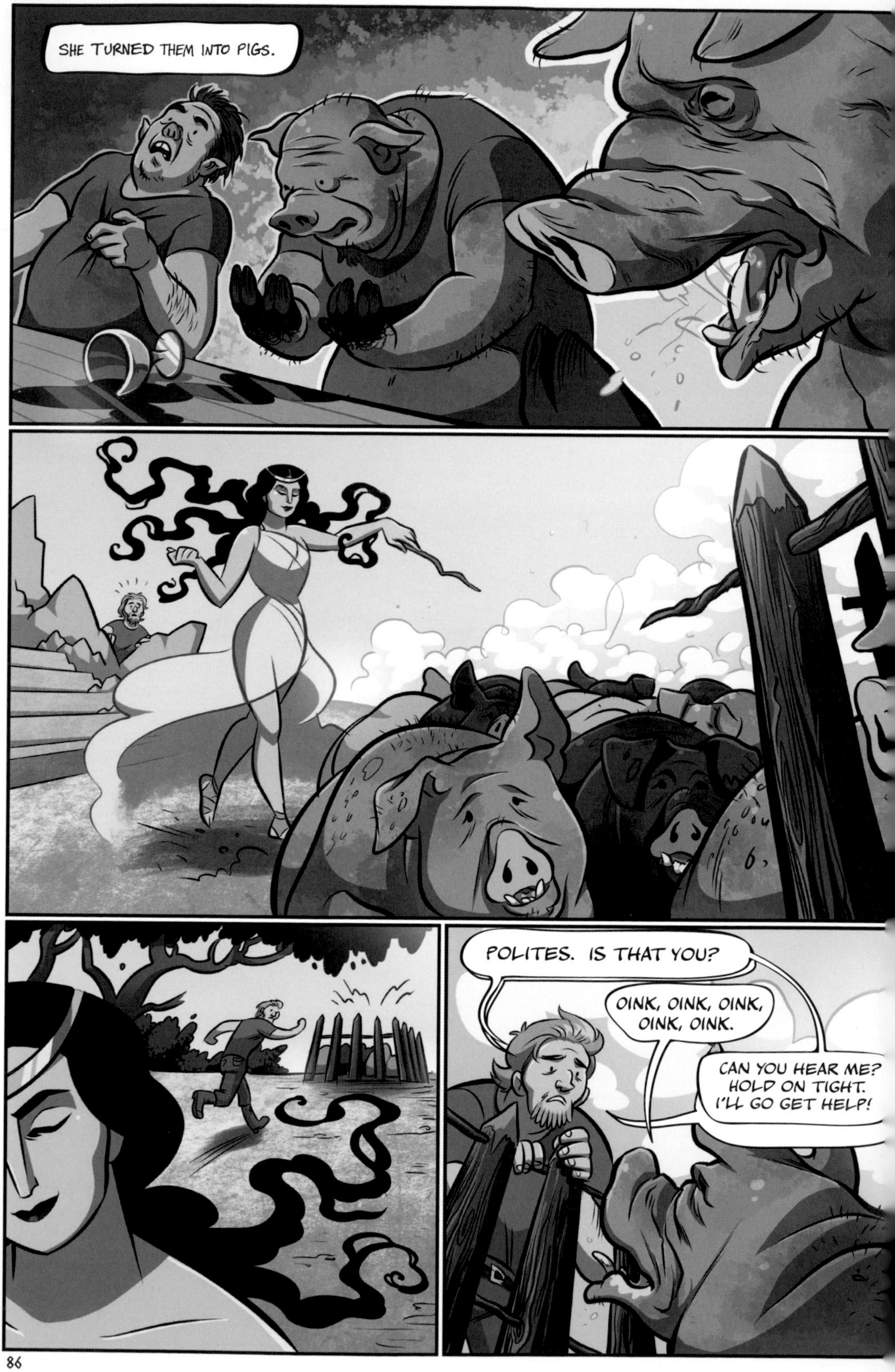
SHE TURNED THEM INTO PIGS.
POLITES. IS THAT YOU?
OINK, OINK, OINK, OINK, OINK.
CAN YOU HEAR ME? HOLD ON TIGHT. I'LL GO GET HELP!

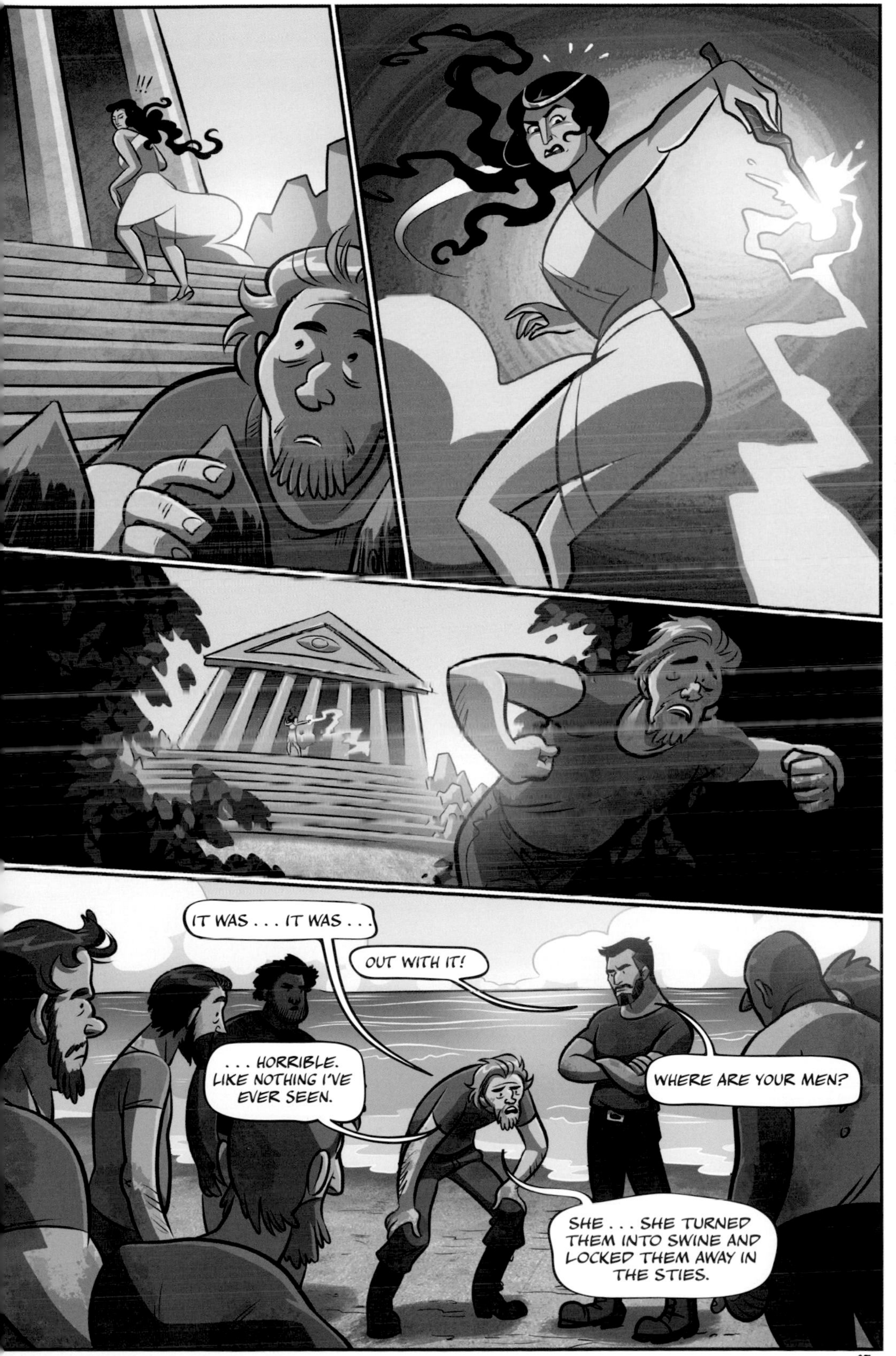

!!!
IT WAS . . . IT WAS . . .
OUT WITH IT!
. . . HORRIBLE. LIKE NOTHING I'VE EVER SEEN.
WHERE ARE YOUR MEN?
SHE . . . SHE TURNED THEM INTO SWINE AND LOCKED THEM AWAY IN THE STIES.

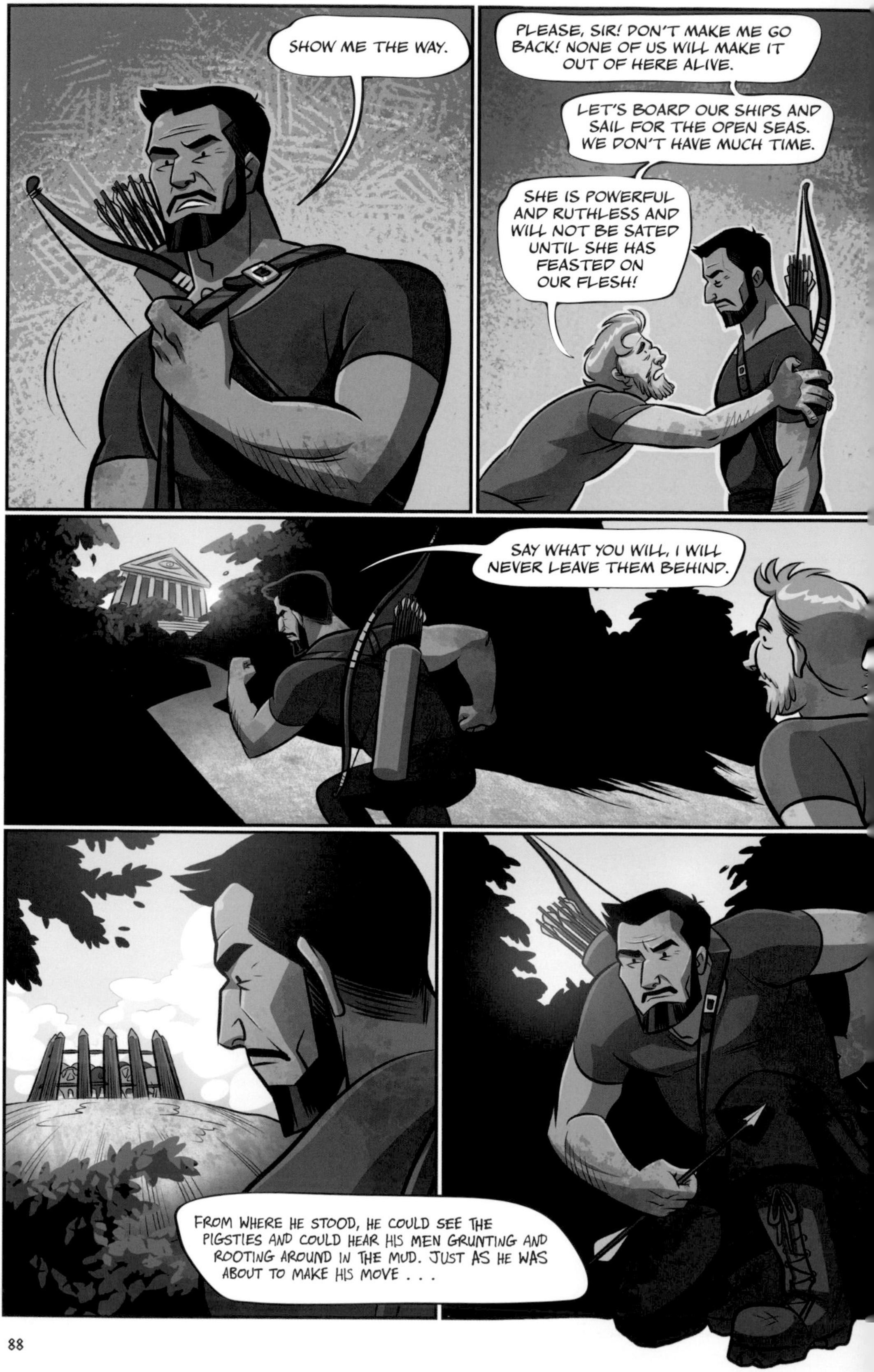
SHOW ME THE WAY.
PLEASE, SIR! DON'T MAKE ME GO BACK! NONE OF US WILL MAKE IT OUT OF HERE ALIVE.
LET'S BOARD OUR SHIPS AND SAIL FOR THE OPEN SEAS. WE DON'T HAVE MUCH TIME.
SHE IS POWERFUL AND RUTHLESS AND WILL NOT BE SATED UNTIL SHE HAS FEASTED ON OUR FLESH!
SAY WHAT YOU WILL, I WILL NEVER LEAVE THEM BEHIND.
FROM WHERE HE STOOD, HE COULD SEE THE PIGSTIES AND COULD HEAR HIS MEN GRUNTING AND ROOTING AROUND IN THE MUD. JUST AS HE WAS ABOUT TO MAKE HIS MOVE . . .

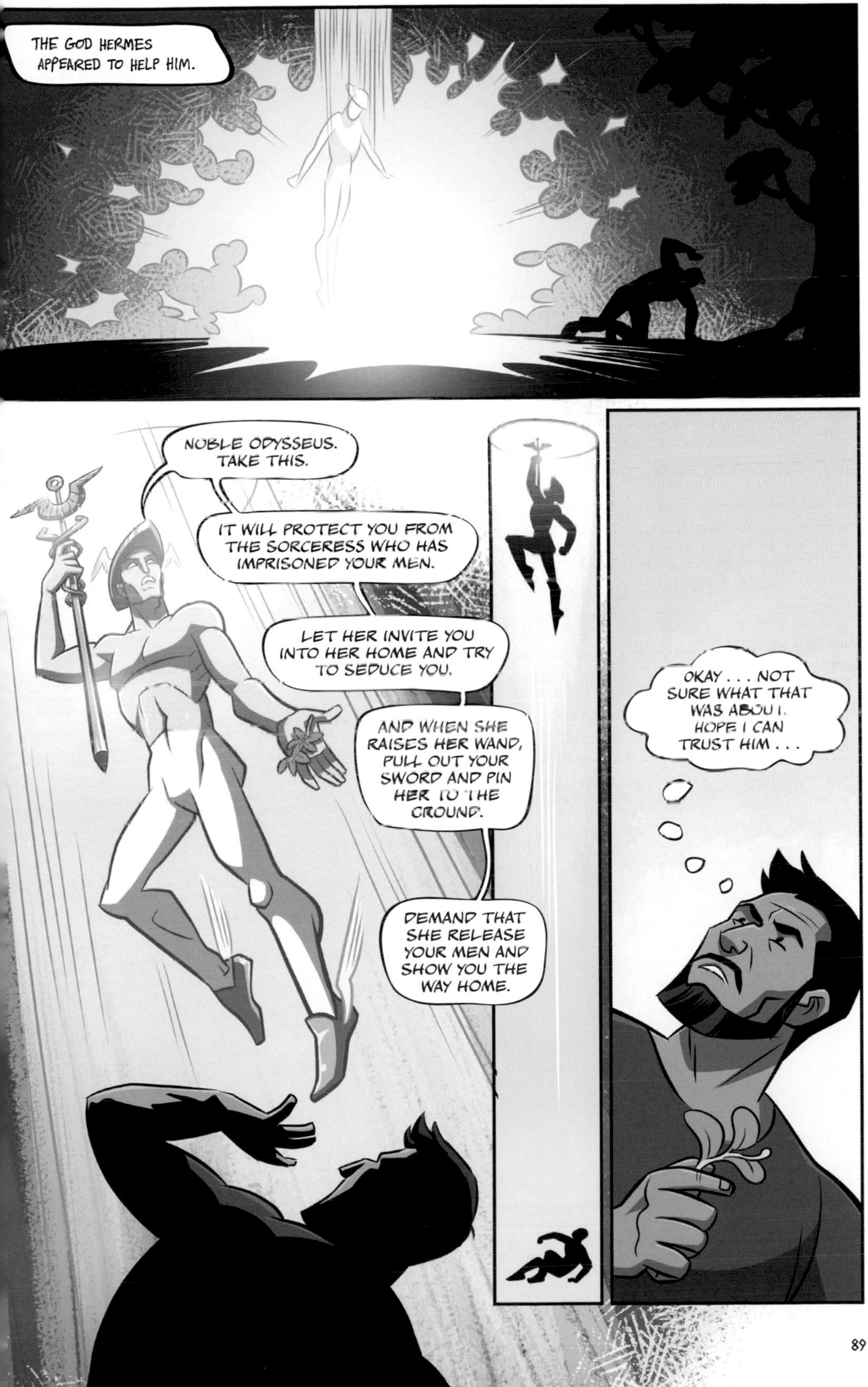
THE GOD HERMES APPEARED TO HELP HIM.
NOBLE ODYSSEUS. TAKE THIS.
IT WILL PROTECT YOU FROM THE SORCERESS WHO HAS IMPRISONED YOUR MEN.
LET HER INVITE YOU INTO HER HOME AND TRY TO SEDUCE YOU.
AND WHEN SHE RAISES HER WAND, PULL OUT YOUR SWORD AND PIN HER TO THE GROUND.
DEMAND THAT SHE RELEASE YOUR MEN AND SHOW YOU THE WAY HOME.
OKAY . . . NOT SURE WHAT THAT WAS ABOUT. HOPE I CAN TRUST HIM . . .

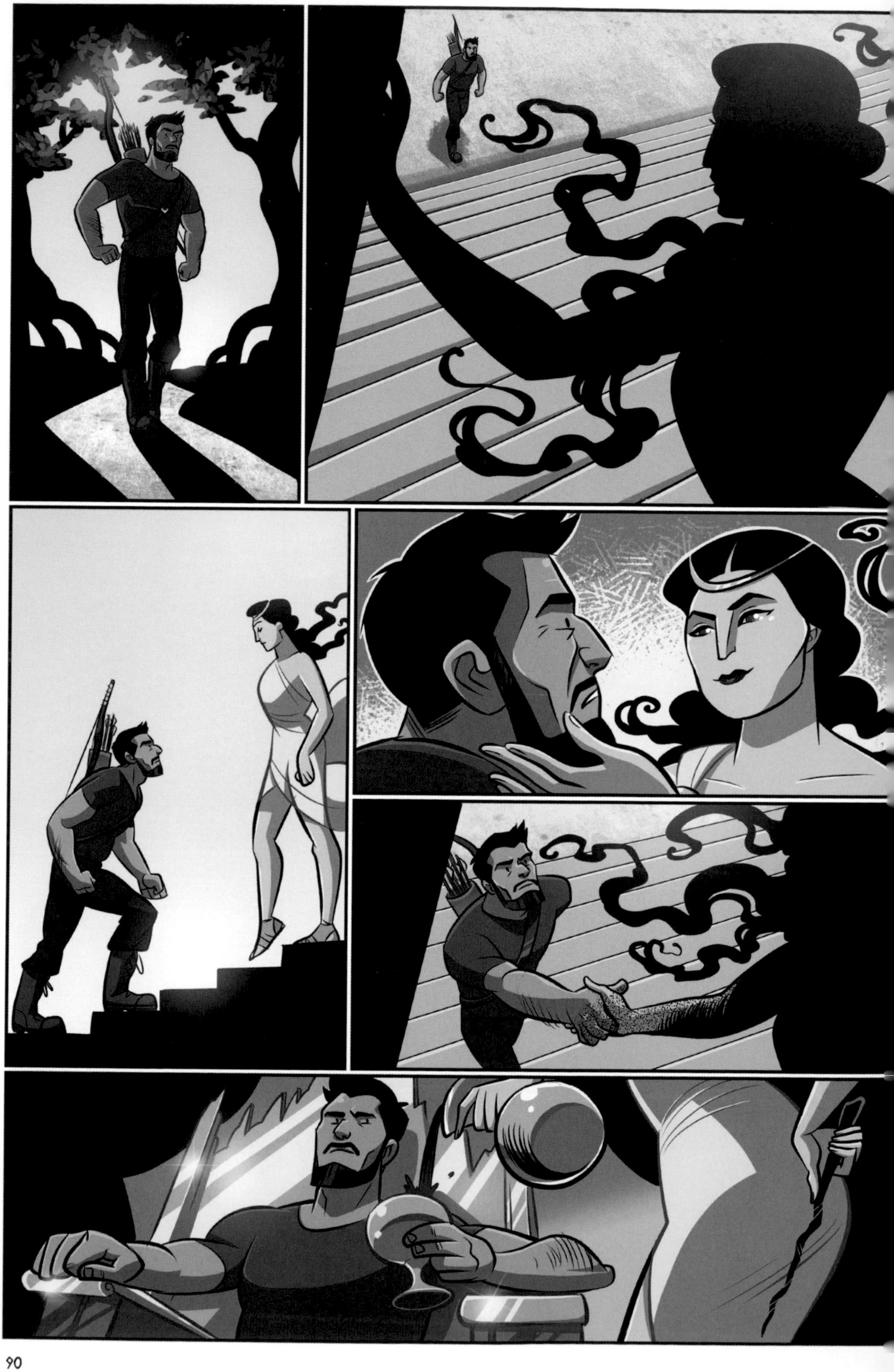

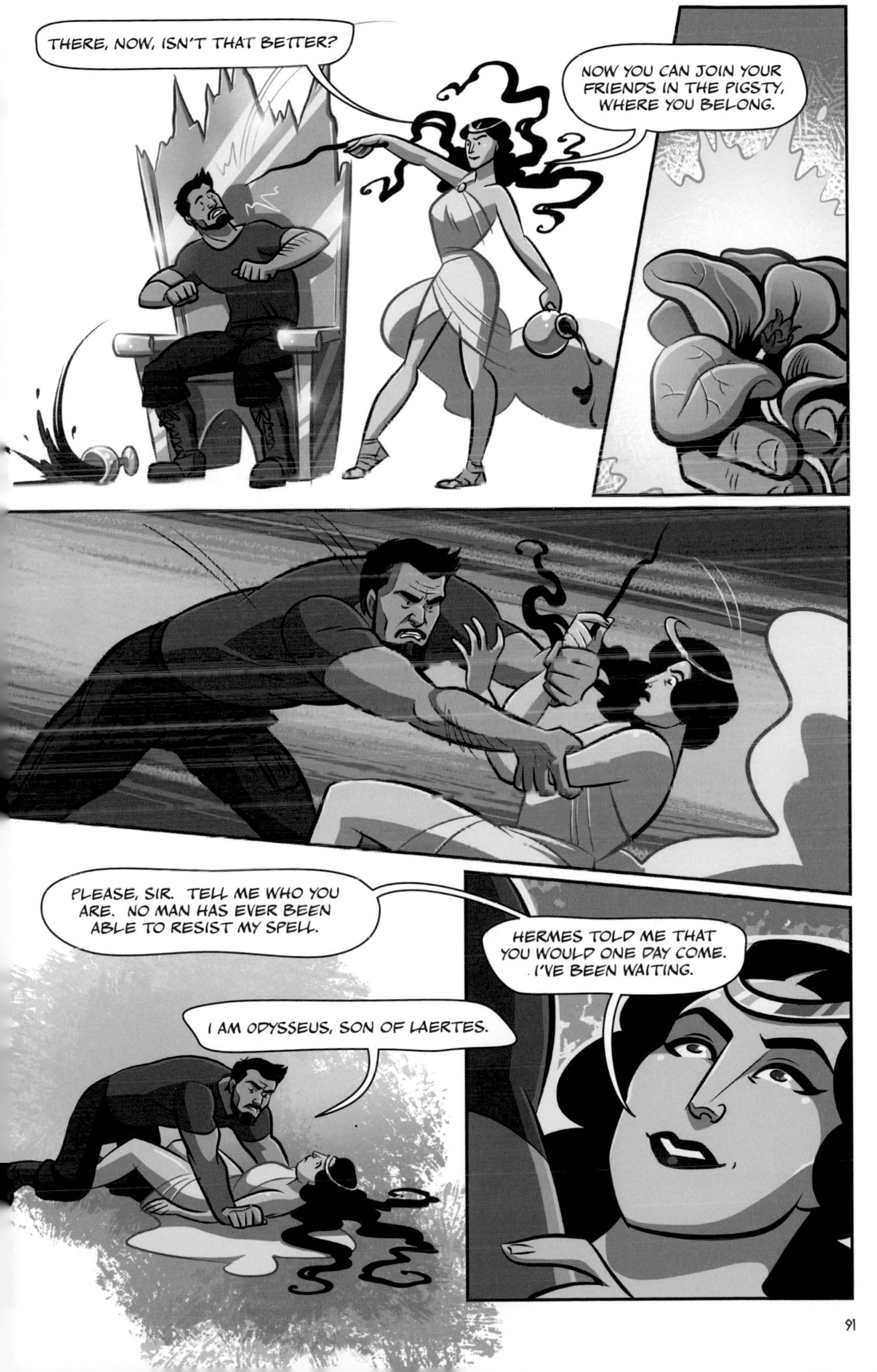
THERE, NOW, ISN'T THAT BETTER?
NOW YOU CAN JOIN YOUR FRIENDS IN THE PIGSTY, WHERE YOU BELONG.
PLEASE, SIR. TELL ME WHO YOU ARE. NO MAN HAS EVER BEEN ABLE TO RESIST MY SPELL.
I AM ODYSSEUS, SON OF LAERTES.
HERMES TOLD ME THAT YOU WOULD ONE DAY COME. I'VE BEEN WAITING.

I HAVE COME FOR MY MEN.

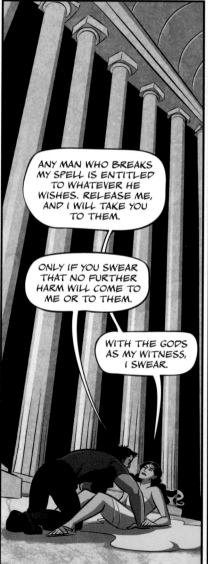

ANY MAN WHO BREAKS MY SPELL IS ENTITLED TO WHATEVER HE WISHES. RELEASE ME, AND I WILL TAKE YOU TO THEM.

ONLY IF YOU SWEAR THAT NO FURTHER HARM WILL COME TO ME OR TO THEM.

WITH THE GODS AS MY WITNESS, I SWEAR.

CIRCE TOOK ODYSSEUS TO THE PIGSTIES. SHE WAVED HER WAND AND RESTORED THE MEN.

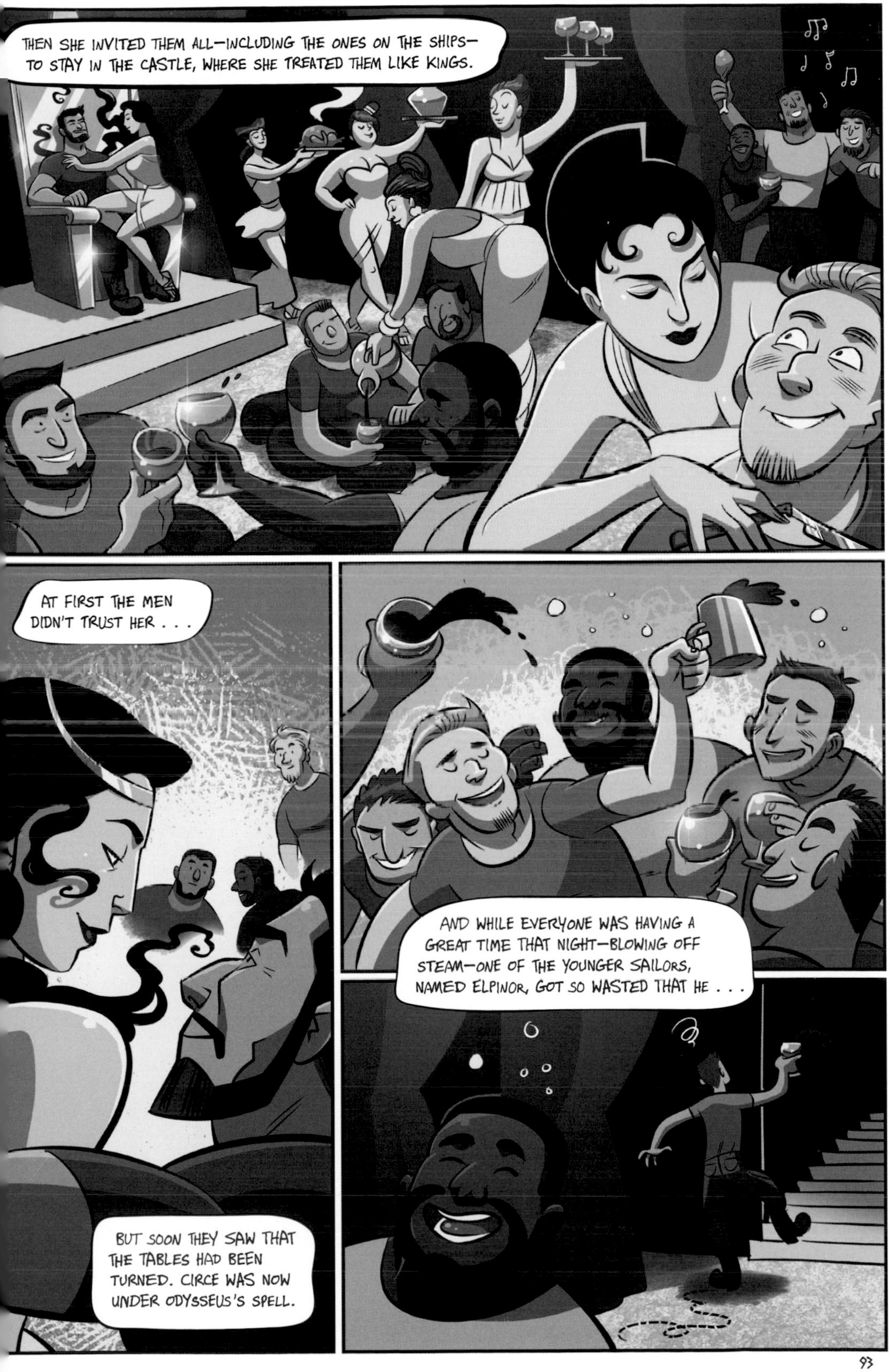
THEN SHE INVITED THEM ALL—INCLUDING THE ONES ON THE SHIPS—TO STAY IN THE CASTLE, WHERE SHE TREATED THEM LIKE KINGS.
AT FIRST THE MEN DIDN'T TRUST HER . . .
BUT SOON THEY SAW THAT THE TABLES HAD BEEN TURNED. CIRCE WAS NOW UNDER ODYSSEUS'S SPELL.
AND WHILE EVERYONE WAS HAVING A GREAT TIME THAT NIGHT—BLOWING OFF STEAM—ONE OF THE YOUNGER SAILORS, NAMED ELPINOR, GOT SO WASTED THAT HE . . .

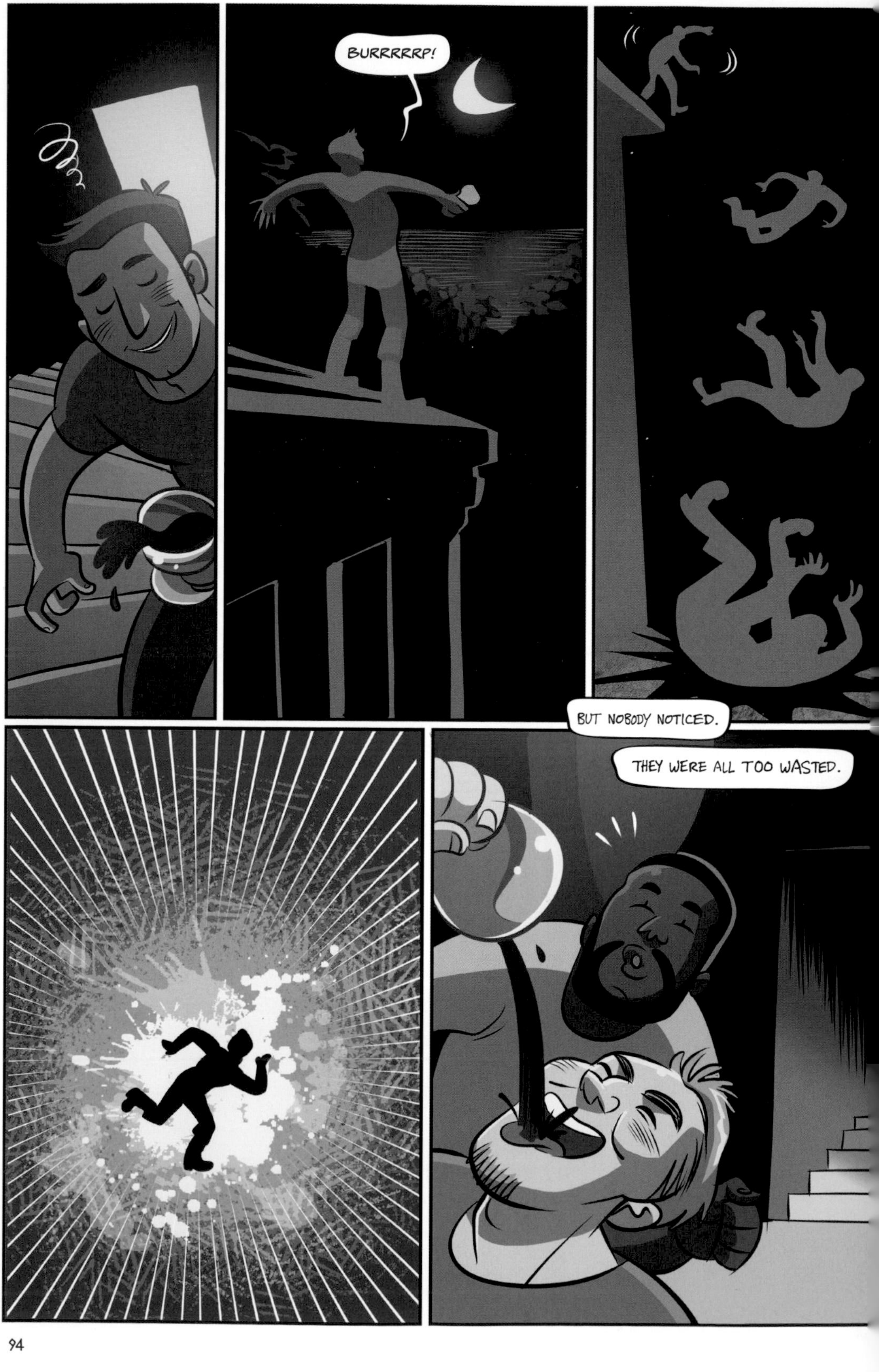
BURRRRRP!
BUT NOBODY NOTICED.
THEY WERE ALL TOO WASTED.

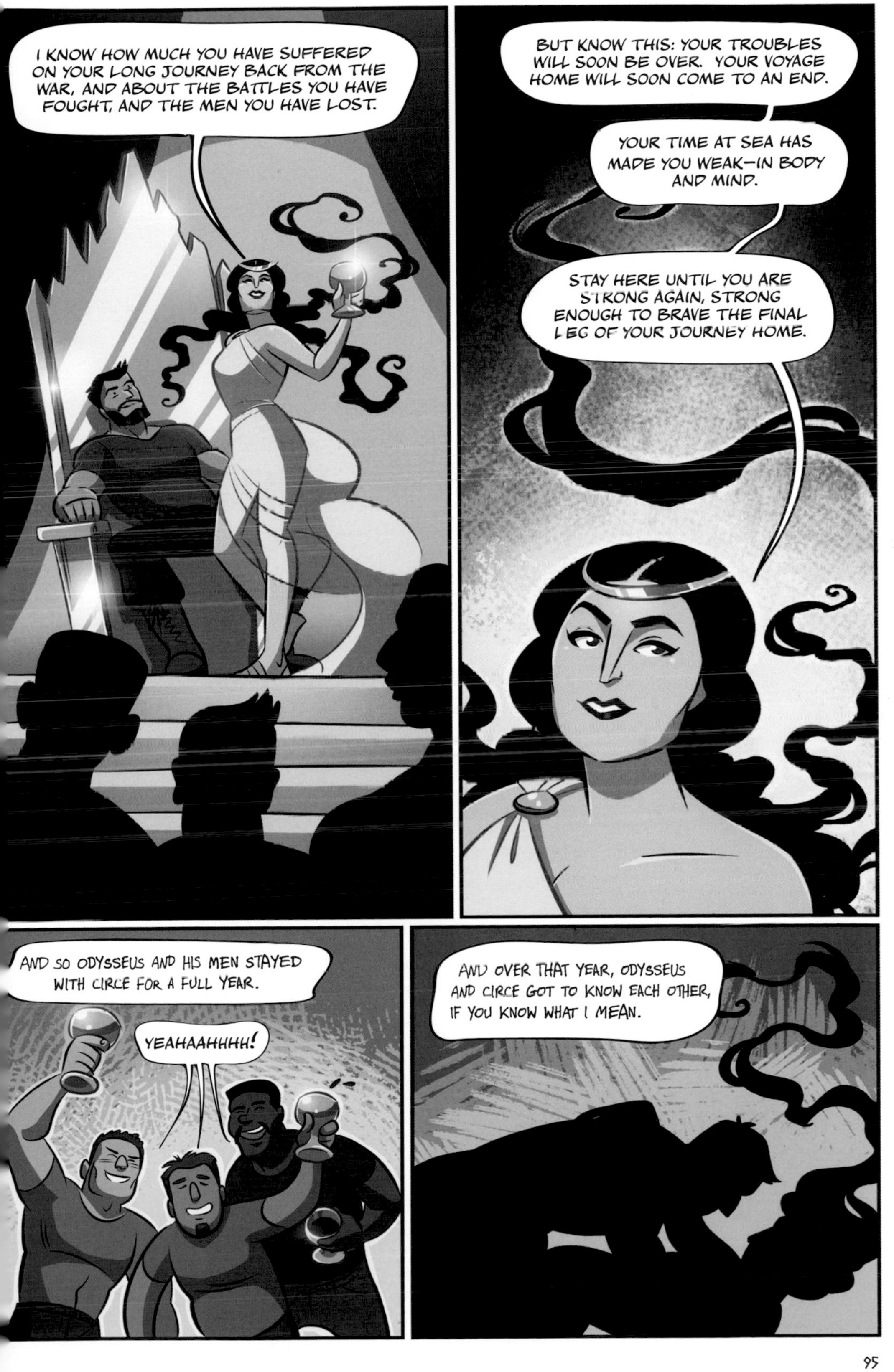
I KNOW HOW MUCH YOU HAVE SUFFERED ON YOUR LONG JOURNEY BACK FROM THE WAR, AND ABOUT THE BATTLES YOU HAVE FOUGHT, AND THE MEN YOU HAVE LOST.
BUT KNOW THIS: YOUR TROUBLES WILL SOON BE OVER. YOUR VOYAGE HOME WILL SOON COME TO AN END.
YOUR TIME AT SEA HAS MADE YOU WEAK—IN BODY AND MIND.
STAY HERE UNTIL YOU ARE STRONG AGAIN, STRONG ENOUGH TO BRAVE THE FINAL LEG OF YOUR JOURNEY HOME.
AND SO ODYSSEUS AND HIS MEN STAYED WITH CIRCE FOR A FULL YEAR.
YEAHAAHHHH!
AND OVER THAT YEAR, ODYSSEUS AND CIRCE GOT TO KNOW EACH OTHER, IF YOU KNOW WHAT I MEAN.

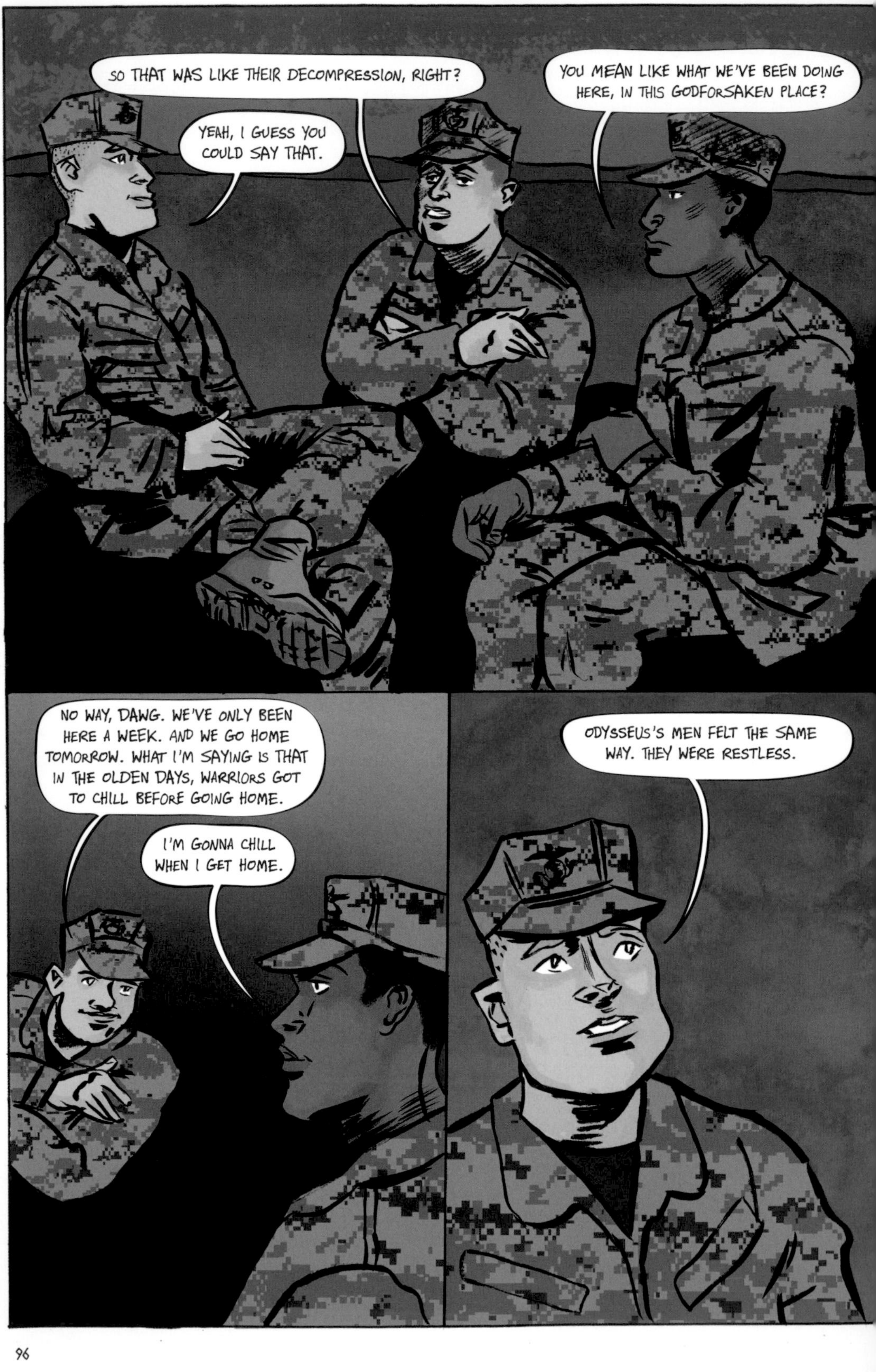
SO THAT WAS LIKE THEIR DECOMPRESSION, RIGHT?
YEAH, I GUESS YOU COULD SAY THAT.
YOU MEAN LIKE WHAT WE'VE BEEN DOING HERE, IN THIS GODFORSAKEN PLACE?
NO WAY, DAWG. WE'VE ONLY BEEN HERE A WEEK. AND WE GO HOME TOMORROW. WHAT I'M SAYING IS THAT IN THE OLDEN DAYS, WARRIORS GOT TO CHILL BEFORE GOING HOME.
I'M GONNA CHILL WHEN I GET HOME.
ODYSSEUS'S MEN FELT THE SAME WAY. THEY WERE RESTLESS.

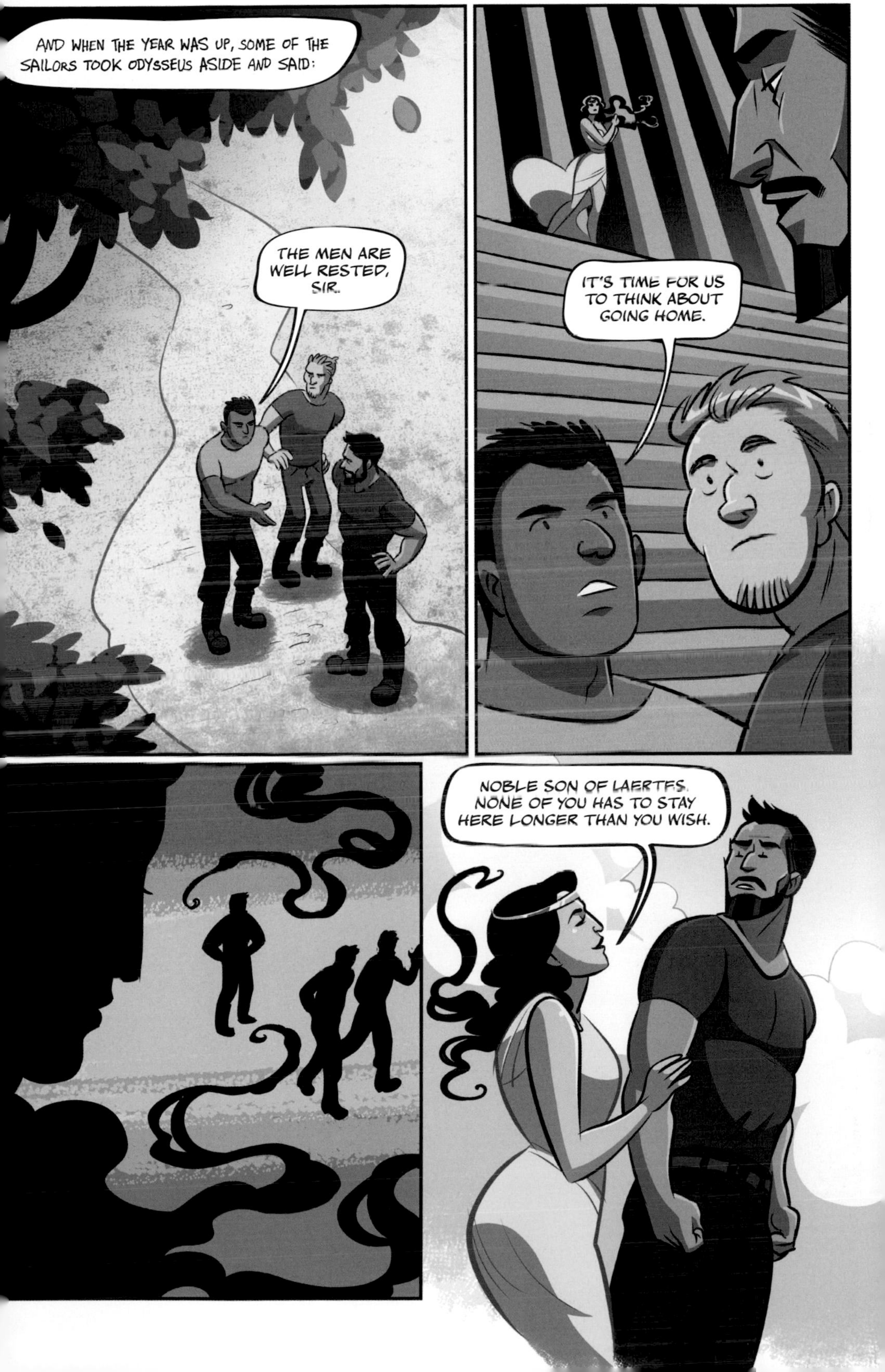
AND WHEN THE YEAR WAS UP, SOME OF THE SAILORS TOOK ODYSSEUS ASIDE AND SAID:
THE MEN ARE WELL RESTED, SIR.
IT'S TIME FOR US TO THINK ABOUT GOING HOME.
NOBLE SON OF LAERTES, NONE OF YOU HAS TO STAY HERE LONGER THAN YOU WISH.

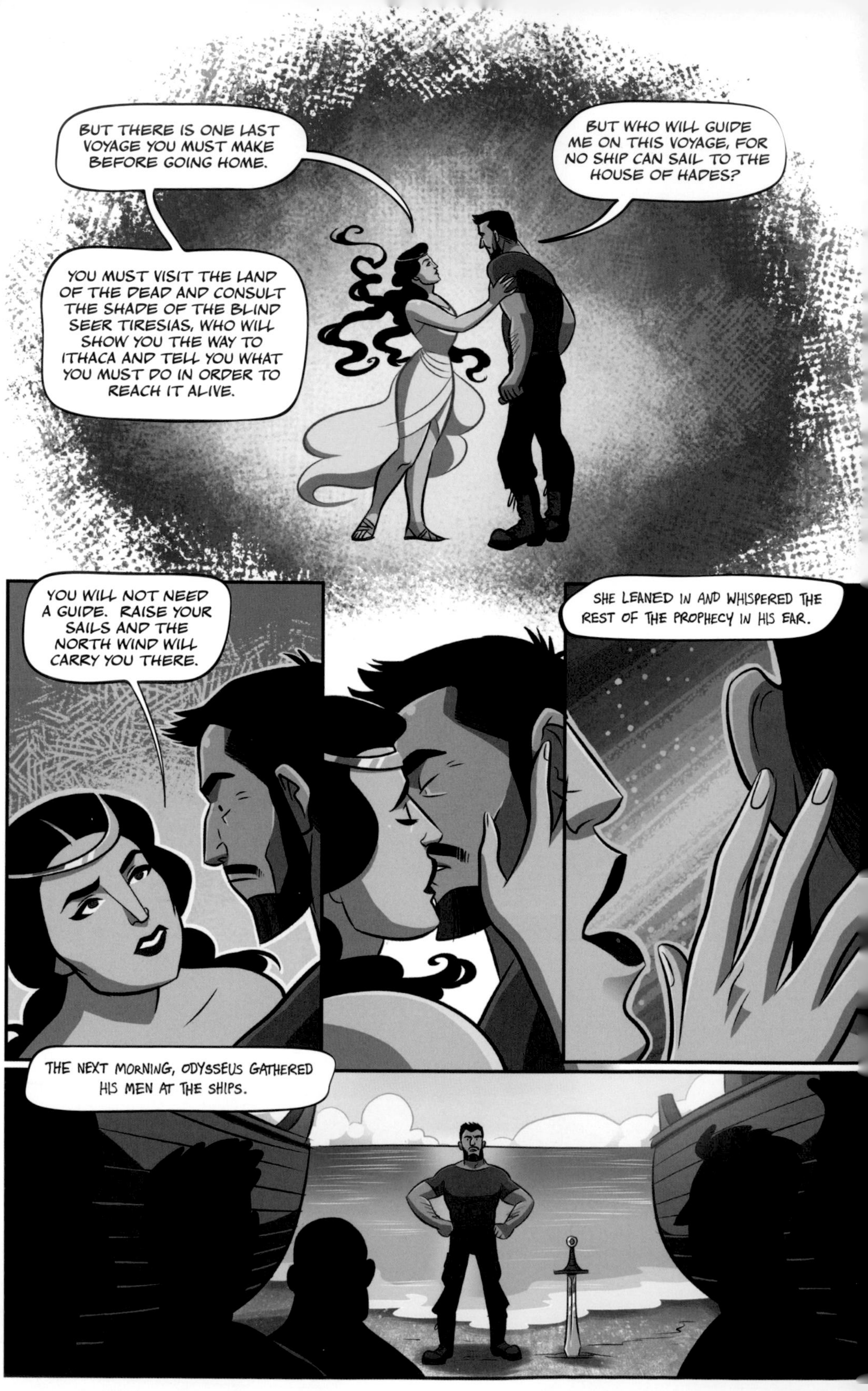
BUT THERE IS ONE LAST VOYAGE YOU MUST MAKE BEFORE GOING HOME.
YOU MUST VISIT THE LAND OF THE DEAD AND CONSULT THE SHADE OF THE BLIND SEER TIRESIAS, WHO WILL SHOW YOU THE WAY TO ITHACA AND TELL YOU WHAT YOU MUST DO IN ORDER TO REACH IT ALIVE.
BUT WHO WILL GUIDE ME ON THIS VOYAGE, FOR NO SHIP CAN SAIL TO THE HOUSE OF HADES?
YOU WILL NOT NEED A GUIDE. RAISE YOUR SAILS AND THE NORTH WIND WILL CARRY YOU THERE.
SHE LEANED IN AND WHISPERED THE REST OF THE PROPHECY IN HIS EAR.
THE NEXT MORNING, ODYSSEUS GATHERED HIS MEN AT THE SHIPS.

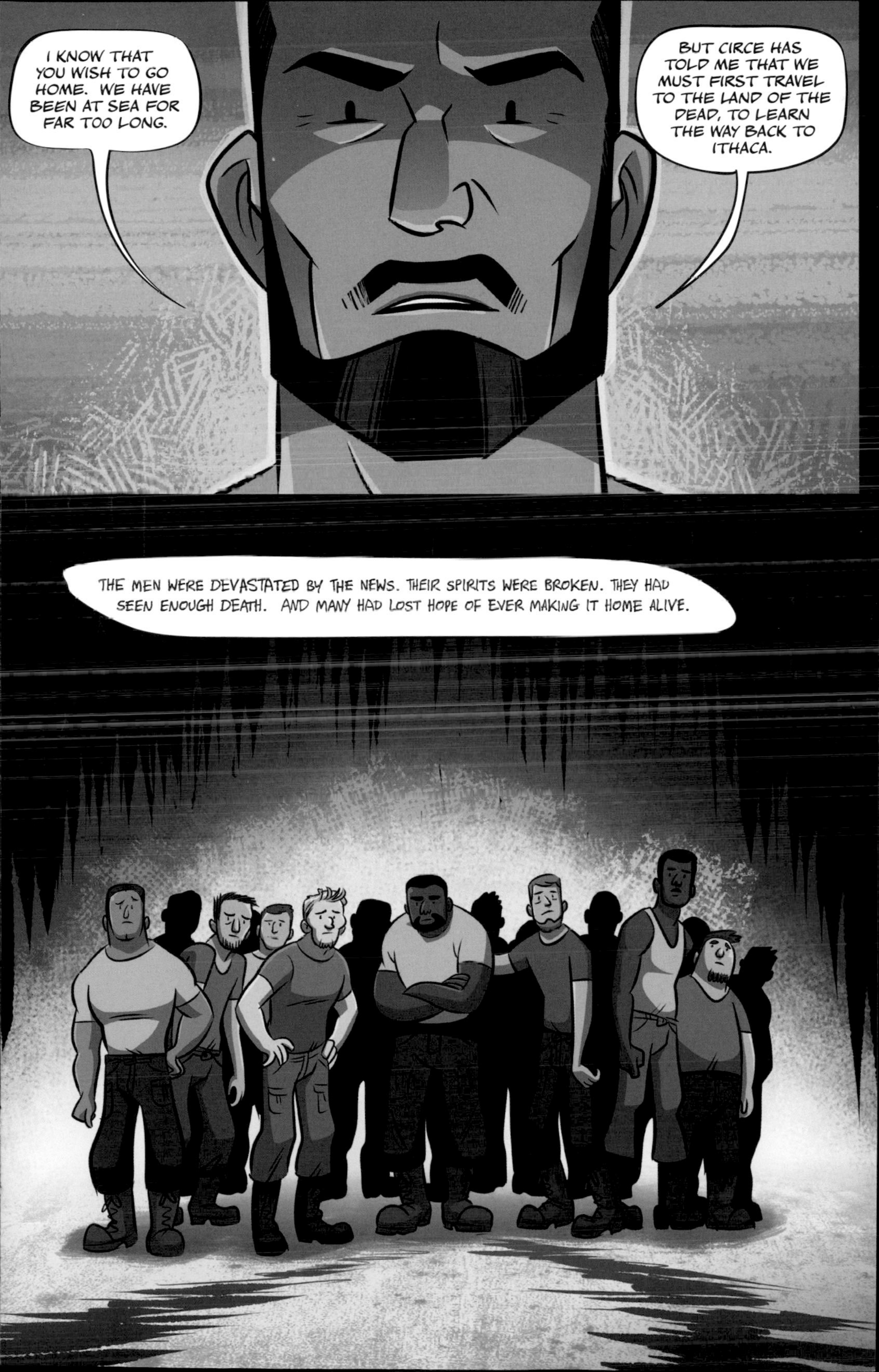
I KNOW THAT YOU WISH TO GO HOME. WE HAVE BEEN AT SEA FOR FAR TOO LONG.
BUT CIRCE HAS TOLD ME THAT WE MUST FIRST TRAVEL TO THE LAND OF THE DEAD, TO LEARN THE WAY BACK TO ITHACA.
THE MEN WERE DEVASTATED BY THE NEWS. THEIR SPIRITS WERE BROKEN. THEY HAD SEEN ENOUGH DEATH. AND MANY HAD LOST HOPE OF EVER MAKING IT HOME ALIVE.

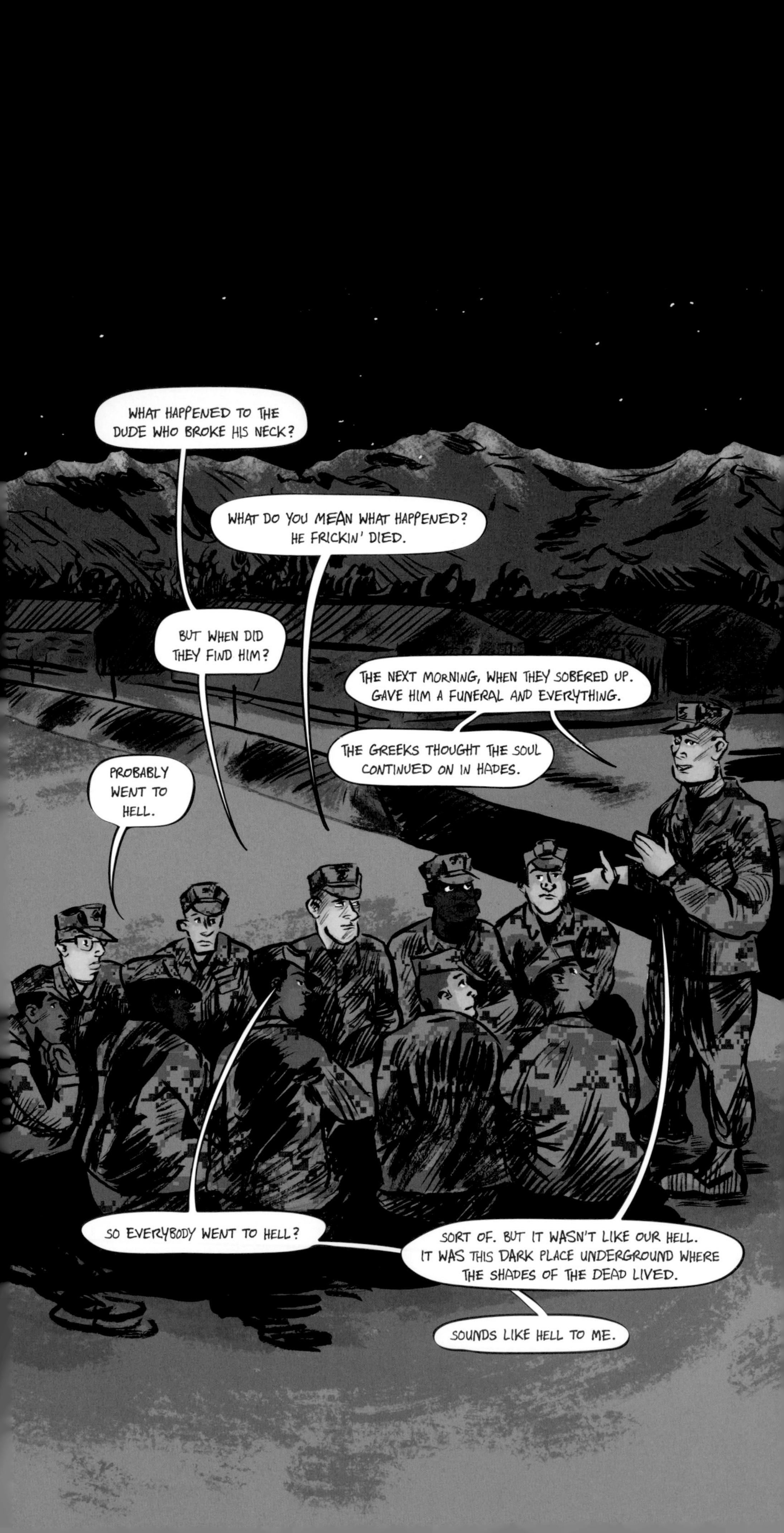
WHAT HAPPENED TO THE DUDE WHO BROKE HIS NECK?
WHAT DO YOU MEAN WHAT HAPPENED? HE FRICKIN' DIED.
BUT WHEN DID THEY FIND HIM?
THE NEXT MORNING, WHEN THEY SOBERED UP. GAVE HIM A FUNERAL AND EVERYTHING.
THE GREEKS THOUGHT THE SOUL CONTINUED ON IN HADES.
PROBABLY WENT TO HELL.
SO EVERYBODY WENT TO HELL?
SORT OF. BUT IT WASN'T LIKE OUR HELL. IT WAS THIS DARK PLACE UNDERGROUND WHERE THE SHADES OF THE DEAD LIVED.
SOUNDS LIKE HELL TO ME.

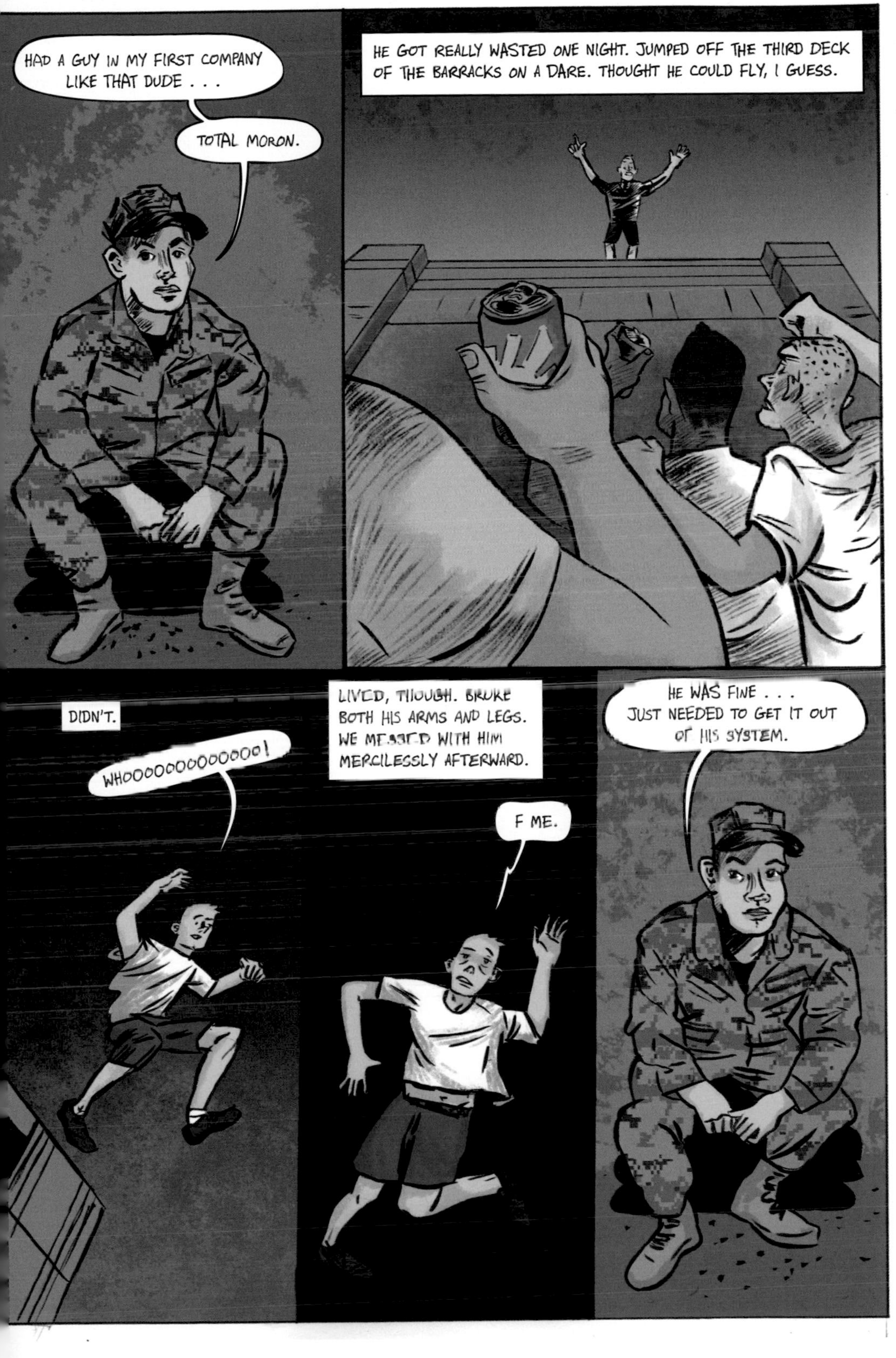

HAD A GUY IN MY FIRST COMPANY LIKE THAT DUDE . . .
TOTAL MORON.
HE GOT REALLY WASTED ONE NIGHT. JUMPED OFF THE THIRD DECK OF THE BARRACKS ON A DARE. THOUGHT HE COULD FLY, I GUESS.
DIDN'T.
WHOOOOOOOOOOOOO!
LIVED, THOUGH. BROKE BOTH HIS ARMS AND LEGS. WE MESSED WITH HIM MERCILESSLY AFTERWARD.
F ME.
HE WAS FINE . . . JUST NEEDED TO GET IT OUT OF HIS SYSTEM.

CHAPTER 4

FACING THE DEAD

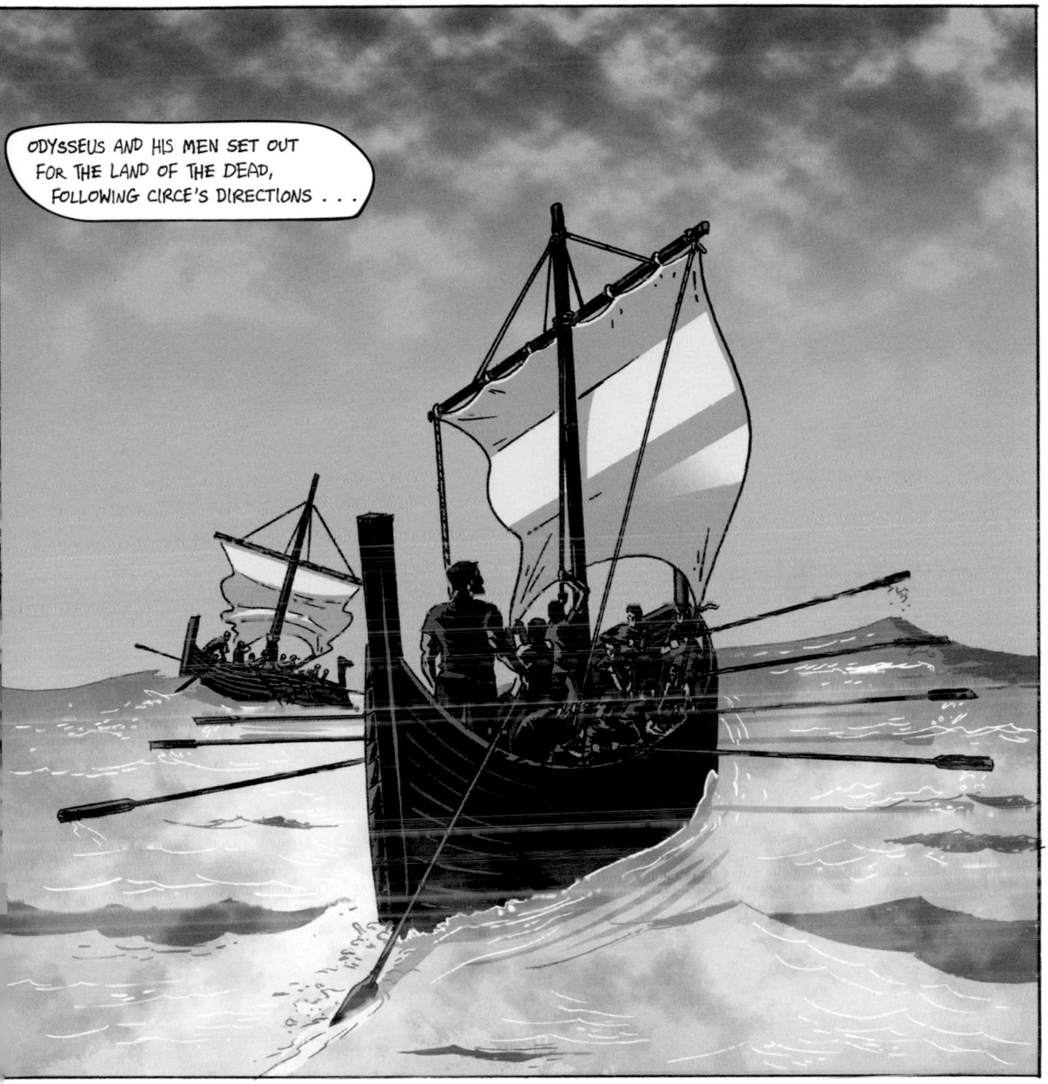
ODYSSEUS AND HIS MEN SET OUT FOR THE LAND OF THE DEAD, FOLLOWING CIRCE'S DIRECTIONS . . .

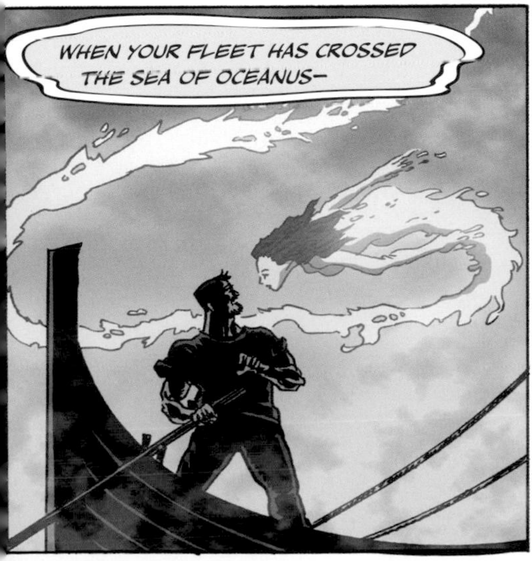
WHEN YOUR FLEET HAS CROSSED THE SEA OF OCEANUS–

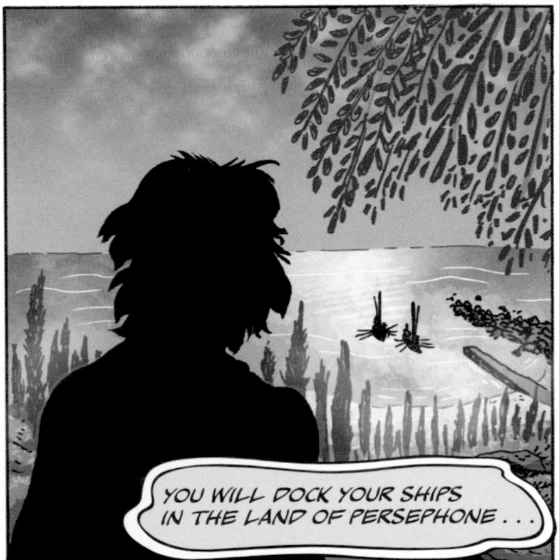
YOU WILL DOCK YOUR SHIPS IN THE LAND OF PERSEPHONE . . .

THERE YOU WILL FIND A DARK CAVE INTO WHICH TWO RIVERS FLOW.

AT THE MOUTH OF THE CAVE, YOU MUST DIG A TRENCH AND CUT OPEN A BLACK RAM AND A WHITE SHEEP—A SACRIFICE TO HADES.

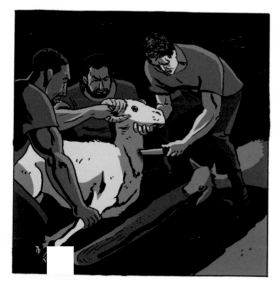

THE BLOOD WILL ATTRACT THE DEAD.

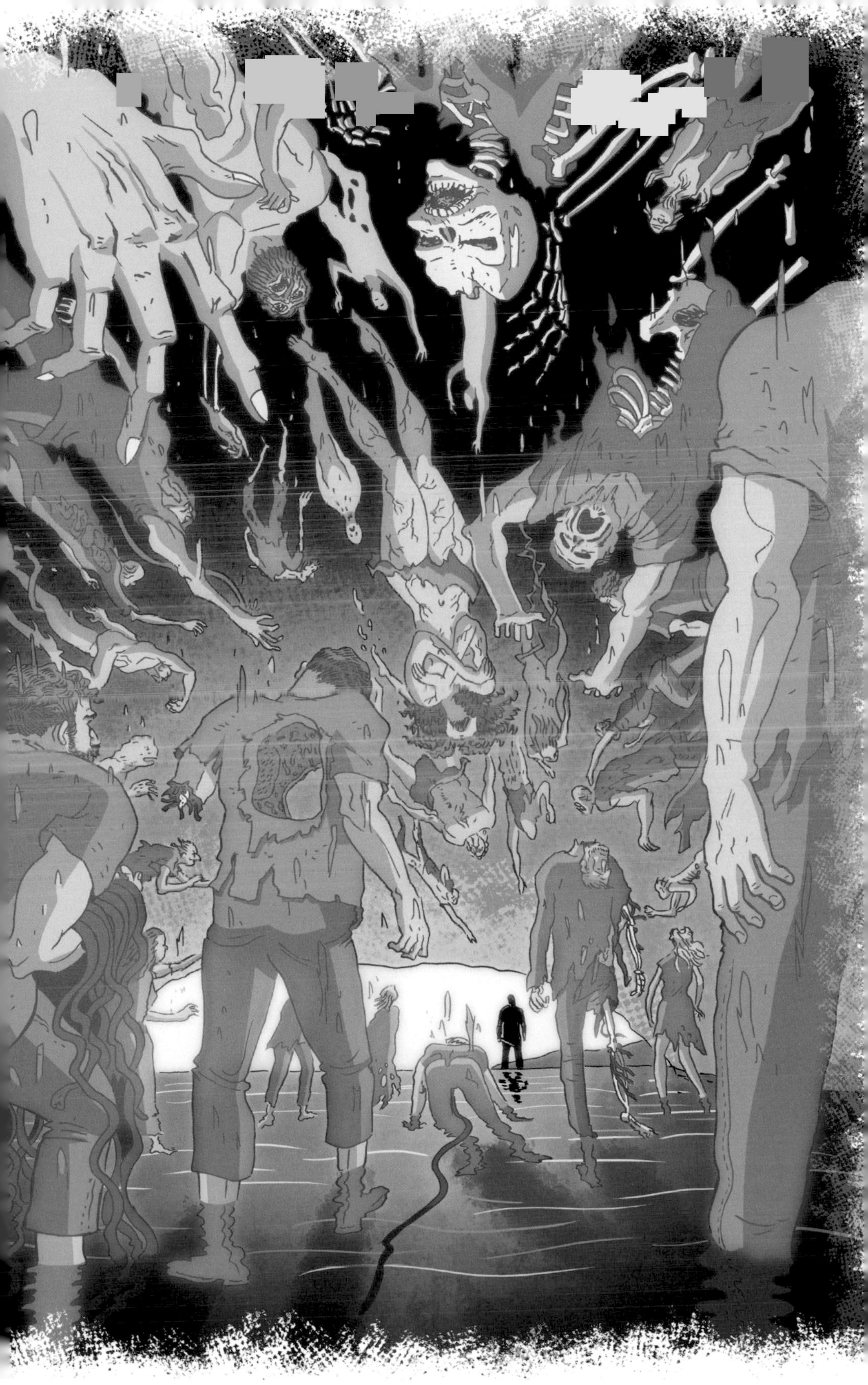

SIT THERE WITH YOUR SWORD DRAWN.

PROTECT THE TRENCH UNTIL TIRESIAS COMES.

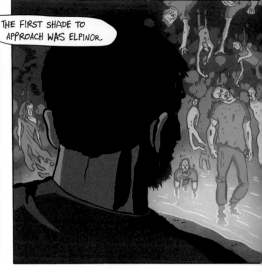

THE FIRST SHADE TO APPROACH WAS ELPINOR.

ELPINOR!

SIR, IT WAS NOBODY'S FAULT BUT MY OWN.

I GOT DRUNK AND FELL OFF CIRCE'S ROOF, AND BROKE MY NECK.

NOW I AM CONDEMNED TO WANDER HADES FOR ALL TIME, A SHADOW OF MY FORMER SELF.

I'M SO SORRY.

PLEASE TELL MY PARENTS THAT I DIED IN BATTLE AND NOT INGLORIOUSLY.

I DO NOT WISH TO DISGRACE THEIR NAME.

YOU HAVE MY WORD.

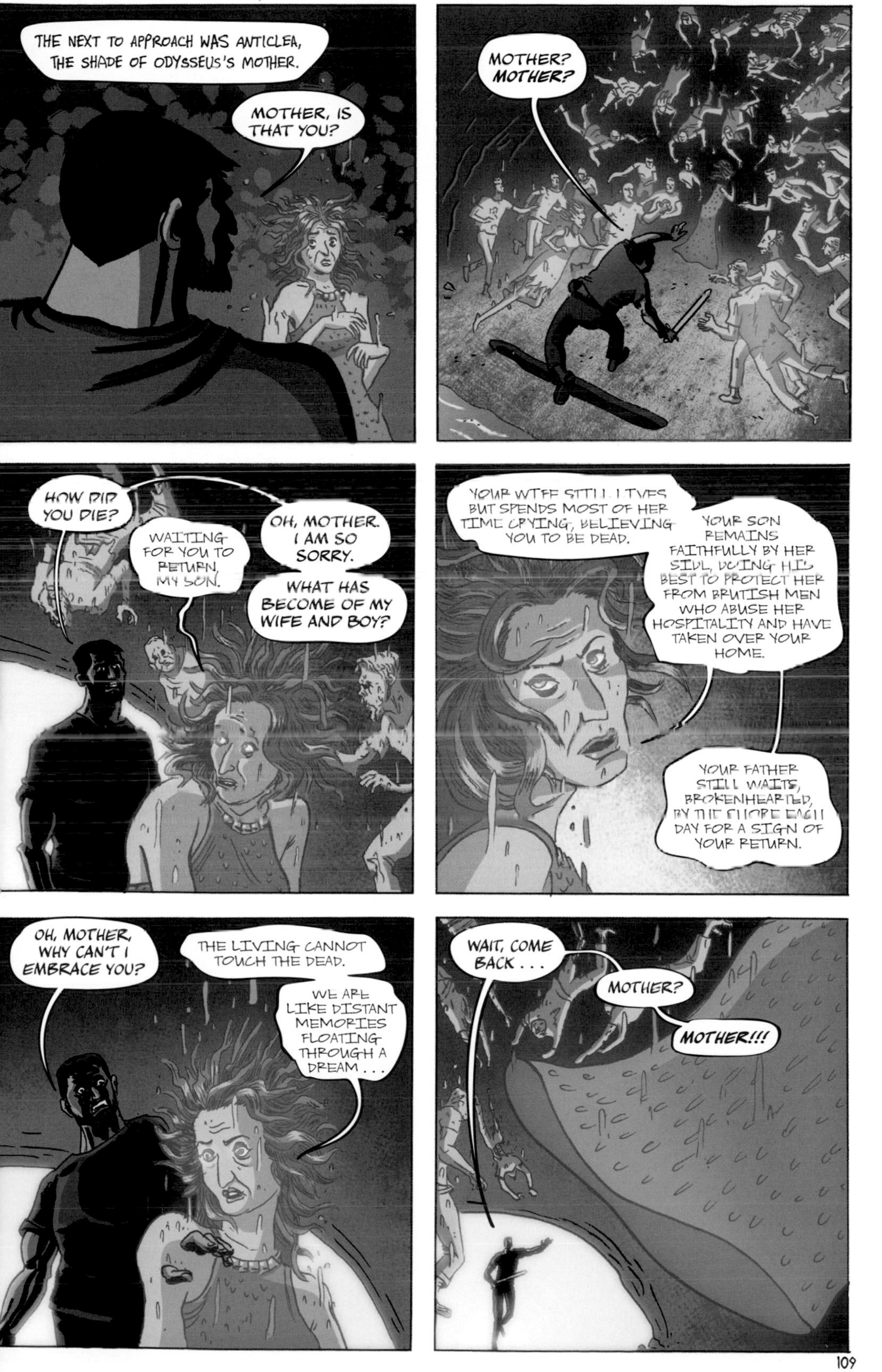
THE NEXT TO APPROACH WAS ANTICLEA, THE SHADE OF ODYSSEUS'S MOTHER.
MOTHER, IS THAT YOU?
MOTHER? MOTHER?
HOW DID YOU DIE?
WAITING FOR YOU TO RETURN, MY SON.
OH, MOTHER. I AM SO SORRY.
WHAT HAS BECOME OF MY WIFE AND BOY?
YOUR WIFE STILL LIVES BUT SPENDS MOST OF HER TIME CRYING, BELIEVING YOU TO BE DEAD.
YOUR SON REMAINS FAITHFULLY BY HER SIDE, DOING HIS BEST TO PROTECT HER FROM BRUTISH MEN WHO ABUSE HER HOSPITALITY AND HAVE TAKEN OVER YOUR HOME.
YOUR FATHER STILL WAITS, BROKENHEARTED, BY THE SHORE EACH DAY FOR A SIGN OF YOUR RETURN.
OH, MOTHER, WHY CAN'T I EMBRACE YOU?
THE LIVING CANNOT TOUCH THE DEAD.
WE ARE LIKE DISTANT MEMORIES FLOATING THROUGH A DREAM . . .
WAIT, COME BACK . . .
MOTHER?
MOTHER!!!

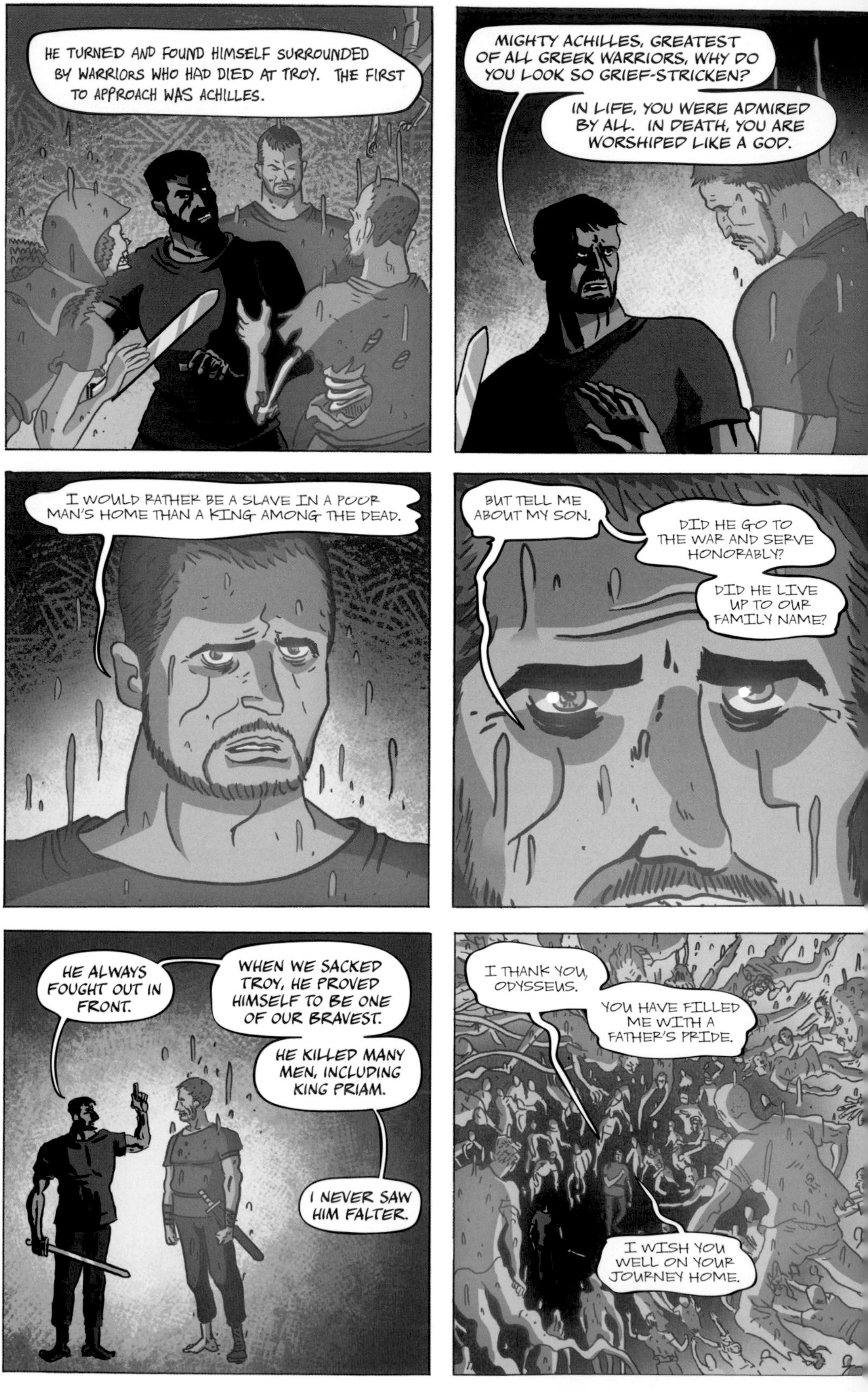
HE TURNED AND FOUND HIMSELF SURROUNDED BY WARRIORS WHO HAD DIED AT TROY. THE FIRST TO APPROACH WAS ACHILLES.
MIGHTY ACHILLES, GREATEST OF ALL GREEK WARRIORS, WHY DO YOU LOOK SO GRIEF-STRICKEN?
IN LIFE, YOU WERE ADMIRED BY ALL. IN DEATH, YOU ARE WORSHIPED LIKE A GOD.
I WOULD RATHER BE A SLAVE IN A POOR MAN'S HOME THAN A KING AMONG THE DEAD.
BUT TELL ME ABOUT MY SON.
DID HE GO TO THE WAR AND SERVE HONORABLY?
DID HE LIVE UP TO OUR FAMILY NAME?
HE ALWAYS FOUGHT OUT IN FRONT.
WHEN WE SACKED TROY, HE PROVED HIMSELF TO BE ONE OF OUR BRAVEST.
HE KILLED MANY MEN, INCLUDING KING PRIAM.
I NEVER SAW HIM FALTER.
I THANK YOU, ODYSSEUS.
YOU HAVE FILLED ME WITH A FATHER'S PRIDE.
I WISH YOU WELL ON YOUR JOURNEY HOME.

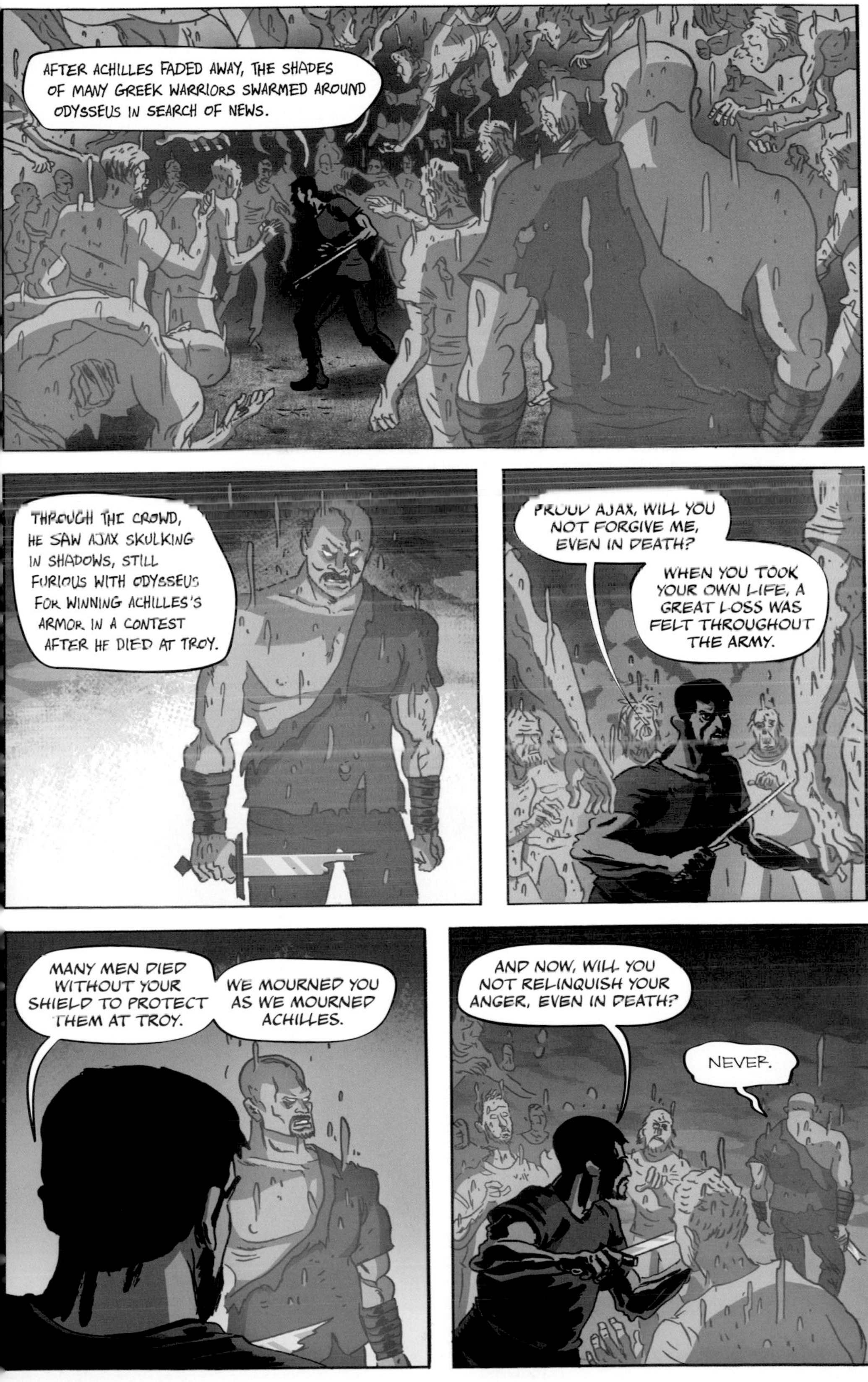
AFTER ACHILLES FADED AWAY, THE SHADES OF MANY GREEK WARRIORS SWARMED AROUND ODYSSEUS IN SEARCH OF NEWS.
THROUGH THE CROWD, HE SAW AJAX SKULKING IN SHADOWS, STILL FURIOUS WITH ODYSSEUS FOR WINNING ACHILLES'S ARMOR IN A CONTEST AFTER HE DIED AT TROY.
PROUD AJAX, WILL YOU NOT FORGIVE ME, EVEN IN DEATH?
WHEN YOU TOOK YOUR OWN LIFE, A GREAT LOSS WAS FELT THROUGHOUT THE ARMY.
MANY MEN DIED WITHOUT YOUR SHIELD TO PROTECT THEM AT TROY.
WE MOURNED YOU AS WE MOURNED ACHILLES.
AND NOW, WILL YOU NOT RELINQUISH YOUR ANGER, EVEN IN DEATH?
NEVER.

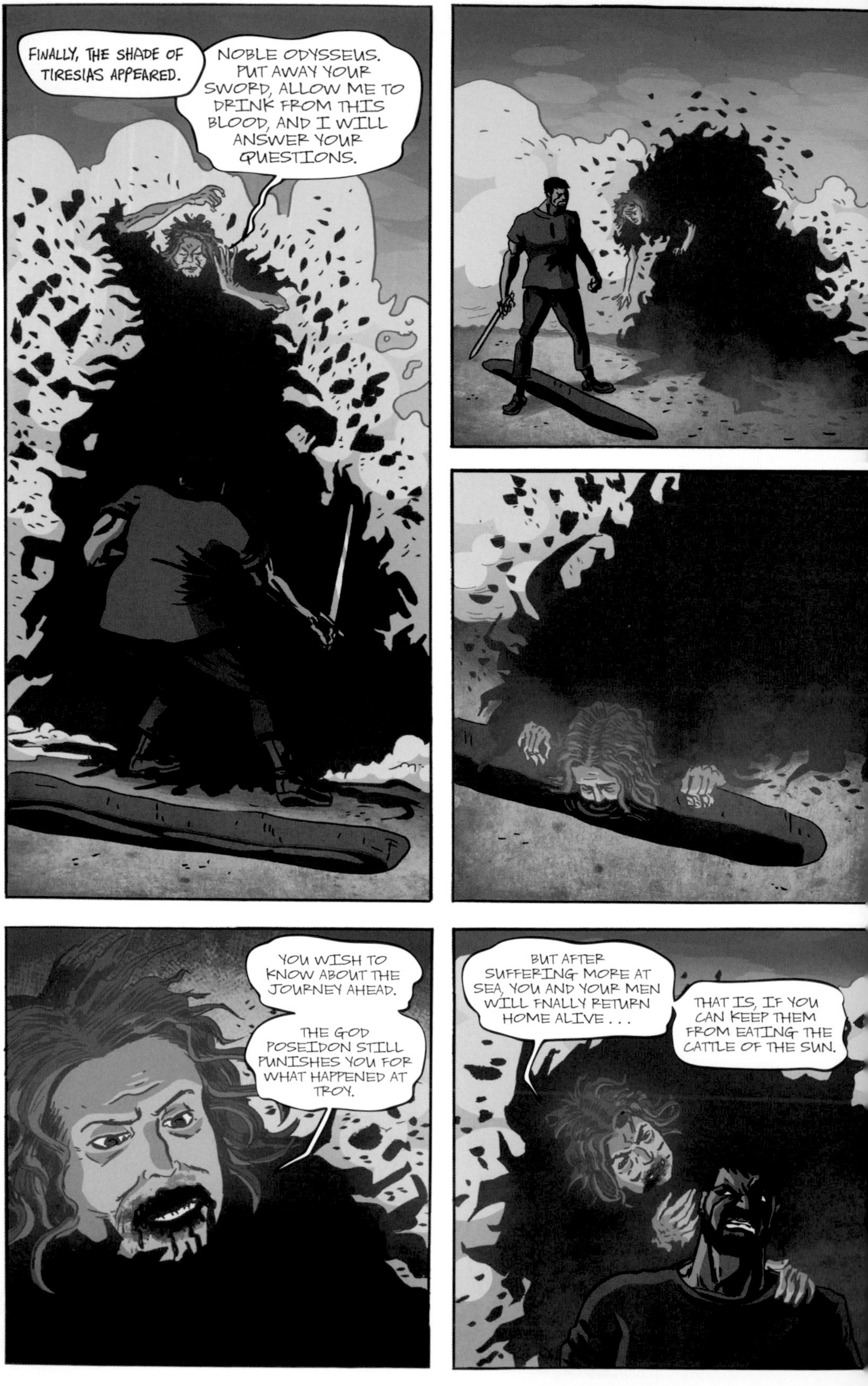
FINALLY, THE SHADE OF TIRESIAS APPEARED.
NOBLE ODYSSEUS. PUT AWAY YOUR SWORD, ALLOW ME TO DRINK FROM THIS BLOOD, AND I WILL ANSWER YOUR QUESTIONS.
YOU WISH TO KNOW ABOUT THE JOURNEY AHEAD.
THE GOD POSEIDON STILL PUNISHES YOU FOR WHAT HAPPENED AT TROY.
BUT AFTER SUFFERING MORE AT SEA, YOU AND YOUR MEN WILL FNALLY RETURN HOME ALIVE . . .
THAT IS, IF YOU CAN KEEP THEM FROM EATING THE CATTLE OF THE SUN.

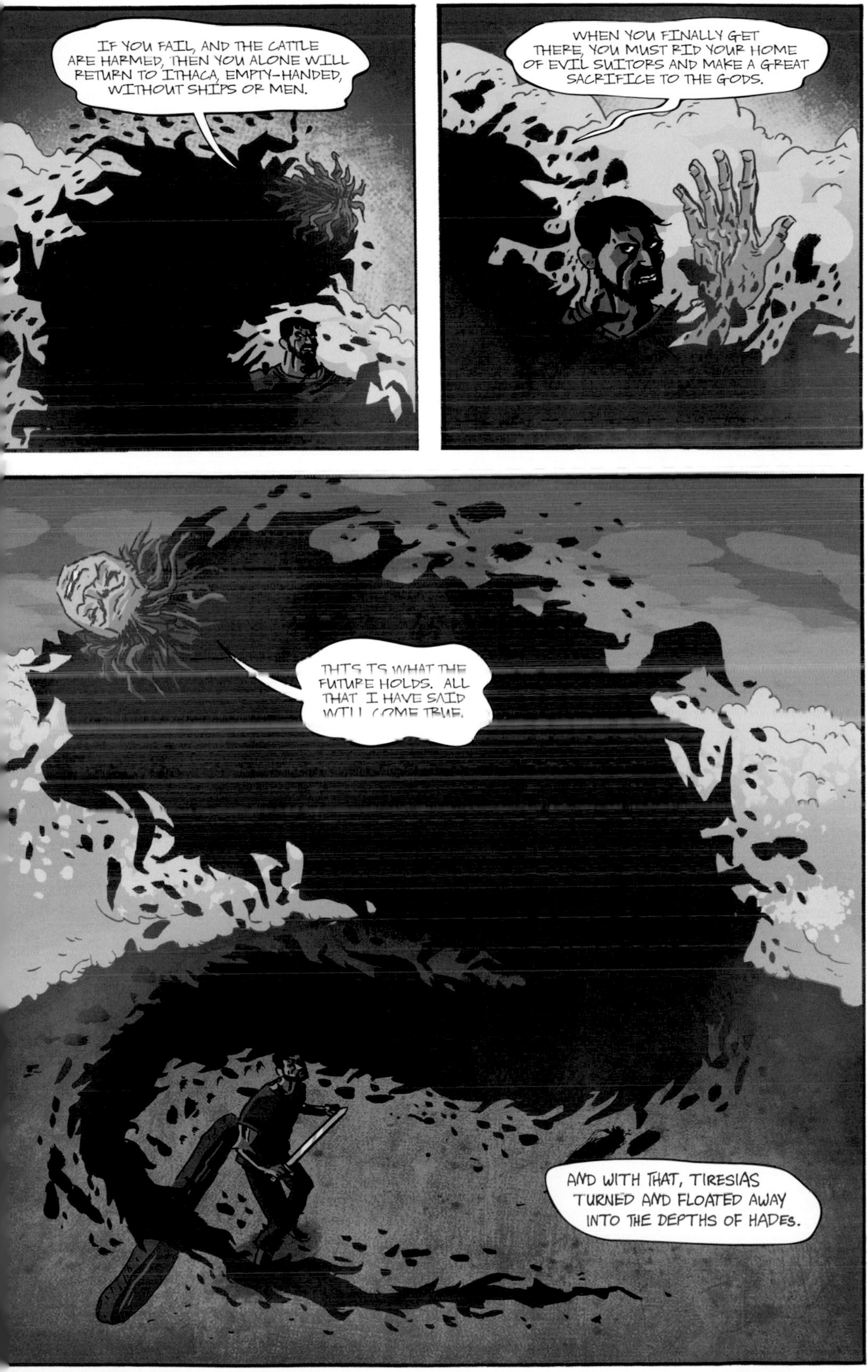
IF YOU FAIL, AND THE CATTLE ARE HARMED, THEN YOU ALONE WILL RETURN TO ITHACA, EMPTY-HANDED, WITHOUT SHIPS OR MEN.
WHEN YOU FINALLY GET THERE, YOU MUST RID YOUR HOME OF EVIL SUITORS AND MAKE A GREAT SACRIFICE TO THE GODS.
THIS IS WHAT THE FUTURE HOLDS. ALL THAT I HAVE SAID WILL COME TRUE.
AND WITH THAT, TIRESIAS TURNED AND FLOATED AWAY INTO THE DEPTHS OF HADES.

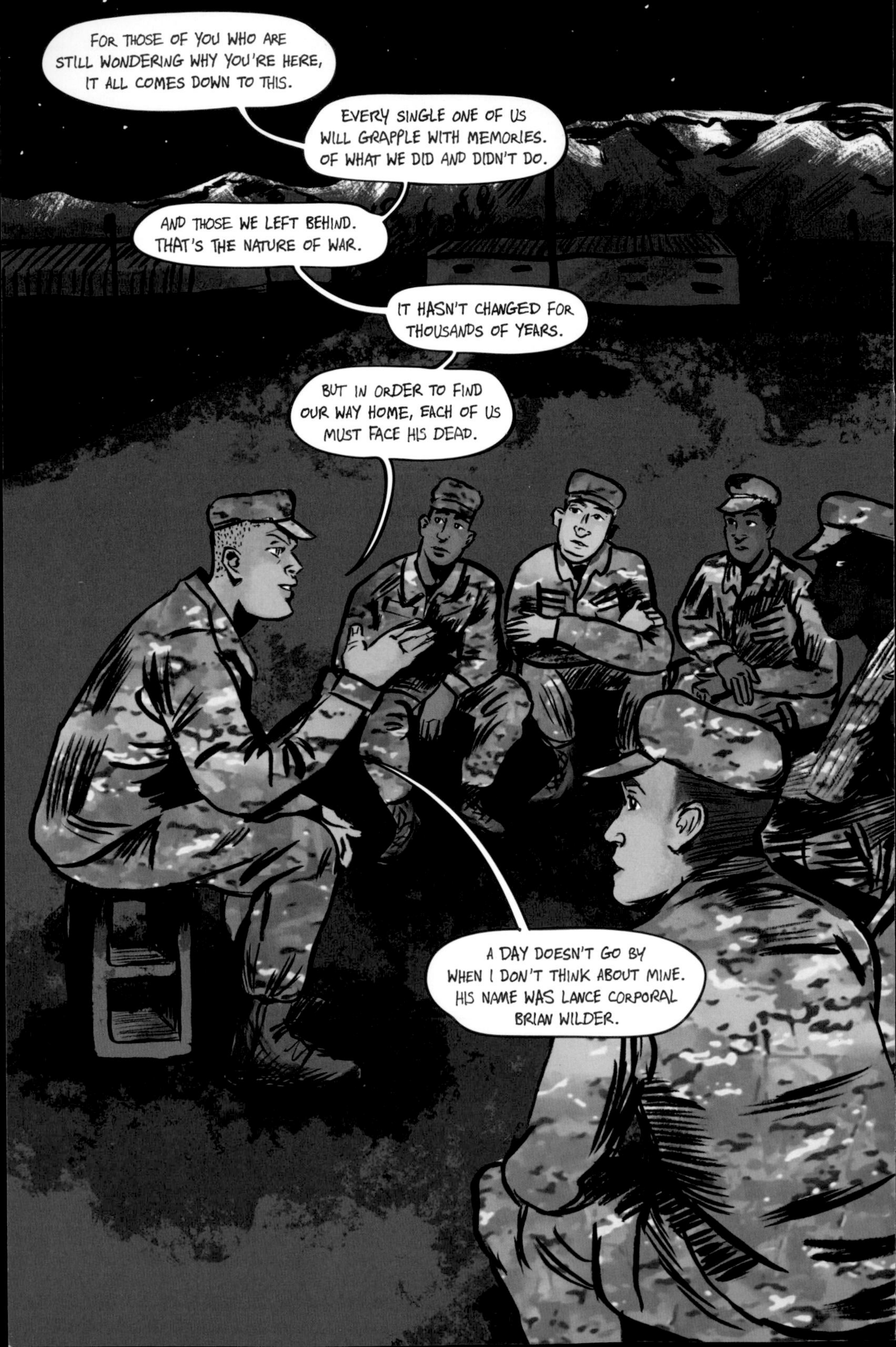
FOR THOSE OF YOU WHO ARE STILL WONDERING WHY YOU'RE HERE, IT ALL COMES DOWN TO THIS.
EVERY SINGLE ONE OF US WILL GRAPPLE WITH MEMORIES. OF WHAT WE DID AND DIDN'T DO.
AND THOSE WE LEFT BEHIND. THAT'S THE NATURE OF WAR.
IT HASN'T CHANGED FOR THOUSANDS OF YEARS.
BUT IN ORDER TO FIND OUR WAY HOME, EACH OF US MUST FACE HIS DEAD.
A DAY DOESN'T GO BY WHEN I DON'T THINK ABOUT MINE. HIS NAME WAS LANCE CORPORAL BRIAN WILDER.

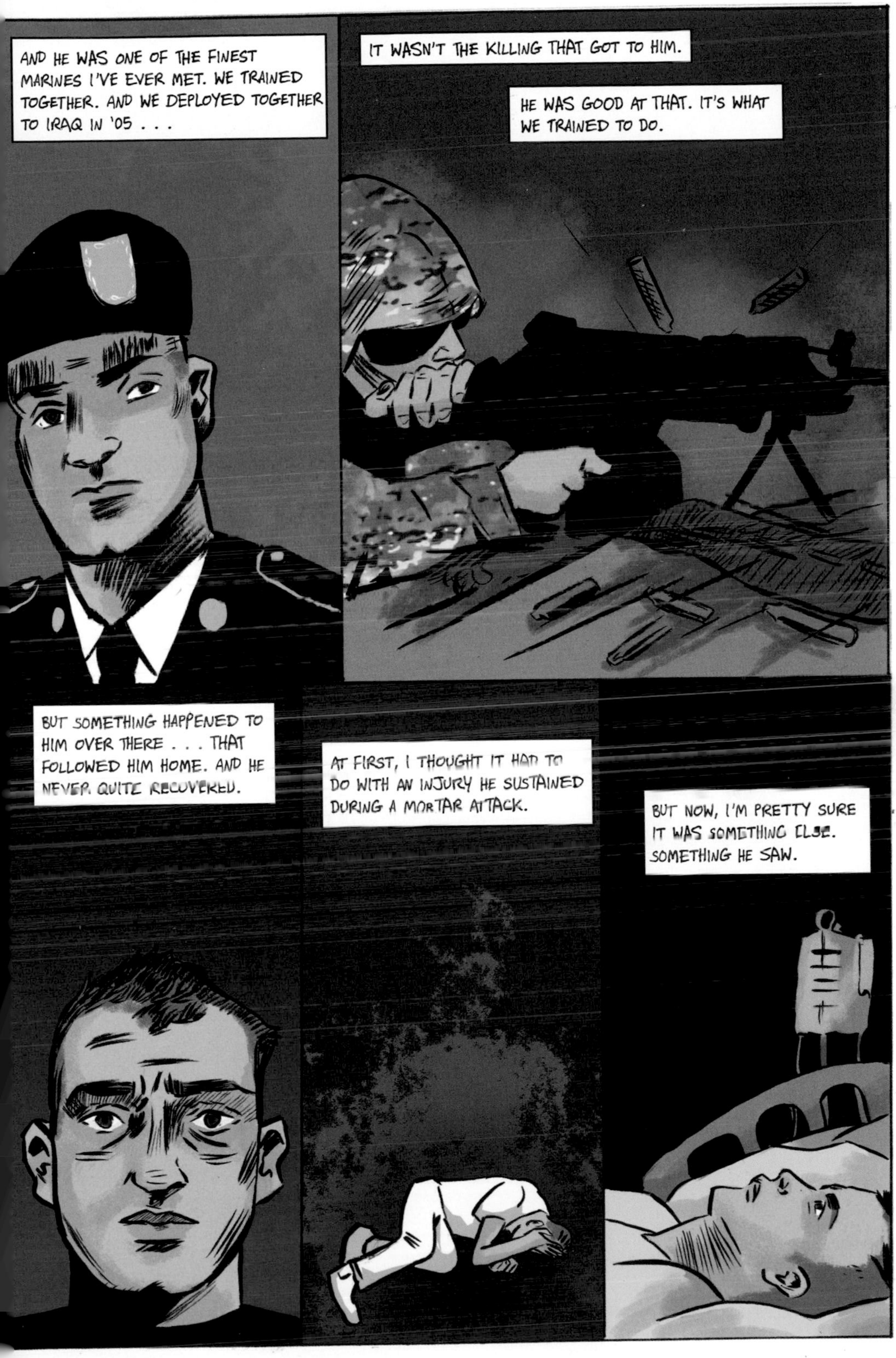
AND HE WAS ONE OF THE FINEST MARINES I'VE EVER MET. WE TRAINED TOGETHER. AND WE DEPLOYED TOGETHER TO IRAQ IN '05 . . .
IT WASN'T THE KILLING THAT GOT TO HIM.
HE WAS GOOD AT THAT. IT'S WHAT WE TRAINED TO DO.
BUT SOMETHING HAPPENED TO HIM OVER THERE . . . THAT FOLLOWED HIM HOME. AND HE NEVER QUITE RECOVERED.
AT FIRST, I THOUGHT IT HAD TO DO WITH AN INJURY HE SUSTAINED DURING A MORTAR ATTACK.
BUT NOW, I'M PRETTY SURE IT WAS SOMETHING ELSE. SOMETHING HE SAW.

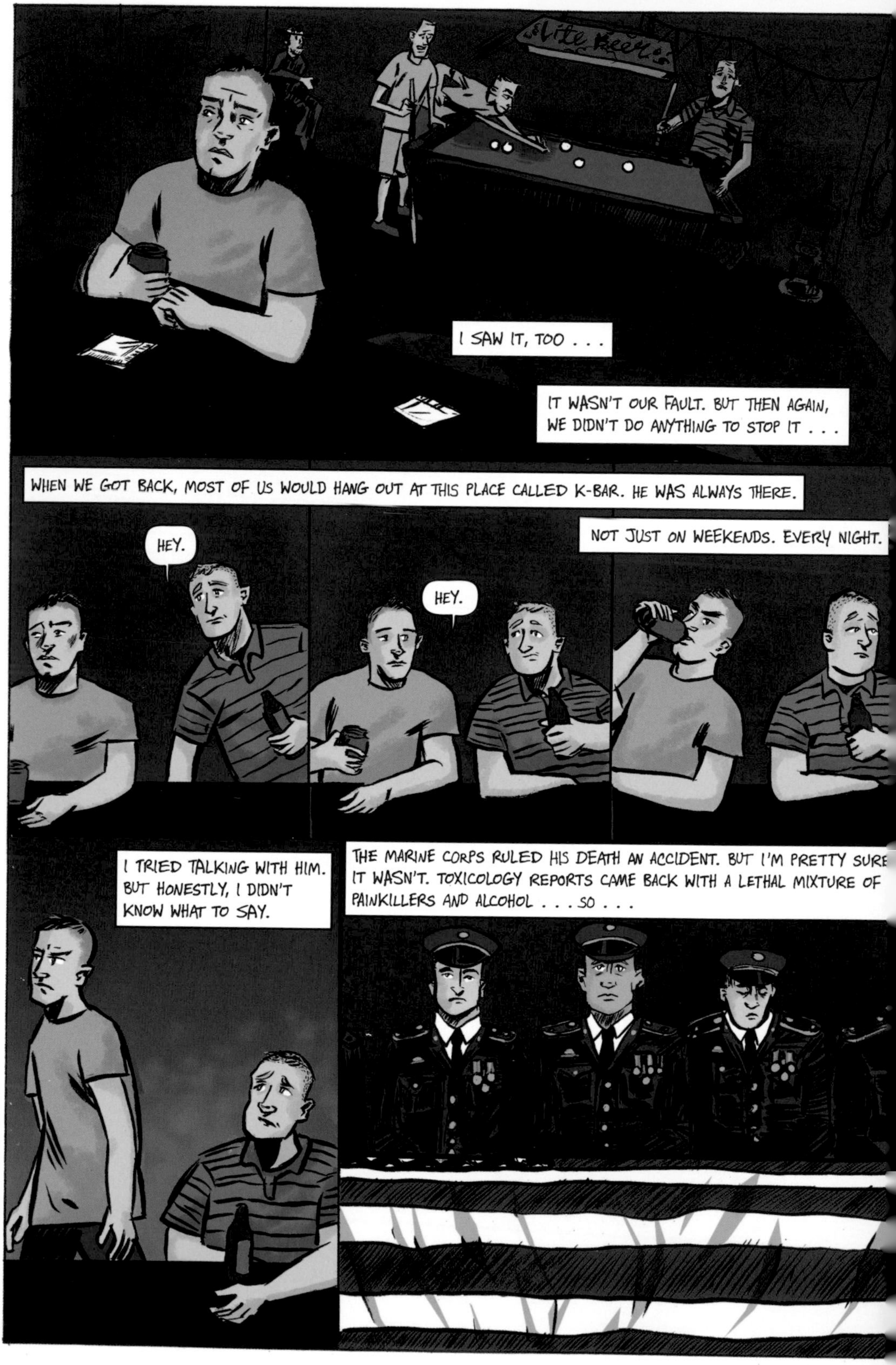
I SAW IT, TOO . . .
IT WASN'T OUR FAULT. BUT THEN AGAIN, WE DIDN'T DO ANYTHING TO STOP IT . . .
WHEN WE GOT BACK, MOST OF US WOULD HANG OUT AT THIS PLACE CALLED K-BAR. HE WAS ALWAYS THERE.
HEY.
HEY.
NOT JUST ON WEEKENDS. EVERY NIGHT.
I TRIED TALKING WITH HIM. BUT HONESTLY, I DIDN'T KNOW WHAT TO SAY.
THE MARINE CORPS RULED HIS DEATH AN ACCIDENT. BUT I'M PRETTY SURE IT WASN'T. TOXICOLOGY REPORTS CAME BACK WITH A LETHAL MIXTURE OF PAINKILLERS AND ALCOHOL . . . SO . . .

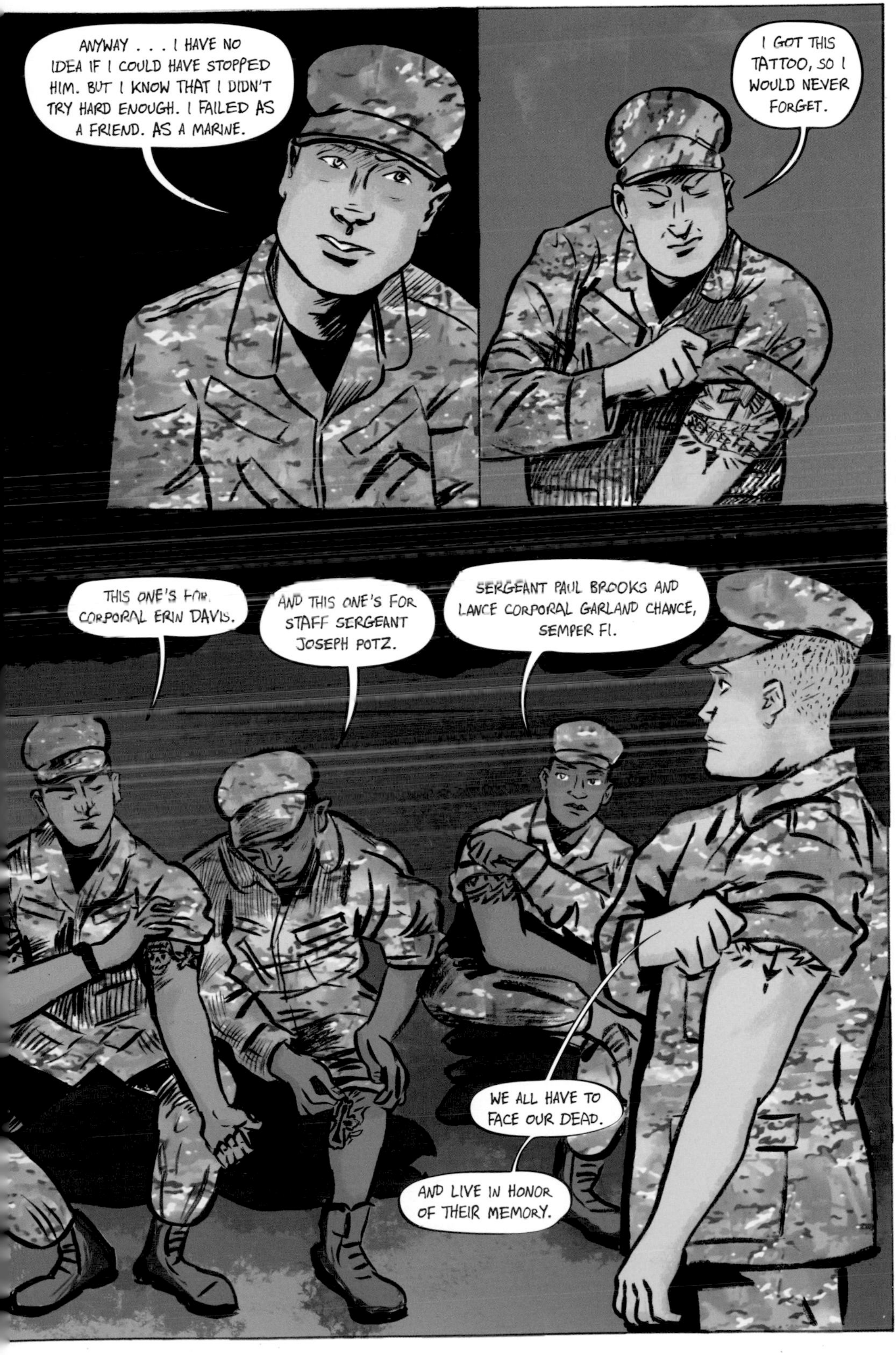
ANYWAY . . . I HAVE NO IDEA IF I COULD HAVE STOPPED HIM. BUT I KNOW THAT I DIDN'T TRY HARD ENOUGH. I FAILED AS A FRIEND. AS A MARINE.
I GOT THIS TATTOO, SO I WOULD NEVER FORGET.
THIS ONE'S FOR CORPORAL ERIN DAVIS.
AND THIS ONE'S FOR STAFF SERGEANT JOSEPH POTZ.
SERGEANT PAUL BROOKS AND LANCE CORPORAL GARLAND CHANCE, SEMPER FI.
WE ALL HAVE TO FACE OUR DEAD.
AND LIVE IN HONOR OF THEIR MEMORY.

CHAPTER 5

MONSTERS AND MEN

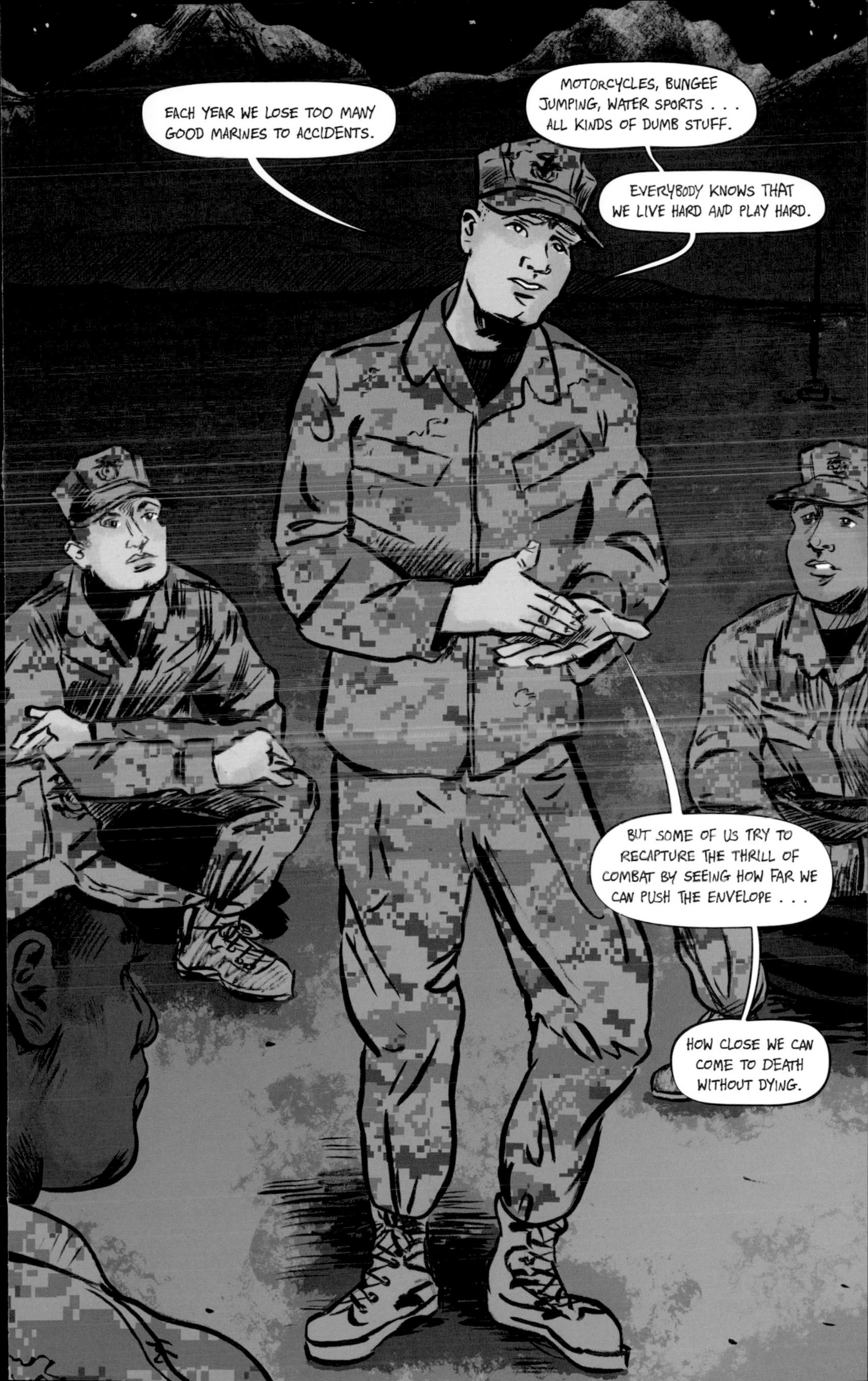
EACH YEAR WE LOSE TOO MANY GOOD MARINES TO ACCIDENTS.
MOTORCYCLES, BUNGEE JUMPING, WATER SPORTS . . . ALL KINDS OF DUMB STUFF.
EVERYBODY KNOWS THAT WE LIVE HARD AND PLAY HARD.
BUT SOME OF US TRY TO RECAPTURE THE THRILL OF COMBAT BY SEEING HOW FAR WE CAN PUSH THE ENVELOPE . . .
HOW CLOSE WE CAN COME TO DEATH WITHOUT DYING.

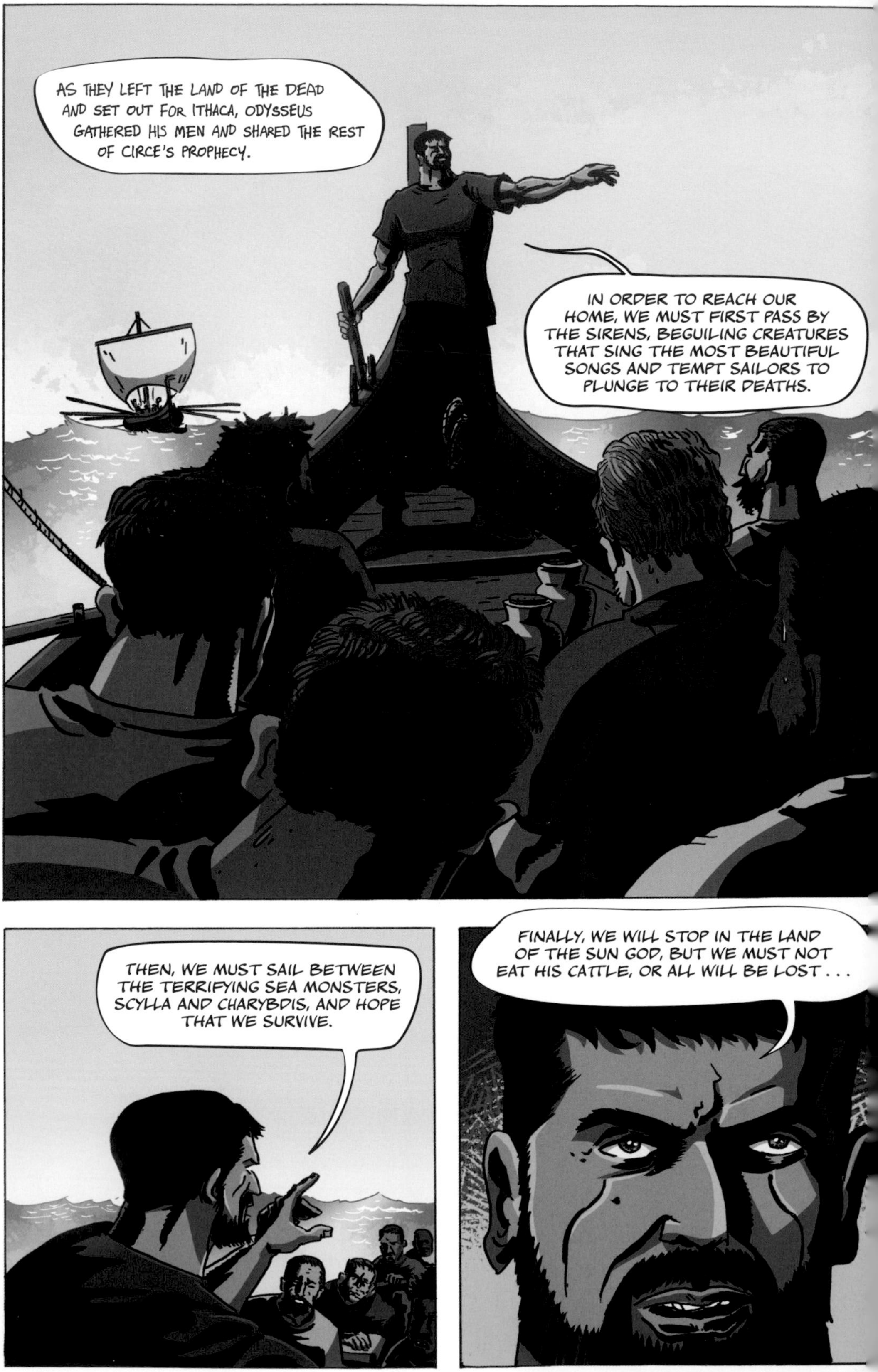
AS THEY LEFT THE LAND OF THE DEAD AND SET OUT FOR ITHACA, ODYSSEUS GATHERED HIS MEN AND SHARED THE REST OF CIRCE'S PROPHECY.
IN ORDER TO REACH OUR HOME, WE MUST FIRST PASS BY THE SIRENS, BEGUILING CREATURES THAT SING THE MOST BEAUTIFUL SONGS AND TEMPT SAILORS TO PLUNGE TO THEIR DEATHS.
THEN, WE MUST SAIL BETWEEN THE TERRIFYING SEA MONSTERS, SCYLLA AND CHARYBDIS, AND HOPE THAT WE SURVIVE.
FINALLY, WE WILL STOP IN THE LAND OF THE SUN GOD, BUT WE MUST NOT EAT HIS CATTLE, OR ALL WILL BE LOST . . .

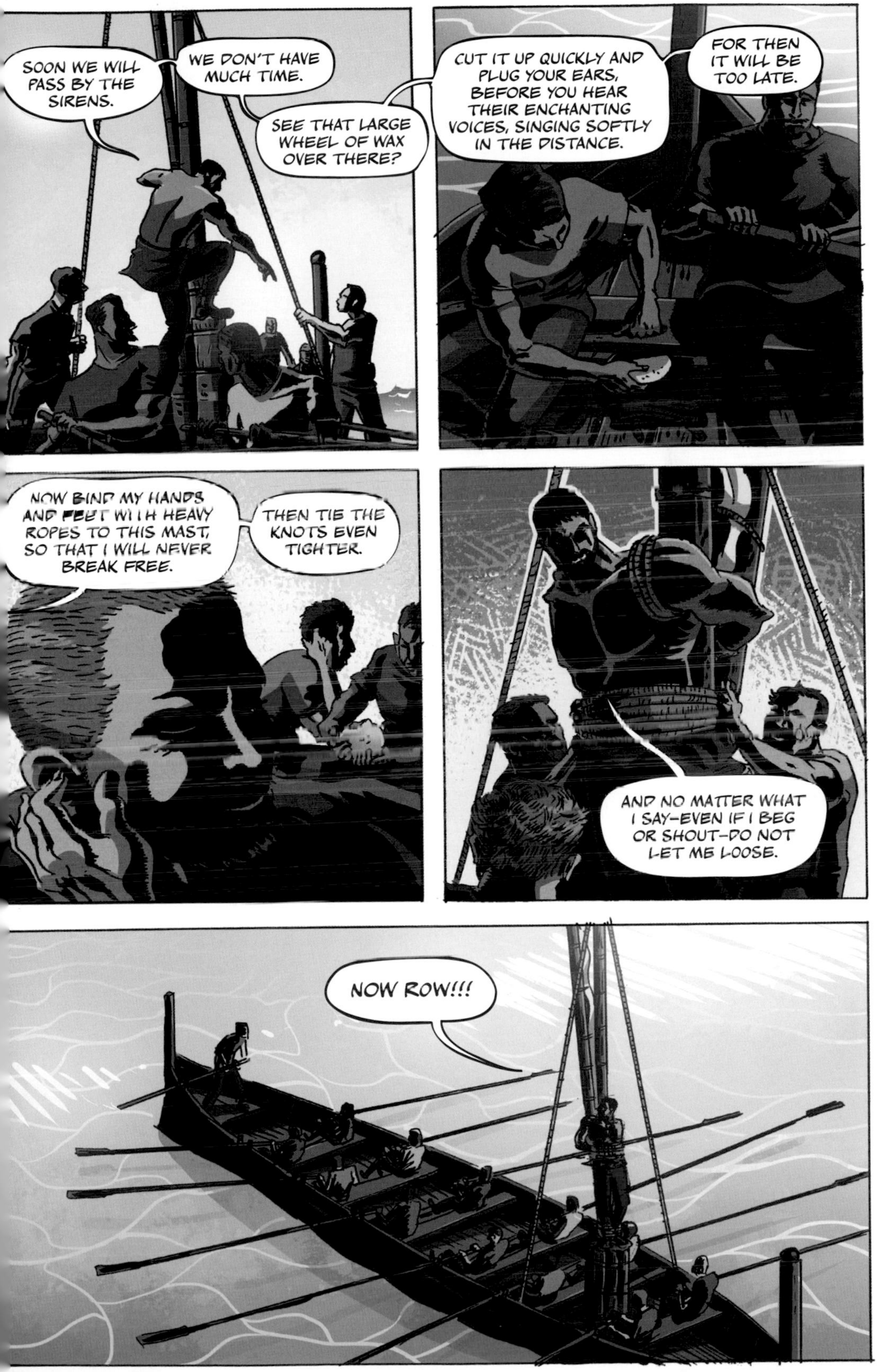
SOON WE WILL PASS BY THE SIRENS.
WE DON'T HAVE MUCH TIME.
SEE THAT LARGE WHEEL OF WAX OVER THERE?
CUT IT UP QUICKLY AND PLUG YOUR EARS, BEFORE YOU HEAR THEIR ENCHANTING VOICES, SINGING SOFTLY IN THE DISTANCE.
FOR THEN IT WILL BE TOO LATE.
NOW BIND MY HANDS AND FEET WITH HEAVY ROPES TO THIS MAST, SO THAT I WILL NEVER BREAK FREE.
THEN TIE THE KNOTS EVEN TIGHTER.
AND NO MATTER WHAT I SAY—EVEN IF I BEG OR SHOUT—DO NOT LET ME LOOSE.
NOW ROW!!!

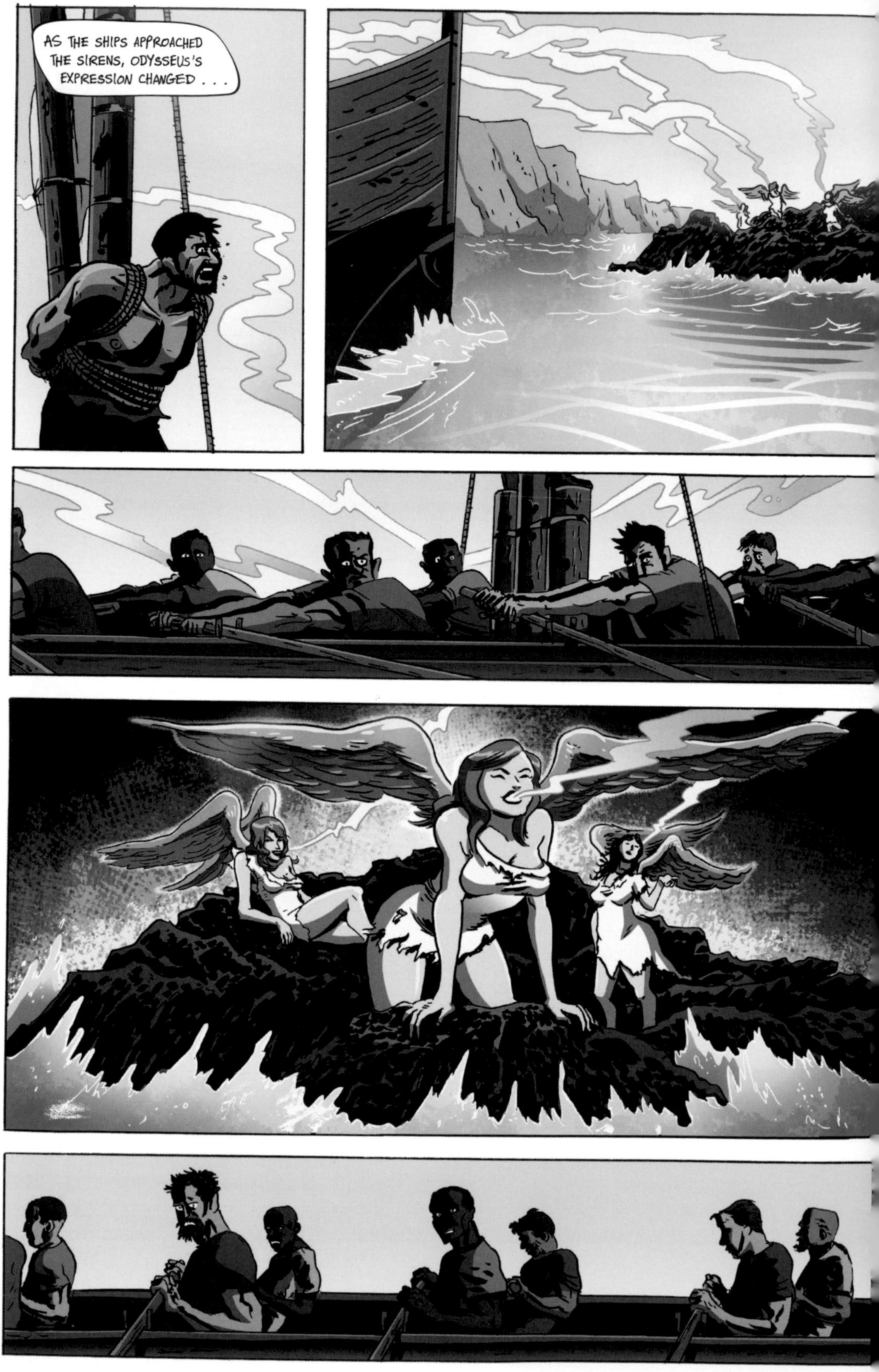
AS THE SHIPS APPROACHED THE SIRENS, ODYSSEUS'S EXPRESSION CHANGED . . .

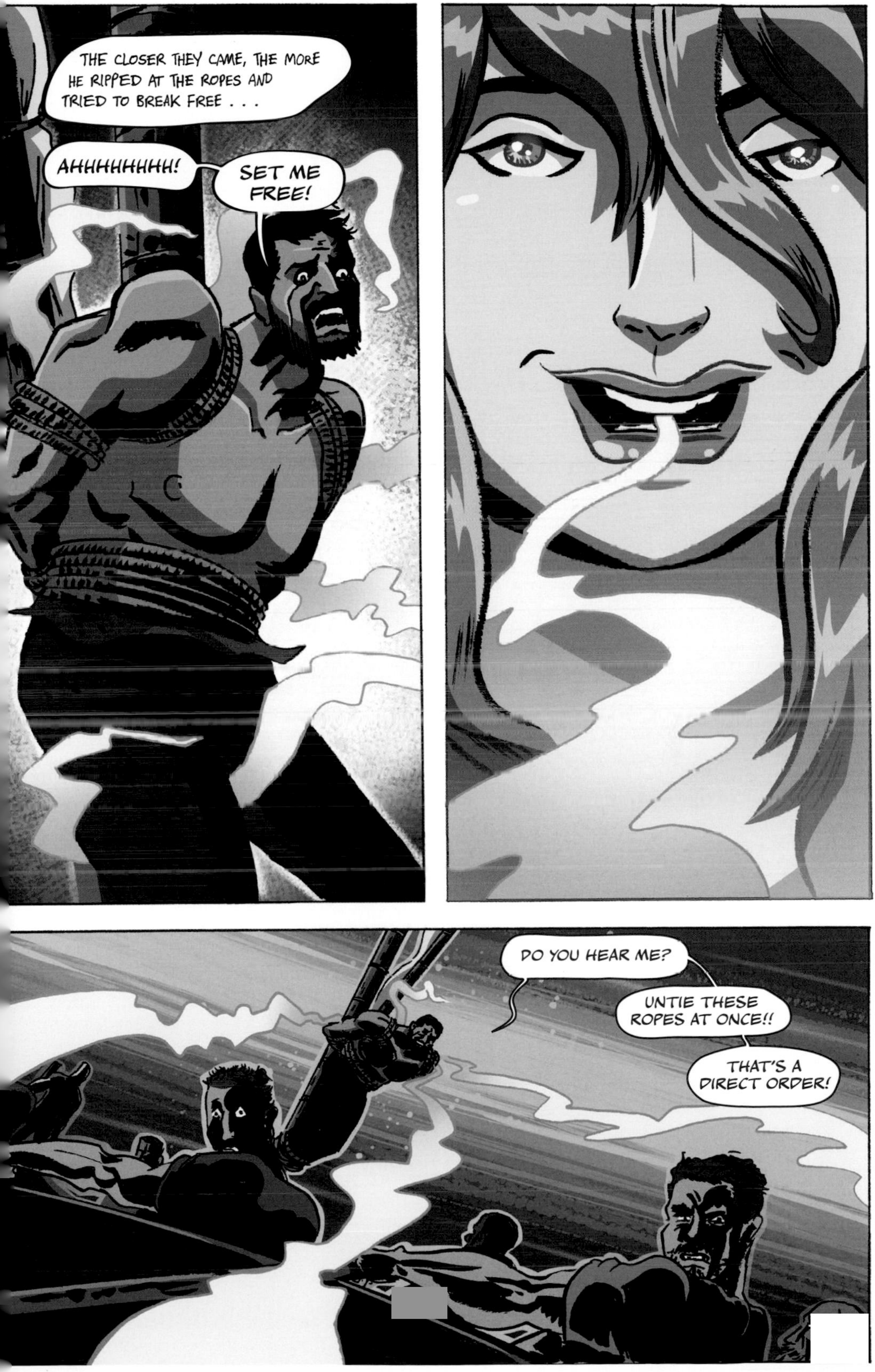
THE CLOSER THEY CAME, THE MORE HE RIPPED AT THE ROPES AND TRIED TO BREAK FREE . . .
AHHHHHHHH!
SET ME FREE!
DO YOU HEAR ME?
UNTIE THESE ROPES AT ONCE!!
THAT'S A DIRECT ORDER!

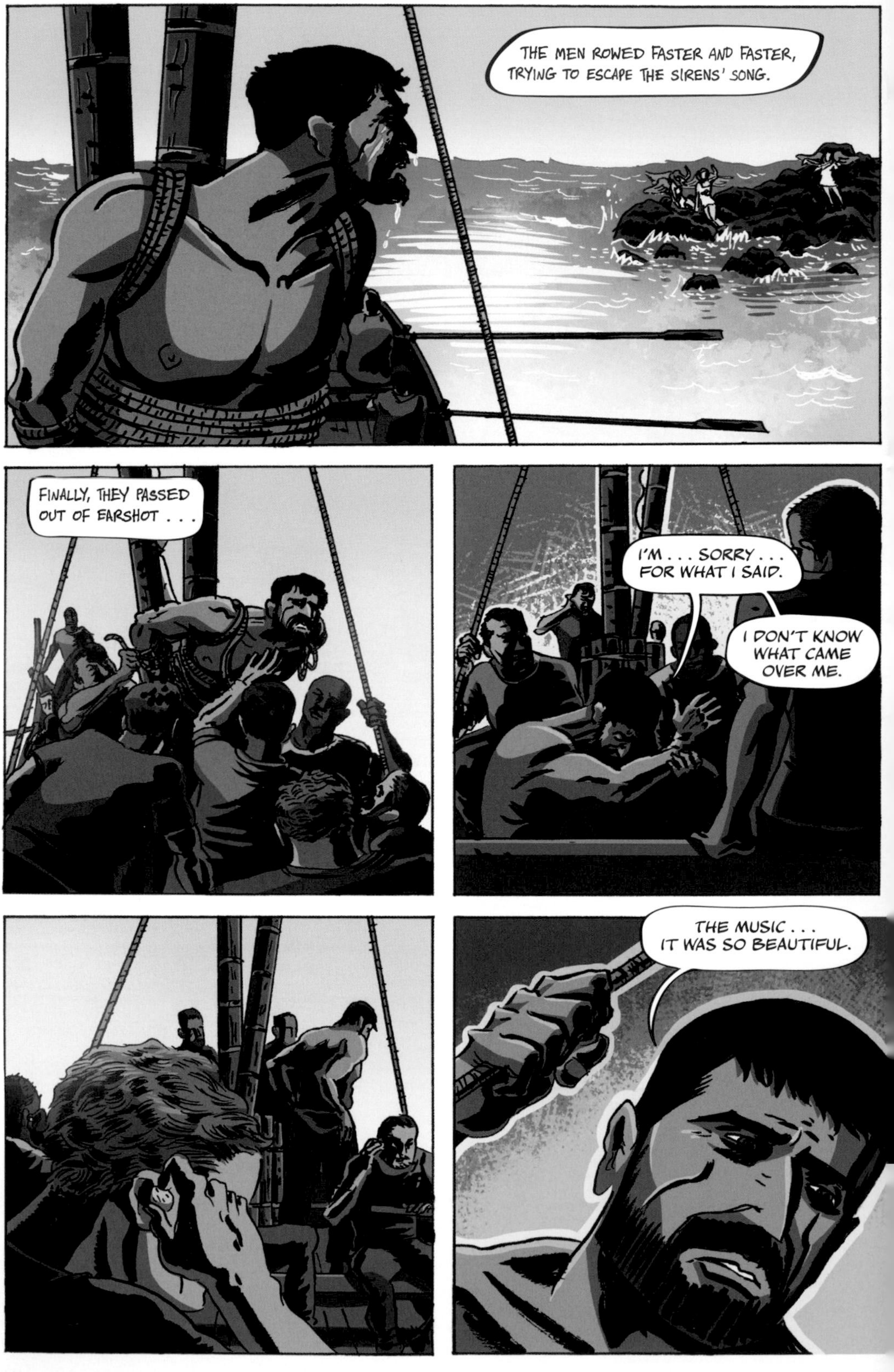
THE MEN ROWED FASTER AND FASTER, TRYING TO ESCAPE THE SIRENS' SONG.
FINALLY, THEY PASSED OUT OF EARSHOT . . .
I'M . . . SORRY . . . FOR WHAT I SAID.
I DON'T KNOW WHAT CAME OVER ME.
THE MUSIC . . . IT WAS SO BEAUTIFUL.

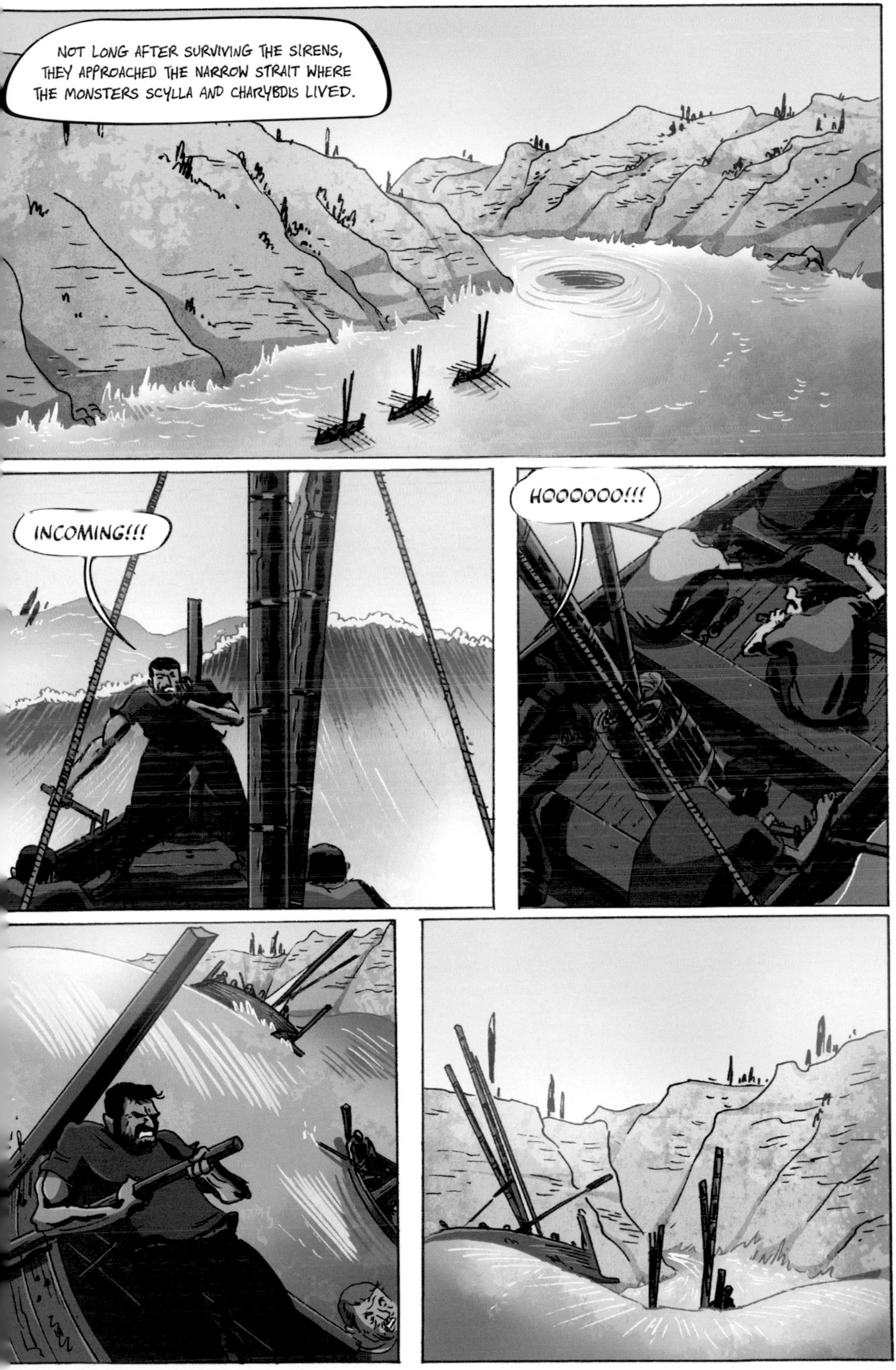
NOT LONG AFTER SURVIVING THE SIRENS, THEY APPROACHED THE NARROW STRAIT WHERE THE MONSTERS SCYLLA AND CHARYBDIS LIVED.
INCOMING!!!
HOOOOOO!!!

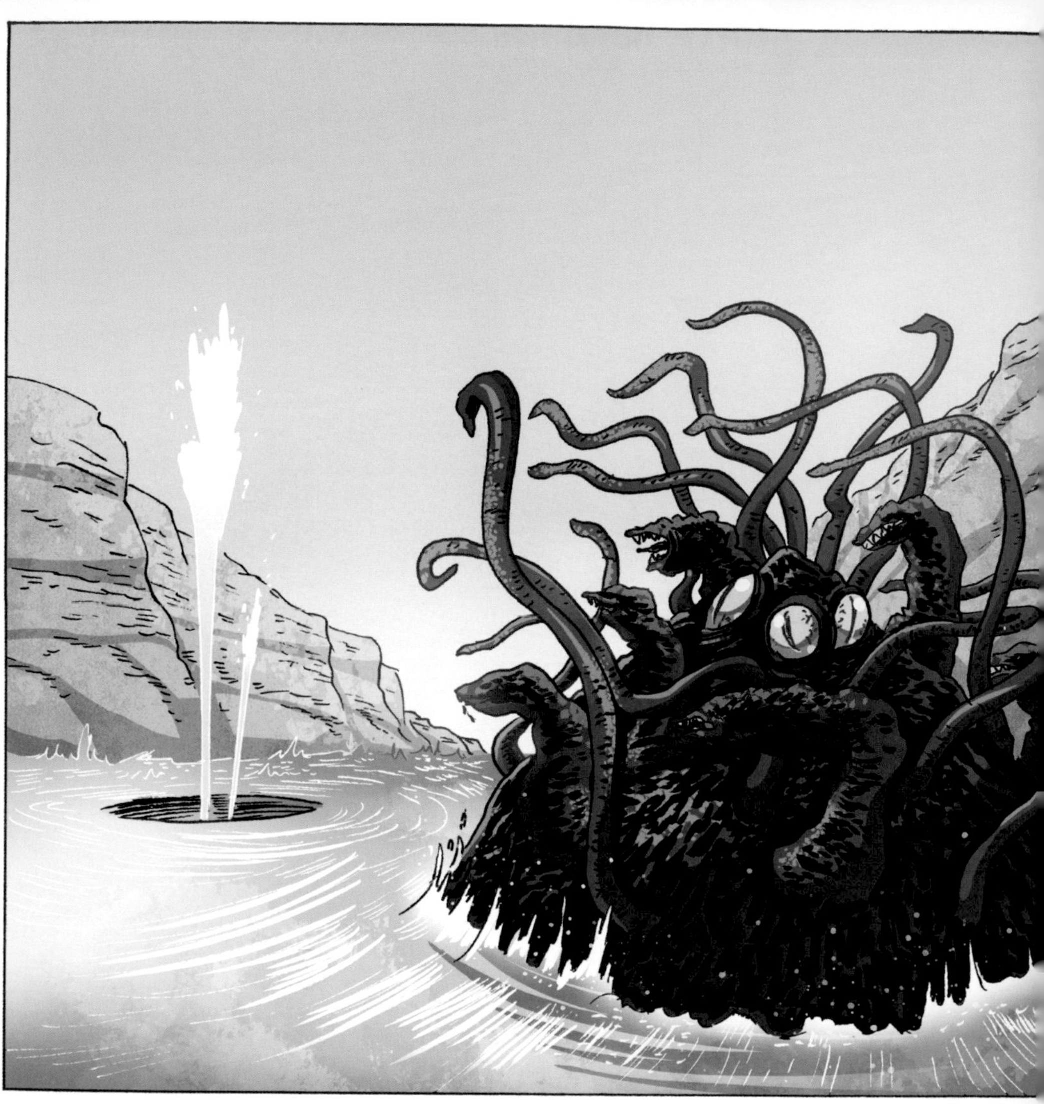

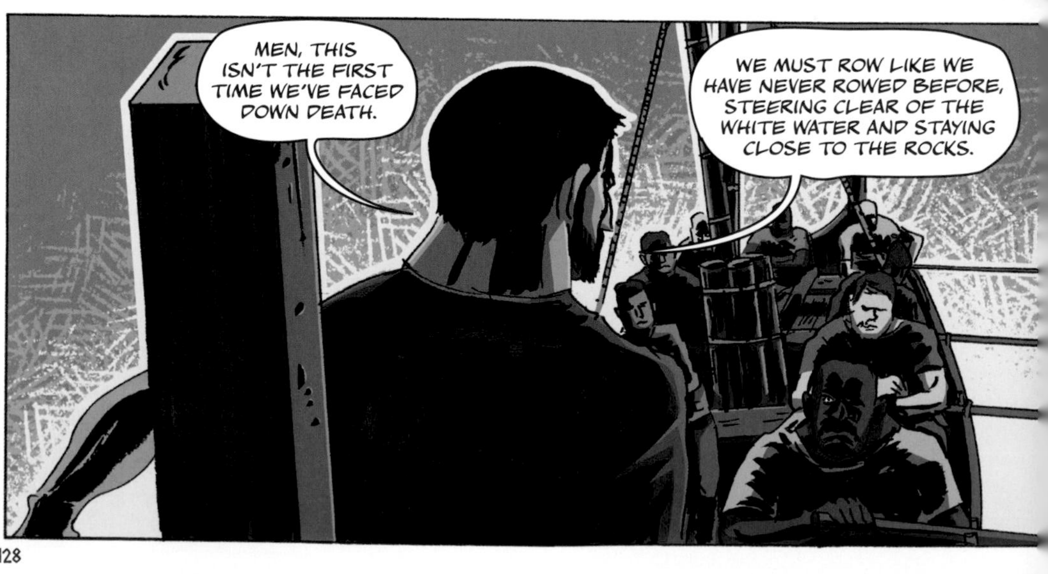
MEN, THIS ISN'T THE FIRST TIME WE'VE FACED DOWN DEATH.
WE MUST ROW LIKE WE HAVE NEVER ROWED BEFORE, STEERING CLEAR OF THE WHITE WATER AND STAYING CLOSE TO THE ROCKS.

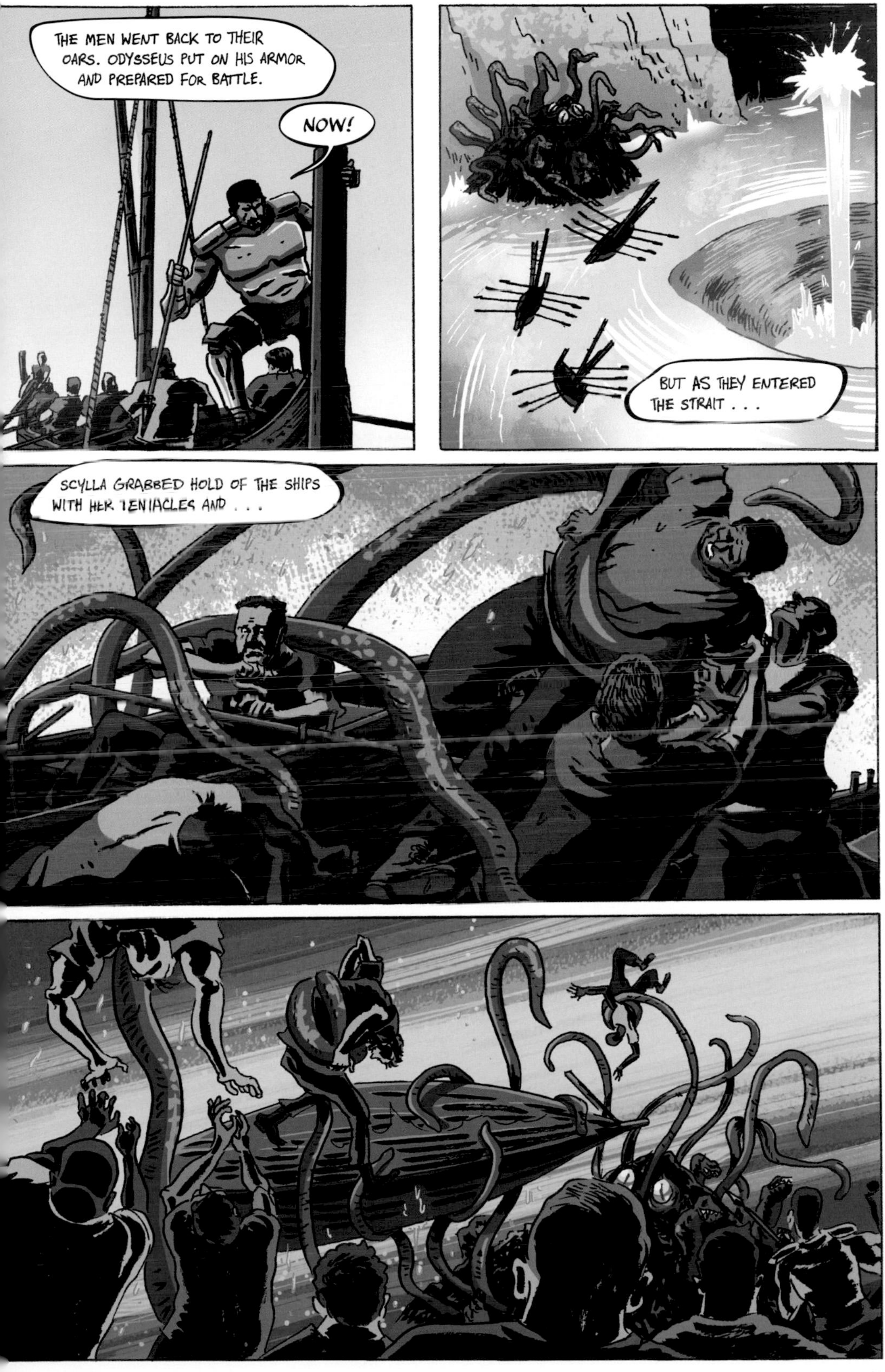
THE MEN WENT BACK TO THEIR OARS. ODYSSEUS PUT ON HIS ARMOR AND PREPARED FOR BATTLE.
NOW!
BUT AS THEY ENTERED THE STRAIT . . .
SCYLLA GRABBED HOLD OF THE SHIPS WITH HER TENTACLES AND . . .

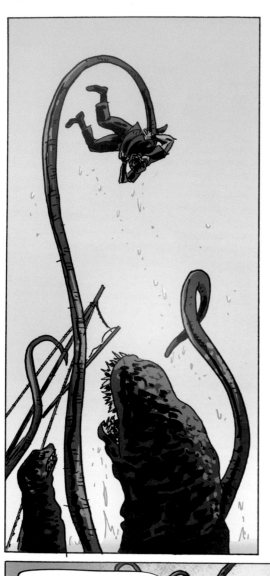

... WHILE ODYSSEUS LOOKED ON HELPLESSLY, SHE DEVOURED SIX OF HIS MEN WHOLE.

HELP US. AAHHHHHHH! HELP US!!!!! HELLLLLLLLLP!

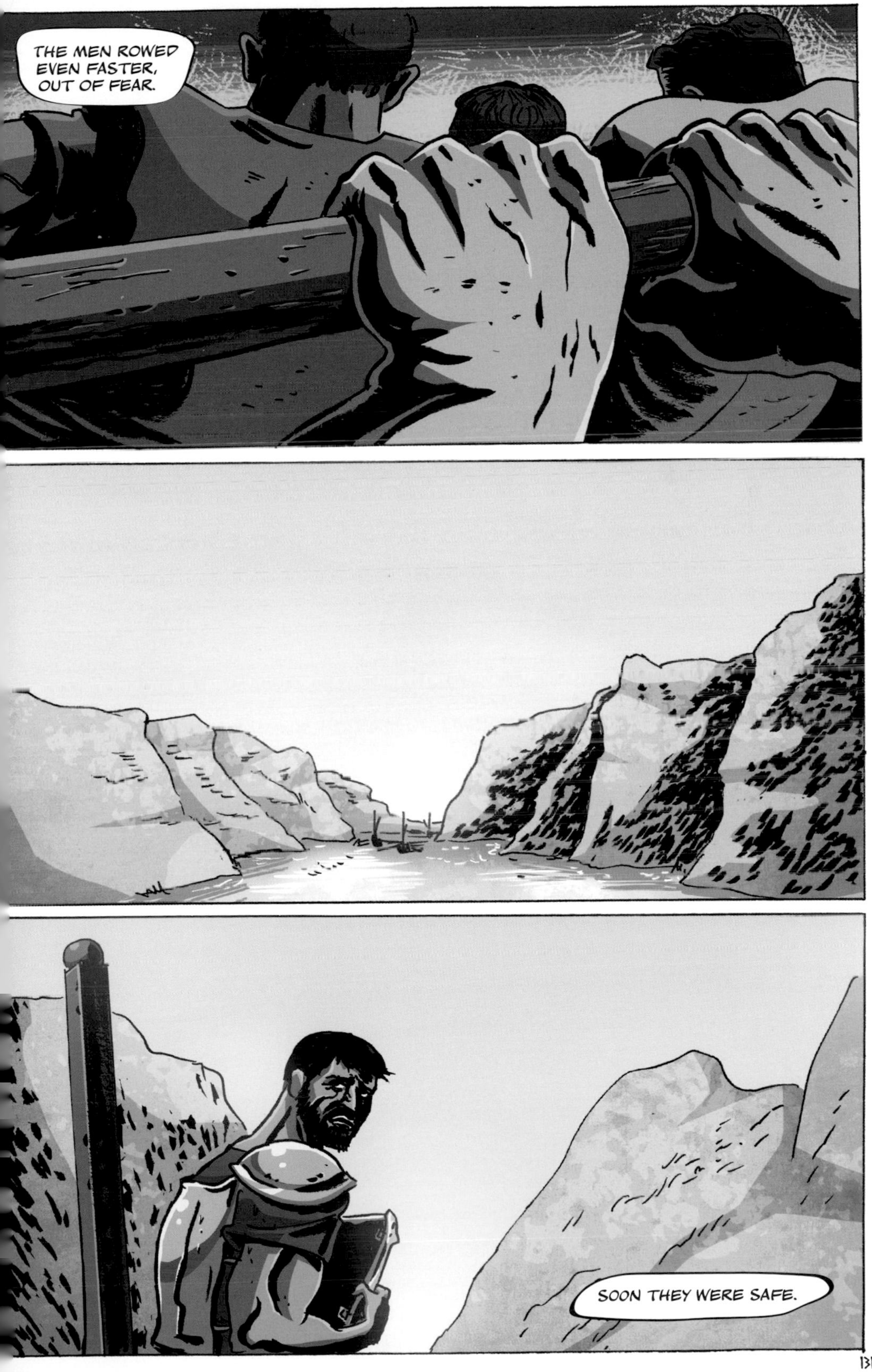
THE MEN ROWED EVEN FASTER, OUT OF FEAR.
SOON THEY WERE SAFE.

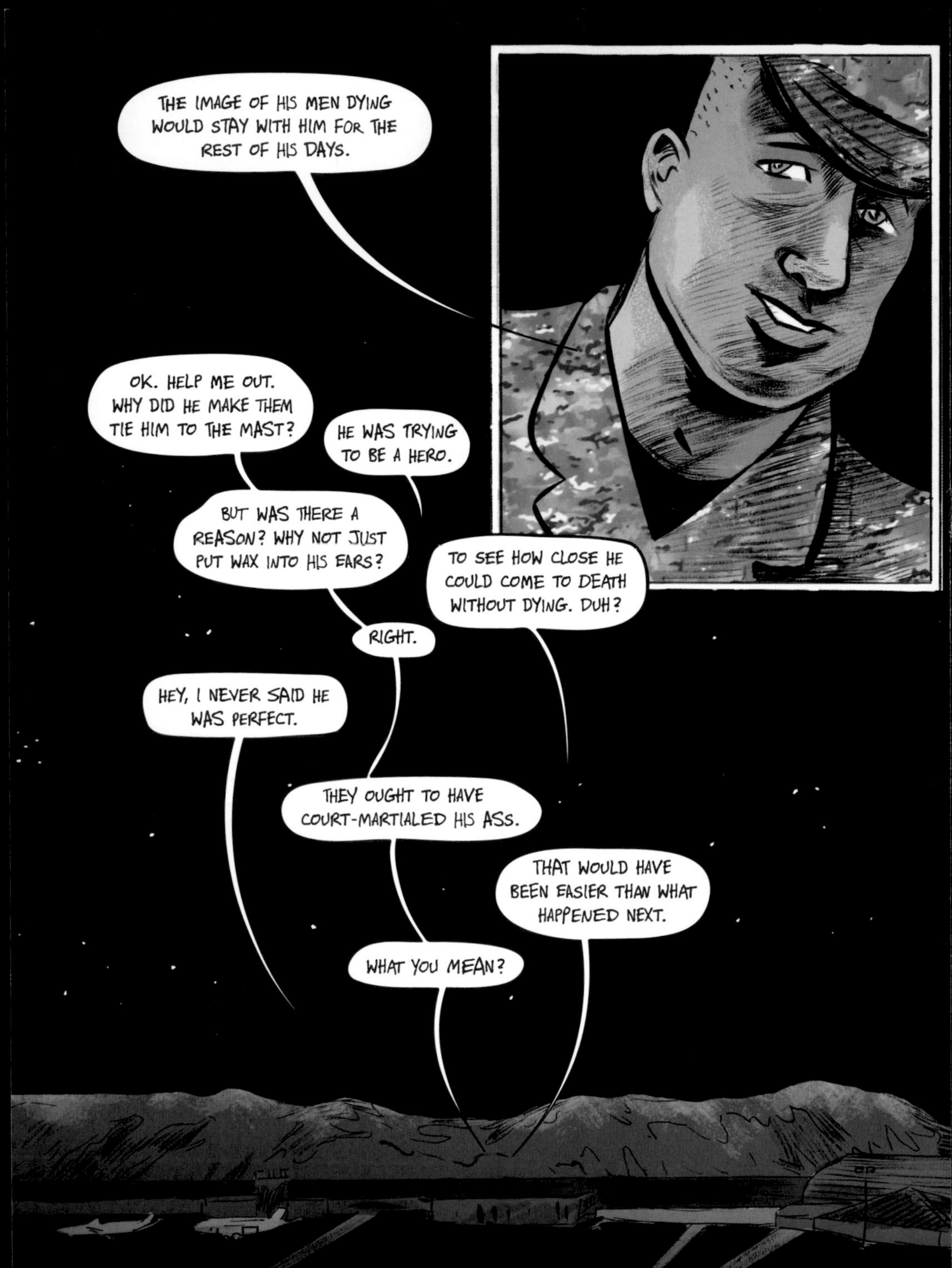
THE IMAGE OF HIS MEN DYING WOULD STAY WITH HIM FOR THE REST OF HIS DAYS.
OK. HELP ME OUT. WHY DID HE MAKE THEM TIE HIM TO THE MAST?
HE WAS TRYING TO BE A HERO.
BUT WAS THERE A REASON? WHY NOT JUST PUT WAX INTO HIS EARS?
TO SEE HOW CLOSE HE COULD COME TO DEATH WITHOUT DYING. DUH?
RIGHT.
HEY, I NEVER SAID HE WAS PERFECT.
THEY OUGHT TO HAVE COURT-MARTIALED HIS ASS.
THAT WOULD HAVE BEEN EASIER THAN WHAT HAPPENED NEXT.
WHAT YOU MEAN?

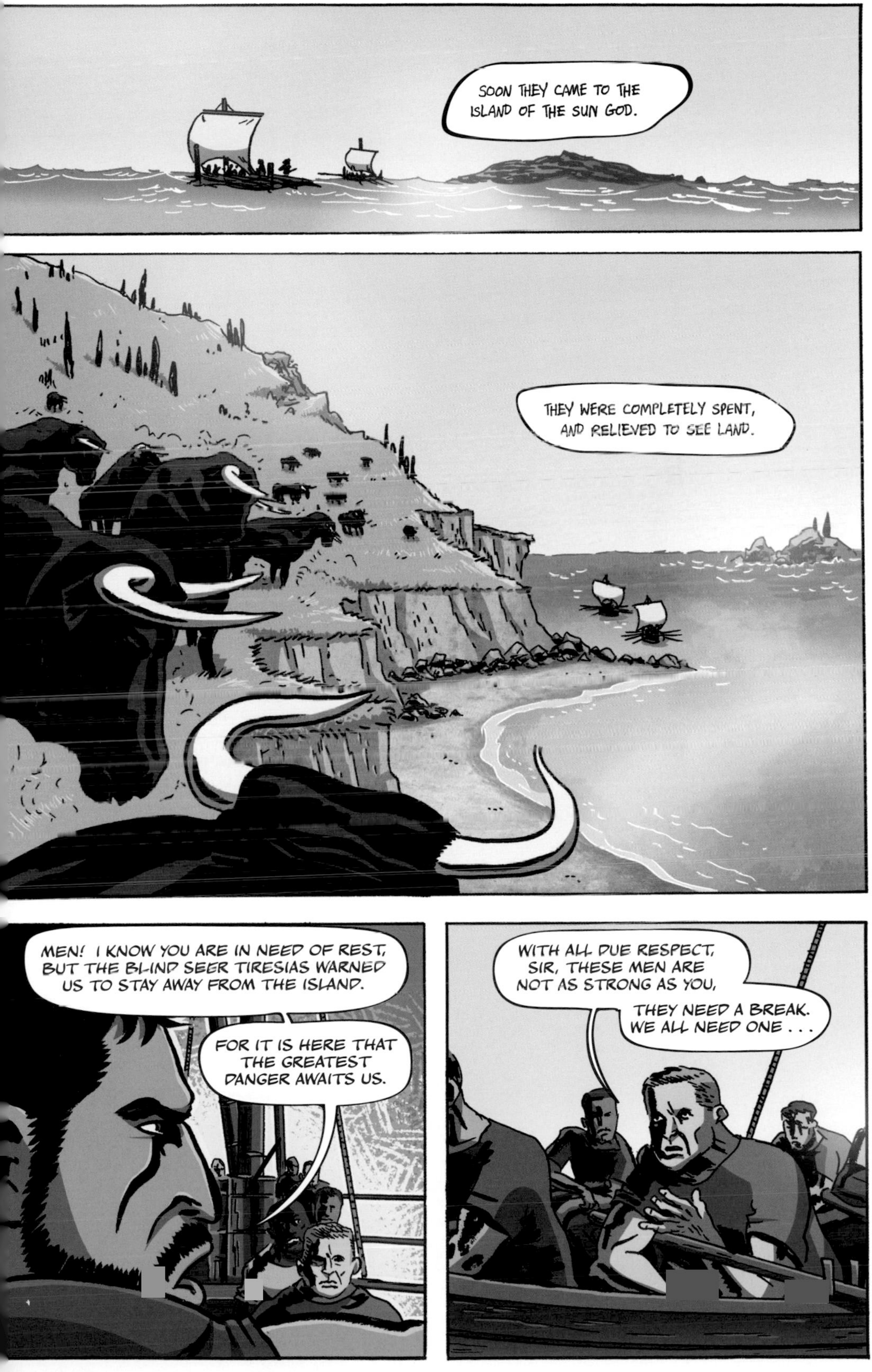
SOON THEY CAME TO THE ISLAND OF THE SUN GOD.
THEY WERE COMPLETELY SPENT, AND RELIEVED TO SEE LAND.
MEN! I KNOW YOU ARE IN NEED OF REST, BUT THE BLIND SEER TIRESIAS WARNED US TO STAY AWAY FROM THE ISLAND.
FOR IT IS HERE THAT THE GREATEST DANGER AWAITS US.
WITH ALL DUE RESPECT, SIR, THESE MEN ARE NOT AS STRONG AS YOU,
THEY NEED A BREAK. WE ALL NEED ONE . . .

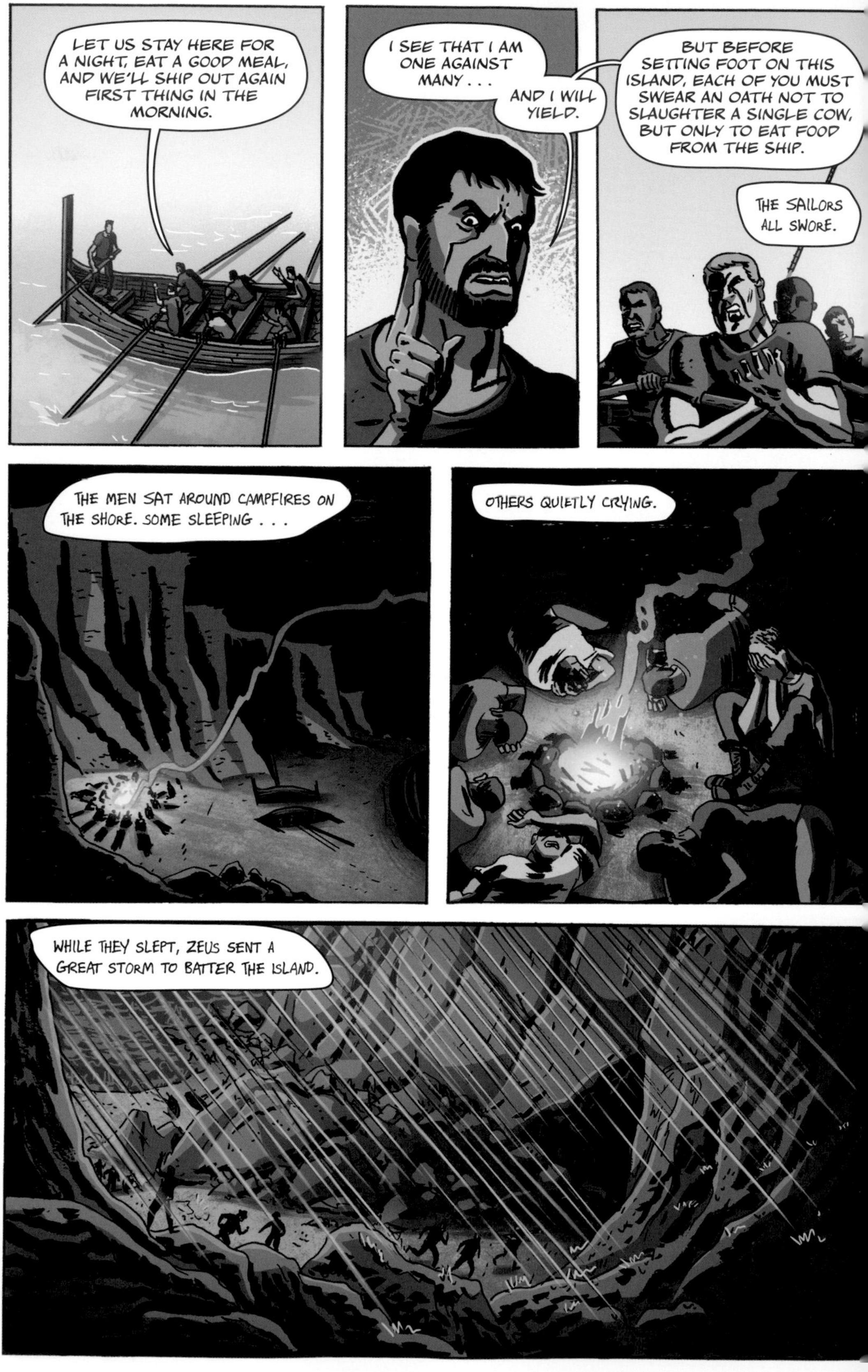
LET US STAY HERE FOR A NIGHT, EAT A GOOD MEAL, AND WE'LL SHIP OUT AGAIN FIRST THING IN THE MORNING.
I SEE THAT I AM ONE AGAINST MANY . . .
AND I WILL YIELD.
BUT BEFORE SETTING FOOT ON THIS ISLAND, EACH OF YOU MUST SWEAR AN OATH NOT TO SLAUGHTER A SINGLE COW, BUT ONLY TO EAT FOOD FROM THE SHIP.
THE SAILORS ALL SWORE.
THE MEN SAT AROUND CAMPFIRES ON THE SHORE. SOME SLEEPING . . .
OTHERS QUIETLY CRYING.
WHILE THEY SLEPT, ZEUS SENT A GREAT STORM TO BATTER THE ISLAND.

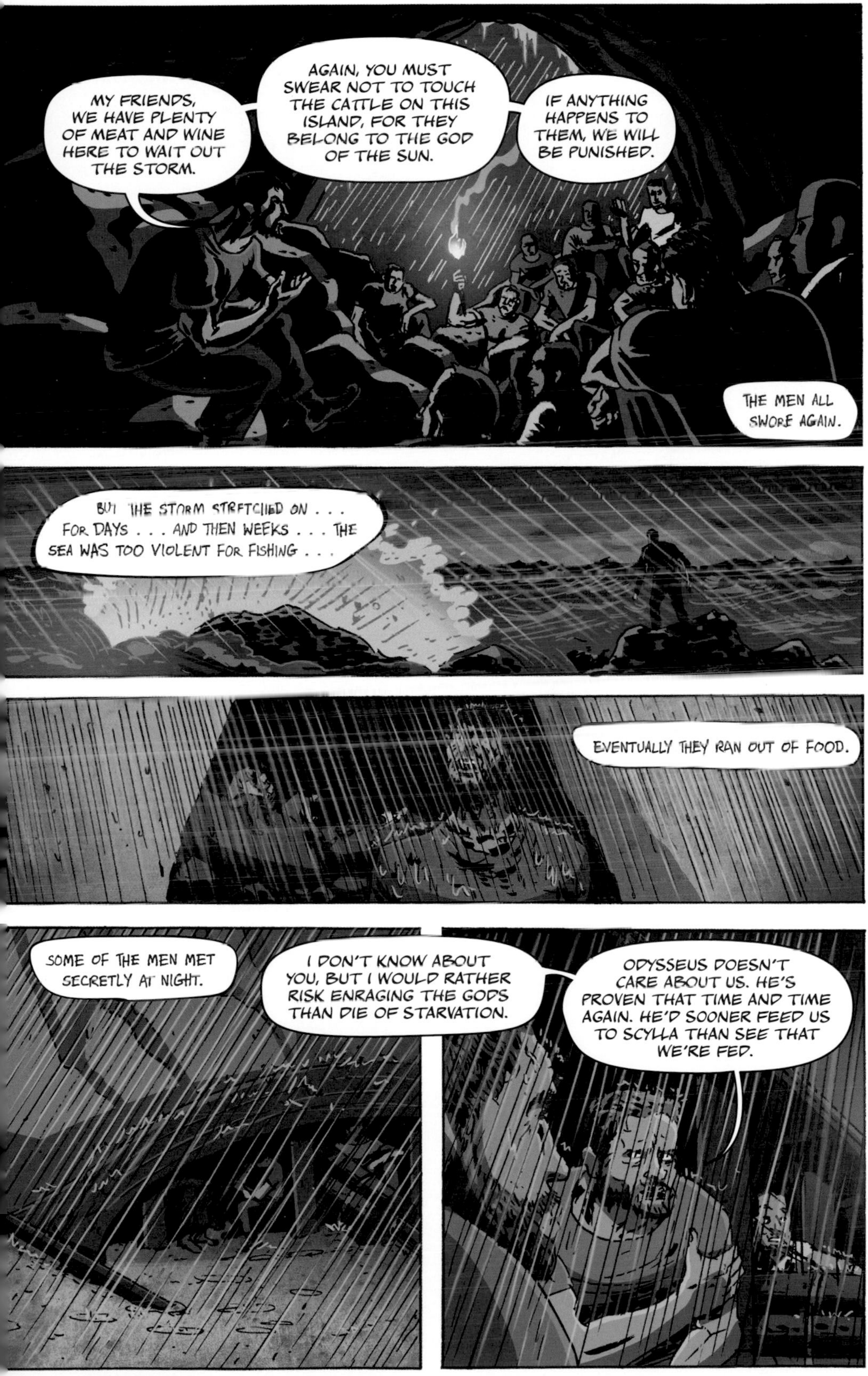
MY FRIENDS, WE HAVE PLENTY OF MEAT AND WINE HERE TO WAIT OUT THE STORM.
AGAIN, YOU MUST SWEAR NOT TO TOUCH THE CATTLE ON THIS ISLAND, FOR THEY BELONG TO THE GOD OF THE SUN.
IF ANYTHING HAPPENS TO THEM, WE WILL BE PUNISHED.
THE MEN ALL SWORE AGAIN.
BUT THE STORM STRETCHED ON . . . FOR DAYS . . . AND THEN WEEKS . . . THE SEA WAS TOO VIOLENT FOR FISHING . . .
EVENTUALLY THEY RAN OUT OF FOOD.
SOME OF THE MEN MET SECRETLY AT NIGHT.
I DON'T KNOW ABOUT YOU, BUT I WOULD RATHER RISK ENRAGING THE GODS THAN DIE OF STARVATION.
ODYSSEUS DOESN'T CARE ABOUT US. HE'S PROVEN THAT TIME AND TIME AGAIN. HE'D SOONER FEED US TO SCYLLA THAN SEE THAT WE'RE FED.

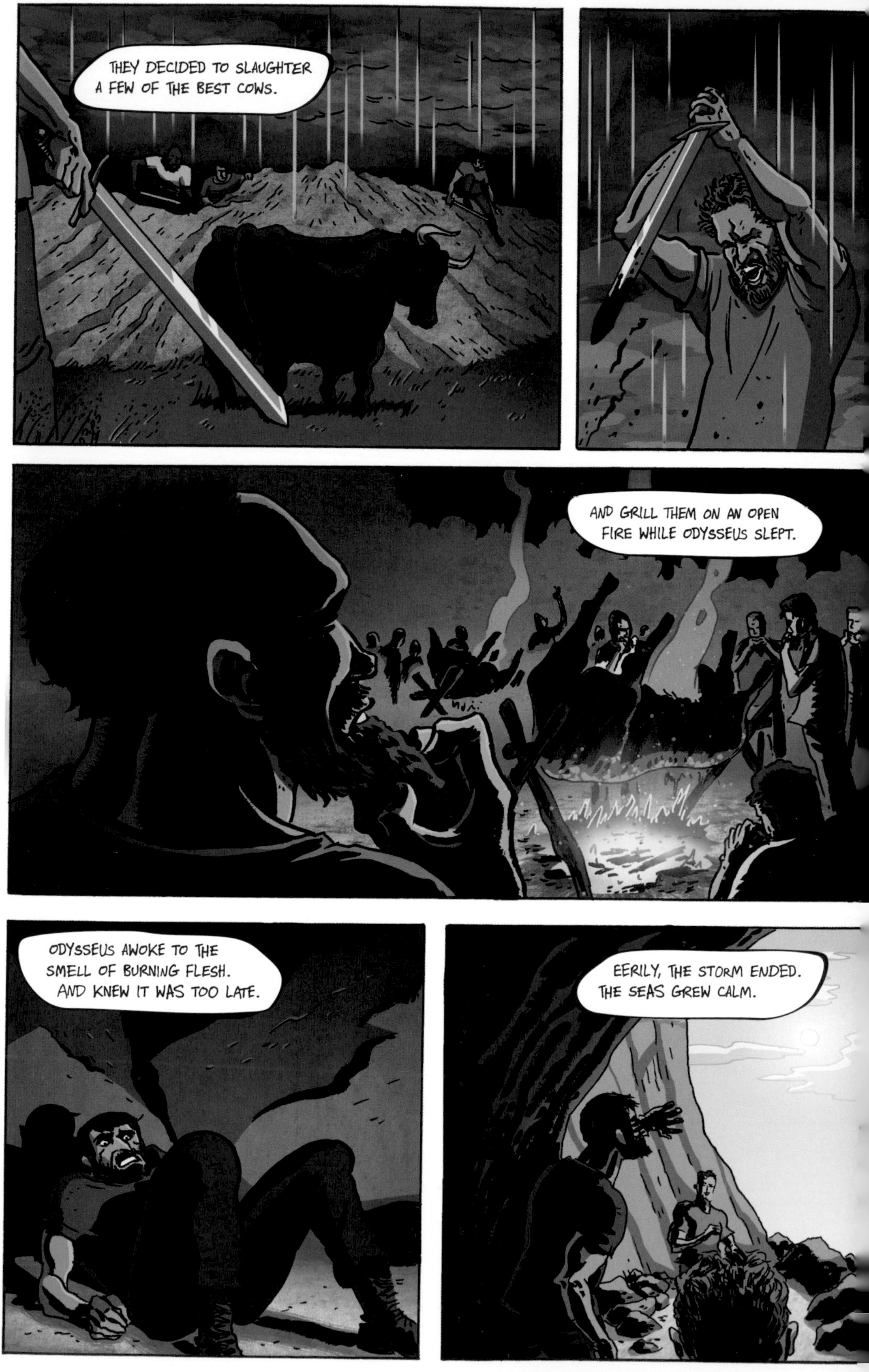
THEY DECIDED TO SLAUGHTER A FEW OF THE BEST COWS.
AND GRILL THEM ON AN OPEN FIRE WHILE ODYSSEUS SLEPT.
ODYSSEUS AWOKE TO THE SMELL OF BURNING FLESH. AND KNEW IT WAS TOO LATE.
EERILY, THE STORM ENDED. THE SEAS GREW CALM.

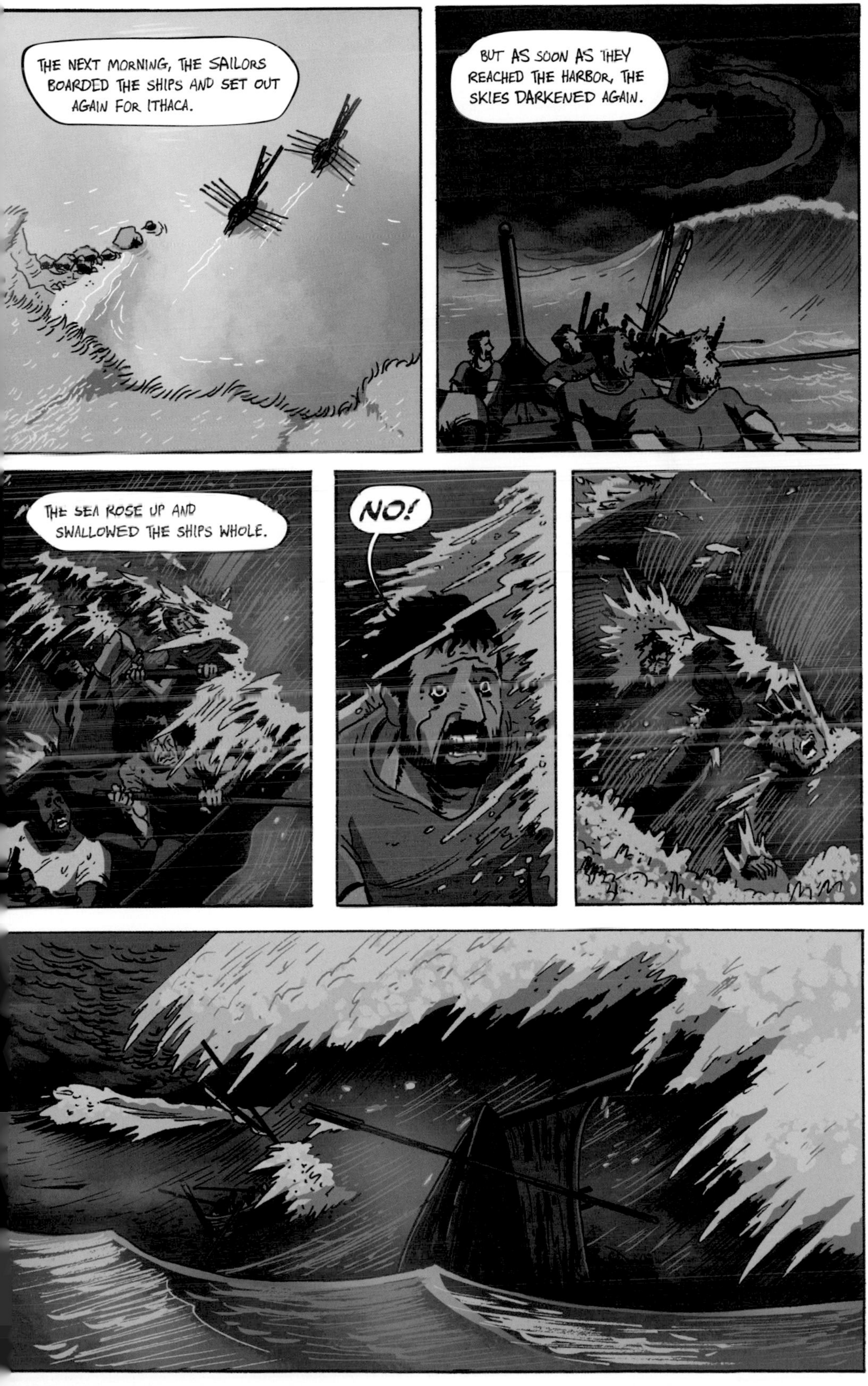
THE NEXT MORNING, THE SAILORS BOARDED THE SHIPS AND SET OUT AGAIN FOR ITHACA.
BUT AS SOON AS THEY REACHED THE HARBOR, THE SKIES DARKENED AGAIN.
THE SEA ROSE UP AND SWALLOWED THE SHIPS WHOLE.
NO!

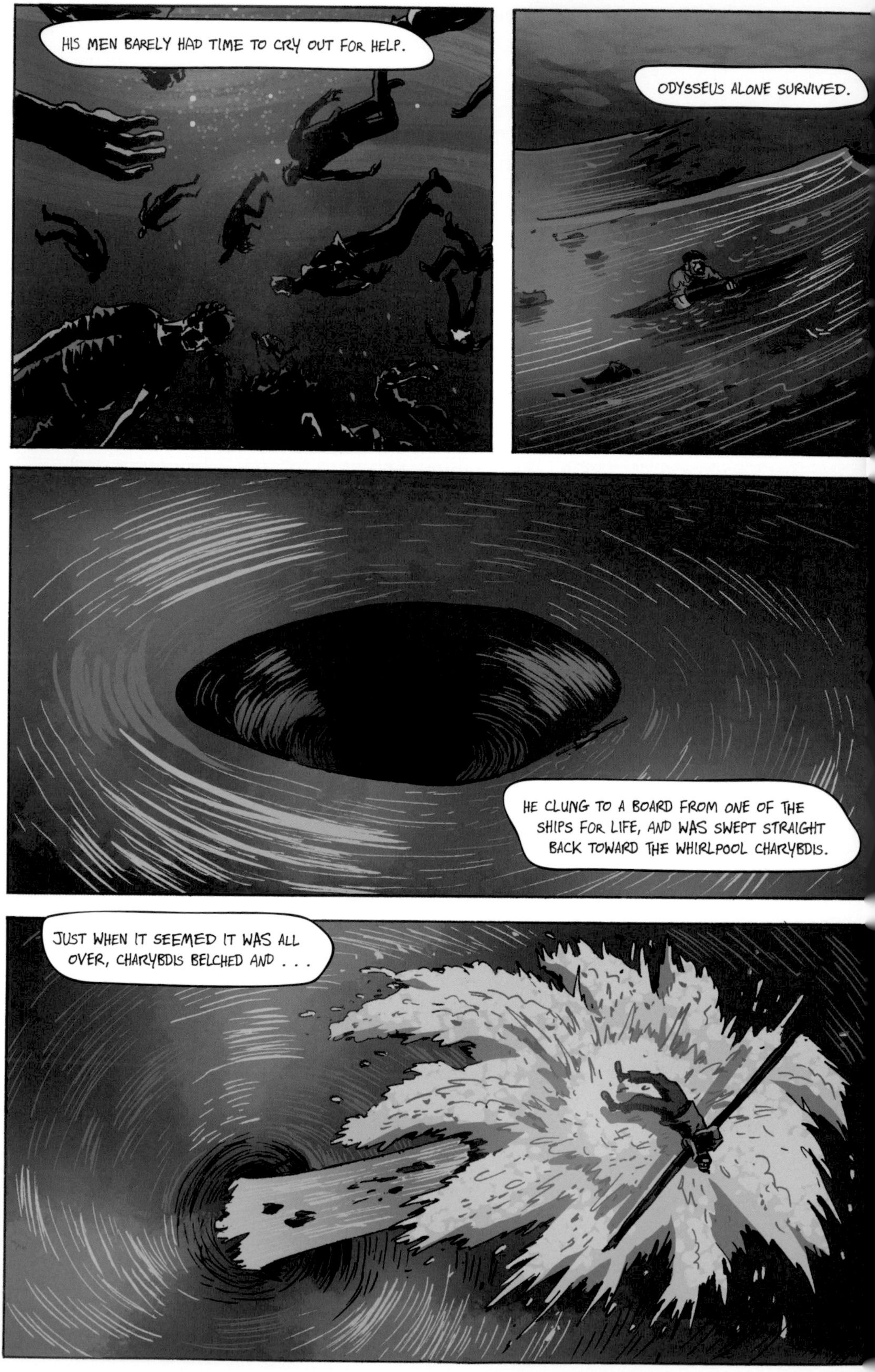
HIS MEN BARELY HAD TIME TO CRY OUT FOR HELP.
ODYSSEUS ALONE SURVIVED.
HE CLUNG TO A BOARD FROM ONE OF THE SHIPS FOR LIFE, AND WAS SWEPT STRAIGHT BACK TOWARD THE WHIRLPOOL CHARYBDIS.
JUST WHEN IT SEEMED IT WAS ALL OVER, CHARYBDIS BELCHED AND . . .

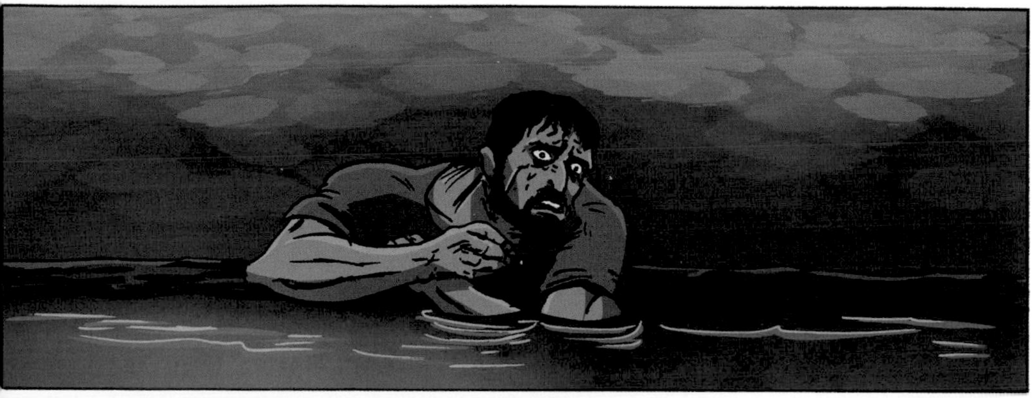

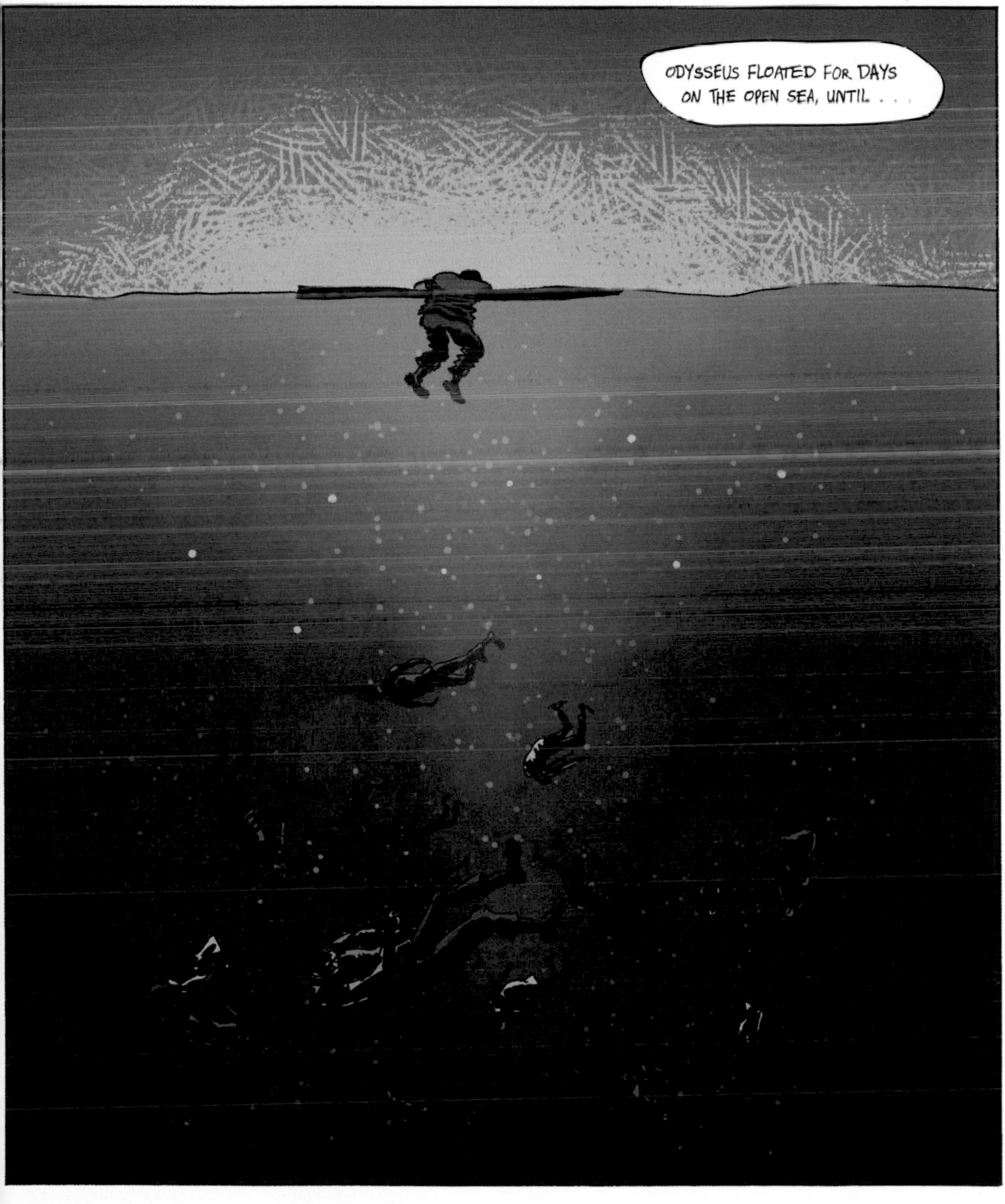
ODYSSEUS FLOATED FOR DAYS ON THE OPEN SEA, UNTIL . . .

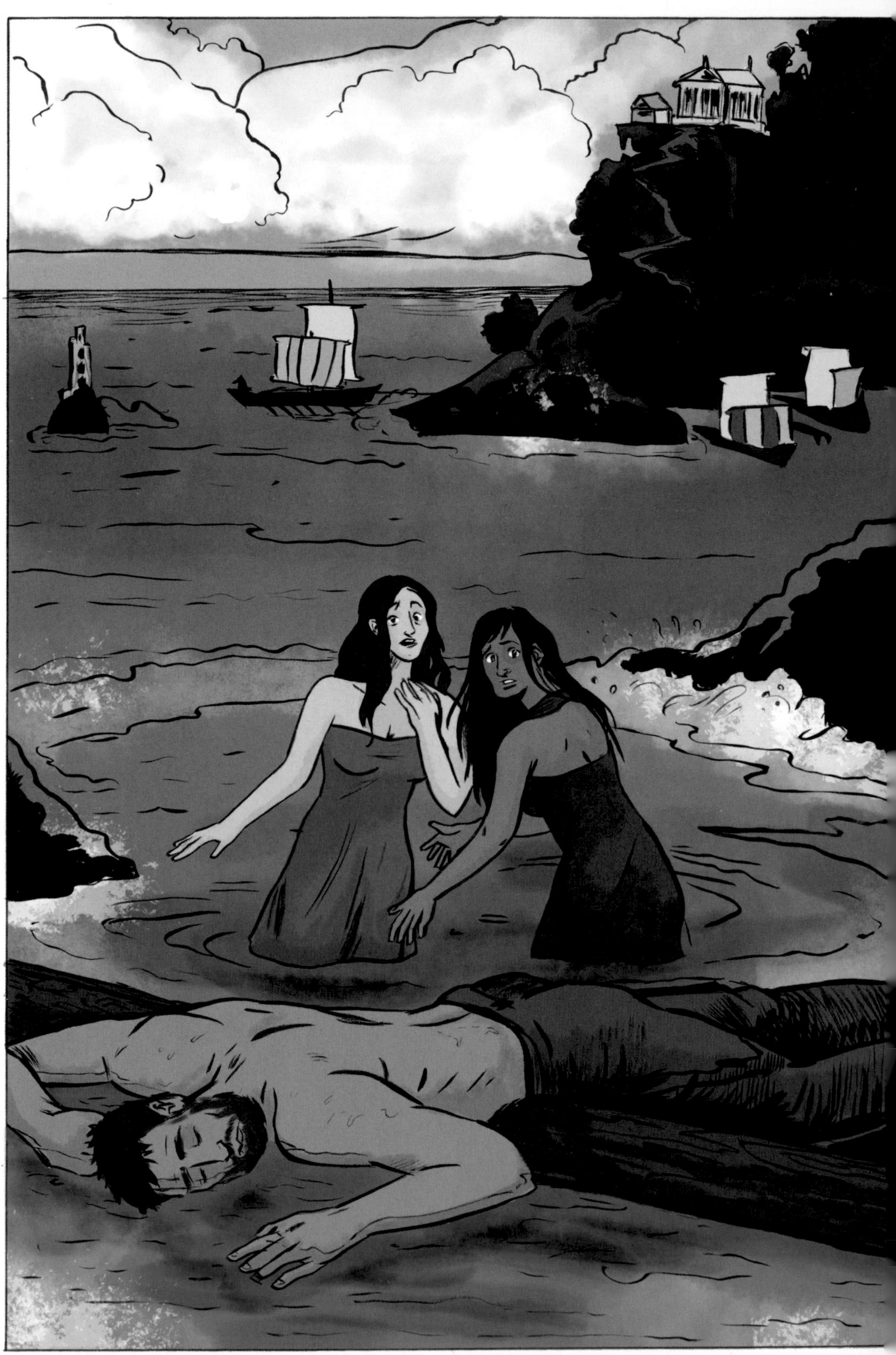

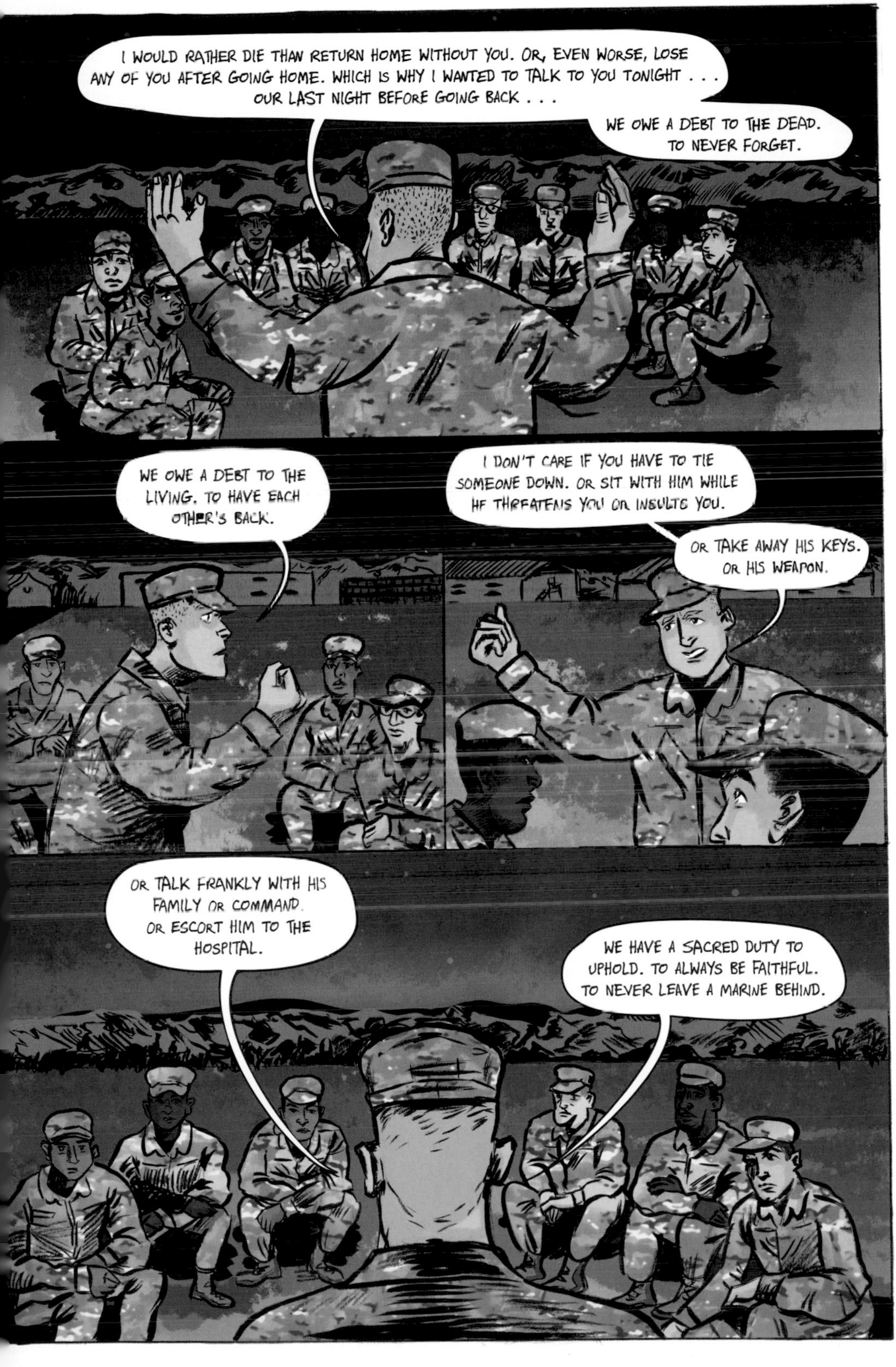
I WOULD RATHER DIE THAN RETURN HOME WITHOUT YOU. OR, EVEN WORSE, LOSE ANY OF YOU AFTER GOING HOME. WHICH IS WHY I WANTED TO TALK TO YOU TONIGHT . . . OUR LAST NIGHT BEFORE GOING BACK . . .
WE OWE A DEBT TO THE DEAD. TO NEVER FORGET.
WE OWE A DEBT TO THE LIVING. TO HAVE EACH OTHER'S BACK.
I DON'T CARE IF YOU HAVE TO TIE SOMEONE DOWN. OR SIT WITH HIM WHILE HE THREATENS YOU OR INSULTS YOU.
OR TAKE AWAY HIS KEYS. OR HIS WEAPON.
OR TALK FRANKLY WITH HIS FAMILY OR COMMAND. OR ESCORT HIM TO THE HOSPITAL.
WE HAVE A SACRED DUTY TO UPHOLD. TO ALWAYS BE FAITHFUL. TO NEVER LEAVE A MARINE BEHIND.

EPILOGUE

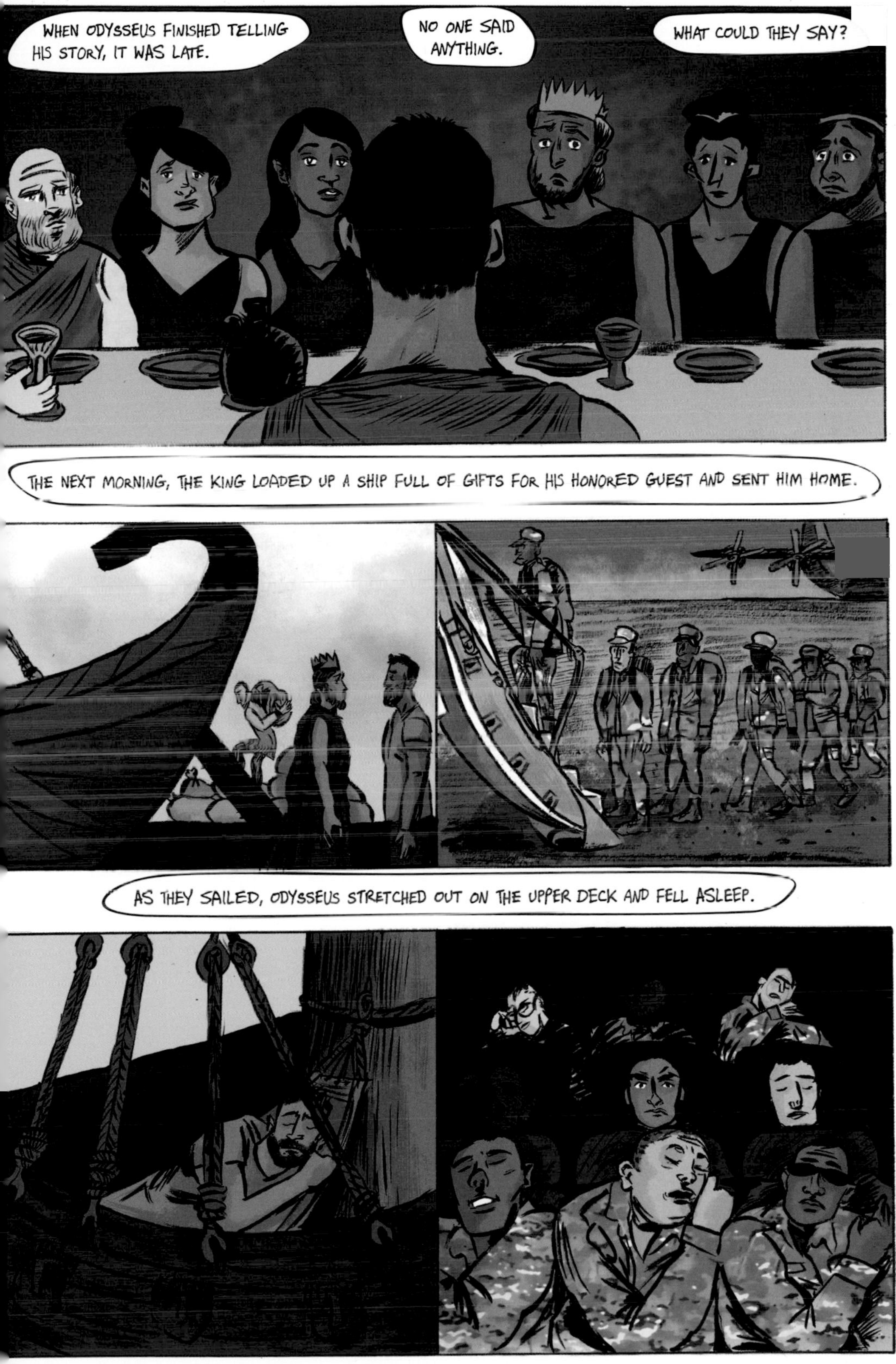
WHEN ODYSSEUS FINISHED TELLING HIS STORY, IT WAS LATE.
NO ONE SAID ANYTHING.
WHAT COULD THEY SAY?
THE NEXT MORNING, THE KING LOADED UP A SHIP FULL OF GIFTS FOR HIS HONORED GUEST AND SENT HIM HOME.
AS THEY SAILED, ODYSSEUS STRETCHED OUT ON THE UPPER DECK AND FELL ASLEEP.

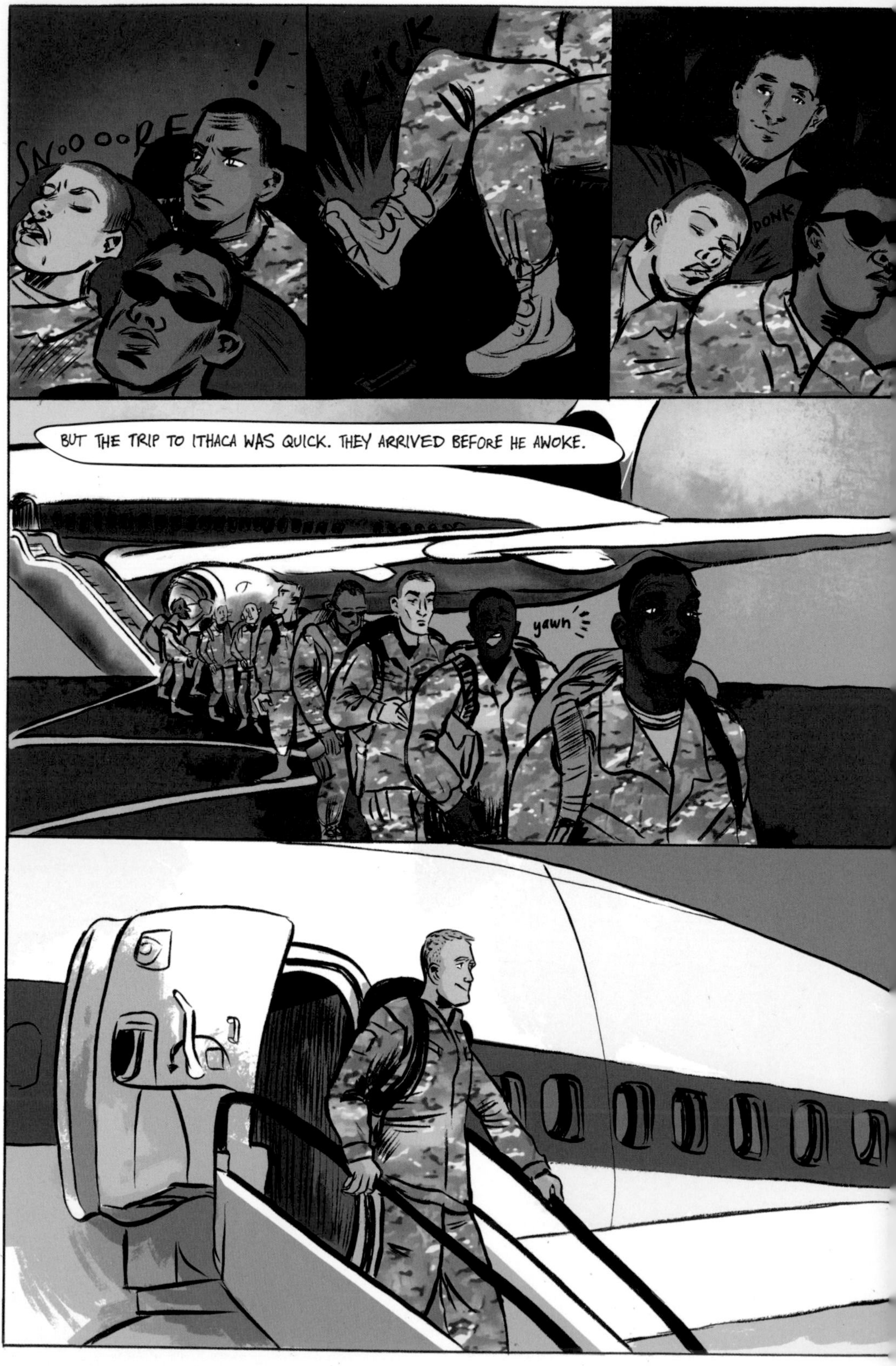
SNOOOORE
!
KICK
DONK
BUT THE TRIP TO ITHACA WAS QUICK. THEY ARRIVED BEFORE HE AWOKE.
yawn

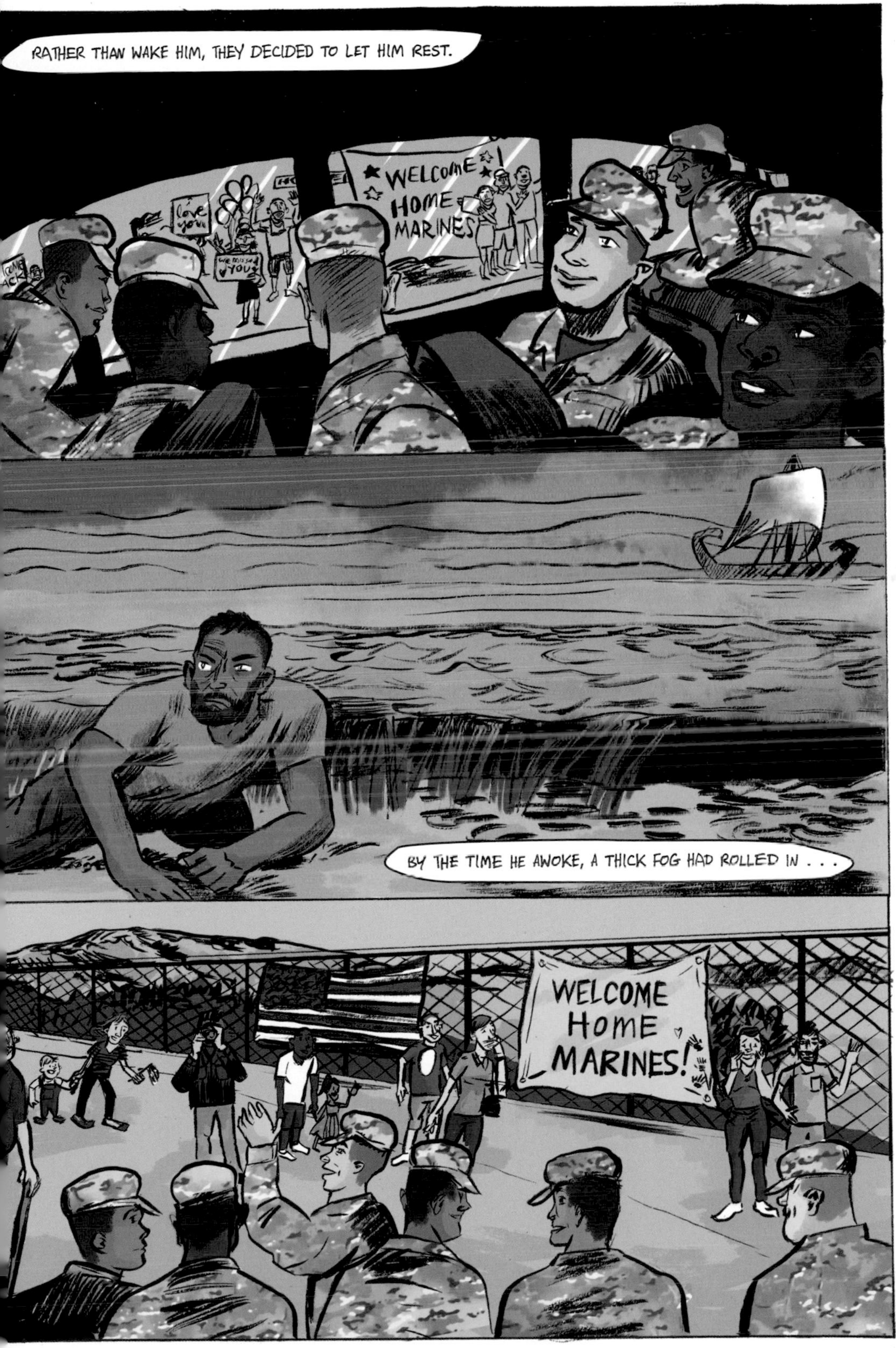
RATHER THAN WAKE HIM, THEY DECIDED TO LET HIM REST.
WELCOME HOME MARINES
BY THE TIME HE AWOKE, A THICK FOG HAD ROLLED IN . . .
WELCOME Home MARINES!

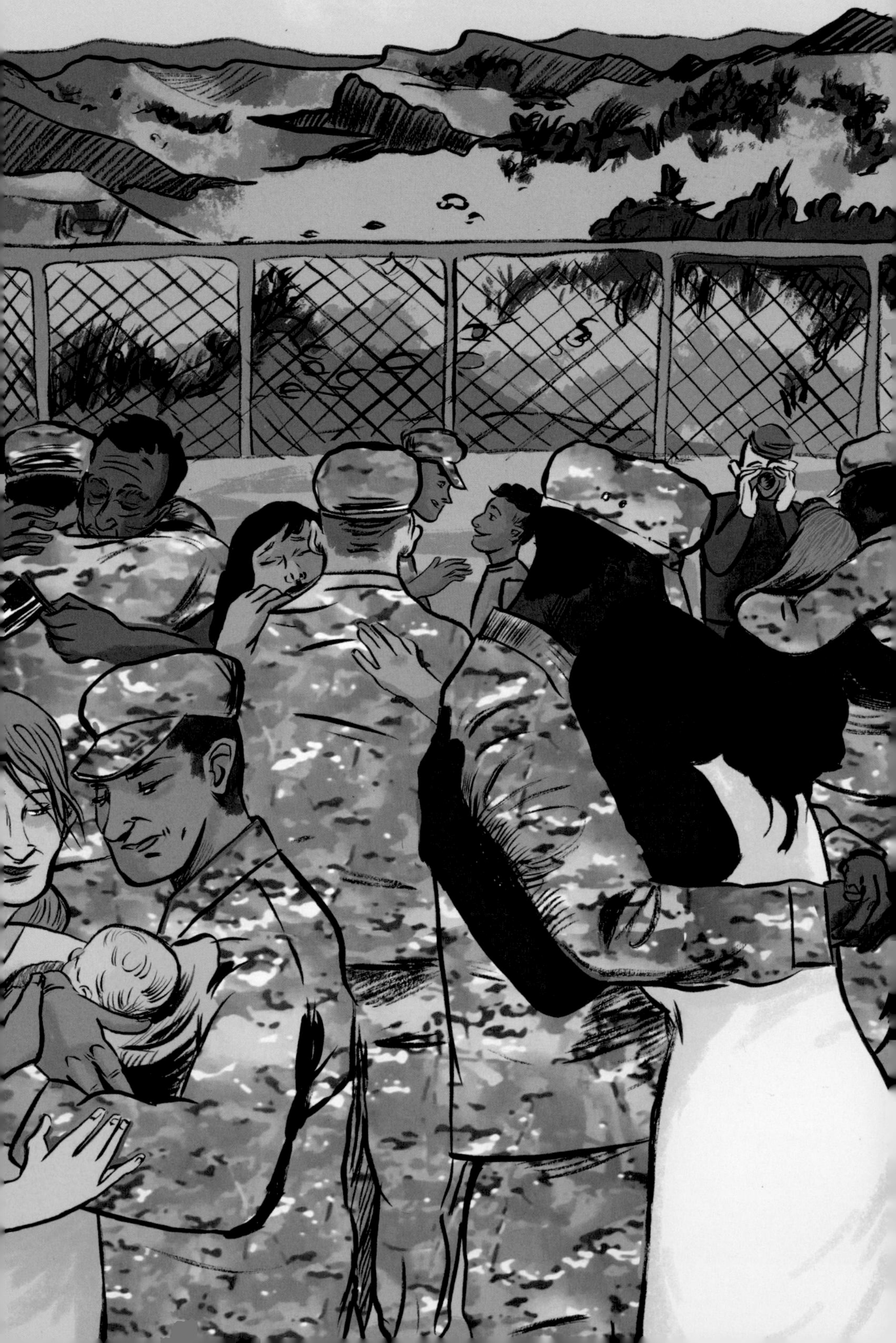

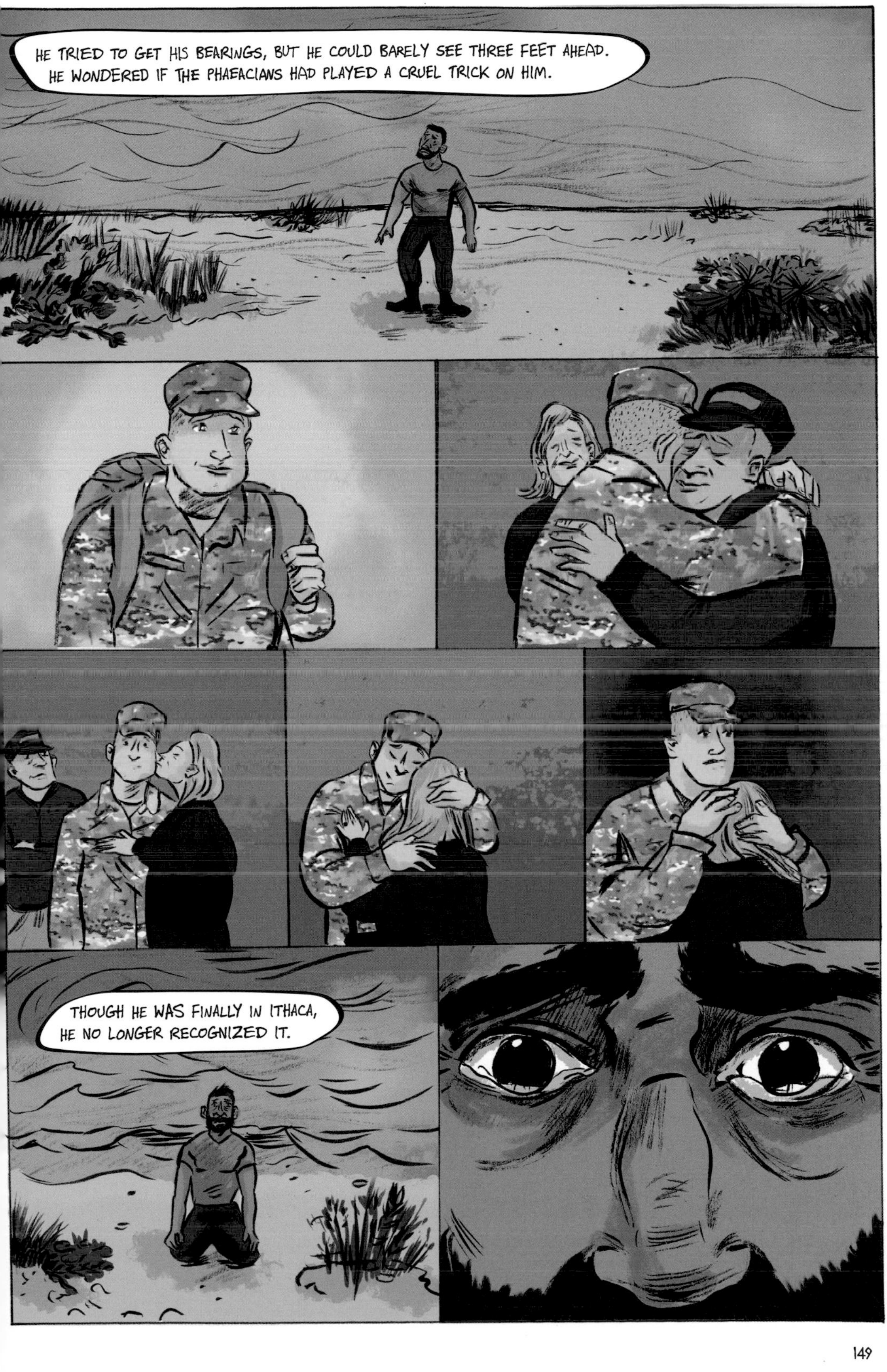
HE TRIED TO GET HIS BEARINGS, BUT HE COULD BARELY SEE THREE FEET AHEAD. HE WONDERED IF THE PHAEACIANS HAD PLAYED A CRUEL TRICK ON HIM.
THOUGH HE WAS FINALLY IN ITHACA, HE NO LONGER RECOGNIZED IT.

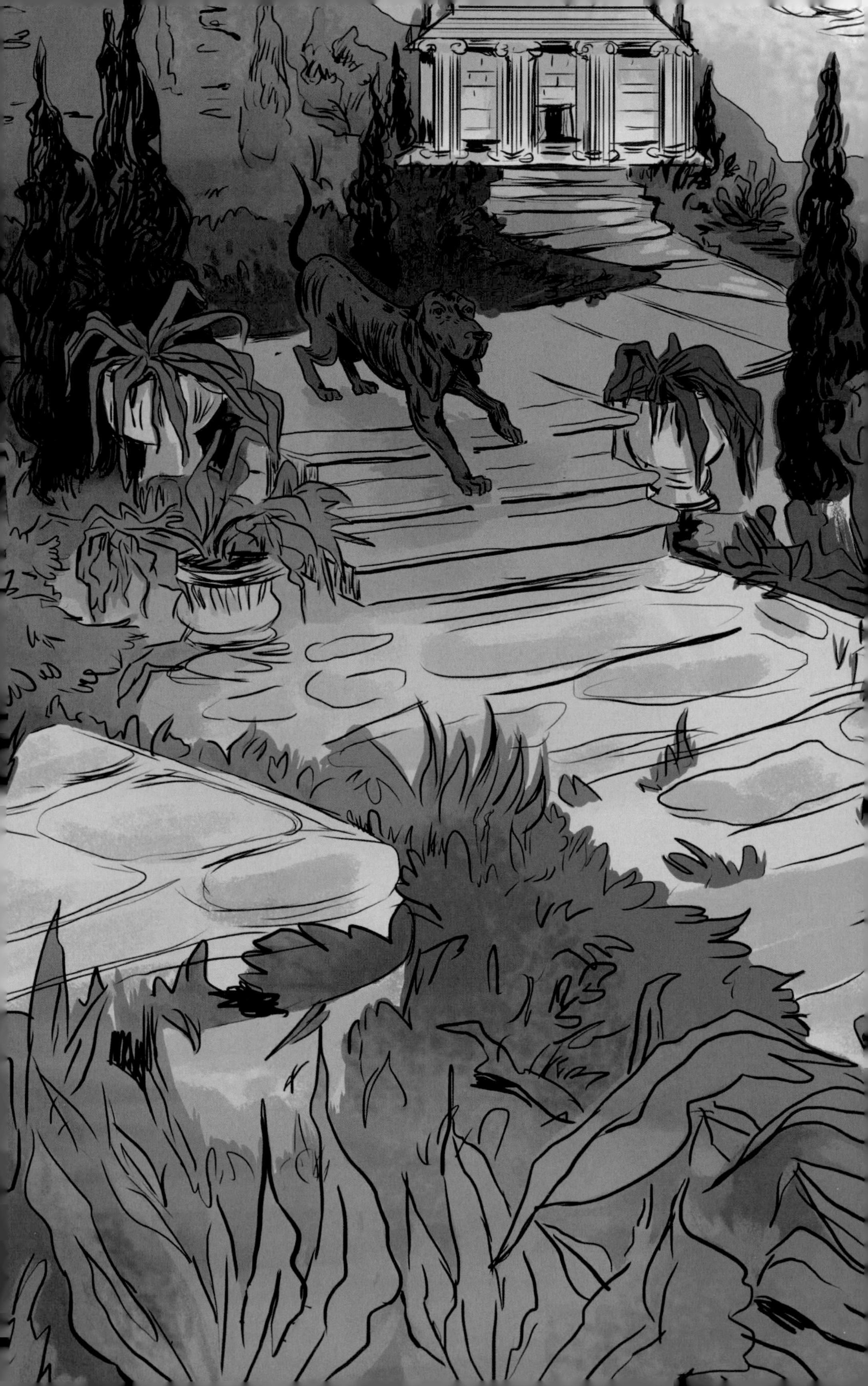

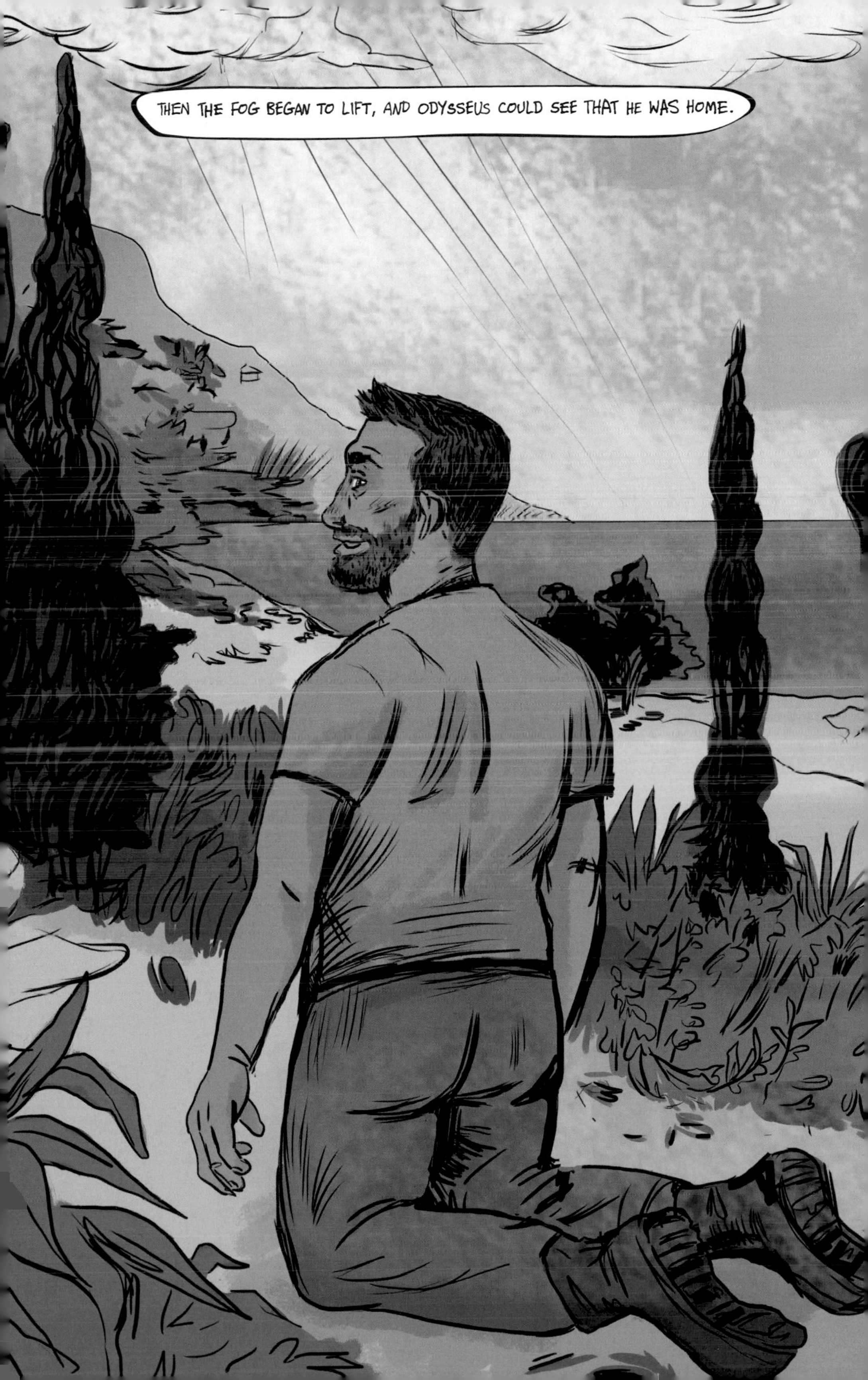
THEN THE FOG BEGAN TO LIFT, AND ODYSSEUS COULD SEE THAT HE WAS HOME.

THE ODYSSEY OF SERGEANT JACK BRENNAN

WRITTEN BY
Bryan Doerries

DRAWN BY
Jess Ruliffson, pages 13–20, 34, 44–50, 64–66, 73–76, 96, 100–01, 114–17, 121, 132, 140–41, 145–51
Joelle Jones, pages 23–33, 35–43
Justine Mara Andersen, pages 53–63, 67–72
Dylan Meconis, pages 79–95, 97–99
Nick Bertozzi, pages 105–13, 122–31, 133–39

COLORING BY
Sally Cantirino, pages 13–20, 34, 44–50, 64–66, 73–76, 96, 100–01, 114–17, 121, 132, 140–41, 145–51
Mike Luckas, pages 23–33, 35–43, 53–63, 67–72, 79–95, 97–99, 105–13, 122–31, 133–39

LETTERING BY
Sally Cantirino

EDITED BY
Bryan Doerries
Tom Hart
Tom Baxter
Joey Manley

PRODUCED BY
Phyllis Kaufman
Alan Gershenfeld
Michael Angst

ABOUT THE CREATORS

JUSTINE MARA ANDERSEN

Justine Mara Andersen is the creator of the series *Mara, Celtic Shamaness* for Fantagraphics as well as as an inker and illustrator for DC Comics, Image Comics, Wizards of the Coast/D&D, Lucasfilm, and other clients. *www.barefootjustine.com*

MICHAEL ANGST

Michael Angst is the CEO and cofounder of E-Line Media, an entertainment and educational publisher harnessing the power of games to help youth thrive in a globally connected and rapidly changing world. Michael formerly served as the chairman of FilmAid International, which uses film and media to bring life-saving information and psychological relief to refugees and other communities in need around the globe. *www.elinemedia.com*

TOM BAXTER

Tom Baxter is the senior editor, comics, at E-Line Media. Prior to joining E-Line, Tom was a member of Bendigo Partners, a private equity firm that invests in early-stage financial technology. Tom holds a bachelor of science in economics from the Wharton School of Business and a Bachelor of Science in Engineering from the University of Pennsylvania's School of Engineering.

NICK BERTOZZI

Nick Bertozzi grew up in Providence, Rhode Island, but now lives in Queens, New York, with his family. He's written and drawn comics about Lewis and Clark and Picasso, and his comics *Shackleton* and *Jerusalem: A Family Portrait* have both spent time on the *New York Times* best-seller list. *www.nickbertozzi.com*

SALLY CANTIRINO

Sally Cantirino is a cartoonist and illustrator who has contributed to numerous anthologies, and whose solo works include *Turnpike Divides, Catifght, Big Dogs, The Gathering Storm*, and *Derby 101*. Her website is *srcantirino.carbonmade.com*.

BRYAN DOERRIES

Bryan Doerries is a writer, director, and translator. He is the founder of Theater of War, a project that presents readings of ancient Greek plays to service members, veterans, and their families to help them initiate conversations about the visible and invisible wounds of war. He is also cofounder and artistic director of Outside the Wire, a social impact company that uses theater and a variety of other media to address public health and social issues. *www.outsidethewirellc.com*

ALAN GERSHENFELD

Alan Gershenfeld is the president and cofounder of E-Line Media, an entertainment and educational publisher harnessing the power of games to help youth thrive in a globally connected and rapidly changing world. Prior to E-Line, Alan served as chairman of Games for Change and as a member of the executive management team that rebuilt Activision from bankruptcy into a profitable industry leader. *www.elinemedia.com*

TOM HART

Tom Hart is a cartoonist and the executive director of the Sequential Artists Workshop, a not-for-profit school and arts organization in Gainesville, Florida. He is the creator of the Hutch Owen series of graphic novels and books, and has been nominated for many industry awards. His memoir, *Rosalie Lightning* (St. Martin's Press), was previewed in *The Best American Comics 2014*. www.tomhart.net

JOËLLE JONES

Joëlle Jones is a comic book artist living in Portland, Oregon. She is currently best known for her work on *HELHEIM*, published by Oni Press. She has worked on various projects with the *New York Times*, Graphic Universe, Vertigo, DC, Marvel, and Dark Horse. You can keep up with her on Twitter @joelle_jones or by checking out her homepage: *www.joellejones.com.*

PHYLLIS KAUFMAN

Phyllis Kaufman is cofounder of Outside the Wire, a social impact company that uses theater and a variety of other media to address public health and social justice issues, and producing director of Outside the Wire and Theater of War. Prior to Outside the Wire, Phyllis was a partner at New York–based law firms, artistic director of a U.S. film festival, and the producer of feature and documentary films. *www.outsidethewirellc.com*

MIKE LUCKAS

Mike Luckas is a cartoonist, colorist, and illustrator living in the New York City area. He works on many freelance projects in addition to publishing his own short stories that can be found at *www.mikeluckas.net.*

JOEY MANLEY

Joey Manley (1965–2013) was the founder of the pioneering online webcomics site Modern Tales, as well as the hosting service Webcomics Nation. He served as the president of E-Line Comics at E-Line Media, hosted the forum and blog TalkAboutComics, and authored the novel *The Death of Donna-May Dean* (St. Martin's Press).

DYLAN MECONIS

Dylan Meconis is the Eisner-award-nominated creator of *Bite Me!*, *Outfoxed*, and *Family Man*. You can find her work online at *www.dylanmeconis.com.*

JESS RULIFFSON

Jess Ruliffson is currently working on a comic book based on interviews with veterans of the Iraq and Afghanistan wars. In 2012, she traveled to Walter Reed to draw portraits and talk with physically wounded soldiers returning home from Afghanistan. You can see more of her comics at *callingthedog.blogspot.com* and *www.jessruliffson.com.*

E-LINE MEDIA

E-Line Media is an entertainment and educational publisher harnessing the power of games to help youth thrive in a globally connected and rapidly changing world. *www.elinemedia.com*

OUTSIDE THE WIRE

Outside the Wire is a social impact company that uses theater and a variety of other media to address pressing public health and social issues, such as combat-related psychological injury, end of life care, prison reform, political violence and torture, domestic violence, and substance abuse and addiction.
www.outsidethewirellc.com

SEQUENTIAL ARTISTS WORKSHOP

The Sequential Artists Workshop (SAW) is a school and arts organization whose mission is to nurture and educate visual storytellers, to support creative investigation, exploration, and excellence, and to promote literacy in cartooning and comic art.
www.sequentialartistsworkshop.org

ACKNOWLEDGMENTS

Our sincere thanks go to the Defense Advanced Research Projects Agency for supporting the creation of this graphic novel, with special thanks to program managers Russell Shilling and Daniel Ragsdale, and their coordinators Jamika Burge and Kevin Keaty for believing in the project and for shepherding us through multiple stages of its development.

We are extremely grateful to the Marine Corps veterans David Blea, Maurice Decaul, Jack Eubanks, and Zachary Iscol for their steady guidance, invaluable insights, and generosity of time and spirit. We would also like to recognize and thank the mental health professionals Bill Nash, Loree Sutton, Ashley Clark, and Charles Hoge for their crucial feedback at many critical junctures.

Heartfelt thanks go to Zoë Pagnamenta, Andrew Miller, Dan Frank, and Will Heyward for immediately seeing the merits of this book and for moving swiftly to find a way to publish it. Thanks also go to Drew Patrick for quickly and elegantly tying up all the loose ends.

Finally, we would like to recognize the contributions of the many artists, editors, and producers who worked on this project, without whose collaboration, dedication, and talent this book would never have been possible. Our thanks go to John Boeck for helping us get the project started. Most of all, we wish to thank Joey Manley, whose untimely death early in the process sent us reeling, wondering how we would ever complete the novel without him, and whose expansive vision and high standards for the project inspired us to create a book of which we hope he would have been proud.

This project was made possible by a collaboration between E-Line Media and Outside the Wire.

This material is based upon work supported by the DARPA Program Office under Contract No. W31P4Q-13-C-0110.

Approved for public release, distribution unlimited.